Nicola Williams is a barrister specialising in Criminal Law. In 1991 she was the first black woman to win a *Cosmopolitan* Woman of Achievement Award for her work at the Bar and she has also appeared in a First Tuesday TV documentary about the legal system. She started writing at the age of fourteen, mostly poetry, and won first and third prizes in the Black Penmanship Awards when she was at university. Born in London of Guyanese parents, Nicola was educated in Georgetown and Croydon. In her mid-thirties, she lives in South London. WITHOUT PREJUDICE is Nicola Williams' first novel and she is currently at work on her second, also featuring Lee Mitchell.

Without Prejudice

Nicola Williams

HEADLINE
FEATURE

First published in 1997
by HEADLINE BOOK PUBLISHING

First published in paperback in 1998
by HEADLINE BOOK PUBLISHING

A HEADLINE FEATURE paperback

10 9 8 7 6 5 4 3 2 1

ISBN 0 7472 5482 6

Typeset by
Letterpart Limited, Reigate, Surrey

Printed and bound in Great Britain by
Clays Ltd, St Ives plc.

HEADLINE BOOK PUBLISHING
A division of Hodder Headline PLC
338 Euston Road
London NW1 3BH

ACKNOWLEDGEMENTS

Writing is a lonely business, but what help and support I had – both human and divine – meant a great deal to me. Thank you: we both know who you are. Some people, however, deserve special mention: Yasmin, for her important professional advice from the 'other side'; Lynette, for visiting me virtually every day that week in April 1996; Udean, a *real* 'sista-friend'; Anne Williams, at Headline, for her patience in chasing me for my rewrites!

And last, but certainly not least, to all my family. May we never take each other for granted . . .

Chapter One

R ay Willis was getting impatient.
   No, he thought, make that very pissed off.

He took a long drag on his nineteenth cigarette of the day, then quickly searched his pockets looking for the Lexigram that had been delivered last night. The now crumpled piece of paper confirmed what he already knew – that he should be at the Crown Court at 9.30 a.m., an hour before his case was to be heard, so that he could have a conference with his barrister. Someone from the solicitors' office should be there too. Well, he was here, and so was his brief, but there was no one from the office, and they were local too. Just what he needed; some student who had been given the file the night before by an overworked solicitor and hadn't bothered to read it until this morning. Now they were making up for lost time – on his time.

He looked at his watch again. Ten o'clock. Half an hour wasted, and he needed all the time he could get, especially as he hadn't turned up for the last conference at his barrister's Chambers. He stubbed out his cigarette on top of the others he had smoked in the last half-hour, pushing it right down into the pile.

'That's the last time I'm going on fucking legal aid,' he said aloud, and walked towards the door. As he touched the handle it swung open, and he looked directly into the eyes of the tall woman barrister who was to represent him.

'Jesus, Ray! How can you breathe in here?' she said as she looked past him into the smoke-filled room.

1

'Never mind that. What the fuck's going on? I've got better things to do with my time, you know.'

Her smile faded instantly. 'Don't speak to me like that. I was here waiting for you this morning. In fact, I also seem to remember waiting for you last week on Tuesday; I had something better to do with my time *then*. If you have a problem with your solicitors, take it up with them, not me.'

Ray looked at her. She was the only woman, ever, who would look him in the eye and speak to him that way. But then, while he couldn't do anything to her, she could do a lot for him. He already had a string of previous convictions when he became one of her first clients, and, although she hadn't got him off everything, her record was good enough – and his bad enough – for him to insist that he would only be represented by her. He didn't like the taste of humble pie, but she was the only thing standing between him and a prison sentence. He couldn't afford to get on her bad side as well.

'OK, OK. Sorry. But you know who we've got – Shervington!' Ray lit his second-last Marlboro, and took two quick drags. 'Fucking bastard must have been rubbing his hands when he saw my name. He knows my face. That shit will send me down for sure.' He looked at his watch again. Five after. 'Look, can't we get started?'

The barrister looked at him. In the six years or so since she had been representing him, she had never seen him so nervous. At twenty-eight, Ray Willis had the kind of hard man reputation that made older seasoned criminals think of him as an equal. He had stared down worse than Shervington before. She found herself wondering whether he had, in fact, committed the offence, then put that thought out of her mind. She remembered what her pupil-master had told her, fresh out of law school, in that year between passing the Bar exams and being 'let loose on the public', as he put it: 'First rule of criminal defence: if your lay

2

client tells you he's pleading not guilty, don't go behind that. If all the evidence indicates that he did it, or if his defence sounds like a pack of lies, then you can advise him as his counsel what you think his chances are. But it doesn't matter if *you* think he's guilty. You're not judge and jury. Unless he actually tells you he's guilty, you'll never know for sure, and not even then.'

She assessed the present situation quickly. 'Look, I've rung Hatton's. Your solicitors don't know where the clerk is. It's not Brendan or Terry or one of their regulars; they would have been here by now. I've already spoken to the usher in Court Four; she says they're running late, so we've got time. If we need any more, I'll apply for it in open court.'

He half turned away from her. She could sense frustration and real fear coming from him, which was unusual. She put her hand on his arm. 'Don't worry, Ray, we're not going to rush this. You know the routine; I can see you without a solicitor present if you sign the back of my brief, stating you've agreed to this.'

'OK, OK, let's just get on with it,' said Ray, stepping back into the smoke-filled interview room.

But she was already opening the door of the adjoining room. 'No, not in there. I'm trying to give up.'

'Since when?' he asked as he followed her.

'Since New Year – three months now.' She carefully lowered her wig, notebook and Archbold, the criminal lawyers' bible, on to the table. It was a pain to carry around. It wouldn't normally be needed in a case as apparently straightforward as Ray's but if it was anything like the man himself, appearances were deceptive. Looking at him in his beautifully cut and obviously expensive black wool suit and silk tie, his blond hair well cut and neatly combed, he looked every inch the successful young professional instead of the successful young professional criminal, someone who had seen the inside of every Juvenile, Magistrates' and

Crown Court in London since he was fourteen, and a few prisons too.

'So,' she said, opening up the rolled bundle of papers tied with red ribbon, 'according to this you were caught with eight ounces of cannabis in the boot of your car and you want to plead not guilty.' She looked meaningfully at him. 'Since you haven't kept your appointments with either your solicitors or me, I don't know anything more than that.'

Ray looked away and reflexively reached into his inside pocket for his Marlboros.

'Mind if I smoke? Just the one,' he added quickly, seeing the look of displeasure on her face.

'If you think you need it,' she said, pushing her chair back from the table as she spoke. Truth was, the smell was making her wish, not for the first time, that she hadn't given up. Especially now, when faced with trying to build a plausible defence from next to nothing. 'I was surprised to see you up on a drugs case, Ray. This isn't your style.'

Silence.

Shrugging, she turned to the papers before her. 'The prosecution case says the police pulled you over in Maida Vale because there had been a spate of burglaries there recently.' She looked down at the statement of PC Lambert, speed-reading it. 'He asked you where you were going. You said, in an aggressive tone, "None of your fucking business." Is that true?'

'No.'

She looked up at him.

'None of it?'

'Look, first he asked me about the motor. "How come a criminal like you can afford this?" He hasn't got *that* in his statement. Then he wanted me to wait while he checked to see whether it was stolen. Then he started to ask me what I was doing so far away from Peckham, where I was going. And he mentioned

4

about the burglaries. I just said "It's a free country" and asked him how long the check was going to take. See, I clocked him straight off; he used to be at Miller Street.'

'*That* Lambert? Who arrested you quite a few times a couple of years ago?'

'Same one. Anyone else, I *would* have told them to mind their own fucking business, and I would have called the solicitors on the mobile as well. But he knew me, and I didn't want to get his back up. I knew the stuff was in the back and I didn't want him to start searching the car.'

'Hang on a minute.' She was writing furiously in her blue notebook, cross-referencing it with Lambert's statement. 'And then what happened?'

'He asked me if he could have a look in the car. His mate had come out of the Panda car by now but was standing just next to it, not up close. I didn't recognise him. Lambert had this smirk on his face, like he was just willing me to say no. And I knew if I did it would look like I had something to hide.'

'Which you did.'

'Well, I was hoping it was well hidden, because I didn't put it there.'

His barrister looked incredulous. 'You let someone put drugs in your car without watching what they were doing, or even knowing whether it was cannabis? Suppose it had been heroin? Or crack? You're too smart for that, Ray.'

'Well, I was doing a favour for someone, know what I mean? I knew they wouldn't do me wrong.'

'Who was it? Family?'

Roy instantly became defensive. 'I don't have to tell you that. You know I'm no grass. I got caught, so it's down to me. End of story.'

'OK, if that's the way you want it.' She paused, then looked at PC Lambert's statement again. 'It says here that no items connected with burglary were found, but in the boot they found the

5

drugs. So where exactly was it hidden?'

Ray took a last long drag on his cigarette, then stubbed it out. 'That's just it. Fucking idiot must've just thrown it in, 'cos when I opened up the boot, there it was, bloody smiling up at me! I tried to explain it was just for my own use, but they charged me with possession with intent to supply. Look, it was a present. I was taking it home to smoke it there. I know it's a lot, but that would have lasted me for a good long time. So many officers know me, I can't afford to go around buying every time I feel like spliffing up. I thought he'd have had the sense to hide it better. I told him to try the most obvious place. But I didn't think he'd make it *that* fucking obvious. Anyway, I didn't think they'd stop a—' Ray halted abruptly.

'What? A white man in a nice car in Maida Vale?'

'Yeah, that's right.' Although no one would describe him as a liberal, Ray looked embarrassed. She wondered why. After all, they both came from the same part of London. They both knew the way things were.

'They probably wouldn't have done, Ray, if you hadn't been driving an M-reg BMW when you have no known income.'

'Yeah, but you know how it is. My uncle's in the trade.'

'Yes, I know how it is. I've represented him too.'

Chapter Two

In the case of Regina v Ray Willis, the Crown was being represented, on this occasion, by Peter Fairfax. He spotted his opponent as soon as she walked, with grace and purpose, through the door of the Bar Mess.

'Ah, Leanne, come and join me. Care for a cup of coffee?'

She smiled as she walked quickly towards the head of the long wooden table where Peter was sitting, and slid in beside him.

'This is a nice surprise. I was just thinking about you.'

'Nothing too terrible, I hope.'

'Just something that you taught me. And it's Lee, not Leanne, please. No one has called me Leanne since I finished pupillage – except my mother.'

Now it was Peter's turn to smile.

'I see you're representing Willis. Again. And I'm prosecuting him. Again.' He waved his prosecution brief. 'Nice to know that, with all the changes at the Bar, there are still some things one can rely on.'

It was good to see a familiar face. Peter Fairfax had been her pupil-master seven years ago, and as such was the man responsible for finishing off her training as a barrister. Although an able and experienced barrister, he was – unusually in the profession – more easygoing and less ambitious than his contemporaries, which probably accounted for the fact that, instead of doing murder trials at the Old Bailey, he was prosecuting a case far below his capabilities against someone more than ten years his junior. Having an independent private income had possibly blunted the edge of his ambition. He was one of the nicest practitioners she had come across since coming to the Bar. He was just what this case needed, a prosecutor, not a persecutor.

'So, what can we do about this young man?' Peter asked, somewhat rhetorically.

'Well, I've taken instructions and my client has authorised me to discuss with you the possibility of a plea.'

'What? To the whole thing? That will make a nice short morning. I can catch my daughter's Sports Day today – she's in the three-legged race.'

In spite of the seriousness of the subject, Lee could not help smiling. He was one of the few barristers willing to sacrifice work for anything remotely concerning family life. Perhaps that was why he still had one.

'I'd like a short morning too, Peter, so if you'll accept a plea to simple possession only, then we'll both get what we want.'

Peter's smile faded. 'I'll have to check with the CPS because they instruct me, as you know, but privately, Lee, this isn't just a couple of joints in someone's back pocket; this is eight ounces of cannabis. Besides, the arresting officer really seems to have his teeth in this one.'

If what Ray Willis had said about PC Lambert was true, Lee wasn't in the least surprised. 'Yes, but that's why barristers prosecute the trials, Peter, not police officers, so we can look at the case objectively. You and I both know that eight ounces of cannabis in nothing to a regular user. It's cheaper to buy it in bulk, then smoke it over a period of months. Besides, where's the evidence of intent to supply? There were no scales, no Rizla papers, no small plastic bags to sell it on with. All you have to prove intent is the amount. It's unlikely you'll get a conviction on that alone, and even if you did, you know I'll appeal.'

'Well,' Peter said, draining his cup and getting up from the ornate table, 'I hear what you say. I, of course, remain neutral on the matter, but I'll convey your views to the CPS.' He looked at his watch. 'You'd better let the usher know what's going on. You know Shervington hates to be kept waiting.'

Ray was pacing nervously outside Court Four, smoking what must have been his thirtieth cigarette. He quickly stubbed it out as Lee approached.

'Well, what's happening?'

'The prosecutor's gone to take instructions. They should accept your plea, but you can never tell with the Crown Prosecution Service.' She took him over to one side. 'If it's no, Ray, what are you going to do?'

'I dunno.' He looked around. 'You know me, I always put me hands up for what I've done, but I wasn't going to supply no one. Trouble is, if I plead not guilty in front of Shervington and I'm convicted, I'll go to prison for sure.'

'You could go to prison on a plea anyway, Ray. This is a lot of cannabis.'

'It *is* a lot . . .' Ray's voice trailed off.

Not for the first time, Lee wondered what the hell was going on.

'It's up to you, Ray,' she said, 'but if what you've told me is the truth, I would advise you to plead not guilty. You've done a lot of things in the past, but supplying drugs isn't one of them. Besides, there's no evidence of intent to supply. Of course, there are no guarantees; a jury could convict you. If so, we'll appeal. But the final decision is yours.'

Ray looked at her, and for the first time in the six years she had known him, Lee saw the same look on his face that she had seen on the faces of many lay clients before – the look that said, 'You're my brief, you sort it all out, tell me what to do, how to plead.' And that she would not do. She would advise them, give them all the options; but ultimately the decision had to be theirs.

Ray took a deep breath, then exhaled loudly. 'Well, you've been all right for me up till now. OK, I'll go not guilty on the supplying.'

Lee nodded. 'Good. I think you've made the right decision. But hopefully it won't come to that. Ah, there he is now. I'll be back in a minute.'

She walked quickly over to Peter Fairfax as he entered the corridor, pushing the heavy wooden doors wide apart in front of him.

'Well?'

'Well,' Peter began slowly, 'Lambert isn't happy, not happy at all. And the CPS aren't too pleased either. But both of them had to agree that there was no evidence of intent to supply – except the amount of the drug which, I had to remind them, was not, in my professional opinion, enough in itself for a conviction on the count as it stands. So, your plea is accepted.'

'Thank you. He'll be pleased.'

'I didn't do it to please him. The man's a criminal, don't forget. But, as you said, most likely simple possession is all he would have been convicted of in any event.'

Lee took her horsehair wig, the mark of her profession, and placed it on her head, making sure it was straight. Of course he was a criminal, but who the hell cared about that?

'Well, we'd better go in. No point in keeping Shervington waiting.'

His Honour Judge Shervington, QC, was living up to his well-deserved reputation.

'*What* course of action have the prosecution taken in this case?' he screeched in a thin, quavering voice.

'Your Honour,' Peter Fairfax repeated patiently, 'the Crown have decided to accept the plea the defendant has just entered of not guilty to possession of herbal cannabis with intent to supply, but guilty to possession *simpliciter.*'

'On what basis?' the judge demanded.

'On the basis, Your Honour, that there is no evidence, in my submission, to prove the necessary intent.'

Judges were supposed to be impartial and above the adversarial debate. Shervington, as expected, immediately got down into the ring, swinging wildly for Her Majesty.

'Have the prosecution taken leave of their senses? This man was found with eight ounces of herbal cannabis in his vehicle. And you seriously suggest that there is insufficient evidence for possession with intent? I'll have you know, Mr Fairfax, this is not the first time this young man has come before me. I believe you are usurping the jury's function and duty to the public to try this case.'

Lee looked back at her client in the dock. Outwardly, he seemed calm – except, that is, for his knuckles which were white from gripping the brass rail of the dock.

'Your Honour, I have no doubt that Raymond Willis is as well known to you as he is to me, but with all due respect, as a prosecutor, I submit that it is my function and duty to the public only to prosecute cases where there is prima facie evidence to secure a conviction on the indictment laid against the defendant. There is insufficient evidence to support the offence with which he was charged.'

Lee paid close attention to the proceedings. It was interesting to watch someone else argue with this judge for a change – prosecutors generally reached new levels of obsequiousness before him. Peter, however, although not disrespectful, was coming close to the line.

'Thank you, Mr Fairfax,' Shervington snapped. He turned to Lee. 'Miss Mitchell, do you appear with instructions? I see there is no one behind you.'

Lee stood up. The judge was referring to her absent solicitor's clerk. They had been at court nearly two hours and still no one had turned up. She was not going to keep Ray waiting indefinitely for them.

'Your Honour, I have made such inquiries as I can. I was told that someone was on their way but that was some considerable time ago. The defendant has agreed both to a conference and to representation if necessary in the absence of his solicitor, and has endorsed my brief to that effect. I did not wish to keep Your Honour waiting.'

'Personally, if I represented this man I wouldn't want to turn up either. It would be a rather nasty case of *déjà vu*. I take it you have no objections to the course proposed by the prosecution?'

'None at all, Your Honour. My learned friend had very kindly indicated as much outside court.'

'Your lack of objection doesn't surprise me in the least.' He turned again to Peter. 'Mr Fairfax, if there is nothing I can do to dissuade you from this course, I shall ask the learned clerk to put the matter again. Of course,' he continued, with a glint in his eye, 'I still have to sentence the defendant. Is there a pre-sentence report ready?'

Lee rose to her feet again. 'No, Your Honour. No pleas had been taken until today. If this matter is to be adjourned for the usual four-week period,' Lee looked over to the court probation officer, a middle-aged, grey-haired man who nodded his assent to her estimate, 'the question of bail arises.'

'Miss Mitchell, I may as well tell you that I am not minded to give your client bail.'

'As Your Honour knows, the Bail Act starts from the standpoint that every defendant has a presumed right to bail unless the relevant exceptions apply. I am sure that Your Honour would not wish to be seen to be pre-judging this issue before you have heard my submissions on this point.'

From his expression, it was perfectly clear that that was

precisely what Shervington was doing, but he was not going to risk being appealed. Instead, he turned his attention to Peter Fairfax.

'Let us hear what the Crown have to say first. Mr Fairfax, I'm sure you have objections.'

'Your Honour, it is clear that the defendant is not a man of good character, and the amount of the drug is, of course, of great concern. Nevertheless, it is a Class B drug, the defendant has turned up at court today and has never failed to answer his bail in the past, has no previous convictions for drugs, and—'

'The man has been to prison in the past, Mr Fairfax!'

'Your Honour is quite right but the Crown feel that, precisely because of this fact, the fear of prison, which is the main reason persons on bail abscond, would not have the same effect on this man.'

Lee held her breath. That was an argument that Shervington would not have countenanced for a second if she had put it forward for the defence, and Peter knew it. But put forward by the prosecution . . .

The silence stretched. Ray stood in the dock, hardly daring to breathe.

'Very well,' Shervington at last conceded with obvious ill will. 'The defendant is granted bail on the following conditions . . .'

The conditions were onerous, as was to be expected, but Ray knew how lucky he was to be bailed at all, and even though there was no guarantee he would not be back in jail in four weeks' time, he was more than happy to agree to them.

As he stood there in the dock, white-faced and sweating, so unlike the Ray she knew, Lee wondered how long it would be before whatever shit he was involved in hit the fan.

A tall, slightly dishevelled figure ran up the stairs and burst through the doors opening on to the long corridor off which the courts were situated. Court Four, Court Four – where the hell was it? He hoped he wasn't late again. Getting legal experience during the holidays before going back to university was all very well, but personally he found the whole idea of criminal law distasteful. Most of his friends had jobs with City firms of Chancery Chambers, which was so much more genteel, not to mention financially rewarding, but he had ended up with some South London legal aid firm. And the clients! Not the sort of people he was used to mixing with socially. The only good thing about it was that he could tell his chums about his walk on the wild side when term resumed.

Ah, Court Four, there it was. On a row of seats outside the court lay a wig and gown, some papers and a copy of Archbold. Standing next to it were two people, a tall, immaculately dressed white man, probably in his late twenties, and a woman the same age or slightly older, also very well dressed, but black. They were smiling at each other and shaking hands. No one else around, so that must be his case. What was the barrister's name? Lee Mitchell.

He rushed up to them.

'Good morning, Mr Mitchell,' he said, interrupting their conversation. 'I'm Jonathan Earle, from the solicitors. I hope I'm not terribly late, but I can take instructions from your client,' he looked at Lee, 'straightaway. I see you didn't turn up for your conference, Ms . . .?' His tone, which had been overly solicitous before, was now just a touch patronising.

'What did you say your name was again?' Lee was amazed at how calmly she asked the question, but then this wasn't the first time this had happened to her.

'Mr Earle. Now, if we could just get—'

'I can't believe this,' Ray burst out. 'It's over. You're too fucking late, mate, and you never bothered to read the papers neither, did you?'

Really, Jonathan thought. The kind of people who were being allowed to practise at the Bar these days. Opening things up was all very well but this chap sounded more like a defendant, not a . . .

Suddenly the full enormity of his mistake dawned on him. He stood there, mouth agape, looking from the angry man to the even angrier woman.

'Ms . . . Ms Mitchell, I'm so very sorry. I had no idea. I just—'

'You just assumed that Mr Willis here was my counsel in this cannabis case,' Lee said, icy-calm. 'You did, I trust, read enough of the papers to know it was a drugs case?'

Jonathan started to say something but Lee waved her hand dismissively.

'Please don't say anything more.' She turned to Ray. He was looking even more embarrassed than Jonathan Earle. 'Ray, we're done here. I'm glad it went well today. I'll see you in four weeks' time.'

With that, she gathered her things and left.

15

Chapter Three

Turning off from Fleet Street into the Temple, it never failed to amaze Lee how quiet it was compared to the surrounding streets. It was something that stirred both positive and negative feelings in her. Sometimes, especially on a summer afternoon, it was so beautifully calm and peaceful that she could not imagine working anywhere else.

She walked towards Middle Temple Hall. Outside it was a group of American tourists avidly listening to a portly man, who looked like a retired sergeant-major, regaling them with its history. As she passed she heard one of the group, an expensively dressed woman, say to a man, presumably her husband, 'You hear that, Harold? This here hall is probably older than our country!'

Somehow, that seemed to exemplify the reverse side of the equation: the feeling that she didn't and never could quite belong, no matter how long she practised at the Bar. When the hall was first built, there would have been no conception that a woman would practise at the English Bar, and the possibility that that woman might be black would have been laughable. Some people still had problems with the concept now. And not only was she black, and a woman, but she hadn't gone to the 'right' school or university and, unlike her moneyed contemporaries, had had to find paying work part-time in the early years while she built up her practice.

But in many ways being an outsider was liberating; no one expected anything of you. It was also nothing new. Hearing her parents talk about what it was like for them when they first left Guyana for England nearly forty years ago, full of hope for the better life they were promised, Lee knew that nothing she had faced came close to the level of exclusion and disappointment they had experienced. When she precociously announced at ten that she wanted to be a lawyer, they were behind her all the way, making sure that at least one of them attended every parent/teacher's evening just to let the teachers know that 'we're watching them good', as her father used to say. And when the school's careers teacher expressed her belief that any kind of legal work, let alone that of a barrister, was an unsuitable and unrealistic ambition for any black girl at the comprehensive, her parents would have none of it.

Thinking back to her Call Night, Lee knew that of all the proud parents, relatives and friends there, hers must have been the proudest. Even her father, sick as he was, smiled fit to burst. She was particularly glad that he had lived long enough to see that.

Lee narrowly avoided colliding with a clerk laden with documents. Four in the afternoon in the Temple was always a busy time, what with barristers coming back from court, couriers delivering briefs from solicitors' offices, and junior clerks hurrying to the post office or to the Document Exchange. In a busy Chambers like Maple Court, the level of activity in the Clerks' Room would reach a kind of controlled frenzy between four and six.

As soon as she walked in, Lee could tell how stressed the clerks were because both of them were smoking furiously, filling the room with a nicotine haze. She liked her Chambers, but she hated to be around when it was like this, particularly now that she was trying to give up smoking. She wondered whether Tom, the senior clerk, who was responsible for keeping the professional lives of the twenty-two barristers who comprised Chambers on track and who was also responsible for hiring junior clerks, had an unwritten rule that any successful applicant 'must be a smoker, or be willing to learn'. Certainly, the only way any of them could give up would be if they both did it together.

'I'm back,' she said, trying to make her voice heard above the din.

She got grunts from Dean the junior clerk, and a wave from Tom, who in his bespoke tailored suit and with his world-weary air resembled an older version of Bryan Ferry.

'Did you hear about the baby Keeley case?' Tom asked.

'How long did he get?' Lee put down her bag. The Keeley case, involving the systematic sexual abuse and eventual murder of an eighteen-month-old girl by her stepfather, had been going on for months, and the depressing details were reported daily in the press and nightly on the evening news. It was, on any view, one of the most open and shut cases in recent years.

'George Amery got him off.'

Seasoned lawyer though she was, Lee's jaw dropped.

Tom held up the latest edition of the *Evening Standard*. 'Read it and weep,' he said.

The headlines screamed, 'KEELEY MAN GOES FREE', and underneath, in slightly smaller type, ' "The Rottweiler" Bites Again'. There was a colour picture of both the acquitted man and Amery, the former looking stunned, as if he could not believe his luck, the latter looking extremely pleased with himself. Lee threw the paper down in disgust.

'That man would represent anyone.'

'Yes, he does. But he's a fantastic lawyer, one of the best. And anyway, isn't that what we're here for, Miss Mitchell? To represent anyone who needs it?' Tom looked at her. They had been down this road before.

Lee sighed. Of course everyone was entitled to a defence, but George Amery specialised in doing the cases no one else would touch; not, she suspected, for any great love of the law but solely for the notoriety and media attention it brought him.

'How did he manage to pull it off?' she asked.

'Legal technicality. You know George; if there is one, he'll find it.' There was something that sounded suspiciously like admiration in Tom's voice. Results, that was all he was interested in. As senior clerk, he received ten per cent of the total annual earnings of Chambers. Lee was under no illusions about him, she knew she was only tolerated because the clients kept coming back. And a little local colour around Chambers did not hurt their image either.

Suddenly, Tom seemed to recall that one of his barristers had been involved in a case, too.

'How did it go with Willis?' he asked.

'He pleaded,' Lee answered. She was looking through the message book as she spoke. 'Goes to show there's a first time for everything.'

'Well, maybe he was bang to rights.'

'You know pleading's not his style, Tom. Look how long I've been representing him. He's had some good results with me, too. I think he was protecting someone, plus Shervington scared the shit out of him.'

'Yeah, he would me, too,' said Tom, taking another drag on his cigarette and gulping down a mouthful of black coffee. 'You've had two messages. Your mother rang, and also some man – Cox, I think – to remind you about tonight.' Tom looked at her expectantly. Lee was aware of Dean looking too. That was the thing she disliked most about Chambers, everyone wanted to know everything about everyone else, especially Tom, who was a true believer in the maxim 'knowledge is power'. It was a veritable gossip factory. Not that there was anything secret about this, she was only going to speak at her old school, but sometimes it was nice to be able to keep something to yourself.

'Thanks, Tom.' She wasn't going to elaborate. 'Anything in for tomorrow?'

'Er, no. We thought you were an effective trial. Oh, I nearly forgot. You know in the last Chambers meeting you said you would take a pupil? We've got someone who's interested in crime – a woman, too. Anne-Marie Green.'

'I've got nothing against a male pupil, Tom. Anne-Marie Green – don't think I saw her.'

'You didn't. She came in twice when you were up on that long affray trial in Manchester. But you did say you would help out by taking her.'

'Yeah, yeah. I would have liked to have seen her first, but OK. Do you have her CV?'

'There's a copy on your shelf,' said Tom, pointing to rows of shelving near the door.

'Thanks,' Lee said, picking it up as she walked towards the door. 'Oh, by the way, is Giles around?'

Silence. Dean, the seventeen-year-old junior clerk, was trying not to laugh and not succeeding very well. Tom looked at him reprovingly before clearing his throat to speak. 'Mr Townsend's not in, Miss Mitchell. Er, you know he wasn't appointed.'

'No, I didn't.' Lee was not in the least surprised. Her Head of Chambers had applied twice before to become Queen's Counsel, an appointment which would have marked him out as a success among his peers, many of whom had already achieved that hallowed status. Unfortunately, in spite of his seniority, his ambition was not matched by either his practice or his brains. 'I'll just ring the solicitors about today's result, then I'll be going.' And with that she left for her room.

Lee's room, which she shared with Mary Fisher, another member of Chambers, was just like the others in her set: beautifully, and very expensively, decorated in a traditional, rather old-fashioned way. However, both she and Mary had added their own personal touches; Mary, with a set of silver-framed photographs of her three children, all of whom had hair as red as their mother's, and Lee with a small carving of an African mother and child, and a photograph of her father taken when he was still healthy and vital. Lee often wondered whether Mary was as surprised as she was how well they got on together. After all, their backgrounds could not have been more different. Probably the only thing capable of embarrassing Mary was any reference to her titled background, the confidence she had was something bred in the bone – unlike her own, which had been diligently and painfully acquired.

Apart from the fact that she was very easy to get along with, Lee liked sharing with Mary because neither of them were around much. Since the birth of her third child, Mary had decided to work from home a lot more, only coming into Chambers once or twice a week. Today was one of her rare days in, which was no bad thing. She could always be counted on to raise your spirits. She was on the phone, her head bobbing up and down as she chatted animatedly to someone, presumably her solicitor, about the result of some long-running landlord and tenant case she had just completed. You could put your ear to the ground and virtually hear, all over the Temple, barristers taking part in the same time-honoured ritual. It was as important as the decision in the case itself: smoothing ruffled feathers if the result was worse than expected, or accepting praise, not too modestly, if it was a win, and looking forward to being sent more cases by a grateful firm.

Today, it seemed Mary fell into the latter category. No false modesty for her. She had won a difficult, lengthy case, and now that she was on the mountaintop she was clearly enjoying the view.

Lee sat behind her desk and rang Brendan Donnelly at Hatton's with her own good news about Ray Willis.

'Ray rang me outside court,' Brendan told her. 'Said he didn't want to ring inside in case the judge changed his mind. I don't know how you managed to get him bail. He always thought you were good, now he thinks you can walk on water.'

'Hard work and preparation, as usual, Brendan.' Lee paused. 'But I think there's more to this than meets the eye. You know Ray, he's not into drugs and I'd never seen him so rattled about anything – and it's not as if he hasn't been inside before.'

'Yeah, well, we'll never know for sure unless he tells us and he's not likely to if someone else is involved. He did tell me about that arrogant Oxford bastard. I can't apologise enough, Lee. We won't be using him again.'

'He'd better give me a wide berth. Next time he won't get off so lightly.' Suddenly Lee couldn't stand it any more. She scrabbled around in her handbag until she found some chewing gum. She put one in her mouth but it wasn't the same. 'Got to go now, Brendan. I've got something to do this evening.'

'OK – hey, before you go,' Brendan paused for emphasis, 'you know the Omartian case?' When the Keeley case had not been on the front pages, it was the fast-living, high-spending Omartians. Theirs was one of the most noteworthy cases in recent memory.

'No, Brendan, never heard of it.'

Brendan gave a deep chuckle. 'The youngest one came in to see me. He's Tail-End Charlie in all this, but from what he tells me, he may actually have a defence. He's still deciding whether to formally instruct us, but if he does, do you want it?'

Barristers far senior to her would turn cartwheels for a brief like that. Lee was no different, but she was damned if she would show it.

'Well,' she said slowly, 'you know I'm pretty busy,' which was the truth.

'Come off it, Lee. No one's too busy for a case like this. Besides, I reckon it won't be heard until this time next year at the earliest. Look, nothing's firm as yet, but if you don't want it—'

'Yes I do,' she interrupted quickly.

'Good. Well, I'll speak to you about it again when I know what the position is. Have a good evening, Lee.' Click.

Lee put the telephone down slowly and sat for several minutes just looking at it, until she saw Mary eyeing her with a grin. Mary reached under her desk and took out a bottle of Bollinger champagne. She opened it and filled two styrofoam cups.

Lee laughed. 'You know, if we both carry on winning our cases we'd better get some decent glasses.'

'Who said you need to win to drink champagne? It's also the best way to drown your sorrows. I know. Mind you,' she said downing hers in one, 'winning makes it taste better.'

'Maybe we should give some to Giles,' said Lee, only half serious.

'I don't know why he applied. All ambition, no balls. But who knows? Maybe fourth time lucky next year, because I'm sure he'll try again. Anyway,' Mary poured herself another cup, 'cheers.'

'Cheers.' Lee raised her cup in a toast. 'I'm off tomorrow.'

'So am I,' said Mary. 'Any plans for this weekend?'

'Not really. It would be good to spend some time with David. But tonight I have to give a careers talk at my old school about coming into the profession, that sort of thing. I suppose they'll say how much support and encouragement they gave me – you know, bullshit like that.'

'Then why are you going?'

Why indeed? Lee slowly took a sip from her cup and looked out of the window. Outside, the evening sunset was turning everything a reddish gold, even infusing the old Temple stones with warmth. 'At my school, just sitting your A-levels was an achievement, never mind passing them. Most of the girls I went to school with were only encouraged to do shop work and many of them are still doing just that twelve years later. So I want to show them that there is an alternative to getting pregnant or working at

23

Woollies. Also, my old careers teacher is still there – in fact, she's the head now. She never thought I would amount to anything so, childish as it may seem, I want to go back to rub her face in it.'

'And so you will. What are you now, thirty? You're a lawyer, and you made it on your own terms with no rich judge for an uncle. You're good at your job – bright, busy. You look the part, sleek and polished. And if that doesn't impress them, there's always the car.'

'The car might swing it. I mean, if you were coming to my old school to convince me, at sixteen, not to leave the place but to carry on studying for another six or seven years to be a lawyer, you'd better look like you were making some money! Anyway, what about you?'

'The children are going to the country to see their grandparents, so Martin and I can do it all weekend and pretend we're still single. You know, turn the clock back to the days before stretch marks and Formula.'

Lee had to laugh. 'Well, I certainly know you'll try.'

Mary grinned, but then her grin faded slightly as she spoke again. 'You know, you haven't been round since we moved. It would be nice to see you again outside this place. Who knows,' she shrugged, 'you might even persuade David to come along this time.'

The chance of that happening was slim. Lee knew that, and by now she was sure Mary did too. David was with her despite, not because of, what she did for a living. As supportive as he was, he could only take one barrister at a time.

'That would be nice. I'll talk to David. And there's no reason we can't meet up even if he doesn't come. Anyway, let's hope you can walk in here on Monday.'

Chapter Four

Fordyce Park, once a secondary girls' grammar school then a secondary modern before its more recent reincarnation as a comprehensive, might have changed its name but little else had altered. Its glory had already started to fade when Lee was a pupil there; now it was a shadow of even those days. The bricks of the large, sprawling main building had turned even greyer with grime and age, and with the school's expansion, a few prefabricated buildings had been added to the main site, like false limbs. They jarred so much it hurt to look at them. At least there was no visible graffiti, but the gates and railings had become even more fortified, giving the school the appearance of having to keep the pupils in by force. Even the beautiful evening twilight could not hide the fact that the reality, close up, was worse than any memory.

Twelve years ago, when she left, Lee had vowed she would never set foot here again. She even avoided driving past it whenever possible, a difficult feat bearing in mind that her mother lived just round the corner. In the ensuing years her life had changed beyond recognition. It was easier to burn your bridges when there was nothing to save; now, the only link to the person she was then and the woman she was now was her mother.

She drove through the old, peeling, wrought-iron gates that framed the entrance to the school. There were speed bumps in the drive that hadn't been there before. A number of other cars were already parked there, all of them modest, and most of them the worse for wear. Lee suspected that the oldest, most dilapidated cars belonged to the teachers. Her own car, a black SAAB, was in marked contrast.

Just inside the hallway near the door was a large, green-painted wooden wall plaque displaying two columns of names, one for every head girl since 1960, the other for every headmistress since 1937. Like a relic of former glories, it hung on a slightly grimy grey wall that could have done with a coat of paint. The last name read, 'Marjorie Cox, 1992—'.

A couple of teachers standing by the door took the names of the arrivals, giving speakers and parent governors their biggest smiles. Scanning the hall, there was not a single face Lee recognised. The pupils were as ethnically mixed as ever, and now, at long last, there were a few black and Asian faces among the staff. It was a pity that at the point when they were most needed, the school was in decline. Mrs Cox was nowhere to be seen; but as had always been the case, Lee heard her before she saw her.

'Leanne? Leanne Mitchell?' That big, booming, bossy voice was unmistakable. It was no wonder Tom had thought Mrs Cox was a man. She took hold of Lee's hand, shaking it vigorously up and down, like a pump, the effort of which caused the material of her floral dress to billow round her large frame. 'So good of you to come. You've returned as one of Fordyce's finest.' The smile she lavished on Lee never reached her eyes. Still clasping her hand but now no longer shaking it, Mrs Cox gave her such a studied, appraising look that for a moment Lee wondered whether she really knew who she was. Her former careers teacher hadn't changed at all: the same large, overpowering presence which, with a few well-chosen words, could eclipse, at sixteen, any dream you ever had of being more than she expected you to be.

'Of course, I always expected you would do well. You had such drive for a young girl. Your parents, too. I was sorry to hear about your father's passing, by the way.' Without pausing for a response, she continued, 'We tell all our girls about you. It's nice to know we provided an excellent education for our former pupils – and still do, within thc limits of our resources, of course. Speaking of which, I think I see the Borough Education chairman. You must excuse me. Oh, Mr Henry . . .' Having made her pronouncements, off she swept, a large flowery blur.

Speakers were already being ushered to their seats on the stage, the same stage where school assemblies were taken and the Christmas play performed. Lee sat with the other speakers and staff as her teachers had done in the past, lined up stiffly in a row against the back of the stage looking out at the pupils and their parents ranged below them. The hall was not full by any means, but a sizeable number had turned up. There was a group of ten or so pupils at the back of the hall gathered round something or someone. As the crowd shifted and parted, it disclosed a tiny black woman with a light, almost olive, complexion, wearing a headdress of African cloth which gave her the look of a young queen. She came forward and took her seat, front row centre. Out of the corner of her eye, Lee could see Mrs Cox looking at this young woman, and wondered at the reason for the frown she was giving her, and the tight set to her lips. Whoever she was, she definitely wasn't a pupil; her confidence, rather than any great age difference, distinguished her from the other students. At the same time, she was hardly old enough to be the mother of a fifteen- or sixteen-year-old. Perhaps someone's sister. She looked vaguely familiar, but then everything was beginning to look that way to Lee. She even recognised one or two teachers now, older and greyer than when they had taught her all those years ago but with the same despondent expressions.

For the first time tonight, Lee felt nervous. She yearned for a cigarette. She smiled at thc others seated there, mostly teachers, she guessed, though she couldn't be sure; so much of the old guard had changed. No response.

27

Then she was being introduced. As Lee listened to Mrs Cox trumpet her achievements, she felt it was not about her. And in fact it wasn't, it was all about Fordyce – how the school had turned out such a good pupil; how she would never have achieved anything if not for the encouragement of the school; how but for Fordyce she would have been yet another "single mother, council flat" statistic.

Lee stood up. She saw rather than heard the applause for her, the "statistic" that had made it. A few mothers near the front of the audience were poking their fifteen-year-olds in the ribs, urging them to listen and emulate. The ones at the back were not paying any attention. In their minds she was far removed from them, and her glowing endorsement by the headmistress only served to emphasise that fact and widen the difference between them. The room became very quiet, all eyes were turned on her, the expectancy almost tangible. And what did they expect? A ringing endorsement of herself as victim? As someone who should never have succeeded but did so by sheer fluke?

Lee turned to Mrs Cox. 'Thank you for inviting me to speak here tonight. You've given the school a ringing endorsement for its part in my success. Unfortunately,' she turned back to the audience, 'none of that part is true.'

That got their attention at the back. And with that statement Lee felt more in control than she had ever done while attending this school.

'Don't misunderstand me. There were a few good teachers here at this school – Mrs Appleby for one. She taught me English Literature. A bit before your time, I suppose – I know she's not here now. But when I was a pupil here, the only work experience we could get was shop work; the highest aim we could have, even the brightest of us, was to be someone's office clerk. You were never, ever encouraged to aim for anything higher.'

Lee took a deep breath. From the look on Mrs Cox's face, she knew it was pointless stopping now.

'This is not about revenge, or ingratitude, or causing embarrassment to the school. But I promised myself that if I was ever invited to address students at Fordyce, I would tell the truth about my experiences here. I'm happy to tell you about what I do, and to encourage anyone who wants to follow in my footsteps. But above all, make your own footsteps. Don't let anyone put you off, or put you down. Just plan to be a better version of what you already are.'

Lee didn't know what reaction to expect, but it wasn't the one she received. The stunned silence seemed to go on for ever. Then just as Mrs Cox was about to approach the microphone, the applause exploded, augmented by whoops and catcalls from the students in the back row, who were standing on their chairs. Everyone was clapping except the petite young black woman in the front row. She looked at Lee and held her gaze for several seconds. Then she looked slowly round the hall, taking in the look of shock and disgust on Mrs Cox's face, the astonished gazes of the other teachers and the sheer delight of all those seated around her. Then she laughed, said something quickly to a man sitting beside her, glanced at Lee again and got up and walked towards the door. She was the only person to leave the hall; such a small figure, and with so much going on, it shouldn't have been noticeable, but it was. Especially when you were trying to remember where you'd seen that face before.

The petite young teacher drifted in and out of the school hall over the next two hours. Sometimes she spoke to the students, both present and former pupils of hers, sometimes to their parents or to other members of staff. But mostly she watched Lee as she worked the room, gliding from one group to another, speaking to anyone who approached her. She looked groomed, polished, expensive; faultless from top to toe. The teacher would never have believed Lee had had any connection with Fordyce until she heard her speak. Voices do not change much, not really, and Leanne had never sounded like a real South Londoner anyway. Then, when she held her gaze, she knew she wasn't mistaken. However poised and smooth the outward appearance, the eyes had a hardness that told not of lack of compassion but of having seen and experienced too much life from too young an age.

She walked back to the main entrance and leaned against it, her back to the hall. She had confiscated some cigarettes earlier that evening from a couple of fourteen-year-olds she used to teach. She scrabbled around for a packet – seven left, enough for tonight – and lit one up. There were few cars left now, and of those that were, she recognised all of them. That meant that shiny black SAAB could only belong to one person. It looked new, or new enough; certainly newer than any car she or Michael had ever had. She suddenly realised that that was the first time she had thought about him today. She must have been busy.

She heard the click of high heels on the stone steps quickly approaching from behind, then pausing for a fraction of a second before continuing more slowly.

'Nice car,' the teacher said, still leaning against the door, not turning round.

'Thanks.' Yes, the voice was the same. Much more assured, of course, but still the same.

As the footsteps came level with her, she took a long drag on her cigarette, half turned and said, 'Want one?'

What a stupid question. 'No thanks. I don't smoke.'

'When did you quit, Leanne? Was it after you dropped all that weight?' For someone so small, she had a surprisingly deep voice.

Lee stopped and turned. 'No, it was after I learned smoking stunts your growth.'

The woman laughed.

'It is Leanne, isn't it? Well, you've certainly got a mouth on you now. Back then you wouldn't have known what to say.' She blew a smoke ring into the night, and that was when the last piece of the puzzle fell into place. Lee remembered her at school, smoke rings drifting from behind the bicycle shed, getting detention yet again.

'Simone? Simone Joseph?'

'Mrs Wilson to my kids. I teach here now. Who would have believed it?' Who indeed? But then she smiled, a big, beaming smile. Everything she ever did seemed to be dramatic, larger than life. She flicked her cigarette on to the gravel path, stepped forward suddenly and gave Lee a big hug.

Lee stood there self-consciously, partly because it took her by surprise, and partly because they had never been friends.

Simone felt the tension in Lee's body and stepped back as suddenly as she had come forward. She looked Lee straight in the eye, a difficult thing to do from her vantage point.

'OK, so I know we weren't good friends before, but I'm so pleased to see you back here you can't imagine. When we heard you were coming, I wondered whether it was you. If any of us was going to make it, my money was on you. Just look at you! Big-time lawyer! God, you look good. And then hearing what you had to say – it's the first time any of my class has paid the slightest attention to any talk of a career . . .'

She was so voluble, it was hard to be immune. Soon Lee was grinning like a fool, her wariness melting away under Simone's warmth. This was so different from the detached air she had affected in the hall.

The sudden chill of the night reminded Lee that even though the days might be sunny, it wasn't summer yet.

'Listen,' she said, as soon as Simone stopped to draw breath, 'did you drive? Or are you waiting for someone?'

Simone's smile flickered for an instant, but her gaze did not waver. That was one thing about her that hadn't changed; she always gave the world that challenging hazel-eyed stare, no matter who you were. That alone got her more detentions than virtually anyone at Fordyce.

'No, I was thinking about ringing for a taxi. I don't live far from here – round the corner from your mum, in fact.'

'Well,' said Lee as she walked towards her car, 'that should be easy to find. Come on, I'll give you a lift home.'

Chapter Five

'It's guerrilla living,' Simone said, without a trace of embarrassment.

Lee was looking at her small front garden. The weeds on the tiny lawn and in the borders were threatening to destroy the path from the rusty gate to the front door as well as the few existing flowers. To cap it all, the house itself was well overdue for a fresh coat of paint.

'Do your house up round here and you're asking for trouble. I'm the only one on my street who hasn't been broken into; they don't think it's worth the effort.' Suddenly Simone burst out laughing. 'It's obvious you don't live here any more, Leanne.'

'I come here nearly every week to visit my mum.'

Simone was surprised at the sharpness of Lee's tone. 'Look, I don't know what you thought I was trying to say. All I meant was that this place has changed, like a lot of things.'

All the air came out of Lee in a rush. She hadn't even realised she had been holding her breath. She massaged the back of her neck. 'Yes, I know. I'm sorry. I'm just sick of being accused of selling out, which is what I thought you were doing.'

Simone knew there was a lot behind that comment – it was the first time this evening that the smooth polish had been disturbed – but thought that now was not the right time to pursue it. In any case, you didn't have to be Einstein to work it out. Personally, she wondered why Leanne ever gave it a thought. There were some people who would always think badly of you if they wanted, no matter what. She knew that better than most.

Lee turned on the ignition and the big SAAB purred smoothly into life.

'You sure you won't come in?' Simone sounded surprised and a little hurt. The journey from school had taken no more than five minutes by car, so there had not been much time to talk.

From the tone of her voice it was obvious to Lee that Simone was bursting with barely contained curiosity, eager to ask her about every detail of her life since she had left school. She didn't want that. And the idea of talking about the good old days with someone who had not been a friend did not appeal either. Too many memories. Her life was different now. But the look in Simone's eyes disturbed her. Many thoughts had flashed through Lee's mind since they had met again, but never had she remembered Simone being lonely or needy. She bent forward and looked up at Simone's house. It was in darkness.

'No, I'd better not. It's been a long day.'

'Someone at home waiting for you?'

Lee smiled. 'I certainly hope so!' She paused, then asked, 'What about you?' Simone had said she was known as Mrs Wilson to her pupils.

'That's a whole other story.'

Lee looked at her. They had been so different at school she doubted they would have anything to talk about, but maybe just her company, and their shared memories, would be enough to take the edge off the loneliness Simone was obviously trying hard to hide. Lee was lucky, she hadn't been lonely for a very long time. Who was she to judge?

'Well, I could come in for a moment. He can wait.'

Instantly the moment of vulnerability was gone, toughness sliding into its place. Survival mode was back, deflecting any feelings of pity. 'No, I'll be fine.' There was a note of finality in Simone's voice. 'But it was nice seeing you again. Now that you know where I live, don't be a stranger.' And then she was gone.

Lee stayed until Simone closed the front door behind her, watching as gradually one by one the lights came on in the house, then she pulled smoothly out into the darkened street. Still acting tough, just like she did at school. Did she live on her own? Where was Mr Wilson?

Lee's house was no more than five miles from Simone's, but it could have been light years away. With every mile the streets became quieter, leafier, and better lit. Simone's house could have fitted into any of the large, double-fronted houses set well back off the road twice over, with room to spare, a fact that was not lost on Mrs Mitchell when her daughter first moved here. This was an area for wealthy, established professionals and their families, and the size and cost of the dwellings made sure it stayed that way. Unusually, however, the house in which Lee lived was divided into two flats, much to the dismay of the local residents. The architect who had converted them lived on the top two floors but was usually absent. The ground and first floor were hers, as was the walled garden. The gravel crunched under the wheels as she pulled into the driveway and killed the engine. The hall light was on. Good. The stuff in the car could wait.

The bedroom was almost in darkness when Lee came out of the shower, but she could still see David's broad muscular back, only partly covered by the sheets, their whiteness making his skin all the more inviting, like rich dark chocolate. And just as enticing. Lee got into bed and ran her hand gently down his back from his shoulder to his waist. Skin so soft, stretched tight over a hard, athletic body – what woman could resist? Certainly not her. She snuggled up closer and kissed him between his shoulder blades. He always slept naked, for which she was eternally grateful. His breathing was so even and regular that she wondered whether he was asleep. Well, he wouldn't be for much longer.

'Now suppose I was sleeping,' a voice came mumbling from the pillow.

Lee slid her hand round his waist and down between his legs.

'You're definitely not sleeping now.'

'You got that right.' He laughed and turned round to face her. 'So why don't I slip inside something more comfortable?'

Sunday found Lee back in the old neighbourhood again, this time parked outside the most impressive building in the area, the local Pentecostal church. When she was growing up, the building had been High Anglican, becoming older, greyer and more neglected even as its parishioners did. Now, like Fordyce Park, it served as a reminder of once prosperous times. Back in those days, the Celestial Church of Christ had had its premises in a former newsagents. They acquired the church building when it fell into disrepair and no one else was interested in it. Painstakingly they had set about restoring it to its former glory.

Lee looked at her watch. Two o'clock. Pastor Matthews never seemed to think that a short service was enough to save his flock, and no one dared leave before he finished. But this was overrunning, even for him. She thought of David, still in bed, which made her all the more annoyed. Then she remembered. Easter service. Damn. At least she'd come prepared. She changed the CD for the fifth time and reached towards the back seat of the car for the Sunday papers which were almost completely hidden under a massive bouquet of flowers.

The last thing she expected to find in a broadsheet newspaper was yet another tabloid-style article on the Omartians. Lee had picked the only newspaper that hadn't had it on the front page only to find it on the inside cover. She made a mental note to speak to Brendan about adverse publicity – that was, if he made good on his promise and sent her the brief. The thought made her heart beat faster and her breathing become more shallow. Some barristers, if they were lucky, got The Case which, depending on the outcome and the lawyer's performance, could either put them in an entirely different class or ensure they never got that chance again. Brendan was usually a man of his word; still, experience had taught her not to count on anything until the brief was on her desk.

'NEW SECRETS OF CITY WONDER BOY' didn't have anything new, or secret, to share. Reporting on this family had reached saturation point. What was interesting, however, was that in spite of the small part Clive Omartian had allegedly played in the fraud, he was getting more than his fair share of media attention. Interesting, but not surprising, looking at a photograph of the accused. It was obviously a family shot, taken in an unguarded moment during happier times. The father was old, and the brother, Hector, looked like a toad. Clive Omartian was neither of these things.

The article itself simply regurgitated the usual gossip about wild parties, high living, and a fast-track lifestyle that attracted women from all over the world. But the tone of the article was different. The tabloid press were clearly fascinated by the life-style. The 'quality' press tried to claim the moral high ground, and so adopted a faint, though distinct, sneer.

'There is something very brash and eighties about the unstoppable rise of the Omartians, all of Eastern European stock, which is totally anachronistic in the nineties. The public watched, fascinated, as they made millions while we struggled through a recession. We didn't know how they could do it, and we couldn't. Now we know. With these allegations, are the chickens coming home to roost?'

So much for impartiality. Lee put the paper aside, feeling disgusted both with the article and with herself for reading it. She looked up, and wondered how all those people could have come out of the church without her noticing. Then she heard a tap on the window and saw a smiling, round-faced woman in a picture hat staring at her.

'I hope you weren't waiting too long, but you know how the pastor stay, specially when it's Easter or Christmas.' Thirty-six years in England had hardly changed her accent, which was still as rich as Demerara sugar.

Verna Mitchell was so short she had to pull the passenger seat as far forward as possible. She smelt of talcum powder and soap, the same brand she'd always used. It was comforting, familiar.

'Pastor Matthews still asks after you, you know. He can't understand why you don't come back.'

'Because I don't believe any more, Mum.' Lee started the engine. 'Isn't hypocrisy a worse sin?'

'I still don't know how that happen. I raise you in fear of the Lord. Must be the company you keeping.'

Lee knew where this was going. Again. 'I hope we're not getting on to David again.'

Verna gave her daughter a long, appraising look. 'You look tired.'

'Didn't get much sleep last night.' It was out of her mouth before she realised. Lee tried, unsuccessfully, to hide a smile.

Verna was no fool. She pursed her lips. 'Don't think I don't know what you smiling about. Just because he got time on his hands doesn't mean you have to keep up with him.'

Lee patted her knee. 'You know, if I didn't know you loved me so much, I could get very offended by this.' Her tone grew more serious. 'I know you don't like him, Mum, but I won't have you criticising him.'

'I'm sure I won't be half as critical if he put a ring on your finger. I don't want no man wasting my daughter's time.'

'I got the flowers.'

'You changing the subject?'

'Yes.'

In the silence that followed, Verna seemed to decide it would be a good idea to leave it. For now.

'They're nice. Your father would have liked them. Red and gold. He always did like bright colours.'

The sleek black car sped into the cemetery. The grounds were extensive, dotted here and there with people paying their respects. A couple of them looked up as they passed. Lee had the uncomfortable feeling that her car looked like an upmarket hearse. They parked as near as they could to the grave, completing the rest of the journey on foot. Neville Mitchell had been laid to rest in a very nice spot which caught the sun most days, as it did now. It was also the most neatly tended grave Lee could see. The work done by the attendants was good, but this was much better. She looked at her mother.

'You've been at his grave again, haven't you, Mum?'

Something very interesting on the next plot seemed to be fascinating Verna, who studiously avoided her daughter's piercing gaze.

'You brought the tools down as well, didn't you? Mind they don't think you're trying to dig him up!'

Verna knelt down and arranged the flowers on the grave, spreading them lovingly over the surface like a colourful blanket. 'Well, of course I can tell them how I want it done when I see them—'

'Of course,' Lee interrupted, drily.

'But sometimes it's just easier for me to put the trowel and fork in my shopping bag and do it myself. Your father understands that, don't you, Neville?' She patted the gravestone affectionately. 'Remember what he used to say? "If you want something done right—" '

' "—do it yourself!" ' they both finished together. They looked at each other and laughed. It was good that they could remember

Neville Mitchell as a husband and father they both loved and missed, but without sadness.

'Self-sufficiency,' Verna continued, her mind still on her late husband. 'In all the years I knew him he was like that. Remember how proud he was when you became a barrister?'

'Yes.' Lee smiled. Her father had never been a demonstrative man, and that had made it stand out all the more in her memory. 'I'm glad he hung in there long enough for that.'

'You think any cancer would have kept him away? All he kept saying was, "Good, now I don't have to worry. She can look after herself." ' Verna looked up at her daughter, so much taller than she was. 'He was so proud of you, baby, just as I am.'

Lee bent down and hugged her mother. She could feel her initial resistance as she fought years of being the loving but stern parent, but it had been melting away ever since Neville Mitchell's death. After all, they were all the family they had.

Verna broke away first, hiding her embarrassment by kneeling down and fussing with the flowers on the grave yet again. When she stood up, she was more composed.

'Maybe I should have buried him in Guyana. He hated the cold so much, you know. That's where we would be now if he was still here. But I wanted him to be close by so I could come and see him when I liked.'

'I think you did the right thing, Mum. Besides, could you count on his family to chase up the graveyard attendants like you do? You'd be flying down there every month to check on them.'

There was a comfortable silence between the two women as they drove back. The sweet melodies of "Sounds Of Blackness" poured from the stereo, filling the car.

'I'm glad you're still listening to some religious music,' remarked Verna.

'I just like the harmonies, Mum. Oh, by the way, I was at Fordyce Park on Thursday.'

'What? So near, and you never did come and see me?'

'Well, I knew I'd be seeing you today. You know who I *did* see? Simone Joseph, as was. Remember her?'

'She used to live at Clairview, the children's home, didn't she? Always fighting.'

'Yes, the same one.'

'In my day we used to say girls like her were too good-looking to be decent.'

Lee looked sharply at her mother. Verna held up her hand, to ward off what she knew was coming.

'Before you say anything, I wasn't talking about her. She couldn't help it if she didn't have much upbringing. Anything she's achieved is no thanks to them. She's a teacher now, I understand. At Fordyce.' Verna chuckled. 'Now she'll be sending people to detention instead of going there herself. This world funny, eh?'

'I'm sure you already know she lives round the corner from you now.'

'Did she say anything about her husband?'

'No, Mum, and I didn't ask. Nothing about children, either.'

'Nice man. Quiet. Not the kind of man you would think she would have gone for. Used to help me with my shopping when he saw me.' Verna sighed. Clearly that was the kind of son-in-law she wanted. 'Haven't seen him around for quite a while now. Look, there's a space over there; that should be big enough.'

As Lee eased her car into it, her mother added, 'And I've already cooked, so don't say you don't have time for some food.' She eyed her daughter critically. 'You look like you need it.'

'You're the only person who would say that. What do you have?'

'Well, I've got some pepperpot from the last time in the freezer, plus some chicken I baked today, rice, yams, sweet potato, cassava, plantain – and some black cake I made yesterday. Not

41

very much,' she concluded, without a trace of irony. 'And the table's all set.'

It was useless to argue. Besides, Lee knew this was her mother's way of saying she wanted her company for a little longer. And she was hungry.

'You always forget, don't you, Mum?'

'What, baby?'

'That I'm a vegetarian.'

Chapter Six

After Thursday's unexpected turn of events, Monday morning was reassuringly familiar.

It was raining. Heavily.

Lee had been awake almost two hours before the alarm rang at 7 a.m., listening to the rain. She thought of the flowers on her father's grave, the rain beating the red and yellow petals into the earth. The thought was profoundly depressing. Now she was wide awake, she could hear the muted sounds of strings from the far end of the hall. That usually set her up for the day, because it was solid and real, like the man himself, the beauty of the music often compensation for the ugliness in many of the cases she handled.

Because of the unexpected way in which Ray Willis's case had been resolved, Lee could have had Monday off as well. Part of her just wanted to go back to sleep, but she was too curious to see whether Brendan had come up with the goods on the Omartian case. And, she suddenly remembered, her prospective new pupil was starting today. Shit!

Lee knew that if she didn't get up straightaway she wouldn't be going anywhere. She went downstairs first to the kitchen, then followed the sound of the music.

The room that doubled as her study and David's music room was Lee's favourite, which was just as well as she spent most of her waking hours there. It wasn't very large, but it was airy and flooded with light from the French windows which opened on to the back garden. When the windows were open in the summer, the muted green decor made it seem like an extension of the garden. Lee paused by the door, listening, even though David was now practising scales. She had to be in love to find *that* attractive. David looked at her across the top of his violin and smiled but didn't stop.

'I thought I heard you playing your piece earlier.'

'You did, but I've got to do this too.'

'I liked it.'

'Wait till you hear the whole thing. Maurice is going to drop a rhythm track on it – Sly and Robbie style. You know, *real* reggae music.'

'You're showing your age; you better start putting some jungle rhythms on it if you want it to sell.'

'Nah, I'm playing what I want to hear. Besides, I'm not pretending to be no sixteen-year-old.'

'Baby, you don't look like any sixteen-year-old I ever saw. I'm making some coffee then I'm shooting straight off. You want some?' He shook his head.

Lee went back to the kitchen and opened the fridge for some milk. Every known type of fruit juice was there – David's doing. She preferred a less healthy start to the day.

The rain had turned to drizzle when she left the flat. As she neared the newsagent's kiosk outside the train station, she saw it was laden with papers featuring yet another story on the Omartian family. She wondered why Clive Omartian had gone to Brendan. As good a solicitor as he was, he was one of two partners in a small legal aid firm in the Elephant and Castle. Why would Omartian money go slumming when the large City and West End firms, with their specialist departments, large staff, and international offices, beckoned? Even if Brendan had picked him up as duty solicitor, families like the Omartians always had a standing brief at the ready to get them out of any difficulties.

Lee was still deep in thought as she got off at Blackfriars

Station and walked up Tudor Street to the Temple. There were two entrances here, a small side gate for pedestrians and a larger one for vehicles. Every morning, but particularly on Mondays, there was a queue to get in. The recent bombings meant that the security checks were now more stringent. A necessary inconvenience, and most people viewed it as such.

But apparently not all.

The driver at the end of the queue was furiously honking his horn. He was driving a large, white Rolls-Royce with personalised numberplates, thus showing that whatever else he had, it wasn't good taste. The driver appeared very agitated, frequently putting his head through the driver's window as he leant on his horn. Usually the security guards ignored that kind of behaviour, but on this occasion they seemed to be falling over themselves to placate the driver. One of them hurried over to him. Whatever he said wasn't audible, but the driver's reply was.

'Well, that's not good enough. Get a bloody move on! I've got to be at the Bailey in twenty minutes.'

The vehicles in front were rushed through in a peremptory manner, without being properly checked. The guards had barely raised the security barrier before 'GA ONE' swept through the gates. 'OK, Mr Amery,' one of them said, with a smile that was both nervous and ingratiating – and infuriating to any onlookers, like Lee, who didn't usually receive such gold-star service. But then, being rich and famous had its privileges.

Apart from the clerks, the start of the week rarely saw many people in Chambers on a Monday morning. Those who were not in court were researching cases in the Temple libraries, or 'doing papers at home', a euphemism used by some for taking the day off. But the telephones and computers were already competing for aural supremacy when Lee walked in.

'Good morning. Any sign of my pupil yet?'

Tom gave Lee a 'Why-are-you-asking-me?' look, but she was

determined not to rise to the bait so early in the morning. She ignored him and instead gave young Dean her most winning smile.

'Have you had any messages from her, Dean?'

'Er, no, Miss Mitchell,' said Dean, hurriedly riffling through the message book. 'Nothing today, and there wasn't anything on the answerphone this morning, so she didn't ring over the weekend. We're still expecting her. But someone else rang for you – Mr Donnelly.'

'Oh.' Lee found she was holding her breath. 'Did he say what it was about?'

'No, he just asked you to ring him.'

Giving in to the urge she had been fighting since she had arrived, she walked over to her shelf to check whether 'Regina v Omartian and others' was there. Although her every professional instinct, as well as her experience of life, had told her not to raise her hopes too high, she was surprised at the depth of her disappointment. When she turned back to Dean, her smile was tight.

'Thanks. When Miss Green arrives, please show her to my room.'

Lee made herself some coffee, and idly tried to read *The Times* but soon found herself staring sightlessly out of the large bay window, the rain trickling down the panes seeming to reflect her mood. Well, that was that. The phone call was probably an apology – wished he could send it to her but she was 'not quite the right stage' for such a brief; 'you're fine with me, but it's the client . . .'; 'your track record's so good, you know I'll always keep you in mind . . .' All of which amounted to the same thing – track record or not, she wasn't getting this case. And the last thing Lee wanted to hear right now was bullshit dressed up as an excuse.

She sighed. Maybe there was such a thing as being too

ambitious for your own good. Her old teachers had warned her about that years ago. After all, she was making good money; she had a nice home, nice lifestyle and, most importantly, she was working regularly. Maybe it was time to start a family – perhaps that was the next step? After all, most people would be happy to be in her shoes.

Most people, but not her. That case would have firmly established her as one of the very best. As a lawyer, Lee knew how good she was; she didn't know exactly why, but she wanted her entire profession to be forced to recognise that fact. For some reason, her thoughts ran to George Amery. She wondered whether that was his motivation too. The idea of having anything in common with him was enough to turn her stomach.

The telephone rang. The internal light was flashing, which was just as well as she didn't feel like talking to Brendan just now, however valid his excuse. It was Tom.

'Miss Mitchell, your new pupil has arrived.' He sounded in much better humour than he had been earlier.

'Fine. Send her in, please.' Lee looked at her watch. Ten twenty. Rain or not, that woman had better have a good reason for being late.

Tom brought her in himself – a noteworthy event; he usually left that kind of menial task to Dean. But one look at her new pupil told Lee why he had made the effort. She would be exactly his type if she hadn't so clearly been out of his league. She looked like a young Grace Kelly, and although she was just starting out on her legal career, her raincoat and umbrella indicated there was no need for economy. Also surprising – as well as irritating – was her air of self-assurance, in spite of being late on her first day.

'Ms Mitchell,' the young woman said, coming forward and extending her hand, 'I'm so pleased to meet you. My name is Anne-Marie Green.' Her hand looked and felt like porcelain. Everything about this woman – her polished accent, expensive clothes, her composure – indicated someone who had led, to date, a closeted, pampered life. Lee hoped there was something more behind that if she wanted to practise criminal law. Still, appearances could be deceiving. She waited a full minute while her pupil took off her coat and made herself comfortable in the chair across from her desk. She watched as Anne-Marie smoothed down her already immaculate suit, the cut and cloth of which confirmed what her outer garments had already indicated.

'Now, could you tell me why you were late?' Lee asked.

Instantly Anne-Marie's smile faded, to be replaced with a look of genuine confusion.

'You did know you were to be here at ten, didn't you?'

'Er, yes. I'm sorry. I tried to get here as quickly as I could but you know how difficult it is to get a cab in this weather . . .'

'I couldn't afford a cab when I was a pupil,' Lee said shortly, 'but I did know how to use a phone.'

'Oh yes, of course. I should have thought . . . I'm sorry . . .' Her voice trailed away.

It dawned on Lee that this was probably the first time her pupil had ever had to apologise for anything. It wasn't that she didn't want to, she just didn't realise it was expected of her. It wasn't a luxury Lee had ever been able to indulge in, and not one she had any intention of accommodating.

She was about to give the younger woman a tart reply but the look of real dejection on her face, so different from her earlier glib assurance, stopped her. She had been right; appearances could, indeed, be deceptive. There was no point in making her cry, she seemed pretty close to tears already. And maybe she herself would have been in a better humour had she got the news she so desperately wanted. Pupils had so little power in the legal evolutionary chain, why take it out on this one?

'Look, judges don't tolerate lateness, and neither do I. So I don't expect it to happen again without very good reason, or at least a phone call. But now we understand each other, let's leave it there. Would you like some coffee, Anne-Marie?'

'Yes,' she whispered, barely able to look Lee in the eye.

'Go to the Clerks' Room and ask Dean to show you where everything is, then we'll talk about what I expect from you for the next six months.'

'OK.' Anne-Marie walked to the door, then stopped. 'Would you like one?'

'No, but thank you for asking.'

The telephone rang again.

'Miss Mitchell?' It was Tom once more. 'I've got Brendan Donnelly on the line.'

A pause. 'OK.' Her pupil was standing there. 'You go and get your coffee, Anne-Marie.'

'Lee? I rang you earlier this morning. Didn't the clerks give you my message?' Lee could tell Brendan was calling on a mobile telephone because the reception was so poor.

'Yes. Sorry, Brendan, I couldn't ring you back earlier. What's it about?' As if she didn't know.

'Clive Omartian. I'm still trying to sort out his brief.'

Still trying? Lee didn't know whether to be sad or mad. 'Oh, yes?'

'Look, I need to see you. Can we meet for lunch in, say, fifteen minutes?'

'Where are you?'

'Right outside your Chambers.'

Lee was astonished. 'Well, why not just come in? Besides, it's too early for lunch.' It wasn't yet eleven.

'You know that shark you call a clerk only wants to see me if I've got work. He wouldn't piss on me otherwise. I'll explain later. Can you meet me or not?' Brendan was normally a mild-mannered man but today there was an edge to his voice that Lee had rarely, if ever, heard before.

'All right. I need to organise my pupil. Make it thirty minutes and I'll be there.'

She didn't need to ask where they would meet. It was an old haunt, near the Old Bailey – where they had first met, in fact. It had been her first big trial, and all she could remember was desperately trying to hide that fact from the other barristers involved. On the day the verdict was expected, everyone else had been too nervous to do anything other than smoke or drink coffee, certainly too nervous to eat anything other than their fingernails. Not Brendan; he had had a full English breakfast. No matter how critical the situation, Lee had never seen Brendan lose his appetite – or indeed eat anything else. It was the same now. Since he was as thin as a rake, you had to wonder where it went.

'Don't you ever fancy a change?' Lee asked as she sat down.

'All the time,' he grinned, 'but the wife would kill me. As far as the breakfast's concerned, at least pork is safer than beef these days – just.' He paused to spear a sausage. 'You're not having anything?'

Lee shook her head. 'Too early for me.'

Brendan gave her a wry smile. 'When I was growing up, you got your meals wherever and whenever you could. Old habits die hard. Thanks for coming.' He put his fork down and stared at her intently. 'I wanted to speak to you about the case.'

'Look, Brendan, if you found someone else to do it, there's no need to explain. No hard feelings.' Maybe if she said it often enough she would even begin to believe it.

'No, it's not like that.' He paused. 'I spoke to Clive Omartian over the weekend, at great length. And, apparently, I've not been the only one.'

'Meaning?'

'He's the most clued-up client I've had, Lee. He knows all the good briefs, he's been following their progress for several months.'

'But he was only arrested two months ago. The papers said he wasn't even in the country then. How could he have known—'

'Who knows? Maybe the shit was getting too close to the fan. The father and brother are involved too, remember? Maybe it was for them.'

Lee couldn't see what Clive Omartian could do for his family from Miami's South Beach that they couldn't do themselves right here, but decided the best thing to do right now was to listen.

Brendan took a long drink from his mug of tea before continuing. 'He's seen Richard Hamilton. And Duncan Forsythe. George Amery. Some others too. Not through me, I might add.'

Lee flinched. As barristers went, these were impressive names. Good as she was, she wasn't in their league.

'What was he doing seeing them? Without you, I mean?'

'He shouldn't have done, of course. But I've never had a rich private client before. Maybe rich private clients always do things their way.' Brendan took a bite out of a piece of toast, dripping with butter. 'He was . . . interviewing them, you could say.'

'*Interviewing* them? What, people of that calibre?'

'They didn't object.' Brendan put down his toast and stared at Lee. 'They want the case, Lee. But he hasn't made up his mind yet.' Another pause. 'I told him about you.'

Lee took a deep breath. 'And?'

'And he agreed to see you too. Before he makes up his mind.'

'He wants to grill me as well? Like all the others?'

'Well . . .'

Lee shut her eyes. 'No.'

'What?'

'No. I won't do it, Brendan.'

'For God's sake, Lee, don't be so bloody hasty. This is just some rich boy's whim, seeing all these briefs. I've spoken so highly of you. Do you know what this case could do for you? For your career? Don't let your pride get in the way.'

'But he's got everyone dangling, grovelling for this case, and he's getting off on it. If he can't choose between men like Hamilton and Forsythe, what the hell do you think he's going to do with me? I won't put myself through that, Brendan.' Lee pushed back her chair to get up. 'There have been times when my pride was all that kept me going in this job. It matters, to me at least. I really appreciate what you've tried to do for me, but I think he's got a bloody nerve asking any of us to behave in this way.'

Outside, the rain had stopped, and Lee welcomed the blast of cold air on her face as she opened the door. She tried to quell the thought that, professionally, she had just made the biggest mistake of her life.

Brendan watched Lee as she left the cafe. Then he took out his mobile phone and dialled.

A male voice answered. 'Hello?'

'I told you she wouldn't go for it. You don't know her like I do.'

'What did she say about me?'

'That you had a bloody nerve.'

'She said that? She didn't even ask about the money?'

'We didn't get that far.'

The voice laughed. 'Well, Brendan, I think you were right. She sounds just the woman for the job.'

Chapter Seven

Never think you've seen everything.

After her last conversation with Brendan, no one was more surprised than Lee when, three weeks later, the Omartian brief landed on her desk – except maybe Tom, who was so impressed he actually brought it to her himself.

'It's a great coup for Chambers, Miss Mitchell,' he said, that long, dour face smiling, as it always did where money was concerned. 'I hear round the Temple that George Amery is none too pleased.'

'I didn't know he was seriously interested in it,' Lee lied. 'Anyway, he's always busy. He's in back-to-back murders at the Bailey, isn't he?'

'He'd make time for this. Anyway, from what I hear he thought he was a front runner. Now he's muttering something about political correctness, or some such.'

So it begins, Lee thought. Who on earth could afford to be politically correct facing ten years in jail? But it could have been worse, he could have said she had slept with either Brendan or Omartian to get the case. Or both. Besides, nothing could dampen her mood now, not even barbed comments from sore losers.

'Well,' Lee smiled sweetly, 'it's just Temple gossip. They can say what they like. I've got the brief, so how much can it hurt? I really don't care. Please, don't get upset on my behalf, Tom.'

Lee's sarcasm went straight over Tom's head. 'That's quite all right, Miss Mitchell.' Still beaming, he turned and left the room.

Having got the brief, Lee thought her quota of surprises was up for the year. She already had two in one day. First, the Omartian brief. Second, a suspended sentence for Ray, Shervington having somehow been persuaded that Ray deserved such a course. But here, waiting outside her room on her return from court that afternoon, was another. Simone Wilson.

It was a month since they had last met. She was dressed very differently today, in a conservative navy-blue suit and white blouse. But the most dramatically different thing about her was her hair. It had been hidden when they last met, now it fell in tiny dark brown curls, waves and ripples past her shoulders. She looked like a sepia-tinted version of an old-time Hollywood starlet. It made Lee feel as awkward as she had ever felt at school – the class misfit watching the perfect petite teenager bewitch all the boys with the strength of her beauty. Even the male teachers had been taken in.

'Bet you're surprised to see me,' Simone said languidly, her eyes never leaving Lee's face.

Lee stared right back. 'Yes, you could say that.'

'Good. I remembered how you hated surprises, even in school. Always liked to plan everything, to know exactly what would happen next.'

'I like it better that way—' Lee broke off and watched, dumbstruck, as Giles Townsend himself, the most senior member of Chambers, came towards Simone with coffee and biscuits.

'It's only instant, my dear. I hope you don't mind.'

'Oh, not at all, Giles. Thank you very much.'

'Do you two know each other?' Lee asked. Never before had she seen her Head of Chambers do anything so menial as to serve coffee himself, not even to his most important clients.

'Oh no. Giles and I have just met. He saw me waiting for you and we got chatting.' The force of Simone's smile at such close proximity seemed to stun Giles; like a deer caught in headlights, he was transfixed. 'I told him I needed some legal advice and he very kindly offered to help, but I told him I was waiting for my lawyer – an old friend.'

'Well . . .' Lee said, lost for words. She hated this, hated the way old memories made her feel.

But things were different now, she reminded herself. She wasn't that awkward girl any more, and never would be again. This was *her* place of work, her own life. Simone had no part in it.

'Let's go to the library, shall we?' Lee's tone was all business now. 'We can speak privately there.' She looked pointedly at Giles and Anne-Marie. 'You can go now, Anne-Marie. Would you excuse us, Giles?'

If, as was commonly believed, you could tell the success of a set of Chambers by the state of its library, or whether it had one at all, then by that reckoning Lee's was one of the more successful ones. The large oak-panelled library was stacked floor to ceiling with legal volumes and texts. Around the ornate central mahogany table were eight leather captain's chairs. Heavy midnight-blue velvet curtains hung from the two large windows. Simone whistled as she took it all in.

'I'm impressed. But then I was as soon as I got here. All these flunkies at your bidding.'

'I wouldn't call Giles Townsend a flunky,' Lee said, drily. 'He's our Head of Chambers.'

'Yes, I believe he said.' Simone was pacing the room now, studying the books intently, though for the life of her Lee couldn't imagine why. 'You always were at home in the library, as I remember.' She sat down.

'That's right.' Lee remembered too. Back then it had been a place of refuge as much as anything else. The memory made her angry. She remained standing.

'And you haven't returned any of my calls.'

'I've been busy. You said you wanted some advice, Simone. What can I do for you?'

'OK, let's get straight to the point.' Simone looked for an ashtray to stub out her cigarette and, finding none, snuffed it expertly with her fingers. 'My husband wants to divorce me,' she said baldly. 'I don't know what to do.'

'You need a solicitor for that, not a barrister.'

'I do know the difference between a solicitor and a barrister, Leanne,' Simone retorted. 'I'm not stupid.'

'No, you were never that. Anyway, I don't do family law.'

'What?' Simone looked around the room. 'All these books and you can't help me? It's still law, isn't it?'

'What do you teach at school, Simone?'

'History.'

'How about if I asked you to teach a geography class tomorrow?' Simone said nothing. 'Well? It's still teaching, isn't it?' When she still didn't reply, Lee said, 'Ask Giles. He has a mixed civil practice. He does a lot of family. I'm sure he'd be only too pleased to help.'

'Yeah, I'm sure he'd like to help the hell out of me. Very much.' Her tone was surprisingly bitter.

Silence. Lee asked, 'How long have you been married?'

'Three years this year.'

'Do you want the divorce?'

Simone hesitated. She put both hands flat on the table. They seemed so little, like a child's. 'He wants it, he can have it. Fuck him.'

'Any kids?'

Again there was that look, the same one Lee had seen in the car that night. 'Why are you getting in my business, Leanne? You already told me you can't help me.'

'That's right. So now will you tell me why you really came to see me?'

'I wanted to find out why you hadn't been returning my calls.'

'I told you, I've been busy.'

'Cut the bullshit, Leanne, OK? We're both too old for that. No one's that busy, not even hot-shot lawyers like yourself. I see your fingers aren't broken, so what's going on?'

If she wanted a straight answer, that was precisely what she was going to get. 'I didn't want to speak to you.'

'Why?' Simone immediately shot back. Clearly she wasn't going to leave this alone.

'I don't know why this is so important to you. You don't seem like the kind of person who has to beg for friends.'

Simone said, in a small voice, 'You can never have too many of those. Real friends, I mean.'

Lee's voice was incredulous. 'I don't believe this. Friends? We were never friends. You made my life a complete misery, and for what? And even Daniel . . .'

'Daniel? Daniel who? Oh, Danny. Jesus, Leanne, that was such a long time ago. And it wasn't as if you were engaged or anything. You still hold that against me?'

Lee tried to get her emotions in check before she spoke again. 'Look, I've gone as far down memory lane as I'm going with you. If you still need legal advice, I'll send you a list of good local solicitors. Otherwise, get out, and don't call me again.'

Lee's voice was calm but Simone felt the force of her anger. It seemed to push her backwards towards the door. Then she turned and ran through it.

It was stupid to still let it get you so angry, Lee told herself as she swung her car out of the Temple and made her way towards Fleet Street. She felt better, somehow, for getting it off her chest, but she also felt uneasy, as if she had hit someone when they were down. Not even Simone deserved that.

It was raining again. Hard to believe it was May. Lee was glad she didn't have to wait for a bus in weather like this any more, especially out here. After six in the evening, the streets around the Temple rapidly became deserted. It was now after eight.

Simone was still waiting, barely visible behind the bus stand. Lee pulled the car over, tooted the horn and wound down the window. The others at the bus stop looked over eagerly.

'Get in, Simone.' She looked like a drowned street urchin.

'What, so you can cuss me again? No thanks.'

'Look, you want to stay out here in the rain? We're both going the same way. Just get in, will you?'

They made the journey in silence. The only sound was the music from Jazz FM. Just once Lee took a sideways look at her passenger. Strands of her hair stuck wetly to her face, and she was biting her bottom lip. Suddenly she looked not like the tormentor of years past but like an abandoned child. The irony was not lost on Lee.

She pulled up outside Simone's house and switched off the engine. The music died. She turned to face Simone.

'Look, I'm sorry. Not for what I said . . .'

'Then why are you apologising?'

'Because I felt like I was kicking you when you were down. With the divorce and everything.'

Simone looked at her. 'OK. So, you coming in this time or what?'

Lee gave her a surprised look, then laughed. 'I wasn't expecting that.'

'Why not? I can't hold a grudge against you now that you've apologised.' A ghost of a smile. 'Anyway, I can't say I didn't deserve it. I know what I was like back then. I don't expect us to be friends overnight, Leanne, but I'd like to try. To be honest, I could really use a friend right now.'

Simone's house was not expensively decorated but the contrast between the deliberately shabby exterior and the tasteful pastel interior made it appear so. Having grown up in such a house herself, Lee knew how small the rooms were, but whatever Simone had saved on decorating the exterior had been well spent internally. The tiny living and dining room had been knocked into one large lounge. There was very little furniture, but what there was was of good quality.. Most surprising of all was that along one wall were shelves filled floor to ceiling with books, just like the Chambers library.

'I'm going to get changed. Help yourself to whatever you like. The kitchen's through there. I've got tea, coffee, wine, rum – something stronger, if you like.'

'No alcohol for me, not if I'm driving.'

'I wasn't talking about alcohol. Though I suppose I can't spliff up in front of you, you might have me arrested or something.'

Lee smiled and shrugged. 'It's your house. Up to you what you do. Just don't give me any.'

The tiny white kitchen was so pristine it looked as if no one had ever cooked in it. Lee made herself some coffee, then changed her mind and poured herself a glass of red wine instead. Then she went back into the lounge, taking the bottle and another glass with her. She could hear Simone in the hallway, playing back the messages on her answerphone. The same man's voice was on three consecutive messages. Simone was fast-forwarding through them. Lee looked at a photograph of Simone and a man who she guessed was Simone's husband. For someone who acted as if she didn't care about her spouse, Lee was surprised to see it take pride of place on the mantelpiece. She picked it up. Judging from the photo, he was of average height, a dark-skinned man with solemn eyes, and he was smiling benignly at his wife. Simone appeared fuller in the face and body than she did now, but still radiant. The love between them was almost palpable. Lee was still looking at it when Simone came back into the room. She had changed into jeans and a big jumper.

'Is this him?' Lee asked, holding out the photo.

'That's right.' Simone made no attempt to touch it or take it from Lee.

'It's a shame. You both look very happy.'

'Yes, we were then. That was taken some time ago.'

Lee replaced the photo. 'You look like you've dropped some weight since then.'

Simone turned away and poured herself some wine. 'It wasn't just weight that I lost. I see you got yourself something,' indicating the wine.

'Yes.' Lee took a sip, then continued, 'When did it start going wrong?'

Simone went to sit down. 'I wasn't talking about the loss of my marriage. I was pregnant when that was taken, and as you can see there're no babies running around this place.'

In the silence that followed, 'I'm sorry' seemed a completely inadequate thing to say, so Lee said nothing. Simone downed her drink in one and poured herself another before continuing, 'We met when I was at teacher training college. He was the chief maintenance engineer on the campus. When we first went out he said he didn't think I would look at him, him being "just a handyman", as he saw it. He thought I would treat him just like the other white students. He didn't realise how much it helped me, seeing another black face every day. We got married as soon as I graduated. When I got the job at Fordyce, we moved down here. We wanted kids straightaway. When I got pregnant, I thought, "finally, a family of my own." I was about five months gone when that photo was taken. Had my due date and everything. Two weeks later, I lost it.'

'You don't have to say any more.' Lee said that as much for her own benefit as for Simone's. The sense of hurt and loss in those calmly spoken words was almost physically painful to hear.

'No, it helps. Anyway, we both took it hard. He's an only child and he really wanted that baby, so we were both grieving for our own different reasons. Perhaps if we'd done it together, he'd still be here. Anyway, after a few months he said he couldn't cope and went back home to Bristol. He left the day the baby would have been born. That was over a year ago.'

'I'd have fucking killed him!' Lee exclaimed. 'How could he leave you alone then? He must have known you had no family.'

Simone's laughter was as shocking as it was surprising. 'Sometimes I can be understanding. Mostly, yes, I do feel like killing him. Especially when I got the letter about the divorce. I always thought we would work it out somehow . . .' Her voice trailed off. Then she said briskly, 'But as I told you before, if that's what he wants, he can have it. I'm not begging no man to stay with me.'

The phone rang. Lee looked at Simone, who made no attempt to pick it up.

'That's what answerphones are for. Besides, I think I know who it is.'

A disembodied voice came from the hallway, muffled but still audible. 'Hey, Sim, where are you? It's nearly ten, why aren't you home yet? I was going to come round, but I know how vex you get if I turn up uninvited. Give me a call when you get this message. I'll keep the mobile on.' Click.

'He's rung three times today already,' Simone said, yawning. She didn't appear to be the slightest bit concerned. Lee wondered whether she should be sorry for this soon-to-be divorcee. Clearly she wasn't that lonely.

'Who is it?' Lee asked.

'Oh, just some guy. Turned out he used to be at Fordyce too, but I don't remember him. Steve Payne?'

Lee didn't remember him either.

'I've been seeing him about four months now. I don't know,

you sleep with someone a couple of times, next thing they think they own you.' She lit a cigarette, then curled up on the sofa. 'He's the only man I've been with since the separation. It was all right when it started but now he seems to want some kind of . . . commitment from me, even though I told him from the beginning that's not how it would go.'

'All the men I've represented in court,' Lee said, 'one thing it's taught me is that you can live to be a hundred and still not fully understand them.'

'My problem is that I understand them only too well. Anyway, how about you? I know you got a man. Have you been together long?'

'We've been living together five years.'

'Anyone I know?'

'No, don't think so.'

'Any kids?'

'Not yet.'

'Are you happy?'

'Very much so.'

'Good, I'm glad. You deserve it.' She paused. 'I'm not surprised you didn't want to keep in touch, Leanne. I was a real bitch to you at school. I was jealous of you, and when you don't know that, it's easy to be destructive. You had a family – a two-parent family. You always knew exactly what you wanted to do, you weren't going to end up on the check-out at Tesco's, that was for sure. You were the only black girl I knew then who liked to study. I couldn't understand what you saw in books until I went to study myself. And now look at you. It certainly paid off.' She smiled. 'I know my pupils were well impressed. Unfortunately, more because they thought you were loaded than by what you said.'

They both laughed. The earlier bitterness was still there but was beginning to lift, the tension eased by drink and gradually relaxing into one another's company.

'Do you keep in touch with anyone else from school?' Lee asked.

'Not really, but I hear things, you know. It's pretty fucking depressing. A lot of drugs and small-time offending.'

'It's still hard to believe you're back at Fordyce. Why teaching?'

'Because I thought I couldn't possibly be any worse than the ones we had. Because I know how much of a difference it would have made to me if I'd had just a little bit of encouragement, from any teacher. Oh, I know the whole class would have benefited from that too, but then everyone else had a family . . . Anyway, as badly as they thought of all of us, I was the one least likely to succeed. Remember Jackboot?'

'I wish I didn't.' As teachers at Fordyce went, Mr Jackson had been so bad he was dismissed after only one academic year.

'One time he took me for detention, just before I left, and you know what he said? When we were alone, of course. He said, "I don't know why you're wasting your time here. There's only one career for girls like you; at least with your looks you'll make some decent money out of it." '

'He said that to you? Did you tell anyone?'

'Who was I going to tell?' Simone said impatiently. 'Anyway, he did me a favour. All I wanted to do was prove him wrong. So I went to college all the way in North London where people didn't know me and I could get away from the company I was keeping, retook my CSEs and surprised myself by getting good grades. So I stayed on, did some A-levels and then went to teacher training college in Bristol.'

'Why there?'

Simone shrugged. 'It seemed far enough away.' She paused. 'I know there's a Bristol connection in my family. I thought I might try and track them down there.'

'And did you?'

'Couldn't be bothered, not after I met Michael. They didn't want to know about me, so fuck them.'

The phone rang again. At the first sound of his voice, a look of real annoyance crossed Simone's face.

'I think that's my cue to leave,' Lee said, getting up.

'Don't leave on his account. I don't feel like it tonight, so he's not coming round.'

'I know, but it's late, and if I drink any more I won't be able to drive home.'

'Yeah, well, I wouldn't leave that car around here if I were you.' Simone stood up and walked Lee to the door. For the amount of drink she had consumed, she was surprisingly steady on her feet. 'It's been good to see you again, Lee, and to talk. I know you can't roll back half a lifetime in one evening, but we're both different people now. I hope we can go forward from here.'

'I had a good time, too. I'll get you those solicitors' names, but you need to decide first whether you want this divorce or not.' Lee put her hand on Simone's shoulder. Such a long way down. 'Take care, Simone. I'll be in touch.'

'You'd better,' Simone smiled. She watched Lee drive off, closed the door behind her, triple-locked it, then switched off her answerphone.

Chapter Eight

'Why do I have to meet him outside Chambers?' Lee asked. She was at her desk, as usual trying to do two things at once, this time picking at her salad while talking to Brendan on the phone.

'Because he wants to. You don't ask a client like Clive Omartian to sit in the waiting room with all the other crims. Also, if he came to Chambers there'd soon be a media circus all round your door. Besides, this isn't a conference about the case as such, because not even you could have read everything I've sent you so far.' He was right there, the initial brief had been just the tip of the iceberg. Since then Brendan had sent her copies of every document he had received from the prosecution, and now there were at least eight lever-arch files stacked on one side of the room. And that wouldn't be the end of it, by any means; they still hadn't had any information from the co-defendants' solicitors, with whom they had to work closely if they had any chance of winning this case. That was a source of concern to Lee; although all the defendants were related, their solicitors didn't appear to be falling over themselves to help her client. She hoped this wasn't the first indication of a cutthroat defence; the surest way to convictions all round was when defendants started blaming each other.

'Come on, Lee. You didn't have to meet him before. You've got the brief now, so indulge him a little.'

Lee thought this time she could afford to be magnanimous. But she was trying to keep up her practice generally as well as prepare this trial. If things went on like this, not only would she need Anne-Marie to work almost exclusively on this case with her, she would have to cut down on her other work too. She made a mental note to speak to Tom about farming out some of her existing cases.

'All right, all right. When and where?'

'He'll pick you up this evening, after work.'

'I can't do it this evening, Brendan. I've got plans.' She hadn't, but legal aid clients didn't get conferences at three hours' notice and there was no reason Omartian should just because he had money. He was already getting too many concessions as it was.

'Anything that can be changed?'

'No.'

'Oh.' Brendan was clearly unhappy. 'Well, it will have to be tomorrow.'

'You know I don't like Friday conferences, Brendan. Anyway, why can't he wait his turn like all the other clients?'

'Because he's not like all the other clients, and well you know it. Besides, he's flying out from Heathrow Saturday morning and he won't be back for three weeks. He needs to see you before then. You're not the only one who has something at stake, Lee. I've got a wife and kids to support on a poxy legal aid practice, which is barely breaking even. This is as important to me as it is to you, so I'm prepared to do anything not to piss him off.'

Score one to Omartian then, Lee thought sourly, as she put down the telephone. With Brendan and by extension herself dancing to his tune, he was running this case, not his lawyers. Experience had taught her that certain clients, especially those with power and influence, had to be reined in or else you ceased to be their lawyer and became merely their cipher. She thought Brendan had learned that too.

Friday evening at 6.30 p.m. found Lee in Chambers, which was empty except for Tom. People usually left as early as decently possible on Fridays, including her senior clerk, and Lee couldn't help feeling he was waiting around to see what would happen. She was wearing one of her favourite suits, one that had been horrendously expensive, even in the sales, but had proved itself time and again whenever she needed to underscore her authority without saying a word.

Promptly at 6.45 p.m., as promised, a middle-aged man of average height, wearing a sober grey suit, arrived. 'Ms Mitchell?'

'Yes?' Lee answered, suspiciously. This was not the man she had been expecting.

'My name's Parker. I'm Mr Omartian's chauffeur.'

'Parker? You're kidding, right? Is that really your name?'

The man looked at her, his face expressionless. Evidently it was a joke that had long ago worn thin. 'It's a very common name, Ms Mitchell.'

'Well, how do I know you are who you say you are? And before I leave here, I want to know where we're going.'

'Mr Omartian thought you might, that's why he told me to give you this.' He handed her an envelope, which, like the note inside, was of creamy thick vellum. It read:

Dear Ms Mitchell,

Yes, Parker is his real name. I thought it was amusing, though he's a bit touchy about it. That's one of the reasons I hired him. I'm sure by now you've asked him to verify both his identity and your destination, or else you wouldn't be reading this. I fully expected this of you. In fact, I would have been disappointed if you hadn't. Parker has worked for me for several years. He'll be taking you to a restaurant in St James's, and when we've finished he'll take you wherever you want to go. As this is not a social call, I fully expect to be billed for your time.

Clive Omartian

★ ★ ★

Lee folded the note and put it in her handbag. She scrutinised Parker. Growing up in her old neighbourhood had given her finely tuned antennae for dangerous situations. Gut instinct told her this was not one of them – not yet, anyway.

'OK, let's go. Goodnight, Tom.'

Judging from the car, Clive's wealth was at least tempered with good taste. True, it was a very large dark blue Mercedes but, mercifully, without personalised numberplates. The leather interior smelt brand new, and was the same colour as the car – such a close match, in fact, that it must have been hand-dyed. As Lee settled back in the car, she had to concede that, in this regard at least, the tabloids had been right.

The restaurant in St James's looked like a private club and was so discreetly appointed that clearly only those who either knew where it was or were specifically invited could attend. Inside, the lighting was discreet, as were the staff who appeared noiselessly to take her coat and show her to the dining room then just as silently melted away.

Clive Omartian was seated at a corner table, which was set somewhat apart from the others, presumably for privacy. From a distance, he appeared just as he did in the newspapers. As Lee walked across the room towards him, he stood up, and she could see he was over six foot, taller than she expected. When she came face to face with him, she had to concede that, on any view, his photographs didn't do him justice. He looked Italian, except for his eyes, which were such a startling blue-green that Lee wondered if he wore contacts. He was wearing a collarless shirt under a suit that was so impeccably cut and fitted so well, it had to be handmade.

'I'm so glad you were able to see me, Ms Mitchell.' He had an anonymous transatlantic accent, the kind you would acquire if you were part of the international jet set.

A waiter came to pull out her chair for her, but he waved him away and did it himself. Lee knew from her brief that he was twenty-seven and therefore three years younger than she was, but he had the quiet confidence of someone twenty years older. Clearly he knew that where charm was concerned it was the little gestures that counted. Lee made a mental note not to be disarmed by her client, now or in the future.

She was impressed by the restaurant. Evidently they were used to the famous and the infamous dining here – anyone, as long as they were rich enough. Omartian's presence did not cause the slightest frisson among either the staff or the other diners.

'Brendan tells me you're going abroad tomorrow,' Lee said, as Clive signalled for a waiter. The movement was barely perceptible but it was enough to bring not one but two waiters over to their table, one for each of them.

'Yes. I have a place in Miami, on South Beach, but I suppose you already know that, from the newspapers. It's about the only thing they've got right.' He sounded rather resigned, as if being misrepresented in the press was something he had learned to tolerate by now. 'What will you have to drink? The wine list here is particularly good.'

'Just tonic water for me, thanks.'

'As you wish. I'll have a vodka tonic,' he told his waiter, and both waiters disappeared as smoothly and silently as they had arrived.

'I don't usually see clients on Fridays, especially at such short notice.'

'Really? No exceptions?'

'Really.'

'Then I'm even more grateful that you were able to come tonight. I hope what I'm paying you will make it well worth such inconveniences, now or in the future.'

Even though it was said very politely, Lee couldn't help feeling that by raising the issue of money she had been put gently, but very surely, in her place. He had proved what she had always suspected was true, that this was a game, and in choosing the time and place for their first meeting, by mentioning the fact that he was paying for her services, he was making sure he had home court advantage.

She was used to playing this game.

'I prefer conferences to be at my Chambers, Mr Omartian. If you weren't going abroad tomorrow, I would not have agreed to see you this evening. Even though you're my biggest client, you're not my only one. My other clients need my expertise as much as you do even if they can't afford to pay for it.'

Omartian looked taken aback, but only for a moment. Then he grinned. He had a very engaging grin.

'Well, Ms Mitchell, I do believe you're trying to put me in my place. It's been a long time since anyone has spoken to me like that.'

'I don't doubt it,' Lee said drily.

'Is my money so abhorrent to you?'

'Not at all. It buys my expertise, but it doesn't mean you'll get preferential treatment, or that I'm at your beck and call.'

'Brendan told me you were very forthright. What he actually said was that you had balls.'

'Coming from him, I'll take that as a compliment. What else did he tell you?'

'That everything in your background militated against your becoming a barrister; no connections, no money, the wrong sex for the job, certainly the wrong colour. That you were a fighter. I need a fighter, Lee.' It was the first time he had used her Christian name.

'And that's why you chose me.'

'I've got to prove my innocence. And you've got something to prove, too. You want to show you can do this. So I know you'll

70

move heaven and earth to win this case for me. Those public school ponces don't have any fire in their belly. I don't want someone to give up on me when the going gets tough.'

'I hardly think George Amery fits into that category.'

'Ah, yes, the Rottweiler.' Clive took a sip of his drink. 'But then he didn't have Brendan Donnelly's recommendation.'

' "Public school ponces" – I seem to remember you went to Harrow, or is that something else the papers got wrong?'

'Yes and no. I was there – my father's way of proving he was a real English gentleman. But I was expelled after three years. So you see, I do know what I'm talking about.' Then he laughed, and Lee couldn't help smiling.

'So tell me what the papers got right, if anything, Mr Omartian.'

'First, I think if you've decided what you want to eat, we should order. Secondly, if you insist on calling me Mr Omartian, this is going to feel like an even longer evening for both of us. Don't worry,' he said, holding up his hand, 'I won't presume any familiarity other than a professional lawyer-client relationship. So you won't have to worry about keeping the rich boy in line.'

She couldn't help smiling again. 'All right, Clive, you win.'

Lee ordered a large salad. Clive ordered steak, very rare. Lee's surprise must have shown on her face because he said, 'I like everything that's bad for me. The papers got that right, to answer your question. I have a lot of money, Lee, and I like a good time. So I spend it. I travel, I like women, I like cars, the faster the better.' Lee didn't know whether he was referring to the women or the cars and decided it was better she didn't know. 'Money buys you a certain freedom,' he continued, 'but not from jealousy and not into the Establishment. I always knew that – I learnt it at Harrow. But my father didn't, not really.' For the first time that evening, he looked sombre. 'That is why this is all so hard on him.'

'And Hector?'

'I really don't care what Hector thinks,' he said shortly.

At that moment their waiters returned, each bearing covered silver platters. They placed them before Lee and Clive and in one fluid, synchronised movement removed the silver domes before retiring. The food looked exquisite, and tasted just as good.

'Why don't you tell me what you know about the case so far?' Clive asked, breaking the silence that had followed his last outburst.

Lee wondered whether he was testing her. Luckily she had done her homework.

'The prosecution say that your father and Hector are two of five partners in an investment firm in the City. Quite small, but with a good reputation, a kind of "boutique" firm with a loyal client base. You've had some good returns, and it's still privately owned. Then a client rings up to ask why the return on his two hundred thousand pound investment is so low. When the books are checked, it turns out that only thirty per cent of the money was invested, hence the low return. One hundred and forty thousand pounds had been withdrawn from the client's account. However, two signatories are needed, not one, and the only one found on it was your father's. He's interviewed twice by police, each time without a solicitor. At first he says nothing, but the second time he says "I did it". That's it; nothing else, no reason, nothing. The police don't believe he did it, or if he did, that he did it on his own. After all, he's seventy-seven and a very rich man who sets great store by his reputation; he wouldn't jeopardise it for that kind of money. But they know about Hector, they know he's got gambling debts. They also know, as does the entire country by now, that the wife he was featured with in all the society pages the previous year has just divorced him, very expensively. So they arrest him, too. In my opinion, they don't seem to have anything on him as yet, so we'll have to find out the score from his solicitors. Anyway, you're not a partner; you just work for the company – when you're there. But a month later, you're arrested too. Now why would they do that, Clive?' Lee asked, looking straight at him.

'Who knows? Maybe they thought if the father and one son were involved, how could the other work for the same firm and not be involved as well? Maybe they thought we were just a bunch of East European peasants with more money than was decent.' He paused, holding her gaze. 'I didn't take the money, Lee.'

'I didn't ask whether you did or not, Clive. The question is, what evidence do they have against you? As I see it, all they have is a signed confession from your father.'

'Does this mean they could drop the case against me before it gets to court?'

'It's possible. Anything's possible. Only don't get your hopes up.'

'Well, I'm a natural optimist, and at present I see no reason not to be. I have every confidence in you, Lee.'

Which is a great way to shift the burden on to me while you kick up your heels in Miami, Lee thought sourly. 'Would you like coffee?' Clive asked.

Lee declined. 'In that case, I hope you don't mind, but I have an early flight tomorrow. Parker will take you wherever you need to go.'

'Yes, of course.'

Again, the waiters noiselessly appeared to help them from the table. They walked to the entrance hall where their coats were already waiting for them. Lee turned to Clive.

'How did you get Brendan as your solicitor?'

'He was the duty solicitor at the police station when I was arrested. Unlike my father, I wasn't stupid enough to be inter-viewed without one. He seemed good, so I just stuck with him. Why do you ask?'

'Nothing, just curious.' It was a good enough answer, she supposed. It didn't entirely make sense, but then very little did in this case, so far.

'Would you mind if I made a personal observation, Lee?'

'Depends what it is.'

'That's a very beautiful suit you're wearing. It's Armani, isn't it?' He smiled. 'So, you see, money does have its uses.'

'You don't miss much, do you?'

'Not about women.' He extended his hand to shake hers. 'Goodnight, Lee.'

A silver-haired man of about fifty had given Lee and Clive such a hard stare as they crossed the room together he was surprised they hadn't noticed him. He wished they had. Cosy tête-à-têtes at the coveted corner table; heaven knows he'd used that table himself often enough for just such a purpose. It had been rumoured Omartian's tastes ran to the exotic in women. Just as he'd suspected, she'd obviously got that case on her back. Why else would he have been turned down in favour of her?

The waiter appeared with the bill.

'Why are you bringing me this?' he snapped. 'Charge it to my account, like you usually do.'

'Certainly, Mr Amery.'

Chapter Nine

'Watch out, sir,' Dean said, just in time to prevent Giles Townsend tripping over a parcel on the floor and falling flat on his face. He sprang out of his chair, as only a seventeen-year-old could, and deftly removed it from beneath the feet of the older man.

'What the hell's that doing here?' Giles shouted irritably. 'I could have broken my neck.' He was always prone to exaggerate.

'Yes, what the hell's that doing there, Dean?' Tom parroted, as he always did when his Head of Chambers was around. 'I thought I told you to move it. You should know better than to leave parcels by the doorway.'

'Sorry,' Dean mumbled, trying to sink lower into his chair. Tom had told him no such thing. He didn't know why the senior clerk was getting at him. After all, the parcel had arrived less than five minutes ago, and well he knew it.

'What is it anyway?' Giles asked testily.

'More papers on the Omartian case, Mr Townsend,' Tom replied.

'You know, it's fantastic for Chambers, isn't it, Mr Townsend?' said Dean. 'If Miss Mitchell pulls this off, they're bound to remember it when she applies for silk . . .' He realised what he had said even before Tom kicked him under the desk, but it was already too late.

That's just great, Giles thought sourly. His mood took even more of a downturn. He went to his shelf. Same old rubbish, he thought. *Bar News, Counsel* – the magazines that were regularly sent to members of the Bar – the usual circulars about expensive books that would be obsolete in less than two years, and other paraphernalia that only came to the Head of Chambers. Nothing important, or new, like a case. He made a mental note to speak to Anne-Marie; he didn't just want to keep abreast of the Omartian case, he wanted to be the first to know.

'Well, Tom, both of you,' looking pointedly at Dean, 'would do well to remember that these Chambers do in fact have other barristers, and other cases. Our reputation depends on more than just one case. I'm going to lunch. I'll be back around three.' And with that, he stalked out of the Clerks' Room.

It had been some time since he'd lunched in Gray's Inn, mainly because it was quite a walk from the Temple, and thus only attempted when he had either a yearning for comfortable, school-dinner type food or a particular reason to be there. Today it was the latter. He saw his dining companion as he entered the large hall.

'Giles,' the man signalled to call him over. 'It's good to see you again.' Both of them knew this last remark was a lie. Oliver Morrison, QC, had three things in common with Giles Townsend: they had both been at Oxford together; they were both members of Gray's Inn; and their daughters were both at Cheltenham Ladies' College. But that was all. Oliver was tall, broad and loud, unashamedly High Tory. He also had a brilliant mind and a truly impressive practice, and consequently was one of the country's most successful, and wealthiest, silks. It showed. By any other standards Giles could be seen as a comfortably off, successful man, but none of this mattered if it was not acknowledged by one's peers. Three times he had applied to take silk; each time he had not been appointed. Oliver, in his bespoke suits, of which he seemed to have a great many, threw into sharp relief everything Giles was not, everything he wanted and did not have.

'Thank you for agreeing to see me, Oliver.' He was Oliver now, not Ollie. The camaraderie they had once enjoyed had all but disappeared.

'That's quite all right, Giles. How's Sarah?'

'She's very well. And Margaret?'

'Splendid. Just celebrated our silver wedding anniversary. Look, Giles, I'm afraid I can't stay long. Something came up just as I left Chambers.'

No time for a long, lazy lunch then. Not like the old days.

'Pressure of work,' Oliver continued. 'You know how it is.'

Giles wished he did. 'I quite understand.'

'Perhaps you'd like to do this some other time, when I'm not so rushed.'

'No. No.' It had taken long enough to pin Oliver down to this date. Giles was damned if he was going to wait any longer. 'This won't take much time. After all,' he added bitterly, 'you know why I'm here.' It was humiliating, seeking advice from someone who had graduated with him and was now seen as his superior, but he couldn't see any other way. He was desperate. He hoped it didn't show.

'Yes.' Oliver looked at him shrewdly. 'But I really can't see how I can help you. In any event, I can't understand why you would want to discuss something so . . . sensitive in such a public place.'

Because no one will know, Giles thought. In the middle of Gray's Inn dining hall on a Wednesday lunchtime, surrounded by other barristers and students, no one will suspect that I'm asking my former friend and contemporary why I've been turned down for silk.

'Well, I was wondering . . . I mean, you're in the know, you must have heard something . . .'

Oliver was mute.

'Damn it, Oliver, you know what I'm trying to say. Three

times I've applied for silk, and each time I've been turned down. I thought the name of Townsend stood for something at the Bar.'

'Having a former high court judge for a father doesn't guarantee your appointment as Queen's Counsel,' Oliver said, a touch reprovingly.

'I know, I know. I'm sorry,' Giles said, calming down as quickly as he had flared up. 'I know that appointments are made on merit. It's just that after nearly thirty years ... and look at Campbell-Blake. Ten years younger than me and he got it on his first try, from what I hear. You can't tell me I'm not at least as able as he is.'

The plain fact was that he wasn't, though it was hard to tell that to someone convinced of his own brilliance.

'Henry has an extremely good medical negligence practice; that's all he's ever done. He has a well-deserved reputation.' Oliver paused, then chose his words carefully. 'It is perhaps ... easier to be publicly acknowledged as a good barrister if you have concentrated your efforts in one area of the law.'

'Are you saying that because I have a mixed practice I'm considered some sort of dilettante?'

'Having a mixed practice is not where the difficulty lies, Giles. There are several silks in that position, as you well know. But every one of them has at least one field in which they're considered pre-eminent. In addition, they all have a good record of outstanding, important cases.'

'And I don't, is that it?'

'You need a winner, Giles. One big case, or at least a noteworthy one. You don't even have to win it, just be seen to be doing your best and make sure the world knows about it. A celebrated case has never hurt anyone's career. Look at Amery; not our sort of person, of course, but there's no denying his success in that regard. Take the Omartian case, for example. That black woman in your Chambers has nabbed Clive's brief, I gather.'

'Yes,' said Giles, morosely.

'It appears then that your liberal instincts were right when you took her on. Now, if you had a case like that, a win there would stand you in very good stead next March. That, of course, is only my opinion. And, as you know, I have no influence in these matters.' Another lie, and both of them knew it.

'Yes, well, that case has already been taken.'

'You could still get on board. Can't you find out whether she needs a leader?'

'Perhaps. To be honest, I don't think I would be her first choice.'

'Good heavens, man. You're her Head of Chambers. Choice doesn't come into it.'

'Maybe.' Giles was noncommittal. Oliver didn't know Lee like he did. 'It's early days yet, though. It might not need a leader.'

'True enough.' Oliver stared at Giles. 'Well, what about ringing her solicitor? Solicitors have been known to reallocate cases, especially where there are . . . doubts, shall we say, about appointed counsel.'

'I don't think it would work. They seem quite friendly. Plus, he's Irish. You know, all immigrants together.'

'I see. Well,' Oliver said as he rose from the table, 'you've heard my views.' He gazed down at his old friend. 'You need that case, Giles. Either get one or make something into one.'

Simone shared her umbrella with the PE teacher as they left school together – no mean feat as Sylvia Thomas was a tall, athletic woman, six foot in her trainers. No matter what she wore, she always looked as if she had just leapt out of a Nike commercial. She wouldn't stay very dry, Simone thought ruefully. Still, it was better than getting completely wet. Besides, Sylvia was such a good laugh, it was almost worth it.

A car horn sounded. 'Simone. Simone. Wait up.'

Simone recognised the voice and kept right on walking. But Sylvia looked round. 'Isn't that someone calling you?'

Simone stared straight ahead. 'Doubt it. Come on, Sylvia, I'm getting soaked with you holding this umbrella.'

One of her students came running up to her. 'Mrs Wilson. Mrs Wilson.'

'What is it, Gary?'

'That man over there said to give you these.' Gary presented her with a bunch of red roses. There was no ignoring him now. Both Simone and Sylvia stared at the sender. Sylvia nudged her. 'Not bad, not bad at all. He looks just like that rugby player, Jeremy Guscott. Flowers too. He's not from around here, then.' She looked at her friend. 'You don't look too happy to see him.'

'I'm not,' Simone said shortly.

As he made his way towards them, both women were still staring, but their expressions were very different. Sylvia's was clearly appreciative; Simone simply looked furious.

'Good afternoon, ladies,' the man said, smiling, but not taking his eyes off Simone.

After a long silence, Sylvia said, 'Well, Simone, aren't you going to introduce us?'

'Sylvia Thomas, Steve Payne.'

Sylvia looked at him as if he was a tasty morsel to devour, preferably slowly.

'Pleased to meet you, Sylvia. I just came by to surprise Simone, see if she wanted a lift from school.'

'Thanks, Steve, but as you can see I'm with my friend here. Plus, it's not far, as you know.'

'Oh, don't mind me, Simone.' Sylvia ignored the look of dismay on Simone's face. 'You don't want to walk in weather like this if you can help it.' Evidently she seemed to think she was furthering some sort of romance.

Steve pulled up the collar of his jacket. 'Please, Simone. My car's right over here.'

As soon as she was inside the shiny BMW Simone turned angrily to face him. 'What the hell do you think you were doing, turning up at the school like that? You know I don't want my work colleagues to get in my business. And that boy was in my class.'

'I know,' Steve replied calmly. 'I had to pay him five pounds to give you the flowers.' His voice took on an unpleasant edge. 'That's the trouble with you black women. You say black men aren't romantic, then when we make a gesture, you don't appreciate it.'

'You think you're the first man to give me flowers?' Simone was shouting. She glanced out of the window and saw Sylvia looking at them, and waving. She waved back, then watched her colleague slowly move away. She took a deep breath to try and get her emotions in check. 'Look, I teach a mixed class of fifteen-year-olds. I lose half my authority as a teacher straightaway if they know who I'm sleeping with.'

'How would they know about us?'

'God, Steve! Gary's not blind and he's certainly not stupid.'

Steve started the car. 'Yeah, but we're not sleeping together any more, are we?' His tone was bitter.

'That's right,' Simone shot back, 'we're not.'

They made the short journey in silence. Steve pulled up outside Simone's house and switched off the engine.

'Look, Steve, thank you for the flowers, but I told you—'

'Yeah, yeah, I know what you told me. You want to work things out with your husband.'

As an excuse it was pure wishful thinking, but she could always hope. God, how she missed him. If only Steve wasn't such a control freak. He was good company when he wanted to be, and good company was in short supply right now – any company at all, come to that.

'Steve, you knew from the beginning I wasn't looking for anything serious. You said you were cool with that.'

'That was then. I feel something more for you now.'

'So give me some space. Back off. I can't handle anything heavy right now. Can't we just be friends?'

'Don't call me, I'll call you, is that what you mean? Fuck that.'

'I'm sorry I can't give you more than that.'

'I know you, Simone. You won't call.'

'I might.'

'Yeah, sure.' Steve turned on the ignition and Simone got out of the car without another word.

As she triple-locked her front door behind her, the hollow feeling she had carried around inside her for so long seemed to grow and expand until it threatened to consume her. Then she remembered Lee, and went to the phone.

Chapter Ten

'I hope he's paying you enough to be working late on a Friday night,' Simone said.

'Well, at least I can do it at home. It's been late every night this week,' Lee replied. 'What with supervising Anne-Marie, plus trying to juggle the rest of my workload, at the moment I have to snatch time to work on Clive's case when I can. Plus, I have to confess, if my room mate's in, we end up talking so much that I don't get very much done.'

'What's she like?'

'Who, Mary or Anne-Marie?'

'Both.'

'Mary's very bright. A shit-hot civil lawyer. Very posh background, but nice for all that. Married with three kids. The last one's less than a year, so she's not in that much, which is just as well.'

'I thought Giles was the man in Chambers for that sort of work.'

'No, he just thinks he is. As for Anne-Marie, she's all right, I suppose. Says she's determined to make a career for herself as a criminal lawyer, but I don't know. I can't help thinking that the first old lag she comes up against will send her screaming for the hills. She has no perception of how the other half live, except in the most abstract sense. She won't be able to identify with the average criminal defendant at all.'

'Is that important, to do a good job?'

Lee thought for a minute. 'Maybe not, but it helps. Anyway, I'm sure you've got better things to do than ring me at ten o'clock on a Friday night. Aren't you going out tonight?'

'No, I'm working too. It's just me and some marking.'

Lee wasn't that surprised by her answer. This was the third time Simone had rung her in as many days. She suspected that loneliness was creeping up on her again; however well-disguised, she could still hear it in her voice, the same way she had that night they had met again.

'What happened to your man?'

'Steve? He seems to have got the message. He's stopped calling. I can't say I don't miss him, but I haven't dared ring him in case the control thing starts up again. Anyway, what's your famous client like?'

'Come next Friday, and I'll tell you . . .' Suddenly Lee's voice became muffled by something that sounded suspiciously like a kiss. When she came back on the phone she sounded distinctly more upbeat. 'Sorry, Simone. About Friday, you are still coming, I hope?'

Simone sounded doubtful. 'I don't know, Leanne. I'll probably be coming alone, and I don't want to cramp your style.'

'Behave yourself. Who said you needed to bring anyone? It's a double celebration, David's birthday and me getting the case. Plus, David's going on tour so you won't get to meet him for another two or three months otherwise.' When Simone didn't reply, Lee added, 'If you really don't want to come alone, why not ring Steve? You said yourself he seems to have got the message. It's been three weeks now. Maybe he's found someone else to control and would be happy just to see you again, as a friend. Anyway, what else are you going to do? You don't want to stay home on a Bank Holiday weekend.'

Lee and Brendan stood outside the tall, imposing building and slowly looked up. It was a modern glass masterpiece that was completely incongruous next to the smaller, more traditional buildings, which appeared shabby in comparison and from a bygone, inglorious age when £100 could retain a lawyer for an entire case. Even the most junior partner in this law firm would earn more than that in an hour. This was the law firm of the future, the type that had mammoth legal teams stretching across five continents and could buy any legal mind it wanted.

'Don't worry,' Brendan said reassuringly, whether to himself or to her, Lee wasn't sure, 'it's just to show who has the biggest balls. That's why Ellenburg suggested we have the conference here.'

'I'm not worried,' she replied. She hoped she sounded convincing. No sense in both of them losing their nerve. She wondered whether he realised she had been up all night with this case. She hoped it didn't show. Lately, it seemed that when she wasn't working on it, she was worrying about it. And this conference was important, not just to establish where each part of the legal team was as regards preparation and the information each had received from the prosecution, but as a test. They might all be on the same side in theory, but there was no doubt that Robbs Ellenburg Bennett wanted to show in no uncertain terms that they intended to be the dominant force on the defence team.

'Anyway,' she continued, 'seeing as I don't have any balls to be concerned about, it doesn't matter to me. I'll just leave you boys to play with each other. And Brendan, I know this is the big time, but try not to look so overawed, will you?'

'It's all right for you. At least you look the part.' Brendan squinted down at his grey suit, perfectly serviceable for a day in the Magistrates' Court but not for a meeting at one of the biggest law firms in the City. Unfortunately, it was also his best suit. 'I feel as if I'll leave a nasty stain on anything I touch here.'

Anne-Marie, Lee's pupil, was waiting for them in the reception area, as arranged. She was visibly displaying the nervousness Lee was trying to hide. Lee walked smartly up to the marble-topped reception desk. The initials R.E.B. were engraved in its surface in large italic script. 'Good morning. Ms Mitchell and pupil, and Mr Donnelly to see Mr Ellenburg. He's expecting us.' Nervousness and being a little on the defensive gave an unnecessary edge to her voice.

But both the security guard and the receptionist were politeness itself. 'Of course, ma'am.' The receptionist looked like a Californian blonde and had the accent to match, perfectly in keeping with the firm's international image. 'The conference room's all set up. Mr Ellenburg and the others are waiting for you. Everyone's here.'

Brendan and Lee looked at each other as they followed the young woman to the lift up to the conference room. They were on time – early, in fact.

The only thing Lee took in about the room itself was that it was very large – Brendan's entire firm would have fitted into it – and very light. There were banks of windows running along its length, providing what was probably a spectacular view, and a table so long that communication with the far end would have required a foghorn. Fortunately, everyone was gathered at the near end of the table. Lee's gaze swept over them. All male. All white. Usual story.

Judging by the documents spread out and the open law texts, the ten people already present had been here some time. At the other end of the table were computers. A couple of assistants had laptops, too. Lee guessed that six of the men were R.E.B. junior solicitors specially deployed to work on this case. The firm could afford to put in those human resources. That left four major players, two of whom Lee recognised as members of her own branch of the profession.

A tall, patrician-looking man of about sixty rose to greet her.

'Ms Mitchell, Mr Donnelly, Ms Green, I'm Marcus Ellenburg.' He had a firm, solid grip, but his hands were as soft as hers. Lee wondered what he would make of Brendan's calluses. She also wondered how he knew who Anne-Marie was. She hadn't mentioned her name – hadn't even said she would be bringing her, in fact.

'It was good of you to come,' he continued, almost as if this was a pleasant social gathering rather than something it was imperative for her to attend. 'I know Counsel usually have conferences in Chambers, but here we have the space and access to material that I thought might be beneficial to all of us, as well as our Lexis link. Now, I'm sure you know Nicholas Robbins and George Amery, by repute, if nothing else. George is a relatively late replacement for Hector Omartian's original trial counsel, whose services have recently been dispensed with.' All three barristers gave each other tight, polite smiles. 'A firm like ours doesn't usually dip its toe into criminal waters, but I've done business with Frederick Omartian for several years. I've instructed Nicholas to act for him. George has been instructed by Forman Miller.' Lee knew this firm was smaller than Robbs Ellenburg Bennett, but of no lesser pedigree. 'Arthur Forman has decided to take time off from his very busy practice to attend himself.'

'Had to be in on a celebrity trial, didn't I, Marcus?' Forman said with a smile. He looked at Lee. 'Since O. J. Simpson, seems everyone wants one.'

Lee took her seat opposite Amery. 'We did say ten thirty, didn't we?'

'Quite right,' Ellenburg nodded, 'but George and Arthur happened to arrive early. As you know, Forman Miller is virtually next door.'

'I see.' Lee didn't believe him for a minute. Despite Amery's late instruction, the two teams were forming an alliance, leaving them out in the cold. She herself had come into the case late, what with Clive's later arrest and then terminal indecision about who was to be his trial counsel. She didn't want to be even more at a disadvantage. She and Brendan would really have to keep their wits about them, even on their own side. 'What did you discuss about the case before we arrived?' she inquired. She didn't think she would get an honest answer, but she had to ask. They would have been surprised if she hadn't.

'Just general points about the state of the evidence,' Ellenburg replied smoothly. She was right. She wouldn't get the truth. 'The Crown's disclosure has been lamentable so far.'

'The videotape from the company purporting to show Frederick with his hands in the till, as it were,' said Robbins, 'hasn't arrived yet.' He slammed his notebook down in disgust. 'That was the whole point of this conference, as far as I'm concerned.'

There was a knock on the door.

'Come in,' Ellenburg called.

A middle-aged black woman, dressed in some kind of uniform, entered, bearing refreshments on a tray. Evidently this was only for the senior members present. She looked quite startled when she saw Lee, who gave her a small smile. The woman quickly regained her composure, placed the tray on the table and withdrew.

'Good,' said Robbins, 'I could use some of that right now.' But he made no attempt to get it. It took some seconds to dawn on Lee that she was being expected to pour. She pushed the tray away from her towards him. 'Please help yourself,' she said coldly.

The embarrassed look on his face told her she hadn't misjudged him. 'Of course. Would you like coffee or tea?'

'Coffee, please.'

'How do you take it?'

'Black, no sugar.'

Beside her, Amery grinned. Lee stared at him.

Ellenburg cleared his throat. 'There were two other reasons, apart from the tape, why I felt a joint conference would be beneficial. Firstly, each of us needs to be brought abreast of the others' cases so far, so that we can reach some kind of consensus on approach; secondly, I realise you've been instructed comparatively late, Lee, so I thought there might be specific matters you would want to raise with us.'

'Yes, there are. I've read your client's interviews. Does he accept he's made admissions?'

'Yes, he does,' Robbins replied.

'And was he coerced by the police in any way?'

'He says he freely volunteered the information.'

'Then what's the basis of his not guilty plea?'

'*He* wants to go guilty. I've advised him against it,' Robbins said.

There was a silence. Then Ellenburg said, 'Frederick Omartian was interviewed without myself or anyone else from the firm being present. Not even the duty solicitor.' This last was said in a tone that indicated he thought this was only marginally better than having no one at all. Brendan looked down. 'There was no evidence that he had been cautioned or read his rights.'

'I thought you said he wasn't put under any pressure by the police.'

Robbins answered. 'The man's seventy-seven. Some would argue that just being in a police station at that age is coercive, particularly when you've never had so much as a driving conviction. Plus, he's a rich man; what's one hundred and forty thousand pounds to him? Yes,' Robbins concluded in a self-satisfied voice, 'I'm sure I could get a jury to believe that.'

'What about the signatures on the cheques?'

'What about them?'

'He was the only one who signed, when every cheque or money transfer was to be validated by two signatories.'

'Precisely my point. He built that company; all the more reason why he wouldn't make such a stupid mistake, even if he needed the money. I've already instructed a handwriting expert.'

'Are you running duress as a defence or just the common-or-garden "He didn't do it"?'

'The latter.'

'In spite of his confession?'

Robbins shrugged. 'I have to agree that makes matters more difficult, but only slightly. He's agreed, reluctantly, to take the advice of counsel. He seemed to think that just because he told the police he did it, he should plead guilty. A matter of honour, you understand. But if we can get his confession ruled out early on a voire dire, and at least cast doubt in the minds of the jury regarding the signatories, we're home and dry, and all the documentation in the case matters not one whit.'

'What if it's ruled in?'

'Same difference. What judge in the country is going to send a business tycoon of his age to jail? Especially when he can make restitution. He'll be ruined, of course,' he added, almost as if this was incidental, 'but he's made his millions. So he won't be invited to the Queen's Garden Party any more; if I can live with that, he ought to be able to.'

Lee turned to Amery. 'What about Hector?'

'What about him? You know he's pleading not guilty, I'm sure.'

'Yes, I know that much. That's why we're all here, isn't it?' she said to the lawyers generally. 'Will we be having a mutual exchange of proofs?'

Silence. Ellenburg and Robbins exchanged glances.

'My client is considering his position as regards that,' Amery replied.

'Meaning?'

'Just what I said.'

'What's the problem?' Lee asked. 'I know what his plea is. You don't need your client's permission for this.'

Brendan spoke, for the first time. 'Have you seen it, Marcus?'

Faced with a direct question, Ellenburg was too gentlemanly to lie. 'I've seen a draft. A very early draft,' he added hastily, 'which I'm sure has been revised since.'

Lee put both hands flat on the table. The surface felt cool. Very slowly and deliberately, she asked, 'Would someone mind telling me just what the hell's going on?'

'Now, wait—'

'No, Nicholas, I want to know. Now.' Looking directly at Amery, she asked, 'Are you going cutthroat against my client, George? Is that what this is all about?' She looked at them all. 'Is that why you were all in here before we arrived, "generally chatting"? Because if it is, my solicitor and I can leave right now.'

'There is absolutely no need for this, Ms Mitchell,' Ellenburg said. It was Ms Mitchell again now, spoken in the kind of ringing tones meant to indicate he would brook no argument.

'Isn't there? Well, seeing as we're all being so honest and open with one another,' she said sarcastically, 'the way I see it, the one with the best motive is your client,' jabbing her finger at Amery and Forman for emphasis. 'He might be an Omartian, but he's not rich. He's fifty-five and still working for his dad who shows every sign of being around for a long time to come. His wife cleaned him out last year, so no early retirement for him. And the police know about his gambling, so they must have been watching for months before they made their move.'

The gloves were off now.

'He's not going cutthroat,' Amery snapped. 'More's the pity, because I think your druggie client did it to pay off his dealers. But the old man is leaning on Hector to keep quiet. He doesn't want his favourite, the prodigal son, going to jail and becoming someone's girlfriend for five years.' He stopped abruptly, as if he had said too much. Forman put his head in his hands. Ellenburg looked visibly shaken, as if the whole carefully orchestrated meeting had slipped from his control.

Lee was stunned. This was the first she'd heard about drugs. Not even the newspapers had said anything about that. 'Dream that up all by yourself, did you? Because he turned you down? Don't think I don't know what went on before I got the brief. I've met Clive Omartian. Believe me, I've represented enough users and dealers to know one when I see one, especially if he's into it for that kind of money. He's no user.'

'Oh, really? Tell me, when did he last go to Miami?'

'That's rubbish,' Brendan shouted. He sounded really angry. 'And unless you can back it up, don't ever let me hear anything like that repeated outside this room.'

Amery laughed mirthlessly. 'Don't worry, I won't. And Hector won't drop your client in the shit, even though that's right where he deserves to be. But he won't do anything, not one thing, to help him.'

'You think I need your help?' Lee replied. 'I've got one co-defendant who's admitted to it, and even if the voire dire succeeds, he's not saying anything against my client.' She leaned closer to Amery. 'I don't care what you think you know about Clive Omartian. You deal with your case, let me deal with mine. Just don't go cutthroat on me, George. I'm warning you.' She got up. 'I really can't see any useful purpose being served by my remaining at this conference with Mr Amery, Marcus. Nicholas, perhaps you and I could speak later. I would like to see the tape if the prosecution serve it on you before we get our copy. But thank you, you were right. I certainly have been enlightened.'

Ellenburg gave a long, slow sigh. 'As you wish. Lionel,' he said to one of his junior solicitors, 'perhaps you could escort them to the lift. I'm sorry you feel you can't stay, Ms Mitchell. Mr Donnelly, perhaps you could ring me tomorrow. Goodbye, Ms Green. Please give my regards to your uncle.'

'Thank you,' Anne-Marie said, in a voice barely above a whisper. She seemed shell-shocked by the intensity of the exchange.

Inside the lift, Brendan leaned against the wall. 'Fucking bastard.' His voice was weary. 'He's going to try and stitch us up, Lee.'

Lee nodded. 'I know he wants to, but the father will stop him, either directly or through Hector.' She paused. 'Did you ever hear anything about Clive and drugs?'

Brendan looked at her. 'Come on, Lee. I was as surprised as you were about that. He's no user.'

'I hope you're right, because if he is, that gives him motive. I need to see him again – in Chambers, this time – as soon as he gets back from Miami.' She turned to Anne-Marie. 'You didn't say you knew Marcus Ellenburg.'

Anne-Marie reddened. 'I don't really, not to speak to, but my uncle does. They play golf together.'

Lee was about to take the matter further, then decided against it. It was none of her business. The conference had fizzled into nothing, and what she wanted most of all now was to go home and take a nap. She would come back to Chambers in the evening to work on the case, see if she had missed something, anything, to indicate drug use. 'Anne-Marie, could you tell Tom I'm not coming back? I'm going home; I'll ring him from the car. Brendan, I'm going south. Can I give you a lift?'

'No, I've got some things to do, but thanks anyway.'

It was a beautiful sunny day, the best one they'd had so far this year. The heat in the enclosed car hit her as soon as she opened the door. Maybe next time she'd get a convertible. As she drove over Blackfriars Bridge, she suddenly thought of Simone. She hadn't heard from her since their evening out on Friday. Simone had arrived with Steve and the evening had gone well. Steve was certainly a good-looking man, Lee acknowledged, but she hadn't really taken to him, though she couldn't pin down why exactly. Maybe he and Simone had got back together. Still, it was unusual for five days to pass without Simone getting in touch. Lee decided to drop in to see her at the school. Maybe she was free for lunch. She could use some honest, friendly company right now.

Chapter Eleven

Lee gingerly picked her way through the mass of weeds that lined both sides of the ramshackle path leading to Simone's front door. She recalled what her friend had said about 'guerrilla living', but this was ridiculous.

The curtains were all drawn, which was strange.

Lee rang the bell several times and was just about to go when she heard the click of the first of the many locks being opened.

The first thing that hit Lee as the door opened was the smell of bleach. Simone must have been doing some serious cleaning.

'Hey, what's up?' Lee asked, feeling her smile dissolving into a frown. Simone looked a mess. She was standing there barefoot, in jeans and a man-sized grey sweater which all but swamped her. The sleeves hung down past her hands, hiding them. Her hair was uncombed, just pushed back haphazardly from her face. These must be her cleaning clothes, Lee reasoned, though how she could stand to wear such heavy clothing on a hot day like this was amazing, and that didn't account for the tired, pinched look on her face. 'I went round to the school, but they said you hadn't been in yesterday, and had rung in sick today. They were worried about you.' Lee looked intently into Simone's face. 'What's wrong?'

'Nothing.' She looked away at first, then back at Lee. Her eyes were dull.

After a silence, Lee asked, 'Well, can I come in or are you going to keep me on your doorstep?' She laughed, trying to lighten the atmosphere, but it didn't work.

It seemed an age before Simone replied. 'All right.' She moved just far enough away from the door to allow Lee to come in.

'Well, you could sound a bit more pleased to see me,' Lee said as she stepped past her into the hallway. The smell of bleach was overpowering. It seemed to be coming from upstairs. 'Why've you got your curtains drawn? It's a beautiful day outside, and you never know how long it'll last in England; you've got to make the most of days like these whenever you get them.'

Simone still said nothing. She was leaning against the wall. The window above the door threw some light into the hallway, but her face was in shadow.

'Look, I can go if you want me to.' When Simone still didn't reply, Lee added, 'Since I'm not getting anything from you now, I'm going to go upstairs, use your toilet, and then when I come back down you can either tell me what's happened or I'm outta here, and you can call me when you're ready.'

The smell of bleach got stronger and stronger as Lee neared the top of the stairs. When she got to the landing, it was so strong it made her want to gag. She was faced with three identical doors, all of which had been stripped as if to prepare them for painting. There was no way to tell which was the bathroom, so Lee went to the one nearest her. It was locked, or jammed, she couldn't tell which. She rattled the handle, pushing against it, feeling it begin to give.

'What the fuck do you think you're doing?' Simone came running up the stairs, her face contorted with fury, and launched herself at Lee, hitting and punching her.

The suddenness of the attack caught Lee completely off guard. Instinctively she backed into the door. It gave way and both of them fell into the room.

The blinding sunlight was such a contrast to the darkened interior of the rest of the house that it took Lee a little while to get her bearings. Once she had managed to focus, she wished she hadn't.

It was a nursery.

Lee stood rooted to the spot. All the equipment looked new – the cot, the Moses basket, the stroller, the toys, the rocking chair by the window. Some of it had been covered in dust sheets. There was a baby book on the table, but Lee didn't have to look at it to know no entries had been made.

The room seemed to trigger something deep inside Simone. She lay in a crumpled heap by the door, sobbing uncontrollably, great wracking sobs that seemed to come up from a place so painful Lee never wanted to hear their like again. She crouched down beside her friend. She felt awkward, not knowing what to do in the face of such raw, acute pain. She hesitated, then gathered her into her arms.

'Oh Simone, Simone, I'm sorry. I didn't know . . .' She rocked Simone back and forth as she cried, saying nothing. It seemed to go on for ever, then very gradually it subsided. Simone slowly moved away from Lee's hold and looked at her. Her eyes were red and bloodshot, her face teary; her nose was running. She wiped her nose with the sleeve of her jumper. 'Steve . . .' she began.

'Steve?' Lee repeated. What on earth did he have to do with this?

Simone turned away from Lee as if she couldn't bear her to look at her. Her bottom lip was trembling and Lee thought she was going to cry again but with a superhuman effort she managed to stop herself. When she spoke again, her voice was flat. 'He raped me.'

'*What?*' Lee couldn't believe what she was hearing. Not Steve. They seemed to be getting on so well last Friday. 'When? What happened?'

'Friday. When he picked me up, he said he'd thought about it a lot, that he respected my decision, and wanted to be friends.' She spoke in bites. Her voice still had the same, flat monotone, as if she was reading a script for the first time. 'He was such good company that evening, like when we first met. He brought me home. Asked to use the toilet. I went into the bedroom to get something, and then . . .'

This time she did cry. Lee held her again. 'It's OK. You don't have to tell me any more.' But Simone shook her head. After a long silence, she continued.

'He let himself out as if nothing had happened. When he left, I stayed where I was until he drove away. Then I ran downstairs and locked the door.'

'Did you call the police?'

'Police? Round here?' She was sneering now. 'You think they're interested in a black woman being raped? By someone she was checking? They think all we do is fuck and breed anyway. And even if they wanted to, they can't help me, not now.' She wiped her eyes. 'The first thing I did after locking the door was take a bath.'

'A bath.' Lee tried to keep the dismay out of her voice. It was perfectly understandable, but it was the worst thing she could have done.

'I ran the water as hot as I could take it, then I threw in Dettol, Jeyes Fluid, bleach – anything I could lay my hands on.' She laughed mirthlessly. 'I even douched with bleach. I could smell him on my skin, so I took the scrubbing brush and scrubbed everywhere he had put his hands on me. I sat in that bath for over two hours. But I could still smell him – smell his aftershave in my bathroom. So I threw bleach on the floor, on the walls, everywhere, until I couldn't smell him any more. But I could still see him . . .' She put her fist in her mouth to stop herself crying once more. When she started speaking again, her voice was trembling. 'That was five days ago, so there's no . . . evidence. Not that I would have told them anyway.'

'Why didn't you ring me?'

'Because you would have told me to go to the police, which is exactly what you're doing now.' Lee looked away. 'And because,' Simone continued in a smaller, quieter voice, 'I didn't think I would live to see today. My husband left me. I've got no baby, no family. And now this. I felt I was so dirty, so . . . used, I wanted to die.'

'And now?' Lee asked quietly.

'I still feel dirty. But I don't want to die. At least not today.' She pushed her sleeve up so that she could run her hand through her hair.

Lee stared in shock. She took hold of both Simone's hands. They were red, blistered, and rough to the touch. Three of her nails were broken. There was a bad bruise on her right wrist.

'Where else did he hurt you?' Lee asked quietly.

'Apart from raping me, you mean?' Simone's tone was acid. She was silent for a moment, then continued, her voice now clinical, detached, 'I've got bruising on both hips and around my left breast. I also have teeth marks on my neck and around my right nipple.'

'Let me see.'

'No!' Simone scooted away from her. 'I'm not exposing my body any more – not to you, not to anyone.'

'But I can say I saw them if I have to make a statement—'

'Leanne, are you deaf? I said I'm not going to the police!' She was shouting now.

'But you don't know how many other women he's done this to – or might do it to in the future.'

'Him? A good-looking man like that? He doesn't need to rape.'

'He raped you, didn't he?' Lee said quietly.

Something flared, then died, in Simone's eyes. 'I'm not going to be a martyr for anyone. Let them complain. I just want to forget it, put it behind me and get on with my life.'

'You call this putting it behind you? Simone, you've been hiding in here with the blinds drawn for five days. You can't face the outside world in here, you can't even face the daylight. You look as if you haven't eaten for days. How long do you think you can go on like this?'

'As long as it takes.' She grew angry now. 'Look, what's it got to do with you anyway? He didn't rape you!'

'What's it got to do with me? I'm your friend. Your friend, Simone. This isn't Fordyce, and you don't have to be the tough girl in the playground. Not around me. Not any more.'

Simone started to cry again, as painfully as the first time. Lee let her lean on her shoulder, her tears soaking into her designer suit. She felt like crying too. She could feel the tears coming but she didn't want Simone to see. One of them had to be strong right now. Gently, she extricated herself from her friend. 'I'll be back in a minute.'

The tears were filling her eyes now, making it difficult to see. She still didn't know which was the bathroom. She tried the next door. The bedroom. The bed had been completely stripped, the sheets and duvet in a pile on the floor in the furthest corner. Lee stepped back out as quickly as she could. She couldn't bear to be in there. The sadness was as tangible as when her father had died. She went into the bathroom, put her hands over her mouth and began to cry, as quietly as she could. When she'd finished, she washed her face. She could see faded and whitening splotches on the pink wall where Simone had flung the bleach. The smell of bleach would stay in here for days. The sadness would last even longer.

She went back to Simone. She was sitting up now, leaning against the door frame, her back to the open room. Lee crouched down beside her.

'At least let me ring for the doctor.'

Simone looked at her. 'I told you I don't want anyone seeing—'

'You might be pregnant.'

Simone's head jerked up, her face stricken. It was obvious she hadn't thought of that.

'It's been five days. Too late for the morning after pill, but . . . Simone, you've got to see a doctor.'

Simone said nothing.

'Look, even if you don't want to do it for yourself, do it for me. And if you do that much, then,' Lee took a deep breath, 'I won't go on about you reporting it to the police.'

Simone looked at her. 'Promise?' She sounded like a little girl.

Another deep breath. 'Yes, I promise.'

Simone sat rigid for several moments. Then she said, slowly, 'The emergency doctor doesn't like to come out round here. They're scared they'll get attacked. The junkies, you see. It'll be quicker if we went to the surgery.'

Thank God. Maybe the doctor could talk some sense into her.

Simone struggled to get up. When she did, she was as unsteady as a newborn colt. She looked at the broken lock on the door. Lee noticed how she carefully avoided looking into the room itself. 'Then we have to get a locksmith.'

Chapter Twelve

Lee stood by the big bay window of her room in Chambers, staring out. If anyone had told her that so much could have happened in her life in the last two months she would have laughed in their face. She had a headache which no amount of aspirin seemed able to kill. It had been ten days and Simone still refused to go to the police. Clive Omartian still hadn't surfaced in spite of Brendan's best efforts. And, although she got more done, her bed was feeling pretty lonely without David in it. She wished she had someone to talk to. Perhaps Mary. But Mary wasn't in this morning. To top it all, her cigarette cravings were back. With a vengeance.

The phone broke into her thoughts.

'Miss Mitchell?' It was Dean. 'I've got Mr Donnelly on the line. He says it's urgent.'

What now? Lee thought. 'Put him through, would you, Dean?'

Brendan sounded both worried and relieved. 'Lee, thank God you're not in court. Clive's been arrested, and the police are refusing bail.'

'What? How long has he been back in the country?'

'Look, does that matter now? He was picked up speeding over London Bridge, off his face on something or other. The police say they flashed him to stop. When he didn't, they pulled him over, smelt cannabis, searched him and found some.'

'How much?'

'I don't know. And that's not all. He had a girl with him, and I

102

mean a girl. Sounds like she's not even sixteen. He was taken to Miller Street. The press haven't got hold of it yet. I know some people, I think I can keep it quiet for another day, max. So we've got to get him out of there before then.'

'Have you told anyone else about this? Ellenburg? Forman?'

'You're joking, aren't you? You think I'd give anything to Forman and Amery that they could use against us? I'm hoping I won't have to. You're the only one I've told, Lee.' He paused. 'It's not the drugs I'm worried about so much; they'll probably just caution him if it's personal use only. But I've heard mutterings about USI.'

Lee buried her head in her hands. Good job Brendan couldn't see her now. 'Did the girl make a complaint? Or her mother?'

'Not yet, as far as I know. They're still investigating it.'

Lee sighed. 'Well, we'd better get down there to see him, Brendan.' She looked at her watch. 'Right away. I'm due at Southwark at two.'

'What? You mean you'll come?'

'I need to speak to him anyway, don't I? Well, now's as good a time as any. At least we both know where he is.'

'It's just that you barristers never usually sully your feet by going to the police station to see clients.'

'We go back a long way, Brendan. You should know by now I'm not the kind of person to stand on ceremony. I'll meet you outside Miller Street in twenty minutes.'

Miller Street police station was in one of the most depressing parts of South London. The building seemed to reflect the attitude of its occupants to the immediate environment, as if it, too, was at war with the locals. Brendan was wearing a shabby beige raincoat over a brown suit, even though the weather was still unseasonably hot for early summer. The face that greeted them behind the custody desk belonged on a bouncer, not a policeman. Yet it was familiar. It only took a few seconds for Lee to place it, even before Brendan addressed him by name.

'Good morning, Sergeant Lambert. I've come to see Omartian.'

'Well, well, if it isn't Mr Donnelly. Again. You'd better watch out, some of your legal aid clients are in here too. You know, the ones who aren't rich, and who don't have their faces all over the papers. Remember them?' He looked Lee coldly up and down. 'I see he gets two for the price of one.'

'This is—'

'I know who this is,' Lambert interrupted Brendan. 'Last time I saw you was at Inner London with that toerag Willis. Put any more filth back on the streets since then, Ms Mitchell?' He emphasised the 'Ms' with a sneer.

Lee looked back at him with a studied calm. 'And it's nice to see you again too, PC Lambert.'

'Sergeant Lambert to you.'

'Yes, of course.' She smiled, too sweetly. 'So glad to see they finally recognised your talents and promoted you, after all these years.'

Lambert at first took the comment at face value, then flushed as he recognised Lee's jibe.

'Yes, well, you see, they've got this positive discrimination policy working here, what with us being surrounded by ethnic minorities in this area. So some of us who've been working long and hard were passed over for promotion just to make the force look good.' He put his elbows on the counter, warming to his theme. His eyes never left Lee's face. 'But now we've got a different problem, you see. We've got so many blacks in the force we've got to be careful we don't get them confused with the villains. Wouldn't want to arrest the wrong ones, would we?'

'Look,' Brendan butted in, 'can we just get down to business? I want to see my client.'

'Well, you can, but I don't know about her. He doesn't need the two of you there, and as you know, Mr Donnelly, I only have to let in the *solicitor*.'

Lee opened her mouth to say something when Brendan tried a different tack. 'Come on, Jack. It seems quiet today. I know you don't have to, but I would really appreciate it. I'd consider it a personal favour, in fact.'

Lambert seemed to take for ever making up his mind. He was clearly enjoying this, having the whip hand over two defence lawyers. 'OK, Mr Donnelly, seeing as it's you, and you're a regular down here, I'll make an exception, just this once. Wait here a minute.'

As soon as he moved far enough away from the desk, Brendan hissed, 'Why the hell did you have to wind him up like that?'

'He started it,' Lee hissed back. 'I'm not going to have anyone talk to me like that, Brendan.'

'This is so bloody childish, Lee. This isn't about you or him. It's about the client. Get your ego out of the way.'

Just then Lambert came back. 'This way.'

Clive jumped up as soon as they entered the cell. He was so glad to see them he didn't register the tension between his legal representatives. Two days' growth of beard made him appear, oddly, even more handsome. He raked his fingers through his hair, pushing it back from his eyes.

'I didn't expect to get both of you,' he said, relief evident in his voice.

Lee eyed the room with distaste. It was a lot cooler than outside, which was its only saving grace. She was dying to sit down, but every surface was so begrimed with ingrained dirt that she didn't dare. The wall looked only marginally cleaner, but it would have to do. She leaned against it. Clive caught her eye and the enthusiasm died on his face. He sat back down on the bench bed, next to Brendan.

'So why didn't you tell us you were back?' she asked.

'I only got back last Friday.' When she said nothing, he continued, 'Look, if it makes you feel any better, not even my father knows I'm back. Is this important now? I just want to get out of here.'

'Brendan tells me you got stopped speeding south over London Bridge with some young girl in a car reeking of cannabis. Police found some on you too. Is that right?'

He hung his head. That told her everything.

'How could you be so . . .' She recalled what Brendan had said earlier, stopped, then started again. 'That was an extremely stupid thing to do, bearing in mind you're up on a trial for fraud in a few months. Don't you think we have enough problems already?' When he still said nothing, she asked. 'What about the girl?'

'What about her?' he muttered sullenly. He sounded like a guilty schoolboy who had been caught out.

'Don't play games with me, Clive; you really don't want to piss me off. Brendan and I can walk out of here any time we like. You? You may well be sleeping in Brixton Prison until your trial. You know they're thinking about charging you with USI – Unlawful Sexual—'

'Wait a minute. I never had sex with her.'

'How old is she?'

'Sixteen. That Sunday was her sixteenth birthday. I had to get her home before midnight – her mother classes it as a school night.' He smiled wryly. 'I'm not saying that I wouldn't have, but the opportunity didn't arise. She was up for it, though. Said she wanted me to be her birthday present. Seems she read about me in the papers and knew that I liked . . . female company, so she must have figured I wouldn't turn her down.' He grimaced. 'She was right.'

'Do you know her?'

'No. I've seen her around on the club scene though. You can't miss her.' He smiled again, turning to Brendan. 'Bet she doesn't look like any sixteen-year-old you've ever seen.'

Brendan didn't return the smile. 'Did she say anything to the police?'

'Not that I heard.'

'Do you think she'll make a complaint?' Lee asked.

'About what? I told you, nothing happened.'

'OK then,' Brendan said, 'what about the drugs?'

'I had some grass on me; I admitted that to the police.'

'Did you give her any?'

'Now *that*, Ms Mitchell, I'm not stupid enough to do. Me having it is one thing. The last thing I'd want is for the papers to say I was corrupting a minor, or some such.'

'You never told me you used drugs,' Lee said slowly. 'Why not?'

'Got a cigarette, Brendan?' Clive asked suddenly. He fished one out of the offered pack, and lit it using Brendan's lighter. His hands were rock steady. He took a long drag, then continued, 'I didn't think it was relevant. How does it relate to a fraud case?'

'Anything that can be used against you is relevant. In future, let me decide what that is. Don't worry, I'm not going to tell the police. I don't care whether you take it or not, frankly. But I don't like being caught by surprise. George Amery knew about it.'

'So he's acting for Hector now, is he?'

'I never said that. How did you know?' Lee asked suspiciously.

Clive took another long drag on his cigarette. 'Who else could have told him? My father doesn't know. He's a prominent man, very old-fashioned and, contrary to how it may seem, I wouldn't want to embarrass him unnecessarily. I'm even quite fond of him.' He leaned back against the wall. 'Now Hector – Hector really loves him. So he won't tell him either, but he knows. Besides, I don't consider cannabis to be a drug.'

'According to Amery, Hector reckons you took the money to pay off your dealers.'

'What? One hundred and forty grand's worth? I could buy it by the field for less than that.' He stood up and started pacing round the cell. 'Haven't you worked it out yet, Lee? Hector hates me. He thinks I'm my father's favourite. Strange that it should matter so much to a fifty-five-year-old man, but he may well be right. I was a happy accident, you might say. When Hector was born, my father was twenty-two, married to a woman from the old country, and just another immigrant struggling to make his way in England. When I came along he was fifty, happily remarried, a financial, professional and social success. I represented all that to him. He could afford to indulge me, and he did. No matter what Hector does, he never seems able to please the old man.'

'Do you take anything you *do* consider to be a drug? Coke? Crack? Es?'

He laughed. 'If I took any of those I wouldn't look as well as I do now. Crack is for those who don't have the money or the class to take anything else, and as for the others, well, let's just say I like to be in control at all times. I can do that on grass. Besides, musicians take it, they claim it inspires their music. I like being around musicians. Don't you, Lee?'

She stared at him. Where did that come from? 'What do you mean?'

'Nothing, nothing. Look, I'm just tired. I start to talk all sorts of nonsense when I'm tired. Please, you've got to get me out of here.'

'That depends on what the police want to do about the USI.'

'But I told you—'

'I know what you told us, Clive,' Lee said, gentler now, 'but they don't have to believe you. I'm hoping they won't charge you. But if they do and if they won't bail you from the station, we'll make an emergency bail application as soon as possible.'

'And how soon can that be heard?'

'Tomorrow at the earliest.'

'Tomorrow!' He sat down again and buried his face in his hands. He looked so dejected Lee felt genuinely sorry for him, even though he had brought this on himself. She put her hand on his shoulder.

'I'll do my best to get it heard quicker, but I don't want to lie to you, Clive; if they don't bail you from here today, don't get your hopes up.'

Slowly, he raised his head from his hands. Looking at Brendan, he said, 'In that case, don't forget to bring what we discussed.' Turning back to Lee, he said, 'I know you'll do your best. I have faith in you.'

As they walked from the cell back to the front desk, Lee asked, 'What was all that about?'

'He wanted a change of clothing for the bail hearing, in case he doesn't get bail tonight. He's given me the keys to the house, in Little Venice. Gorgeous place it is, too.'

Lee nodded. 'Look, you'd better speak to Lambert; you seem to get on better with him than I do.' She smiled slightly. ' "Best interests of the client" and everything.'

'Lee, about before. I—'

'Forget it. It's not the first time we've had our differences. Besides, if you were a pushover, I'd probably hate you.' They had reached the desk by now. Lambert was waiting for them.

'I'll be outside, Brendan. Nice to see you again, Sergeant.' She didn't wait for a reply. She hoped this sweetness was killing him. It was certainly killing her to have to do it.

It was at least fifteen minutes before Brendan joined her.

'Well, if you've come out this quickly the news can't be good. He's staying in there tonight, isn't he?'

'Yes. In spite of what he tells us, they're taking the possible USI seriously. They know who the girl is; they sent a police car round to her house to take a statement, but apparently they haven't managed to find her, or her mother. God alone knows why. So they're producing him at Southwark tomorrow.' He looked at her. 'Think you'll be available to do it?'

'Don't see why not. Better ring Tom now to book me in.' She looked at her watch. 'In fact, that's where I should be going now. But one more thing, Brendan. Why do you think they took him to Miller Street? I mean, Southwark is nearer. They would have had to drive right past it to get to Miller Street.'

'Who knows? Maybe Miller Street officers were off their patch.' He gave a tense little smile. 'You can go back in and ask Lambert if you want.'

'You think he'd tell me if he knew? No, thank you very much. See you tomorrow morning.'

Brendan nodded, and watched her thoughtfully as she drove away.

Chapter Thirteen

His Honour Judge Hugo McCallum was clearly unimpressed. 'Well, Ms Mitchell, when you prefaced your arguments by saying you were making a bold request, you were right. Are you seriously suggesting I should release this man on unconditional bail? In view of the seriousness of the charges?'

'Your Honour, the defendant has pleaded guilty to simple possession of a small amount of herbal cannabis, consistent with personal use only. The Crown are not proceeding with any other matters arising out of that night—'

'Ms Mitchell,' the judge interrupted, his voice taking on the patient tone he normally reserved for small children and defence barristers, 'let's not go there again, shall we? Less than two minutes ago I sentenced him to a forty pound fine, in case you weren't listening. You know very well I'm referring to the far more serious fraud allegation this defendant faces. Now, can you give me any good reason why I should release the defendant on bail at all?'

No, I can't, Lee thought. 'Yes, Your Honour, I can give you several. Firstly, apart from the relatively minor offence to which the defendant has pleaded guilty here today—'

'Which puts him in breach of bail,' McCallum interrupted.

'Your Honour's quite right. I do not seek to make any excuses for it, neither would the defendant wish me to.' Lee hoped Clive was looking suitably remorseful in the dock behind her. 'But, apart from this offence, the defendant is a man of good character.

Secondly, whilst not seeking to minimise the seriousness of the matter to which the defendant has just pleaded guilty, it is a relatively minor offence of an unrelated character. Thirdly, the defendant has been on bail for several months now, and this has been his first legal infraction. It will doubtless be several months more before the trial is heard. Under the circumstances, therefore, it would, in my respectful submission, be wholly unfair for the defendant to remain in custody until trial.'

The judge looked at prosecution counsel. He was so young and so obviously inexperienced that plainly he had just been sent along to hold the fort.

'Mr Singh, what is the present position as regards this trial?'

The young man jumped up and fumbled with his papers.

'Er, if Your Honour would just give me a moment . . . the Crown expect to be ready for a plea and directions hearing in approximately four to six weeks, and the matter could, as far as the prosecution is concerned, be set down for trial as soon as possible thereafter. There are no prosecution dates to avoid.'

Shit! Lee thought. Shit! Shit! Shit!

'Thank you. Well, Ms Mitchell,' said the judge, turning back to her with a smile that looked suspiciously like a smirk, 'it seems that your estimate of several months in custody is somewhat pessimistic, wouldn't you agree?'

Lee tried a different tack. 'If Your Honour is not minded to grant unconditional bail, I have discussed the matter with the defendant, and he is willing to abide by any reasonable conditions the court would impose.'

'Ms Mitchell, I doubt whether any conditions I would be inclined to impose would be considered reasonable by the defendant – that is, if I am to grant him bail at all. At present I have still to be convinced that he deserves it in any form. Mr Singh, what do you say as to the matter of bail?'

Lee held her breath. If the prosecution raised even the slightest objections, McCallum would have no hesitation in locking Clive up.

'The Crown object to unconditional bail,' her heart sank, 'but have no objections to bail with stringent conditions.'

Behind her, Brendan exhaled so loudly she hoped the judge did not hear.

'I see.' The displeasure was obvious in McCallum's voice. 'Anything else you want to say, Ms Mitchell?'

'Unless I can assist Your Honour any further, those are my submissions.'

It seemed an age before the judge said anything. He pursed his lips and wrote for a full minute, then he put down his pen in a deliberate manner and looked at Clive, who was being signalled to rise to his feet by the dock officer even before ordered by the judge to do so.

'Clive Edward Omartian, stand up. I have listened to everything your counsel has ably said on your behalf. I must say I disagree with her. I do not consider the possession of any drug, even one in such common usage as cannabis, a minor matter. It is a serious matter when it comes before me, and I treat it as such, in particular when the offence was committed whilst on bail.' He paused to let his words sink in. 'However, on balance I am just persuaded to grant you bail, with conditions,' he added sternly. 'One, you must surrender your passport forthwith. No more foreign trips for you until the trial is over. Two, you must live and sleep each night at your home between the hours of eleven p.m. and six a.m. Third, I require one surety in the sum of five thousand pounds, to be taken either at this court today or at a police station. Is there anyone here today?'

Lee turned and looked at Brendan. He shook his head.

'No, Your Honour. If I might just have a few moments to confer with the defendant . . .'

'You can have all the time you need, Ms Mitchell. The

113

defendant is going nowhere until those conditions are satisfied. Take him down.'

The court usher jumped to her feet. 'All rise.' Everyone in court stood silently as the judge retired to his Chambers. It was too late to speak to Clive now; he was already on his way down to the cells. Just before he disappeared from view, he looked at Lee and smiled. He didn't seem too disappointed; in fact his spirits seemed to have dramatically improved since she last saw him. He must have realised, as she did, that he was lucky to get bail at all.

As Lee and Brendan left the courtroom together, she waited until they were safely out of earshot of prosecution counsel and his CPS representative before she spoke.

'Well, that curfew will certainly tie a knot in his tail. We could try and vary it, I suppose, if he wants, though I think he's less likely to get into trouble this way.'

Brendan shrugged. 'We'll see what he wants.'

'What about the surety?'

'We've got one on the end of a phone.'

'One of his father's rich friends, no doubt.'

'No, one of his own. Neville Ellenburg.'

'What?' Lee guessed she must have looked as astonished as she sounded. 'Ellenburg, as in Marcus Ellenburg?'

'His son. Apparently he's a friend of Clive's from Harrow.'

'He told me he hated his school,' Lee mused. 'Made it seem like he had no friends there . . .' She caught Brendan giving her a puzzled look. 'Why would the son of a co-defending solicitor stand bail for our client?'

'I don't know,' Brendan replied, 'but I'm not looking a gift horse in the mouth, and I suggest you don't either. He's on his way to his local police station even as we speak.'

Lee shook her head. 'I don't like this, Brendan. It's a bit too close to home.'

'Where in the Bar Code of Conduct does it say we can't do this,

114

Lee?' Brendan said impatiently. 'If it was Marcus, now I would be more inclined to say it might look strange, but even then I wouldn't turn it down. But this is the son we're talking about. He's got his own money, from what I understand. What could be the objection?'

'I still don't like it.'

'We don't have to like anything about our job, Lee. We just have to do it.' For a moment Lee thought she saw a look on his face she had never seen before, but it passed so quickly she must have imagined it. 'Look,' he continued, 'I'm going to ring him now to give him the result. He should be parked outside Hampstead police station any minute. The sooner he does the business, the sooner Clive can get out.'

Lee watched Brendan go off towards the telephones. Something about this case was beginning to make her very uneasy. Good thing she had Brendan on her side, otherwise she wouldn't know who to trust.

'Back here again, are you?' said a voice right behind her.

She whirled round, a sharp retort on her lips, when she recognised who it was.

'Where I grew up, Ray, you don't sneak up on people. Not from behind. What are you doing here, or shouldn't I ask?'

'Well, it's nice to see you and all,' he grinned, and Lee couldn't help smiling. He looked impeccable, as usual. Next to Clive Omartian, he really was the best dressed defendant she had ever represented. 'I'm up here with Darren this time.'

'Your cousin? He's barely out of trainers, isn't he?'

'Still in them. That's why he hardly gets caught. Never liked them meself, though, even when I was his age. No style, know what I mean?' He looked over to the door of the courtroom where his cousin was being dealt with even as they spoke. 'Just turned seventeen. Balls barely dropped but thinks he's a hard man. He's shit scared though. He's trying to hide it, but he can't fool me.'

'What's he up for?'

'Handling. Nothing much, but it's his first time in the Crown, you see. I can't sit in court with him because as soon as any of these judges see me, that'll be it for him.' He paused. 'You're up here on Omartian, aren't you? Heard about your big case.'

'How?'

'You know, word gets around.' He paused. 'Had the brief long?'

'A couple of months – right after I last represented you, in fact.'

'You two getting along all right?'

'How do you mean?'

'Well, he seems hard to pin down. Thought you'd have to be chasing him up and down the country – all round the world, even. Still, can't believe everything you read in the papers.' He paused again. 'How well do you know him?'

'As well as I need to. About as well as I know you or anyone else I've represented, I suppose. Is this going somewhere, Ray?'

Ray looked at her intently. 'How well does he know you?'

Before Lee could say anything Brendan approached them hurriedly.

'Looks like you're wanted,' Ray drawled. Again, that intent look. 'Look after yourself, Lee.'

Brendan had by now come close enough to recognise Ray. His step slowed. He gave Ray a half-smile in greeting. Ray eyed him coldly. 'Be seeing you,' he said to Lee, his eyes still on the Irishman. 'Remember what I said.' Then he was gone.

'Remember what?' Brendan asked as he watched Ray's retreating back.

Lee was about to tell him, then stopped herself. Tell him what, anyway? Far better to work it out for herself first. It was probably nothing, anyway.

'Haven't the faintest idea,' she said. 'Anyway, what's happened between you two? He's been with you man and boy, hasn't he?'

Brendan shrugged. 'A lot of my clients are getting pissed off because of the time I'm spending on Clive's case. They don't want any of my assistants, just me. There's a limit to what I alone can do, even for old clients like Ray. If he doesn't like it, he can take his work elsewhere. It's only legal aid, anyway.'

Lee had never heard him talk about legal aid clients like this before, not even in jest. 'They're entitled to good representation too, Brendan. Besides, that's our bread and butter.'

'Yes, but this is cake, Lee. This is cake. Speaking of which, here comes our boy now.'

Clive wore a plain white shirt and the black suit Brendan had brought in for him. Even from a distance it was obvious from its cut and drape that it was expensive, but discreetly so. Having spent two nights in custody he should have looked like shit. In fact, he looked anything but.

As he walked across the large open waiting area to join them at the door, heads turned in recognition. Muted whispers floated all round them.

'Ready?' Lee asked him.

He smiled and nodded. He look out towards the entrance. The sunlight was streaming in through the glass doors. 'Thank you for what you did for me in there.'

'Well,' Lee began, 'I'd like to take all the credit, but—'

'So take it,' Clive interrupted.

Why not? she thought. It wasn't every day she was able to bask in the adulation of a rich, handsome man. Then she remembered what Ray had said.

'I've got the car,' she said. 'Do you need a lift anywhere?'

'No, Parker should be pulling up for me any minute – ah, there he is,' Clive said, as the navy blue Mercedes pulled into view, right on cue.

They left court through the revolving doors. Lee was about to turn to Clive when she saw a flash out of the corner of her eye. She turned back and was stunned to see half a dozen photographers and journalists running towards them.

'Fucking hell!' Brendan exclaimed.

Lee turned back towards Clive. In the instant she had looked away from him, he had put on his sunglasses – whether to shield him from the sun or from the press, she wasn't sure. It was such a studied action, it should have made him look like a third-rate playboy. Instead, it made him look tantalisingly remote.

She put her hand on his arm. 'Let's get back inside.'

'No, I'm not running. Just think how it would look. They'd only come after us anyway.'

'I don't care how it looks. I don't want you talking—'

A young female reporter shoved a microphone in Clive's face. It was too late.

'Mr Omartian, how does it feel to be free?'

From the back, someone shouted, 'Tell us about the girl, Clive. She says she went down on you while you were driving over London Bridge. Bit young for you, isn't she?'

Where was the training for this in Bar School? Instinctively, Lee put her hand over the microphone. 'No comment.'

'I didn't ask you,' the woman snapped. She turned to Clive. 'Hiding behind your lawyers, Clive?'

If she was trying to goad Clive, she certainly succeeded with Lee. 'Listen, if you don't want to be wearing that thing, get it out of my face. I said—'

'It's all right, Lee.' Clive sounded as if he was used to dealing with this sort of thing. What he didn't sound was surprised. In fact, when he spoke he sounded not only as if he had expected it, but almost as if he was enjoying it.

'First of all, I don't need to hide behind anyone. Secondly, nothing of the sort happened between me and that young woman. If it had, I'm sure I wouldn't be talking to you here now. Finally, yes it feels good to be out. Believe me, two days locked up is enough to last me a lifetime. And it's all due to my barrister, Lee Mitchell, in whom I have total confidence, and who I know will prove at my trial what I've said all along, that I'm not guilty of any fraud.' Security staff and other solicitors and barristers had by now come out to see what all the fuss was about. They, plus the assembled journalists, looked at Lee with new-found respect. 'That's all. Thank you.' Clive moved quickly down the steps towards his car where Parker was standing by the rear door, waiting to open it for him. Lee was right behind him. Brendan seemed to have disappeared somewhere. Where had he gone?

'Let me get in, Clive. I need to speak to you.' Pause. 'Now, please.'

She slid in beside him and the car pulled smoothly away. She was glad the windows were tinted. No one could see the frustration on her face, or the trembling.

'You OK?' Clive asked.

'No. No, actually I'm not.' She took a deep breath to steady her nerves. She needed to regain her composure, fast. 'I asked you not to speak to the press. I told them "no comment", yet you ignored me. Why?'

'Well, I had to say something. What you said to that reporter wasn't exactly tactful.'

'I don't care what she thinks about me.'

'Well, I do. As my lawyer, you're a reflection on me as well as my case.'

'A reflection on you? You think I'm your cypher, Clive? You think you can tell me to say or do anything and I'll just do it, like some trained monkey? You've got the wrong woman for that.' When he said nothing, she continued, 'I think you've got this relationship all wrong. *I'm* the lawyer. *I'm* supposed to advise *you*, and when it comes to anything that can adversely affect your case, including publicity, you're supposed to do as I say.'

Slowly, deliberately, he took off his sunglasses and looked at her. His blue eyes were glacial. 'You can't control me, you know, though I must say it amuses me to see you try.'

'So what was that "total confidence" stuff back there all about? Just bullshit for the cameras?'

'No, it wasn't. It's just that I'm not some legal aid oik who'll simply do as he's told.'

Lee paused before she spoke. 'I need to have free rein if I'm to represent you, Clive. You're not a fool, and I hope I've never treated you as one, but I can't have you second-guessing me and courting publicity all the time. Neither should I be finding out things from other lawyers about my client. I'm not a mushroom – you can't keep me in the dark and feed me shit. If that's what you want, we'd better call it a day now. You won't have any problem finding someone else to act for you.'

The silence seemed to go on for ever. Finally, Clive spoke.

'I'm not going to sack you, Lee. Of course, you're right. I'll remember in future.'

She didn't believe him, but for now it would have to do. 'Put me off here, please. I'll make my own way back to my car.' She looked at him. 'I hope we understand each other.'

She left the car, shutting the heavy door behind her. Clive leaned back into its cool interior. 'Oh yes,' he said to himself. 'I think we do.'

Chapter Fourteen

'Today is Tuesday the tenth of June at eight a.m. This interview is being tape recorded. I'm Detective Sergeant Scott, and this is . . .'

'WPC Murphy.'

'Right, and the person being interviewed is . . . could you state your full name and address for the record, please?'

'Steven Beresford Payne.'

'And your address, please?'

'You know my address. You dragged me out of there this morning.'

The detective fixed him with a steely look. 'Please,' he said again. It was more order than request.

'Twenty Harold Court.'

'Right. Mr Payne, it's right, isn't it, that you were cautioned this morning at your home when you were arrested?'

'Cautioned?'

'Yes. You were told you did not have to say anything—'

'Yeah, yeah, yeah.'

'Well, for the purposes of this interview I must remind you that you don't have to say anything, but it may harm your defence if you do not mention when questioned something on which you later rely in court. Anything you do say may be given in evidence. Do you understand?'

'Yes. I've got nothing to hide. Just get on with it, will you? I've got things to do.'

'So have we all, Mr Payne.'

'Yeah, but you two are getting paid to sit around here wasting your time talking to me. I'm not.'

'Before I ask you questions about the allegation that's been made against you, I must remind you that you are entitled to legal advice at any time.'

'Yeah, but you said it could be ages until the solicitor comes. I can't wait that long.'

'For the purposes of this tape, I want this to be clear – do you understand your entitlement to legal advice?'

'Yes.'

'And do you wish to go ahead with this interview without a solicitor being present?'

'Yes.'

'If at any time during this interview you feel you need the services of a solicitor, please say so. Now, Mr Payne, you have today been arrested on suspicion of rape occurring—'

'I didn't do it.'

'Occurring in the early hours of Saturday the fourth of May – Bank Holiday weekend. The complainant is Mrs Simone Jean Wilson. Do you know Mrs Wilson?'

'Yeah, we were seeing each other, know what I mean?'

'By "seeing each other", do you mean you were having a sexual relationship?'

'Yes, we were.'

'At the time of the alleged rape?'

'Yes.'

'She said she'd broken it off with you about a week before.'

'Well, she did say something like that, but we went out a week later. How serious could she have been?'

'Why would she do that?'

'How should I know? You'll have to ask her. Missed getting it regular, I suppose.' Steve smiled. 'She made it very clear right from the start that she didn't want any big commitment.'

'And how did you feel about that?'

'You mad? Like it was Christmas and my birthday all rolled into one! You've seen her, haven't you? When a woman like that says she just wants to fuck you, you'd be crazy to turn it down.' He paused. 'She didn't say it quite like that, of course.'

'Maybe she didn't say it at all.'

Steve's face hardened. 'Go and ask her then.'

'What about Mr Wilson, then?'

'She told me they were separated. She never liked to talk about him.'

'She claims that on that Saturday morning, she only let you in to use the toilet, but while you were in her house you attacked her.'

'Where was she when she claims this happened?'

'In the bedroom.'

'Well, there you are, then.' Steve leaned back in his chair and folded his arms. 'What was she doing in the bedroom, anyway?'

'You needn't look so smug about it,' the female officer interrupted. 'Last time I checked, you didn't need permission to go anywhere in your own house, no matter who else was in there.'

'Look, when I'd finished, she called me into the bedroom. She was there waiting for me. She didn't even give me time to put my business on – though I don't like wearing those things, anyway.'

'How did she get those marks on her?' DS Scott asked.

'What marks?'

'On her hips and her breast. She's got some nasty bites, too.'

'What can I say? We both got very . . . excited.'

'Strange, seeing as you both "got excited", there's not a mark on you.'

'Well, there was,' Steve said defensively, 'but they're gone now.'

'Did you go to the doctor about them?'

'No.'

'Well, she did. We've spoken to the doctor and we've seen the notes. We also saw her yesterday. Those bruises are still there.'

'So? Maybe it was someone else in the meantime. Ever think of that?'

'We're asking the questions here, Mr Payne. So, are you saying that it wasn't your energetic lovemaking that resulted in those injuries, but another man's?'

'Look, all I'm saying is I didn't rape her. I don't need to rape. I was seeing other women while I was with her. We had no holds on each other. I don't know what she was doing. I don't have a problem getting women – you saw who I was with today, right?'

'All that shows is that you're not very fussy.'

'What's the matter, officer? Didn't get any last night? No,' Steve looked at him, 'I know what your problem is. That woman this morning, Lynne; can't bear it, can you, a black man fucking one of your women. Especially when they like it.'

WPC Murphy looked at her superior officer. Evidently something had hit home. His manner was still calm and controlled, but his face and neck were so red he looked as if he was about to explode. The atmosphere in the room was getting uglier by the minute.

'Let's get back to why you're here, Mr Payne. Mrs Wilson had some pretty nasty marks on her for something that had happened two weeks earlier, even if she did like it rough. She's at least a foot shorter than you. The doctor says those marks are consistent with being grabbed from behind. You make it sound like she gave as good as she got, but there isn't a mark on you.'

'I told you, I did have.'

'Where?'

Steve said nothing.

'Can the woman you were with the next night back that up?' WPC Murphy asked.

No answer.

'Well? You said you'd had a woman in your bed every night since Mrs Wilson. Can she corroborate your story?'

'No comment.'

'Oh, so it's no comment now, is it? And just as things were getting interesting.'

'No comment.'

'Well, you see, Steve,' DS Scott continued, leaning in closer now, 'the general public, particularly these feminists, they're getting really touchy about date rape – a woman's right to say no and all that. There's even a programme on telly tonight about it. Seems you picked the wrong time to be arrested. Now, if you know some woman who can help you, I suggest you tell us her name. Or is she married too?'

'Yeah. Matter of fact, it's your missus.'

WPC Murphy saw the murderous look in her colleague's eyes. She caught his arm just as he was about to lunge at Steve. 'Calm down!' she hissed in his ear. She hoped the tape wouldn't pick it up.

Steve had seen the look, too. He turned to the woman. 'Did you see? Did you see what he was about to do?'

'Dunno what you're talking about, Mr Payne,' she replied smoothly. 'What exactly do you mean?'

'He was about to attack me.'

'I didn't see anything like that. You see anything like that, Sarge?'

'No, nothing like that,' DS Scott said. The look was still there, but the voice was as calm and controlled as before.

'I want to make a complaint.'

'WPC Murphy will show you where to go as soon as you're released from the station. Meanwhile, is there anything else you want to say to us, Mr Payne?'

'You must be fucking joking.'

'I'll take that as a no. Anything you want to ask, Constable?'

'No, Sergeant Scott.'

'I'm now offering you our notebooks, describing what happened at your house this morning, to read and sign if you agree with the contents.'

'You're having a laugh, ain't you? I'm not signing anything.'

'Up to you.' Scott looked at his watch. 'The time is now eight thirty-five a.m. and this interview is being concluded.' Click.

When WPC Murphy rejoined DS Scott, he was leaning with his forehead against the wall.

'That's how not to do an interview. If I'd have got hold of him . . . anyway, thanks.'

She shrugged, embarrassed. 'Well, what do you think? About the case, I mean?'

But Scott's mind was still on the interview. 'Stupid black fuck. You get so many of them come in here. Brains in their knobs, and all they want to do is fuck. I swear, every time they come, it kills off part of their brains.' He saw her slightly disapproving look. 'And you can take that look off your face, Gill. I don't feel like being very PC at the moment. You heard what he said about my wife. Anyway, who knows with these people? Maybe she did like it rough. It did take her two weeks to get off her arse to talk to us.'

'Those bruises were pretty bad, Sarge. Plus we've got the doctor who says they were worse when she saw them.'

'Yeah, I know, I know. But you know the problems with these date rape cases, it always comes down to who they believe.'

'Or rather what they believe about the victim.'

Scott looked at her shrewdly. 'You're not going all soft on me, are you, Gill? If she had broken up with this man, what's he doing in her house at two o'clock in the morning if not to renew old acquaintances? Why didn't she tell him to take a piss round the corner?'

'When you invite someone in your house, you don't expect them to attack you.'

'You don't go in your bedroom either; you wait downstairs until they go.'

'If what she says is true, she didn't deserve what happened to her, Sarge. At least we can give her the benefit of the doubt.'

'I can see you're not going to let this one go, are you, Gill? As if our caseload isn't heavy enough already. Trust me to be stuck with the bleeding heart.' Scott sighed. 'OK, you win. I owe you one from before, anyway. Let's kick it upstairs and see what the CPS think of it.'

Chapter Fifteen

Lee woke with a start. The sunlight was streaming through the window. On David's half of the bed lay a number of witness statements and financial records, and a volume of Archbold. She had fallen asleep over the brief. Again. She groped for the clock: 5.45 a.m. She'd had exactly three and a half hours sleep, total, partly due to David's late-night call from the States, oblivious of the time difference, but mostly because she was going over and over, checking and re-checking all the points to be covered today in the Omartian case. Today, the first day of July, was the plea and directions hearing, in all likelihood the last court appearance before trial and possibly the last time the defence team could ensure they got everything they were entitled to from the prosecution before the trial started.

Lee turned over and tried to go back to sleep. With any luck, she could get another hour and a half before she had to get up. When 6.15 found her still wide awake, she gave up. She stumbled into the kitchen and was reaching for the instant coffee when she realised she had enough time this morning to make the real thing today, a fortifying, special treat at the beginning of what promised to be a challenging day.

She took her coffee, and the telephone, through to the study, opened the French windows and sat out on the patio. She was not an early riser by nature, but sitting out in the garden on a summer morning more than made it worth the effort. The air was so fresh, and it was so quiet and warm, that she could have been a million

128

miles away. And, right now, she wished she was.

There was only one other person she knew who would also be up this early.

Simone answered on the third ring. 'This is a bit early for you, isn't it?' she asked.

'Yes, but I knew you'd be up.' Lee paused, then said, 'You know, my usual. Just checking to see how you are.'

'Leanne, you've been ringing me every day for the last six weeks. Nothing very dramatic can happen in twenty-four hours . . .' She stopped suddenly. They both knew that was wrong. After all, it had happened to her.

'Anyway,' she went on with forced cheerfulness, 'I'm fine, honestly. You don't have to keep ringing so often, you know. I know you're busy with your big case. Some kind of big review today, isn't it?'

'PDH,' Lee said automatically. Her voice softened. 'And it's no trouble, though I'd rather you were staying here with me. I'm just hanging about in this big flat by myself, and to be honest I could do with the company now David's away. It would be nice to have another black face in this building – and dahling,' she continued in an affected accent, 'we could have breakfast every day on the terrace!'

Simone laughed, the first genuine laugh Lee had heard from her in weeks. 'If it's company you want, why not ask your mum? That sounds right up her street.'

'You mad? I love her but she'd drive me crazy. She'd bring her Bible and those bridal magazines and start leaving them in places where I can "accidentally" find them, and try to force-feed me into the bargain. It's bad enough when I see her on Sundays.'

'Nice try, Leanne, but I know you just want to keep an eye on me. But if you want company, you're more than welcome to come and have breakfast overlooking my weeds!'

Lee wondered in what part of the house Simone was sleeping.

How could she stay in such a place? One bedroom a shrine to a dead child, the other the scene of a brutal rape by someone she knew and had once trusted enough to willingly let into her bed. Unless she hadn't . . . Lee wanted to kick herself for such a treacherous thought. 'You know,' she said, 'I'm really proud of you for what you did. I've said this to you before, but I wish you'd told me. You didn't want to go to the police. I could at least have come to the station with you. No one should have to go through that alone.'

'Deciding to go was far more difficult than actually going. I had to convince myself the police couldn't make me feel worse than I already did. And I suppose in a way that's why I went. Nobody should be made to feel like that, go through what I did, and I kept remembering what you said – that Steve might do it again, to somebody else. Besides, I've done things on my own for so long, Leanne, I don't think I know any other way. And it wasn't as bad as I thought. They were more sympathetic than I expected, even the men.'

'Listen,' Lee said, 'after this trial, I'm thinking about going to the Gambia for a couple of weeks. I've never been to Africa, and I know your father's family are from there. You want to come?' She knew that Simone would find that hard to refuse. She'd often mentioned wanting to trace her family there.

'I'd love to, but you know I can't afford it on a teacher's salary.'

'My treat. After all, I should be a moderately rich woman once this is over.' Lee paused. She knew Simone was battling with her pride. 'Don't say no, Simone. God knows we could both do with the break.'

'Maybe after Steve's trial,' she said, finally. 'I don't want to go away with that hanging over my head. Look, I've got to go. Best of luck today.'

'OK.' As she hung up, Lee made a mental note to go and visit Simone that evening. There was something unnerving about the way in which she seemed determined to go it alone. She glanced at the clock. Only quarter to seven. Nothing was to be gained from sitting here any longer. Time to put the Omartian show on the road.

Traffic was terrible, as it usually was on a Monday morning, but Lee was determined not to let it disturb the equilibrium she was trying to maintain. Co-defending with George Amery would put paid to that soon enough. The hearing itself shouldn't last more than an hour; much of the important work would be done beforehand in negotiations with counsel, before any barrister set foot in court. Worse than that was waiting. The PDH was due to be heard at 10.30 a.m., before Judge McCallum, but according to Dean, the junior clerk, so were five other cases, and Lee knew from bitter experience that it was entirely possible still to be at court at lunchtime, still waiting for your 10.30 listing. As she stopped at yet another traffic light, she flicked the radio idly before finally settling on Choice FM. At least the journey from her flat to court was relatively short; even if the traffic continued nose to tail, she would certainly be there by nine at the latest.

In the event she arrived a full twenty minutes before that. At that time of the morning, the only other people she expected to see were the cleaners and the security guards. The last person she expected to see was her client.

Her surprise must have shown on her face because he said, 'Well, you did tell me to keep my head down. I thought I was sure to beat the cameras if I got here early. They're bound to be out in force later on. It'll be the first time in ages we'll all be together – one big happy family,' he added cynically.

Lee went over and sat next to him. He smelt as expensive as he looked. However he felt, he looked the picture of confidence, as if victory was assured, it was merely a matter of time.

'What time did you get here?'

131

'Just gone eight.' He gave her a long, appraising look. 'You look very nice this morning.'

Instantly Lee's hackles went up. 'Thanks,' she said crisply. 'You must have left home very early to get right across London by eight o'clock.'

'Parker always knows a back way. That's why I hired him. He did the Knowledge a few years ago.' He smiled. 'But I offered him more money.'

'Of course,' Lee replied drily. 'Traffic was a bitch, especially coming up to London Bridge.'

'What route did you take?'

Lee outlined the most direct route from her home to court, along the main roads.

'Try this one next time,' Clive suggested, and described in detail a short cut.

Lee looked at him sharply. The route he had so accurately given her was familiar, it was one she had herself used when she was in a real hurry. 'Who told you where I lived?'

'You did. Don't you remember? The first time we met. I said Parker would take you wherever you wanted to go.'

'No I didn't. I never give clients my home phone number, much less my address. Besides, Parker didn't take me home.' She looked at him, hard. 'Have you been following me, Clive? Spying on me?'

'Oh, for God's sake, Lee, stop being so paranoid. Why would I need to do that? I'm more than happy with what you've done for me so far. You must have told Parker in anticipation of going home, then changed your mind – I don't know.'

Lee was positive she had never given him or Parker her address. Well, nearly positive.

She stood up abruptly. 'Is Brendan around?'

'Haven't seen him yet.'

'Time to robe up,' she lied.

'What, already?'

'Yes, already.'

'I don't know why you're angry. I won't tell anyone. It's a mistake anyone could have made.'

'Not me. Excuse me.'

As she walked to the lift she could feel his eyes boring into her back. She jabbed at the call button. After what seemed like an eternity, the doors trundled open. She couldn't get to the second floor fast enough.

The female counsels' Robing Room was cool and deserted. By the time she got there, whatever doubts she had about having given Clive her address had disappeared. Never in all her years of practice had she ever told a client where she lived. But Brendan knew where her flat was. Surely he wouldn't have told him.

She was halfway through dialling Brendan's mobile number when she had second thoughts. If Brendan had told Clive, knowing her as he did, he would expect her to confront him and tell him what she knew. Instinct told her to keep her mouth shut. Time enough to tell him later, if she had to.

Instead, she dialled Chambers.

Tom answered the phone. 'Miss Mitchell? No problems with the Omartian case, I hope?'

'No, it's not that. I need a big favour from you, Tom. You know all those briefs I had for Ray Willis? Have you re-allocated them already?'

'No. Didn't Mr Donnelly tell you? He rang up and asked for them back.'

'Recently?'

'No, this was soon after you got the Omartian case for definite. Said something about you being too busy to do them. The odd thing was, he went mad when I said I would re-allocate them. He never minded before, and he didn't with all the other cases you've got for him, just these ones. He was back on the phone to me a couple of weeks ago, soon after your bail hearing, I think. Threatened to come down himself and forcibly remove them if I didn't send them back.'

Lee's heart was in her mouth. 'Are they still in Chambers?'

'They're going back today.' Uncharacteristically, Tom sounded almost apologetic. 'Look, I'm sorry about the delay. I know he's a friend of yours, but he's got some good work. I was just trying to keep it in Chambers.'

'No, no. You don't know how glad I am they're still there. Can you dig out Ray's phone number for me?'

'What, right now? I'm in the middle of billing—'

'Please, Tom. I wouldn't ask if it wasn't important.'

'OK.' He was clearly reluctant, but after a long pause he came back. 'I've got a home number for a Peckham address, and a mobile – no, two mobile numbers.'

'Give me all of them. Then send the briefs back. He sends too much work to Chambers for us to piss him off.' And, she added silently, any further delay would be bound to make him suspicious, particularly after the obvious hostility Ray had shown towards him at the court. 'I'll ring you later when I've finished here.'

'The case was all over the news this morning, Miss Mitchell. Did you catch it?'

'It's the first time the whole family will appear together. Plus, there's a lot of speculation about the pleas.'

'Not Clive's?'

'No, the father's. Seems they think he might be pleading guilty.'

A guilty plea from any one of them could mean that the prosecution would drop the case against the others; they had lost too many high-powered fraud trials involving prominent City businessmen to risk losing another. It would also mean she could get shot of Clive, Brendan, and everything else surrounding this case. She didn't know whether to be glad or sorry.

'But don't count on it, Tom. I just don't have that kind of luck.'

'What? I would have thought you'd be gutted.'

She shrugged. 'It's not all it's cracked up to be, Tom. 'Bye.'

She went back downstairs, carrying her wig but wearing her gown. She needed to exert her authority over Clive, and there was nothing like a barrister's robes to do that, but it was still too early in the day for the full regalia. After all, it would be nearly two hours before she got anywhere near a court, and the others hadn't even arrived yet.

Brendan was deep in conversation with Clive, but they both smiled at her as she approached. She smiled back, scrutinising them carefully all the while, but there was nothing untoward in either of their expressions. What had she expected to see, any-way? She hadn't a clue what was going on. That was precisely the problem.

'Well, it makes a pleasant change having both the barrister and the client before me.' Brendan rubbed his hands in anticipation. 'All raring to go, Lee?'

'Let's just say I'll be glad when this whole thing is over.' She looked at Clive. 'No offence meant, Clive.'

'None taken. I feel the same way.'

It was still early, but the large foyer was already starting to fill up. Of the rest of the defence team there was no sign.

'Do you know who's prosecuting today?' Brendan asked.

'No. I know I should have asked Tom to find out, but then, how likely is it that the person doing the trial brief would be coming down here to do a piddly PDH? Look what happened at the bail hearing.'

'Well, you're wrong about that, Ms Mitchell,' came a deep voice from behind her.

Startled, they all turned round, and Lee was both surprised and deeply grateful when she realised who it was.

'Peter! You're prosecuting this case?'

'The very same,' her former pupil-master smiled. 'And you needn't sound so astonished about it. I have got quite a few years under my belt, you know.'

'Oh, you know I didn't mean it like that. It's just . . . I'm very glad to see you. Very glad.' She turned to Clive and Brendan. 'Would you excuse me, please? I just want to have a quick word with Mr Fairfax.'

Clive watched the two of them walk away, talking amicably. Without taking his eyes off them, he said to his solicitor, 'Those two know each other?'

'Peter used to be Lee's pupil-master when she first qualified at the Bar.'

'They seem very . . . comfortable together. I thought he was something more. Maybe an ex-lover?'

Brendan snorted. 'Believe it or not, Clive, it is possible for men and women to be on good terms without shagging each other.'

'Is it really? I must try that one day.'

'Besides, you've seen what she's got at home. Who would you choose?'

Clive shrugged. 'Absence makes the fond heart wander. And who knows? It takes all types. He's still in America, isn't he?'

'Yeah. He won't be back until long after the trial's over.'

'You know, I hear he's actually quite good. So my money wasn't wasted after all. Who knows, I may even make a profit. Ah,' the tone of his voice changed. 'Look who's here.'

Brendan turned and saw Frederick and Hector Omartian with their respective solicitors, Marcus Ellenburg and Arthur Forman, and barristers, Nicholas Robbins and George Amery, all arriving together. That had to be more than coincidence. Many of the other lawyers and defendants who had been milling around in the foyer awaiting the start of their own trials recognised at least one of that group, the lawyers feigning nonchalance, the defendants not even trying to hide their interest.

Hector was the first to see Clive and Brendan. The dislike on his face was plain. He tapped George Amery on the shoulder, jerking his head towards where his brother was standing. Amery looked over at the two of them briefly before scouring the foyer, no emotion registering on his face. Brendan guessed he was looking for Lee.

Frederick Omartian was deep in conversation with his lawyers when he turned to say something to his elder son. With a start, he realised whom he was looking at. Even from this distance, Brendan could see his hands were shaking as he took out his glasses from his breast pocket and put them on to have a better look. While Amery's face had shown nothing, Frederick's face betrayed a range of emotions. Joy at seeing his younger son, sadness at finding himself in this position, the pain of having his loyalties torn between two sons who evidently hated each other – it was all there, and something else too, something indefinable.

Brendan watched as Frederick said something quickly to Hector, then started to cross the floor towards Clive. Halfway across, he turned back and looked at Hector who had stayed rooted to the spot. Whatever was in that look was enough for him to move towards his father. After some hesitation, the lawyers followed.

All eyes were on them now.

Frederick spoke first. 'Good morning, Mr Donnelly. Marcus has told me a great deal about you.'

'All good, I hope,' Brendan said, attempting a smile.

'Oh yes. He has great admiration for someone who can provide the quality of representation you do without all the resources and support that are considered vital to a firm like Robbs Ellenburg Bennett. I'm very glad to meet the man to whom my son has entrusted himself, though I wish with all my heart that the circumstances were different.'

Frederick Omartian had a very precise way of speaking, as one would expect from a man in his late seventies, whose first language was not English and who was used to having to make himself clearly understood, particularly in transactions where millions of pounds were at stake. Brendan's heart felt as if it was being squeezed in his chest. Frederick Omartian was proud and dignified, courteous to the last. To think that such a man should be reduced to this. God, but this was a dirty business.

'Everyone has a . . . strong suspicion, shall we say, that my sons actively dislike each other,' Frederick continued, this time speaking more to the entire gathering than to Brendan, 'but, to my knowledge, nobody, least of all the press, has any concrete proof of this, and I don't intend to give them any. The Omartian name has been dragged through the mud enough as it is. At the very least, whatever the final outcome, I want us to show a united front, but,' he said, looking at his two sons, 'I cannot do this without your help. This has been going on so long I don't expect miracles,' he sighed, 'but will you at least indulge an old man and keep whatever differences there are between you hidden?'

'Yes, of course.' Clive's voice was bland.

Frederick turned to his elder son. 'And you, Hector?'

Hector took a long time before answering. Finally he said, in a dull, flat voice, 'You know I'll do whatever you want, Father.'

Frederick put his hand on his son's arm. He knew what that had cost Hector. 'Thank you. Both of you.'

Amery's harsh voice cut sharply across the intensity of feeling among the Omartian men. 'I'm glad you've papered over the family differences, Frederick, at least temporarily, but I'm much more concerned about the business at hand.' He looked at Brendan and Clive. 'Where's your Ms Mitchell?' he asked nastily. 'Not sacked her yet, have you?'

Brendan nodded towards the far end of the lobby, by the bank of lifts. 'There's your answer.'

Amery's smile died on his lips as he saw Lee and Peter Fairfax, deep in conversation. From his reaction it was evident that he knew precisely who Fairfax was and his part in the case. Without taking his eyes off the pair, he said to Brendan, 'Shame you couldn't find anyone better, Brendan.' Turning to Clive, he said, 'She looks very nice today, don't you think?'

Clive wasn't rising to the bait. 'I really hadn't noticed.'

Amery gave him an appraising look. 'But of course you did. Nicholas, I think it's about time we found out what our co-defending counsel has been saying while we weren't here. Excuse us.' And with that he strode off in Lee's direction.

Lee saw Amery, with Robbins trailing in his wake, before Peter did. Suppressing her first instinct, she smiled at him. As close as she was to Peter, she and Amery were still on the same side. It wouldn't do for the prosecution to see the divisions before they even got started. Bad for negotiations.

'Good morning,' Amery said. He gave them a smile that never quite reached his eyes. 'Hope you don't mind if Nicholas and I join you.' He turned to Lee. 'I just wondered if you two were talking about anything interesting before we arrived.'

Lee knew exactly what he meant. All pretence of solidarity disappeared. Embarrassed that Amery should behave in such a fashion in front of Peter, she said, 'About the case, you mean?'

'You ought to know I don't operate like that, Amery,' Peter said crisply. 'I would consider it very improper. And besides, I would just have to repeat the information once you two got here.'

'Ah, yes, but you two do know each other, I understand.'

'I know you too, George. The Bar's a small place.'

'Well, you can't blame me for looking out for my client's interests.'

Nicholas Robbins looked aghast at what Amery was saying, especially in front of their opponent. He had not expected their differences to be so plainly exposed. Fairfax looked uncomfortable, clearly disapproving of the insinuations that were being made. He appeared about to say something when Ellenburg approached them.

'Nicholas, I wonder if you could join us for a moment. Frederick has a matter he wishes to raise with us both.'

As if on cue, a message came out over the Tannoy system for Peter. Lee watched him go, then looked over to where Brendan and the others were still standing. They seemed curious about what was going on but made no attempt to approach. She smiled at them, then, still smiling, turned to Amery. To any onlooker, it would appear as if they were getting on famously.

'What the hell do you think you're playing at?'

'Don't use language like that to me,' Amery snapped. 'You're not on the streets of South London now.'

'Oh, you think that's bad? What the fuck do you think you were doing trying to embarrass me like that? You were way out of order. I would never, ever cast doubt on your professional credibility like that. I don't need to damage Hector's case to get my client off. His own barrister will see to that.' She looked back at the group. She was still smiling. Amery wasn't.

'Just listen to yourself. Do yourself a favour, dearie, and take that big chip off your shoulder before you collapse under the weight. You're not representing a couple of muggers, you know. You're in the big league now.'

'George, I really don't give a shit what you think about me, and I'm sure you don't mind that I think you're the biggest self-serving bastard I've ever had the misfortune to co-defend with. But because you're good, and you're Hector's choice, I'm prepared to put up with you. But you and I both know that I know what I'm doing, otherwise I wouldn't be here. Now I'm warning you, don't ever pull a stunt like that on me again.'

Amery's eyes narrowed to slits. 'You don't have a monopoly on street-fighting.'

'Yes, but I still remember it, George. Do you? You'd better

smile, the others are watching. Wouldn't want them to think we've fallen out, would we?' she added and walked back to Brendan and Clive.

'Bloody bitch,' Amery said as Robbins joined him.

'I admit I find her rather abrasive, but I can't believe you said what you did in front of Fairfax.'

'It's nothing you weren't thinking yourself, Nicholas. We're not playing by Queensberry rules here. You can afford to think all this is beneath you. Me, I just want to win. So does she. So if you know what's good for you, you'd better stick with me.'

'The family don't want that. "United front" and all that. You know the old man's little speech was as much for our benefit as for his sons'.'

'Who cares what they want? It'll be a sad day when defendants run the show. The only thing they're entitled to is an acquittal. How I decide to go about getting mine is of no concern to anyone, including Hector. She used to be Fairfax's pupil. Didn't know that, did you?' he added derisively on seeing Robbins' shocked face. 'That's the trouble with you Establishment types, you never do your homework on anything but the case. You really trust her not to use her influence to cut some deal? I'd do the same in her place.'

'I know Fairfax of old,' Robbins began. 'He's a very principled man and—'

'I'm not taking any chances. I'm not letting the two of them out of my sight.'

The body language says it all, Lee thought, as she took her place at the large dining table. Looking at the assembled company, it never ceased to amaze her how adversarial barristers could be, both in and out of court.

And that was just among your own side.

'I always find the methodical method works best with these

forms,' Peter said, waving a blue and white document in the air, 'especially where there are multiple defendants. If we get this right, McCallum will merely rubber-stamp it, so we won't spend any more time here than we have to. That's if we're all agreed, of course.' He looked at his opponents gathered round the table. All attempts on his part to lighten the mood had failed miserably. They had left the Omartians downstairs with the solicitors, and were in the Bar Mess now, the dining area reserved for barristers, where they could all talk freely on a counsel to counsel basis; in other words, nothing said among them would be repeated outside their circle without prior agreement.

'So, ladies and gentlemen,' he continued, 'what are the pleas?'

'Come on, Peter. You know none of my clients is ever guilty,' Amery said with a smirk.

'Clive's is still not guilty,' Lee said crisply.

'My lay client also wishes to maintain his not guilty plea,' said Robbins, in his usual ponderous manner. With Frederick Omartian first on the indictment and Robbins laying the groundwork for the entire defence team, this trial would drag on for weeks, Lee thought despairingly.

'Yes, I recall seeing correspondence from Robbs Ellenburg Bennett indicating this right from the outset,' Peter remarked. 'I must say I'm surprised that that plea is being maintained, bearing in mind his voluntary confession.'

'Frederick Omartian is acting under legal advice.'

'Doubtless you've told him he'll lose credit for any guilty plea entered subsequently.'

'Really, Fairfax. With all due respect, it's not your place to question my client's plea or the advice upon which it's based. I'm not a pupil, you know. I know what I'm doing.'

Privately, Lee wondered if he did, but what the hell. Frederick Omartian wasn't her client. Besides, she was relying on his confession to get Clive off. If he maintained his not guilty plea, the prosecution would read it out before the jury. That would do more for Clive than anything he could say for himself.

'Of course. I didn't mean to imply otherwise.' Peter raised his eyebrows slightly at Robbins' outburst but didn't pursue it. Instead he asked, 'Are you all agreed on witnesses?'

'For my part, I only want the two officers who arrested Clive, the officer in the case, and the interviewing officers,' Lee said. 'That's five altogether. Keep it nice and simple.'

Given his usual laboured approach to everything, Lee was surprised to hear Nicholas agree with her. 'I take the same view. The fewer witnesses the better. Less complicated for the jury,' Nicholas said.

'Well, I want everyone fully bound,' Amery said.

They all turned and looked at him.

'What?' Peter exclaimed. 'There are thirty-seven prosecution witnesses. You can't possibly require all of them.'

'I don't recall you starting to represent my client, Fairfax. Hector Omartian is heavily implicated in a serious allegation of dishonesty, one which, if proved, would mean he could never work in the City again, quite apart from any jail sentence he might get.'

'Or might not,' Lee said. 'When did they last send anyone away for this sort of thing?'

'But at least ten of the witnesses don't directly deal with your client at all,' Peter continued.

'Then I'm sure my learned friends here will request them as live witnesses. For my part, I want everyone who has ever made a statement even mentioning Hector's name to be available for me to cross-examine.'

'But you don't need them. The case is strongest against the father anyway.'

'I disagree with that,' Robbins interjected.

Amery gave him a sidelong look. 'Why? He was the only one stupid enough to spill his guts.'

Robbins went very red in the face. Before he could reply, Peter went on, 'For example, you know several of the officers who searched the premises and seized documents made substantially the same statements.'

Amery leaned back in his chair. 'Now why aren't I surprised to hear that?'

Peter's usually affable voice suddenly took on an edge that Lee hadn't heard for a very long time. 'Look, Amery, I know what you're up to. You can waste your client's money by spinning this trial out for months if you want, that's between you and him. But I'm not going to let you use this case to get your face all over the front of the *Daily Mail* again. This is not about you, it's about the man in whose best interests you're supposed to be acting – or have you forgotten?'

Amery, still leaning back in his chair, now folded his arms across his chest. 'Have you quite finished?'

'Yes.'

'Good. My position's still the same. I want them all.'

'Then be prepared to argue it in front of McCallum, as I shall make it quite clear that, in my opinion, many of them are superfluous and unnecessary.'

'Fine.'

There was a pause before Peter, clearly annoyed, continued. 'Well, in the light of what's just been said, there seems to be no point in asking whether any documentary evidence can be agreed. Obviously it can't.'

'If we can get back to the matter in hand, please,' Lee said, determined to stay focused on Clive's interests while the others fought. 'I want the interview tape played, Peter. I've heard it; I don't want anything edited, and the summary isn't nearly full enough.'

'But the summary indicates that he denies any involvement, and he had a solicitor present throughout.'

'Which is more than his father had,' said Robbins.

'I know what you're saying, Peter, but the summary doesn't indicate exactly what he says or how he says it. I want the jury to hear that. He's well enough known for them to be tempted to fill in the gaps with their own speculations; I want to avoid that as much as possible.'

Peter let out a weary sigh. 'Very well.' He jotted it down on the form, then turned to Robbins and Amery. 'What about you? Do you also want your tapes played?'

Both men nodded.

'What about the company's security videotape which is supposed to show Frederick doing the deed?' Amery asked. 'You've been promising us that for ages.'

Peter shifted ever so slightly in his seat. 'It's no longer in the Crown's possession.'

'Which means either you never had it in the first place or you've lost it,' said Amery.

'We no longer have it, and we won't seek to rely on it. You can all draw your own conclusions from that.'

Amery started to laugh. 'Well, well, well, Fairfax; looks like your "strong case" is beginning to crumble all round your ears. Go on then, tell us what happened. Did the exhibits officer forget to tag it properly?'

'I can do without your sarcasm. There are ninety-three exhibits in this case. Accidents do happen, you know.'

'Strange. They never do to me. So where does this leave your case, then? You've got no witnesses to this alleged fraud, no videotape, now,' Amery emphasised, 'no handwriting evidence—'

'Yes we do.'

Since most of the recent developments hadn't concerned Clive, Lee hadn't been paying much attention. Now she was.

'Since when?' she asked.

'I got the statements this morning, when I was called away downstairs, remember?'

'And you've only now told us? You made us wait until now?'

'That was barely an hour ago, Lee,' Peter said quietly. 'I'm disclosing it now.'

Robbins looked thunderstruck. 'When did the analysis actually take place?'

'Six weeks ago.'

About the time of Clive's bail hearing, Lee thought. Strange, the prosecuting counsel, Mr Singh, hadn't mentioned it then.

'Let me look at that.' Robbins leaned over suddenly and snatched the statement out of Peter's hands.

'As you will see,' Peter continued calmly, 'the first statement clearly implicates Frederick Omartian in the first set of bogus transactions, totalling one hundred thousand pounds. As for the other forty thousand, well, it's still not clear.'

'Meaning?' Lee asked.

'Two experts have looked at those. One thinks they're Frederick's but the other thinks they may be extremely good forgeries, most likely by someone who knows his signature very well.'

'Why was this done so long after the fact?' Robbins demanded.

'It wasn't felt necessary. After all, we had your client's confession. It was I who advised that it be done. You see, if *I* were representing old man Omartian, given his age, the number of interviews and the fact that he had no solicitor present, I would try to argue out the interview under the PACE codes,' he said, correctly guessing Robbins' intended approach. 'I just wanted to be prepared for every eventuality.'

'Is it the Crown's case that Clive forged his father's signature?' Lee asked.

'What I'm prepared to say at this stage is that it's possible either of the two co-defendants could have done it, but we think it's Frederick.'

'That's not good enough. You'll have to nail your colours to the mast, Peter.'

'Well, that's the best you're going to get for now, Lee, so prepare your case accordingly,' he said shortly. 'Of course, if the situation changes before trial, I shall let you all know.'

'Like you let us know about this,' Amery said. He was holding the statements now. He threw them on the table in disgust.

'As I've already told you, I only received them this morning, same as you. If you'll observe, they're dated yesterday.'

The despair on Robbins' face was so evident he might as well have buried his face in his hands and held up a white flag. But still he tried to bluff his way out.

'I'm not prepared to go ahead with this trial until *my* experts have had a chance to properly analyse all the documents mentioned here.'

'Of course.'

'The originals, Fairfax. You know you can't do analyses from copy documents.'

'Let me know who your expert is and they'll have access to everything they'll need.' He looked at Lee and Amery. 'It goes without saying this applies to you too, if you want it.'

'That'll push the trial date back a good couple of months,' said Amery. 'Mind Frederick doesn't croak before we get started, Nicholas. Of course, that would greatly help whoever's left standing at the end,' he said, looking meaningfully at Lee.

'Oh, do shut up, George,' Robbins snapped. It was the first sign of spirit he had shown towards Amery. Amery wasn't in the least concerned.

'The thing that will delay the start of this trial is your insistence on unnecessary witnesses – if the judge rules in your favour,' Peter said. 'We'll be lucky if we get a date before the end of the year. We could have wrapped this up in a month once we got started.'

'We'll need at least six weeks,' Lee said. 'If the Crown isn't prepared to say now that Clive isn't in the frame for the forgery, I want an analysis done as well.'

'I think eight to ten weeks,' Amery said.

'We won't get a ten-week fixture until next year,' Peter stated. 'I don't want to wait that long. Plus, McCallum is stuck with the trial once he starts, and you know the word is he wants to retire in December. I'll make inquiries as to prosecution witness availability so we'll know where we are with dates to avoid, at least from the Crown's point of view. Now, I can tell you I have no objections to bail continuing as before for all three defendants. Are there any other legal issues we can usefully discuss?' When no one answered, Peter got up, saying, 'Please feel free to talk about me after I leave.'

Peter had been right about one thing. Judge McCallum was prepared to accept everything that was agreed, and only listened to legal argument on two points. The first was a half-hearted application by Robbins to exclude the handwriting evidence produced by the prosecution – one doomed to fail, but nonetheless supported by Lee and Amery. The second was Amery's argument for the witnesses described by Peter as being superfluous and irrelevant to be called to give live evidence at court.

Amery's nickname might be the Rottweiler, but on present form the Grindstone might have been more appropriate. With a mixture of clever legal argument and dogged persistence, he wore the judge down.

'Mr Amery, this is the eighth time you've presented this argument. On each occasion the Crown has raised the same objections. Do you have anything different to add?'

'As Your Honour knows, no two arguments are ever exactly

alike, no matter how similar the circumstances.'

Judge McCallum's voice took on a deliberately patient tone. 'Do you have anything *significantly* different to add, Mr Amery, or do you seek to adopt the same argument in respect of each contested prosecution witness?'

'Well, Your Honour . . .'

The judge fixed him with a gimlet-eyed stare. 'You're knocking at an open door, Mr Amery. It may not remain open for much longer.'

That was what Amery had been waiting for. First blood to him. He looked over at Peter, barely able to keep the mocking expression off his face.

'In that case, no, Your Honour. I'm grateful for that indication.'

Judge McCallum turned to Amery's opponent. 'Anything you want to add, Mr Fairfax?'

Peter stood up. 'Not unless there is anything I can say to persuade Your Honour to reconsider.'

'Unless you have new and additional argument, Mr Fairfax, I rule that the defendants are entitled to test any and all such prosecution witnesses as they require in cross-examination. Now, I can see from the form, Mr Fairfax, that by some miracle, bearing in mind the number, you don't have any immediate witness difficulties.'

'Not between now and October, Your Honour.'

'So why can't we get it on as soon as possible? August is usually a quiet month. The List Office is crying out for work, I understand.' He looked over to the listing officer, who nodded sagely. 'There's nothing I have in my list that can't be moved around, and if anyone's going to hear this case, it had better be me.'

Now it was Peter's turn to look mockingly over at the defence. 'I quite agree, Your Honour. I for my part am ready to start the trial as soon as Your Honour would like, but my learned friends have all stated they would need some time to examine the handwriting evidence.'

'Yes. It's a pity this wasn't served much earlier, Mr Fairfax. I know your position, but there's no reason the Crown couldn't have done something about this months earlier. It seems a glaringly obvious line of inquiry to me. I see it also extends time estimate for the trial by at least half its original length. Is there any way we could speed this up, Mr Robbins?'

Robbins stood up ponderously. 'None that I can see, Your Honour.'

McCallum nodded. 'Of course. It's not your fault that this evidence was served rather late in the day . . . Yes, Mr Amery?'

'I wonder if Your Honour would give us a moment. It may assist matters considerably.'

'Would you like me to rise?'

'Perhaps that would be best. It will only take a few minutes.'

'Less than ten, I hope, Mr Amery, because that's all you're getting. I have a full list today.'

The court usher announced, 'All rise!' as the judge stood up and left the court. As soon as he did, Amery motioned for Lee and Robbins to join him in the far corner of the courtroom. Peter showed no signs of going anywhere and Amery didn't want to be overheard.

'Sorry, Nicholas, but we need to talk about this some more. I want to keep this judge.'

'Well, that's as may be, but I need to get the analysis done and I'm not starting the trial—'

'I know, I know. You've said that already. Look, he let me have all the witnesses I wanted, and I was chancing my arm with half of them. What other judge would have allowed that? Anyone else would have made me sweat blood for them and still knocked me back. Believe me, the best chance we have of an acquittal is with McCallum.'

'I'm still opposed,' Robbins said. 'What do you think, Lee?'

Both men looked at her. Casting vote.

'I agree with George,' Lee said. Amery stared at her. This was help from an unexpected quarter, but he wasn't completely surprised. After all, whatever else she might be, she wasn't stupid. Her desire to win was so tangible you could almost touch it. 'We'd all benefit if we kept McCallum. If we don't get it heard before October, chances are it won't be till next year, as Peter said, and McCallum won't be around then if the rumours are true. Besides, do you think Frederick can take much more of this?'

Robbins glanced over at the dock. While his sons were both still standing – Hector stiffly upright, Clive leaning against the wall – Frederick was now seated. Even in the short time since they had all been in court he looked as though he had aged. His head was bowed, and his frail hand clutched the rail for support.

'Look,' Lee continued, in her most persuasive tone. It was important to win Robbins round. If he felt aggrieved, he could still insist on the trial being delayed, and the judge would have no choice but to accede to his request. 'They've got witnesses available until mid-October. Let's say the trial takes eight weeks. That's a mid-August start, six or seven weeks away. Surely we can get the analyses done by then. I know Peter. He's embarrassed enough by the late service of the statements, he won't sit on the originals.'

'And I know a very good expert, someone I've used many times before. Once he gets the documents and samples of the defendants' handwriting, he can do a joint report for all of us within, say, four weeks. That keeps us on line for a mid-August start,' Amery added.

The court usher approached them. 'Judge wants to come back in,' she said.

'Well, what's it to be, Nicholas?' Amery asked impatiently.

Robbins still looked wary. 'You can guarantee four weeks?'

'Yes, I can.' There was no way he could, of course, and both he and Lee knew it. But it seemed to satisfy the older man.

Before Robbins could answer, they heard, 'All rise!' They barely had time to resume their positions before Judge McCallum came back in. As he sat down, so did everyone else – except Robbins.

'Your Honour, having conferred with my learned friends for the defence, we envisage we would be ready to commence trial Monday the nineteenth of August, provided my learned friend for the Crown can serve the original documents on the defence within seven days.'

'Glad to hear it. It's the best chance you have of getting a fixture of this length all year. Mr Fairfax, you can comply with that, I trust.'

'Your Honour, could the Crown have fourteen days to serve—'

'Why? No. Seven days from today. Now, bail.' McCallum looked at Lee, clearly remembering their recent encounter, but said nothing. 'I see the Crown has no objections to bail continuing for each defendant as before.'

'That's correct, Your Honour.'

'Very well. Bail on the same terms. Anything else?' He looked at each of the four barristers in turn. All shook their heads. 'Very well. It's a pity I can't do anything about the inevitable publicity. No doubt I'll see you all in August.'

'Well, looks like we've got them on the ropes,' Amery said to no one in particular. All three defence barristers were now standing outside the courtroom, Robbins some distance away from them.

Lee looked around idly at the assorted lawyers, police officers and members of the public milling around in the wide corridor. It seemed busier than usual today. 'I'd be a lot happier if they didn't have that handwriting evidence.'

'But that's all they have in the way of hard evidence. Anyway,

Nicholas is the one who should really be worried. Looks like he'll actually have to do some work now. Ah, here they come.'

Hector left the courtroom first, holding the door open for his father who came haltingly after him. He seemed disorientated and unsteady on his feet. For a moment he looked as if he would collapse. Both sons saw this and automatically extended a hand to help him. Frederick accepted Clive's.

Hector's face seemed to set and harden. He turned his back on them and strode over to Amery.

'What's all this about handwriting evidence?' he demanded at once. 'How does it affect me?'

Amery looked at Lee and immediately drew Hector to one side. At first it was impossible for Lee to hear what they were saying, but very soon this became progressively easier – for her and, unfortunately, everyone else present. By now Clive had joined her.

'No! No! I'm not carrying the can for him. Not this time!' He whirled round and saw his younger brother. There was a look of real hatred in his eyes. He advanced towards him, shouting, 'You bastard, Clive! Why don't you be a man about this? Are you really going to let Papa take the blame? Are you?'

Everyone was listening now, and looking. Even Clive seemed shaken by this onslaught. Out of the corner of her eye, Lee could see someone writing furiously in a spiral-bound notebook. Probably a journalist. Oh God. She had to get Clive out of here. Now!

'Come on.' Lee, Brendan and Clive walked as quickly as was decently possible towards the Bar Mess. Hector couldn't follow them in here, though what damage he was continuing to wreak outside was anyone's guess.

'What the hell was that all about?' Clive asked.

You're asking me? Lee thought. But the priority now was to get him as far away from the court building as possible.

'Brendan, get him away from here. Use the stairs. Quickly. I'll speak to you later.'

She looked at Clive but didn't say a word. Before she spoke to either of them about this, there was someone else she wanted to talk to first.

Chapter Sixteen

Giles Townsend scowled as the eastbound District Line stopped yet again on the journey into Chambers. Wimbledon Village was the only part of south-west London he would countenance living in, but on days like this, surrounded by the great unwashed, he wondered whether it was too high a price to pay. He attempted to read the paper again. His scowl deepened as he turned the page. Even the *Telegraph* had something on date rape. He didn't think they would have followed suit. Since the television documentary, every newspaper and current affairs programme had done a feature, an article or a 'special' on the subject. He had recognised the name of the producer from his university days – one of those feminists, as he recalled, a woman he had actively disliked. Always denying her Oxbridge roots. Even Sarah, his wife, not known for her social conscience, was talking about it. Ad nauseam. He was as sympathetic as the next man; after all, he had gladly prosecuted violent rapists who had attacked unknown women, late at night, and left them for dead. But those were the real victims. This was completely different. One could tell it was the newspaper silly season.

As Giles marched into the Clerks' Room, Tom took one look at the expression on the face of his Head of Chambers and decided the best thing to do would be to stay well out of his way. Again. It wasn't his fault Townsend's forward progress at the Bar seemed to have slowed to a crawl. Lately he was beginning to wonder whether it was all worth it. They both earned the same amount but

Tom knew that, to Townsend, he would always be a working-class lad made good. He didn't want to hear him bleating on about his lack of work, not today. Hopefully what he had would stop it before it started.

'Good morning, sir,' he said quickly. His forced smile was bright. 'This just arrived for you.' He held up a substantial-looking brief, tied with white ribbon. Seeing the puzzled expression on Giles's face, he tried to phrase his next words as delicately as he could. 'I know you, er, decided not to prosecute for some time, but it seems they specifically asked for you.' Tom was still surprised by the fact; he hoped it didn't show.

Giles took the brief. Tucked inside the ribbon on the front was a white envelope. 'Personal' was written on it in blue-green ink, clearly from a fountain pen. There was no stamp, no postmark. Now he was even more intrigued.

'Thank you, Tom. Get Dean to make me some Earl Grey and have him bring it to my room.' He started to walk out of the Clerks' Room, then paused, and turned in the doorway. 'No, on second thoughts ask that new pupil – what's her name again?'

'You mean Anne-Marie?' Tom wondered why Townsend was feigning ignorance. He didn't have to pretend, not with him. Didn't he think he knew?

'Yes, that's the one. She can bring it.'

Space in the Temple was at a premium. In most Chambers the only person who was guaranteed his own room was the Head of Chambers, and Giles was no exception. Today he was particularly grateful for that fact. No one could see the relief on his face, nor the slight trembling of his hands as he placed the brief on his large leather-topped desk. He sat back in his chair for a long time, simply staring at it. A new case, and a criminal one at that. He picked up the letter again. Its position in front of the brief had hidden the title of the case: 'Regina v Payne'. He was just about to open it when he heard a knock on the door, followed almost immediately by Anne-Marie entering, carrying a small tray.

'Ah, come in, Anne-Marie.' Giles put the letter aside. 'Just put it down there.' He pointed to a corner of his large desk where the young woman carefully set down the tray. As she turned to leave, Giles said, 'Don't leave just yet.' He motioned for her to sit. 'We haven't had a chance to talk properly yet. How have you been settling into your pupillage? It's been, what, three, four months now?'

More than half over, Anne-Marie thought silently. He'd never bothered to ask before. In any event, she was sure he knew.

'Oh, fine, thank you. I'm doing a lot more work in my own name now.'

'And Lee Mitchell. How do you get along with her?'

Anne-Marie shifted uncomfortably in her seat. 'All right, I suppose.' But the tone of her voice indicated otherwise. 'She's perfectly civil to me, and very bright but, well, she's awfully hard, don't you think?'

Giles smiled indulgently. 'Something that afflicts many women at the Bar, my dear. They always seem to feel they have something to prove. I hope you won't find it necessary to emulate them in that respect.' Having dispensed this wise counsel, he took a sip of his tea. 'What about the Omartian case? Any developments?'

'Nothing that you wouldn't have heard already, Uncle Giles. I told you, I've—'

'Never call me that in here! Not even when we're alone.' Giles looked around sharply, almost as if he feared being overheard, even though they were the only two present. 'I think Tom suspects as it is. I don't want your pupil-mistress to hear about who you are. I've no doubt she'd have plenty to say on the matter, none of it good.'

'Anyway, as I was saying, I told you I've been busy with my own work. I was rather hoping to get a look at Clive Omartian myself,' she added wistfully, 'but all I've been doing on the case is research. There's been at least one conference and two appearances on the case that I know of since I've been her pupil—'

'That's all? On a case of this magnitude?'

'It's not really as complicated for Clive as it looks, Unc—sorry, Giles. Though it is for the co-defendants. Clive's really just been roped in with the others. In my opinion—'

'When I want a *pupil's* opinion, Anne-Marie, I'll ask for it,' Giles snapped. 'Perhaps you've misunderstood your purpose here. I don't want to hear about developments in this case the same as everybody else; I want to be the first to know anything that happens. Do you understand?' Anne-Marie shrank back in her chair as he raised his voice. And she wanted to practise criminal law? He pitied the poor bastard to be defended by her.

'But why?' she asked. 'What difference could it make to you?'

'Because I should have got it, dammit.' He paused, making an effort to control himself. When he spoke again, his voice had lowered, but the force behind the words was still there. 'Do you think if I had a case like that I would be worrying about whether or not I would take silk? Now, if there's a parting of the ways between Clive Omartian and his counsel, someone will have to take over at short notice. Who better than her Head of Chambers?' He took another sip of tea. 'Tom's told me the case has been adjourned.'

Anne-Marie nodded silently.

'I've taken the precaution of asking Tom to keep you free once the trial starts.'

This was going too far. No one, apart from the senior clerk and Lee herself, had the right to do that, not even Giles.

'What? That could be six weeks. What about my own practice?'

He ignored her. 'You just do your little research and keep me informed. You can leave now. And Anne-Marie,' he added as she hurried to the door, 'don't think of countermanding me with Tom, or through your pupil-mistress. Just remember who you have to thank for this pupillage.'

Anne-Marie bolted from the door like a frightened rabbit. Giles sat back, satisfied. Maybe now he'd see some results. He picked up the letter again.

Odd, really, that he didn't recognise the penmanship immediately, but as soon as he started reading it he knew who it was.

Townsend,

Herewith, a little rape for you. I remembered our conversation. Don't say I never help you. I spoke to some people I know in the CPS; nothing too complicated, I've been assured, but in the current media climate, something you can make a mountain out of and, who knows? At the summit just might be your silk.

Regards,

Morrison

Giles leaned back in his chair. Relief washed over him. Oliver had come through after all. And his timing couldn't have been better. Old university chums always came in handy. Even old university enemies.

He picked up the telephone and tapped out a number.

'Channel Four? May I speak to Lezli Markham, please? . . . Oh. When will she be available? . . . Well, I'm sorry to have missed her. My name is Giles Townsend. I'm an undergraduate contemporary of Lezli's. I was ringing to commend her on "The Rules of Engagement". I thought it was a very fine piece of journalism about a controversial topic, most sensitively done. As a lawyer, I'm particularly sympathetic to the plight of victims of this most grievous violation of trust. In fact, I have some information about a similar case I'm currently working on which I'm sure will be of interest to her. Please ask her to telephone me.' As he gave his Chambers number, Giles smiled to himself. He had begun the climb.

Lee didn't want to use her car. Too conspicuous. She had borrowed David's old estate instead. The car smelt like him. She tried not to get too maudlin. She had to be sharp tonight. Driving that, and dressed in jeans and a black leather jacket, she looked like any other black woman taking care of business. Which was precisely what she hoped to do today.

She'd agreed to meet Ray at a pub in Brixton, one where a black woman and a white man talking together would not attract too much attention, and away from their respective immediate areas.

He was already there when she arrived, seated at a small table in the furthest corner, away from the window. Judging by his full beer glass, he hadn't long preceded her.

He looked up as she pulled out a chair and sat down.

'So what's all this about?' he asked, without preamble.

'I was hoping you'd tell me. That's why I rang you.'

'What are we talking about, exactly?' His tone was evasive.

'Look, Ray. When I saw you at Omartian's bail application, you asked me how much he knew about me. Plus, I thought you and Brendan were friends, but the atmosphere was so cold between the two of you, I'm surprised I didn't need my thermals. Now I find my client knows exactly – and I mean exactly – the quickest route from where I live to Southwark Crown Court, which I *know* I didn't tell him. Something's going on, and I don't like not knowing what it is.'

'So what makes you think I know anything?'

Lee sighed. 'No bullshit, Ray, please. You agreed to meet me. Of course you know something. The only question is how much. And even if it's just a little, it's more than I do right now.'

He sat back in his chair and considered her, as if weighing up whether to tell her anything. Finally, he spoke.

'I don't know much. And if I tell you, things could get really nasty. I mean, seriously. But— All right, Mick?' Ray was looking up and over Lee's head. 'I didn't know you drank round 'ere.'

'I don't really. Not my kind of area, know what I mean?' The man was tall, muscular, with cropped blond hair. As their eyes met, his antipathy towards Lee was obvious. 'Just doing a favour for a friend.'

Ray turned back to Lee. His face was completely closed now. 'Mick and I used to go to school together,' he said. He did not introduce them. 'Hated it, but the teachers hated me too. Couldn't wait to kick me out of there first chance they got. The only thing I liked was English Literature – well, just one book, really: *Julius Caesar*. I remember you telling me you liked it too. I wanted the power, but he got weak in the end; I wasn't going to end up like him. Anyway, that was the only subject I worked really hard at, but when I got good marks they couldn't believe an oik like me could have done so well – I must have cheated.' His smile was bitter. 'I didn't bother after that. Just walked out and never went back. Saved them a job, I suppose. I wasn't missed, I know that.'

Lee wondered where this was going. Mick showed no signs of leaving. Ray had never spoken like this to her before. And the one thing she was sure she'd told him about her schooldays was that she'd hated Shakespeare.

'Anyway, you really helped me out in my last case. And I saw this in a second-hand shop, so I picked it up for you. Don't worry, I paid for it.' He laughed, but it sounded tense, forced. He pushed a dog-eared book across the table towards her. Mick watched his every move. As Lee took the book, she looked at Ray. His expression was unreadable.

He stood up abruptly, scraping his chair back on the wooden floor. 'Anyway, thanks again. You walking out, Mick?'

Mick grunted his reply, and the two of them left together. Lee was tempted to throw the book after them in frustration, except there had to be something more to this.

She flicked through the book. It was so old, some of the pages were falling out. She was surprised to see 'Ray Andrew Willis, 4th Year' inscribed inside the front cover. One page was completely folded over. Two lines were highlighted with Magic Marker, in such a garish yellow that it was clear it was done recently:

Yond' Cassius has a lean and hungry look.
He thinks too much: such men are dangerous.

Involuntarily, an image of Brendan's wiry body and its capacity for large English breakfasts rose in Lee's mind.

Chapter Seventeen

The last working day before a big trial was usually fraught, and this Friday was no exception. There was always a nagging sense of not having quite done enough. And the prospect of a weekend full of work didn't exactly lift Lee's spirits. But in spite of everything, she was looking forward to Monday. Everything she had worked for for the past four months was finally coming together. Now everyone would just see what she was capable of.

It was 6.20 p.m. Virtually everyone had gone home, as usually happened at the end of a long week. Anne-Marie had been happy to stay, but she had been working so hard recently, Lee had taken pity on her and sent her home. After all, she had arrived ready to work unexpectedly early – at 8 a.m., only thirty minutes after Lee, in fact – and they had both worked nonstop throughout the day, right through lunch. A twenty-three-year-old ought to have better things to do on a Friday evening than to work late. So should a thirty-year-old, come to that, Lee thought ruefully. But at least she was getting paid for this.

Her shoulders felt tight. She got up and stretched, then decided a break was in order. She wandered into the Clerks' Room where Tom was seated at his computer. He was contractually bound to stay until six thirty but she was pretty sure that, whatever else he was doing at that computer, it wasn't work.

The slightly guilty look on his face as she walked in told her she was right.

'Miss Mitchell. I thought you'd left. Big day on Monday.'

'I know. Just came to check the diary, Tom. Carry on with whatever you were doing.' She opened the large, heavy, leather-bound book and idly began flicking through its pages. She'd often thought that the way to bring Chambers to its knees would be to hide the diary, containing as it did the trial dates and conference appointments with solicitors and clients for each member of Chambers. A good clerk needed the skills of a diplomat and an air traffic controller combined to prevent trials from clashing and keep as many people as possible in work. And whatever his faults, Tom was a good clerk. Sometimes the diary served as a damning indictment: the space against Giles Townsend's name was clear once again. Lee was glad she at least was busy, particularly where it involved a newsworthy trial due to last six weeks or more. But so many other cases, fixed for the same time, had had to be sacrificed. It was an occupational hazard, but there was always the danger that, once lost, the work would never return.

Anne-Marie's work seemed to have tailed off as well, which was strange. She hadn't said anything. As well as helping her on the Omartian case, she had been in court nearly every day recently, and the work she'd been doing, though not of any great consequence, was still plentiful as far as she knew. As Anne-Marie was the only working pupil currently in Chambers, if she didn't do it, it would have to be sent elsewhere, and Lee knew how much Tom hated doing that.

'How's Anne-Marie been getting on?' she asked, still looking at the diary.

'OK, I suppose,' Tom replied, not looking up from the screen. 'She's no star, but I've had no complaints so far.'

'Are we still busy at the bottom end?'

'Aren't we just. We could do with at least one more working pupil, to tell the truth.'

'How come she's not in court, then? I wouldn't want her to lose any work because of this trial. Did she ask to be kept free?'

'No.' Tom quickly glanced at Lee, then ducked his head behind the computer screen. 'Mr Townsend suggested she be kept free.'

'Really?' Lee's tone was acid. 'For six weeks? Strange he didn't see fit to discuss it with me, seeing as she's my pupil. Any particular reason why?'

'I can't recall.' Which meant no. Tom's memory was legendary. 'Perhaps he felt she could learn more from watching such a big case.'

'Not for six weeks, Tom. That's a long time when you're just building a practice. And it could go longer. She could lose an awful lot of work in that time, not to mention goodwill. She can't afford to piss anyone off, not at this stage.' Lee paused. 'I wouldn't mind, but she never asked to go with me. Not once.'

'Maybe she just assumed you'd expect her there.'

'She's done her own work when I've covered other cases. Besides, you know I would make it perfectly clear to her whether I wanted her there or not. We probably won't even get to any evidence concerning Clive until the end of the first week.' Lee made a mental note to speak to Giles. 'If I rang her now, do you have anything for her on Monday?'

'No, it's all been allocated. But we'll have work for Tuesday.'

'I'll speak to her when I see her.' Lee stood up and glanced at the clock on the wall. Six forty-five. She'd been here eleven hours. 'I think I'll get my things and go, Tom. I hope you have a better weekend than I will. I'll be back in here tomorrow.'

'Goodnight, Miss Mitchell. Oh, this came for you earlier.' He bent down and retrieved a large Harvey Nichols bag from behind his desk.

'How much earlier?' Lee looked inside. It contained a large white box, tied with ribbon. There was no card. She didn't know anyone who would be sending her such an extravagant gift – except for one person. She hoped she was wrong.

'Someone brought it in about four o'clock. You did say you

165

didn't want to be disturbed.' Tom sounded ever so slightly defensive.

'Who was it?'

The person described by Tom didn't match either Clive or Parker. She was about to open it when she realised that her clerk was paying far more attention than was necessary.

'Thanks, I'll take this home. Goodnight, Tom.'

By the time she arrived home, she could barely restrain herself from ripping the box open, but the answerphone was flashing. Two messages. One was from David. He was in Chicago now, apparently. This tour was turning out to be much longer than either of them had expected. She was pleased for him. It hadn't been easy, him not working consistently. But it was bad enough that he wasn't there; she didn't want to miss his calls as well.

The other was from Simone.

'Hi, it's me. Just to let you know I found out the name of the barrister who's prosecuting Steve – someone called Townsend. I don't think they were supposed to tell me, but I kept on at them until they did. I don't know the date yet. The name sounds familiar. Does he work with you? I feel much better now I know something's happening. I may even go and see that rape counsellor like you suggested, though if I felt like speaking to anyone about it, I'd rather talk to you. I don't like to chat my business to just anybody. Ring me when you can.'

Lee felt more than a little guilty. Previously she had been ringing Simone almost every day, but not lately. She made a mental note to do so, just not tonight. Tonight called for a shower, a shot of rum, and an early night. But first the box. She opened it right where she stood in the hall. There was a card in the box itself, but she scarcely looked at it. It could only be from Clive. And besides, the item inside completely took her breath away.

It was a black suit, so impeccably cut and constructed and of such beautiful wool/cashmere that she didn't have to look at the label to know it was very expensive. She rushed into the bedroom, almost tripping in her haste. She stood in front of the mirrored wardrobe and tried it on. It fitted as if it was made for her. She recognised it as one she had seen in *Vogue* only that month, from the Armani collection, top of the line, so expensive that she would never have been able to justify buying it, not even at half the price – should it ever have been reduced that far. As she looked at her reflection, she spotted the card on the floor. She picked it up again.

> The first time I saw you, you were wearing Armani. This is the best of his new line. I thought it would suit you. It will look good on camera. Like it or not, we're both going to be famous after Monday, whatever happens, so I'm sure you would rather we were the stars of this media circus than the sideshow. I think you'll find it's not so bad. Who knows? You might even enjoy it.
> Clive
> P.S. Don't get on your high horse about not accepting gifts. After all, I won't tell if you don't.

That postscript, both its content and its familiar tone, brought her back to reality. She sat on the bed and stared into the mirror. What was she thinking of, even trying on a £2,000 'gift' from a client? Someone about whom she knew so little that she was forced to seek information from a career criminal? What was happening to her?

And how did he know her size?

Carefully, she took off the suit and slowly folded it back in its tissue-lined box. It really was lovely. It would be hard to give this back . . .

At Lee's suggestion, Brendan and Clive were to meet her at Chambers at 8.15 on Monday morning. The reason was twofold: not only would they have time to discuss any last-minute matters, they could travel to court together. A show of unity would be especially important today.

She was the first to arrive. Chambers was empty, as she expected. Anne-Marie would, in all likelihood, meet them at court, and not even the clerks arrived this early.

Brendan and Clive arrived shortly afterwards. Together. Lee didn't know what to make of that. Ray's obscure warnings, about both of them, flashed into her mind. She was still no closer to understanding what exactly he had been warning her against. Mentally she shook herself. This was not the time to be distracted.

Brendan looked both nervous and elated, which was exactly how she felt. Unlike her, however, he wasn't trying to hide it. Clive smiled at her, but said nothing. He was as calm as ever, the same as he'd always appeared apart from his time at Miller Street police station. In spite of everything, Lee still believed he was innocent. Not that it mattered, of course. She didn't have to believe in his innocence to do her job, though it helped. She only had to believe what he told her.

'All set, then?' Brendan asked, rubbing his hands.

'Yes.' Lee looked at him. Their relationship had changed, however much she tried to avoid that fact. She wondered if he'd noticed. Previously, although they had been work colleagues first and foremost, they had become friends as well, meeting for the occasional drink, speaking to each other about non-work-related topics. They hardly did that at all now.

She turned to Clive. 'You look well.' She was stating the obvious. Clive looked rested and as faultlessly dressed as ever. Clearly he hadn't spent the weekend worrying about his trial. 'Is there anything else you want to ask me before you leave? Or tell me?'

'Nothing at all, Lee. I have every confidence in you, you know that.'

'Well, in that case, we should leave right away. The sooner we get there, the better.'

'Parker's outside,' Clive said. 'I thought we could all travel in my car.'

The journey from Chambers to court was a short one, even in rush-hour traffic. All three were able to sit comfortably in the back without touching each other. Clive watched as his barrister sat further away from him. The view was unremarkable, but she seemed to find something particularly interesting in it this morning; she stared out of the window for the entire journey. As the car turned smoothly into the side road leading to Southwark Crown Court, he remarked, 'Pity it's not the Old Bailey. Still, Sting and Liz Hurley were here, so I suppose I shouldn't complain.'

Lee turned and glared at him. Clive gazed back steadily. He appeared to be scrutinising her face. 'You look tired,' he said finally. 'Drained. Evidently I had a much more restful weekend than you did.'

'If you want glamour, hire Naomi Campbell. I'm sorry if the hours I spent working on your case mean I won't be photogenic enough for you.'

'Well, it's a good thing I'm not hiring you for your pleasant disposition. As for the cameras, I think you'll do. Nice suit. Armani, isn't it? Looks new.'

She gave him a steady look. 'Yes, it is. One of my own.' Minutes later the car pulled up at the steps of the court building. Two photographers were already there. Evidently they were taking no chances this time. So much for an early start.

'Clive! Clive! Over 'ere, Clive.'

As they got out of the car, Lee knew that Clive wouldn't turn away or walk any faster than he had to in order to get away from them. But, after the last time, she knew he wouldn't talk, either.

On entering the foyer, she was surprised to see that, far from being the first to arrive, Amery, Robbins and their respective solicitors and clients were already there. Peter Fairfax was also there, deep in conversation with a man in a charcoal-grey suit whom she did not recognise. Judging from his shoes, he was probably a plainclothes police officer. Peter was as far away from any of the defence as possible; that was only to be expected. It was unusual, however, to see Amery's group some distance away from the others. Unusual and worrying. It could be first night nerves, of course. Everyone reacted to the first day of a big trial differently. But she didn't think men of such seniority would be affected that way; Amery in particular was an old hand at big media trials. Instinct told Lee that something was very badly wrong. For a second, she hesitated as to whom to approach first. Then Amery looked over and saw them and decided it for her by deliberately turning his back and ushering Hector Omartian and his solicitor into the open lift.

Lee turned to Brendan and Clive. They, too, had picked up on the heightened tension. 'What's going on?' Clive asked. For the first time, he sounded worried.

'I don't know,' Lee replied. 'Wait here a minute.'

Robbins and his party were seated near the stairs to the first floor. She walked quickly over to them. She tried not to stare at Frederick Omartian, but he seemed much older than she remembered. The fight seemed to have gone out from him. He looked frail and deathly pale.

'Excuse me, Nicholas. Could I speak to you for a moment?'

As soon as they were a safe enough distance away, she asked, 'What's going on between you and Amery?'

Robbins looked surprised by the question. Clearly he hadn't noticed anything amiss. 'Pressure of the first day, I suspect. He hasn't said anything to me.'

That was just the point. 'You don't think there's anything

unusual in that? And what about Frederick? He looks terrible.'

Robbins gave her an indulgent half-smile. 'Lee, please don't imagine problems where I'm sure none exist. As for my client, he is nearly eighty, you know. He won't be able to withstand the tension as well as you or I. But you needn't worry about him. I've taken the precaution of asking my solicitor to fetch him a glass of water.'

A glass of water had no more chance of curing whatever ailed Frederick than she had of getting useful information out of Robbins. 'Well, Nicholas, you know best.' She looked over to where she had left Brendan and Clive. Brendan was helping Parker bring in the many files that constituted Clive's part in this case. Clive himself was watching her. 'Excuse me. I must have a quick word with Peter.'

As she approached her former pupil-master, the man to whom he was speaking looked at her and moved away.

'Morning, Peter,' she began. She studied his expression carefully. His face was as blandly pleasant as ever, but she knew from experience that that was a very effective disguise. 'Looking forward to today?'

'If the right person is convicted, Leanne, yes.' He smiled slightly. 'Ask me at the end of the trial.'

'Surely you don't think that's *my* client,' she replied, mock seriously. When he didn't reply, Lee immediately became very serious. 'Peter, is anything going on with Amery that I should know about?'

Peter hesitated, then said, 'When I know anything for certain, I'll tell you.'

'That means something is going on. I knew it. What is it, Peter? I've got to know.'

'You heard what I said, Leanne. Don't worry. You'll know as soon as I do. Must dash. I've got to make a phone call.'

Lee watched Peter's retreating back as he walked towards the lifts. She tried to reassure herself. She had already guessed something was wrong, hadn't she? So whatever it was, she wouldn't be caught completely by surprise. And, as part of his duties as prosecution counsel, Peter would have to inform her of anything materially affecting the trial before it started.

As she walked back towards Brendan and Clive, she could see Brendan was very agitated. That wasn't like him.

'What the hell's going on?' He was almost shouting. Lee didn't want him anywhere near their client if he was going to act like this.

'Brendan, why don't you give me a hand taking these papers up to court?'

'It's Hector, isn't it?' Clive said, more a statement of fact than a question. He gave Lee an intense stare. 'You ought to know by now that I'm no fool, Lee. Don't hide anything from me, however bad it is.'

She put her hand on his shoulder. 'And you ought to know that if I knew anything, I'd tell you. Don't worry, Clive, I won't let anything happen to you. Come on, Brendan.'

As soon as the lift doors closed behind them, Lee turned to him. 'I don't know what's happening either yet, Brendan, but I intend to find out before we start. Meanwhile, you can't go losing it in front of Clive. We've worked too hard to let anything throw us off balance now.' The look that flickered across his face shook her to the core. It was a look of such fear and hatred that she actually stepped back from the force of it. But then, just as quickly, it was gone.

'Yes, of course. You're right. Sorry.' He put a hand on each side of his head, and Lee sensed he wasn't only trying to get a grip on himself physically. He was behaving like a trainee solicitor on his first case, not the seasoned head of a criminal law firm. She had never seen him like this before. 'But I reckon Hector must have changed his plea. The old man looks totally defeated. A united front, that's what he wanted. And now I think his son's lost his nerve and broken ranks.'

Lee thought about her conversation with Peter. He *had* certainly been more cagey than he usually was with her. 'You could be right.' She suddenly felt very tired, and the trial hadn't even begun yet. 'Look, all this speculation is giving me a headache. After you've helped me with this, could you go back downstairs and see how Clive's doing? Maybe go over his proof again with him; once more can't hurt. If he asks what's going on, tell him whatever you like, as long as it keeps his spirits up. That's if you're OK, of course. Are you OK?'

Brendan tried to smile. 'Don't worry about me, Lee. Call that a momentary lapse. It won't happen again.' He stared at her. 'How do you do it? Keep cool under all this pressure? This is the biggest case of your life so far. You must have ice water in your veins.'

She was glad he didn't know her as well as she had thought. She shrugged her shoulders and smiled. 'Trade secret.' The lift doors opened and they carried the mass of paperwork into the courtroom.

'Right,' said Lee. 'Better go and put my robes on. I'll see you later.'

The first thing Lee noticed when she went back to the courtroom after robing up was the massed ranks of journalists who had already taken their seats. Some were chatting among themselves, others seemed to be straining to catch anything said by anyone significantly involved in the case, even though not a word of actual evidence had yet been uttered. The second thing she noticed was the equally full public gallery. There were a lot of young women present. Anne-Marie, looking distinctly nervous, was waiting for her.

All three defence counsel usually sat at one end of 'counsel's row', the long wide table that was at least half the width of the courtroom. The area reserved for the defence was full of papers, documents and files. The overflow was placed directly behind the barristers, where the defence solicitors would sit. Lee watched as Brendan came in with Clive. They spoke to each other briefly before Clive went into the dock. His brother and father were already there. All three sat stiffly apart from each other, staring straight ahead at the area soon to be occupied by the judge. Robbins had already taken his seat nearest to where Peter would sit, which reflected his place as first on the indictment. Peter himself was nowhere to be seen. Amery was still near the door, speaking to his solicitor. Lee waited for him to take his place next to Robbins – no point in sitting down only to get up again. Amery saw her looking at him and, as he had done before, deliberately turned his back. Lee sucked her teeth in disgust.

Robbins noticed and arched his eyebrows. She leaned across the space between them.

'Still haven't figured out what's going on, Nicholas?'

Before he could reply, an officious looking clerk entered the courtroom from the direction of the judge's Chambers, an anteroom at the side of the court. He scanned the room, frowning when he realised that not only was everyone not yet seated but prosecution counsel wasn't even present.

'Where *is* Mr Fairfax?' he asked irritably. 'The judge wants to come in right away. You know how he is about starting on time.'

As if on cue, Peter burst through the double doors into the court, almost hitting Amery in the process. Lee turned round, and saw the look that passed between them. Just one look, but it was enough. Brendan was right. After all these months, Hector Omartian was pleading guilty.

As Peter took his place at the opposite end of the row, he turned and spoke to his opponents. 'I'm sorry I couldn't speak to you all together beforehand. There's been a significant development—'

'Judge wants to come in, Mr Fairfax,' the clerk said.

'Could I just have a few minutes to confer with my learned friends?'

'If you want more time, ask His Honour,' said the clerk as he took his place. 'He's coming in now.'

'All rise!' announced the court usher.

Everyone in the courtroom stood as His Honour Judge McCallum entered.

'Are we ready to proceed, Mr Fairfax?' he asked, without preamble.

'Not quite, Your Honour.' At the sight of McCallum's quick glance at his watch and his deepening frown, Peter quickly continued. 'There has been a significant development in the case that I was unable to communicate to my learned friends Ms Mitchell and Mr Robbins—'

'Why not?' McCallum interrupted. Before giving Peter time to answer, he continued, 'That's why courts start as late as ten thirty, Mr Fairfax, to enable you to have these discussions beforehand and so not waste the court's time.' He let out an impatient sigh. 'Any reason why I can't hear what you've got to say?'

Peter was clearly unhappy but he replied, 'No.'

'Good. Sounds like a Chambers matter, so let's have the court cleared, Usher.'

There was a low moan from the journalists and muttering from the public gallery but within minutes the court was cleared. As soon as the last person had left and was safely out of earshot, McCallum turned back to Peter. 'Well, let's have it, Mr Fairfax.'

It was almost unnaturally quiet. Peter took a deep breath. 'Your Honour, earlier this morning I spoke to my learned friend Mr Amery, who represents Hector Omartian. As a result both of that conversation and of earlier discussions with solicitors instructed by Hector Omartian leading to further investigations which took place last week, the decision has been taken not to continue the case against that particular defendant.'

'What?' Clive's voice rang clear across the courtroom. McCallum looked at him but said nothing.

'Mr Omartian has decided, of his own free will, to assist the prosecution.' Peter turned and looked at the defence team. Amery looked smug, Robbins blanched. Lee felt shell-shocked, and didn't bother to hide it. She didn't want to look at Brendan; it was already clear what Clive felt. Hector had betrayed his own flesh and blood, and he wouldn't have to serve a day in jail. Peter's voice sounded as if it was coming from far away.

'I appreciate this has taken my learned friends by surprise—'

'So why didn't you tell them before, Mr Fairfax?'

'The final decision not to prosecute was only made this morning, Your Honour.'

'On the day of the trial? This is a most unsatisfactory state of affairs, and I want you to be sure to convey my views to those instructing you. Now, what will Mr Omartian be saying?'

Peter hesitated. 'I would rather serve the new statement on the defence in the usual way, Your Honour.'

'Oh, you will be doing that, Mr Fairfax, make no mistake about it. But I now have to consider whether this trial should be adjourned. I don't expect you to divulge your entire case, but I want the gist of what is to be contained in that further statement now.'

'I have a copy for Your Honour,' Peter said and handed over a number of pages, stapled together. 'As you can see, it largely exculpates the first defendant, although there is still other, independent, evidence of his guilt, most notably the handwriting evidence and his own confession. But it would appear the blame is not largely his. However, it greatly strengthens the case against the third defendant, in particular as to the possibility of coercion used by him on his father.'

McCallum gave Fairfax a shrewd look. 'These are serious offences, Mr Fairfax. How do you know he's telling the truth?

People have been known to approach the Crown and say anything to get themselves off the hook, especially when a trial is imminent.'

'We have good reason to believe he is telling the truth, Your Honour.'

McCallum seemed unconvinced. 'Well, you must conduct your case as you see fit. Ms Mitchell, I take it you haven't had an opportunity to read this.'

'It's just been handed to me, Your Honour.' Lee almost forgot to stand as the judge addressed her. She felt strangely detached, almost as if this was happening in a play she was watching.

'Then I don't feel I should read it before you do, considering its potential effect on Clive Omartian. Doubtless you'll want more time to consider both this statement and his position.'

'Yes, Your Honour.' That seemed all she was capable of saying right now.

'You too, Mr Robbins, although apparently it greatly assists your client.'

Robbins rose. 'I would like to read the statement, yes, Your Honour.'

'Very well.' McCallum paused, then turned back to Peter. 'In that case, I have no choice but to grant an adjournment. I cannot see how the Crown can object, in the circumstances.'

'No, Your Honour.'

'Mr Amery, do you wish to say anything?'

Amery stood up. 'Can my client leave the dock, Your Honour?' he said bluntly.

Even before Peter rose to his feet, McCallum firmly replied, 'No.'

'Your Honour—'

'I said no, Mr Amery. It looks as if your client will be rowed out of this sooner or later. I don't want to take any further steps in this trial whatsoever until both co-defending counsel have had the benefit of information you're already fully apprised of. Any discontinuance, or even changes of plea, if they are forthcoming,' here McCallum looked at Lee, 'can be made on the next occasion. Which had better be soon. I think we need to list this case for Mention, so everyone knows where they are.' He paused. 'Although it now looks as though this trial may be considerably foreshortened, I don't know now whether I'll be hearing it. As you have all no doubt heard, I'll be retiring at the end of the year. I'll try and accommodate counsel as much as I can; if the trial is now going to last less than the allotted six weeks, there is a greater chance that it can be slotted in somewhere, but a decision on any further progress has to be made very soon. I think two weeks from today for the directions hearing. Is that convenient for all parties?' When he heard no dissenting voices, McCallum concluded, 'Very well then. Bail for all defendants as before.'

'All rise!' said the usher as the judge left the court.

Lee made sure that at least the expression on her face was upbeat before she turned to face Clive. She walked over to him confidently as he left the dock behind his father and brother. She reached him just as he appeared to tap his brother on the shoulder. At least she hoped that was what the gesture was. 'Clive, I think the three of us could do with an early lunch. And then we'll go back to Chambers and discuss Hector's statement in detail.'

He looked at her and tried to smile. He appeared very tired. 'It's looking bad for me, isn't it, Lee?'

Her reply was firm. 'I'm not saying anything until we go through this together. Now come on, let's get out of here. I never like being around courtrooms longer than I have to.'

As they reached the corridor, Lee saw, to her dismay, that the press were still there, even though she was sure that the usher would have informed them by now that the show was over for today. None of the barristers would repeat what had been said in what had been a closed court. But a gesture could speak volumes.

As Frederick Omartian seemed to falter, Hector instinctively took his arm, as he had tried to do once before. Instantly his father shook it off and looked at his son with such contempt that Hector recoiled as if he had been struck.

'But Papa,' he said. There was a crack in his voice. 'I did it for you. I know you didn't do it. I couldn't stand by and watch you go to jail. I did it for you,' he repeated as his father walked away from him.

The journalists started writing furiously. Both Lee and Amery looked on. Despite herself, Lee almost felt sorry for Hector. Amery, however, made no attempt to console his client. His only regret was that he was losing the fee for a six-week trial. He had been planning to spin it out for at least another week as well. Still, for what he had done so far he would be paid handsomely. And anyway, he was now free to do that rape his clerk seemed so keen on. He had defended so many of them in the past, that would be a walk in the park compared to this.

Chapter Eighteen

He had been right, Giles thought to himself. It *was* the same woman. It had been a devil of a job trying to arrange this conference because she wasn't a client, just a witness. An important one maybe, but that was all she was. Seeing a witness in a case like this was almost unheard of, but he wanted to satisfy his curiosity.

Sitting in his office now, Simone didn't know whether to be glad or sorry that she had come, or that Giles Townsend was prosecuting her case. Although his manner was sympathetic, there was something about the way he looked at her . . .

'It's written all over your face,' she said flatly.

Giles was taken aback. 'My dear, whatever do you mean?'

'Please, don't patronise me. And don't bother to lie. The kids I teach are better at it than you, and I can see through them too. You don't believe me.' Simone rummaged around in her large leather holdall until she found her lighter and a packet of cigarettes. When she was unable to light it after the fifth empty click, the young solicitor who had attended on behalf of the Crown Prosecution Service gently took it from her trembling hands and ignited the flame on her first attempt. Simone leaned in to put the tip of her cigarette to the flame, then stood up suddenly. If she moved quickly enough towards the window, maybe she could get there before they saw the tears in her eyes. She could always blame their redness on the smoke.

Giles exchanged glances with the CPS solicitor. So what if he didn't believe her? He wasn't trying this case because he felt her complaint was justified. He wished she wouldn't smoke. He didn't like smoking in his office, and in fact refused to keep an ashtray in here, but what was one to do when faced with a hysterical woman? Besides, it gave him a chance to compose himself. Her outburst was disconcerting, but if she'd mistaken the expression on his face for one of doubt, she'd obviously been around children far too long. Maybe that was how she got herself into this mess in the first place.

He watched her silently for a few moments, then asked, 'Are you ready to continue, Mrs Wilson?'

'In a minute,' she replied.

'Take your time.'

The young solicitor looked nonplussed, but Giles was quite happy for his witness to stay there as long as she wanted. She looked most becoming silhouetted against the large open window. She was dressed in the same dark suit she had been wearing when he first saw her, all those months ago. She was so little, almost like a young girl, except there was nothing girlish about her body. And as he watched her shape her mouth to blow smoke rings out of the window, his thoughts began to take an even murkier turn . . .

Suddenly she turned and looked directly at him. Giles could feel his face reddening under her gaze.

'Unseasonably warm, don't you think? For early September, I mean,' he said conversationally, to no one in particular.

'Really? I don't think so.' It was Simone who spoke. It had been hard enough not to cry in front of them, now it was all she could do not to run screaming from the room. She had hoped she was wrong. She had hoped that this older, established man, with the shiny gold band on his left hand, was someone in whom she could place her trust, someone who would fight her corner in the courtroom and represent her interests before what was likely to be another older, established white man. But he had That Look – the look she had seen on the faces of more white men than she cared to remember. One of speculation. Appraisal. Sometimes subtle. Sometimes not. But always underpinning the same question: is it true what they say about black women? How could someone who looked like that possibly believe she had been raped? If only Lee were here.

She flicked her cigarette butt through the open window, then walked back to her seat.

'We don't have very much more to do,' Giles said. He was trying to calm her down. Himself too, for that matter. 'We've already been over your statement three times, and you've been absolutely consistent.'

'That's because I'm telling the truth,' Simone's eyes were red but she was still defiant. 'Though that's not a requirement for you barristers, is it? To believe what people tell you in order to do the job.'

Giles managed to look offended. 'As it happens, I do believe what you say,' he lied, 'though it's true that it's what I can prove that matters, not what I believe. I'm not your enemy, Mrs Wilson.'

She seemed to accept what he said, because all of a sudden the fight went out of her. Her shoulders slumped, and she sagged into the soft armchair. She looked for all the world like a child sent to sit in the corner for something she hadn't done. A child who had just been crying.

'Now, I have to ask you some rather more personal questions,' Giles continued. 'I'm sorry, but the defence will, and forewarned is forearmed.'

'Believe me, there's *nothing* more personal anyone could ask me about this.'

Giles cleared his throat. 'The defendant – how long had you known him?'

'Do you mean when did I first meet him or when did I first start sleeping with him?'

'Er, both.'

'He went to school with me. He remembers me, but I don't remember him. We met just over a year ago, at the Notting Hill Carnival.'

'And is that when your relationship began?'

'Not long after. But as I said, we weren't having a relationship. I was having sex with him. My husband and I were separated. He knew I was hoping we would get back together.' On seeing Giles's startled expression, Simone remarked, 'I'm a very plain speaker.'

Giles and the solicitor looked at each other. Neither of them was sure that a jury would appreciate such candour.

'An admirable trait, Mrs Wilson, but perhaps it would be better to describe it as a relationship, given the circumstances.'

'Why? It wasn't. Does that give him the right to rape me?'

'No,' Giles replied slowly, 'but it might make the jury more sympathetic towards you.'

'I don't care about their sympathy. I just want them to do the right thing. This is the nineteen nineties, not the eighteen nineties. Since they kicked me out of the children's home at sixteen, I've been fending for myself, even when I was still with Michael. When I was sleeping with Steve I was very much a single woman. I don't see why I should have to justify my actions to them, or to anyone else.'

Giles sighed. This was going to be more difficult than he thought. Her attitude was typical of someone who had never been involved in the criminal justice system before. If this young woman thought merely telling the truth was going to win this case, she was much more naive than she appeared.

'What about your previous sexual history with the defendant?'

'What about it?'

'Was there anything . . . unusual in your sexual relations?'

Simone looked at him, her eyes hard. 'I don't like it rough, if that's what you mean.' She leaned back in the chair and closed her eyes. She was perfectly still for a moment, then she said, in a small voice, 'I don't like to be hurt.'

'I'm sorry, but I have to ask, was there anyone else at the time?'

She stared at him. 'No, I wasn't sleeping with anyone else. I wasn't even sleeping with him any more.'

'Is there anything in your past that he knows about that could be used against you?'

'You mean my sexual past?'

'Yes.'

'I thought you would be able to stop his barrister asking me questions like that.'

Really, Giles thought. Everyone thought they were a lawyer nowadays. 'And who told you that?'

'I've been speaking to Leanne; she *is* my friend, you know.'

'Well, I'd rather you didn't.' Giles tried to keep his annoyance out of his voice. 'It only confuses matters, two different approaches to the same thing. Besides, to my knowledge Miss Mitchell has never defended a rapist, nor prosecuted in any kind of criminal case, as she considers both to be against her principles – a misguided view that I do not share. So she can hardly speak from experience on that score.'

Simone thought about what she'd been like, all those years ago. She supposed that constituted her 'sexual history'. She wasn't about to discuss that with the man in front of her. Anyway, maybe Steve didn't know, or couldn't remember – he'd never mentioned it to her. Affection, that was all she'd ever wanted.

'I wasn't a virgin when I married, if that's what you mean,' she said, 'but as you know, I married young, straight after teacher training college. I was faithful to my husband until he left me. Tell me, is Steve going to be asked about *his* sexual history? What he can't get with his looks he gets through his job. He's a music promoter. The business provides plenty of opportunity. He was sleeping with at least two other women that I know of while he was with me.'

'And you didn't mind?' Giles asked.

'If he had been my man, if it had been serious, then yes. But as I keep telling you, it was just sex. For me anyway.' Why did men have so much trouble understanding that concept coming from a woman?

'And what about your husband?'

'What about him?'

'Do you keep in touch?'

'If you call asking me for a divorce keeping in touch. I last heard from him about Easter.'

'You may be estranged but you are still married. It might be good if he came to court. Show of support for his wife, that sort of thing.'

She looked doubtful. Part of her wanted to see him again, but not like this. Yet she could see the force of the argument. 'He'd have to hear about how I was raped, wouldn't he?' she said, choosing her words carefully. 'Worse, he'd hear about how I was raped by a man I had been sleeping with while legally still married to him. No, I wouldn't want to put him through that.'

The solicitor looked at her and smiled gently, touched that she wished to spare the feelings of her estranged husband, even now. But Giles was insistent.

'At least let us contact him. Don't worry, I'll make sure he knows the full circumstances so he won't be taken by surprise if he does decide to come.'

'Besides,' the solicitor spoke for the first time, 'if you're worried what the jury might think – you seeing another man while still officially Mrs Wilson – you could always tell them the reason for your sep—'

'No!' She hadn't meant to shout, but she wasn't going to be

swayed on this one. 'That subject is completely off limits. And it has nothing to do with me being raped, anyway.'

Giles was about to say something but the look on Simone's face told him this was not an issue to be pursued. Not now, at any rate. 'As you wish,' he said. 'Are there any character witnesses you might want to call?'

'What? To vouch for my morality?' Simone asked bitterly.

'No, just as to the kind of person you are,' Giles said calmly. Did she have to act so tough all the time?

'Sorry.' Simone paused before continuing, 'Yes, people at school. I'd like to speak to them first, though.'

'Of course. Well, unless there's anything you want to ask, that's all I'll need for now. You realise we don't know yet when the case will be heard, but it will be sometime before Christmas, in all likelihood. I think the sooner the better for us, with all the recent publicity about this particular kind of assault.'

'My name won't be in the papers, will it?' Simone asked. 'The kids I teach—'

'Don't worry about that,' Giles replied smoothly. 'It's more the jury I'm thinking about; they'll be more sensitised to the plight of the victim, I feel. Anyway, you'll be given as much notice as possible.' He stood up and extended his hand. Simone stood also. 'Goodbye, Mrs Wilson. Think about what I said as regards your husband.'

'I'll think about it, at least,' Simone replied. 'Well, I suppose I'll see you in court.' It was a dismal attempt at a joke. She couldn't even raise a smile herself.

'How are you getting back?' the solicitor asked.

'Leanne said she'd take me home. Thanks for asking.' She looked at them both. 'Well, goodbye then.'

As the door closed behind her, the solicitor turned to Giles and asked, 'So, what do you think?'

He made sure Simone's footsteps had receded before he spoke.

'Tough, isn't she? Personally, I would have liked more tears.'

'But she *was* pretty upset.'

'Yes, I know,' Giles said impatiently, 'but no tears. Juries like that; wronged woman, teacher – pity she's not a mother, that would have helped. She's petite – that's good; easy to see how she could have been overpowered. But this sexually independent attitude has got to go. She won't have a jury of *Cosmo* readers. I don't care what year it is, most people are still uncomfortable about women sleeping with men with whom they're not madly in love. Especially when the ties of matrimony are still there, however unravelled they may be.'

'Yes, but do you believe her?'

Giles looked at her. 'I don't think that matters, do you?'

'Clearly it does to her.'

'Well, she's forgotten one important thing. She's not my client, the Crown is. That's who I represent. Mrs Wilson is just a useful witness. But don't worry,' he smiled, 'I have every intention of winning this case. Every intention.'

'Any chance of bail, then?'

'Doubt it. It's a serious charge, you've got previous for violence, and you live near her. Is there anywhere else you could stay?'

'Not out of the area, no,'

'Well, then, that's that.' George Amery threw the packet of cigarettes across the table at the man he was to defend, who deftly caught it in one hand. A lefty, Amery noticed. He didn't smoke himself, but in his entire career he couldn't remember representing anyone who didn't. If they didn't at the start of their trial, they were puffing away furiously by the end. So, like most barristers, he always carried some around. Marlboro and B & H – they seemed to prefer those, the men especially. Not that wimpy Silk Cut; that was like the white wine of the cigarette fraternity. And his client was someone who obviously prided himself on being a man. All bantam-cock machismo. Given any encouragement, he would probably pull it out so they could all see how big it was.

Amery walked over to the door. He hated conferences in prison. Formica tables. Bad lighting. Terrible coffee, if you were lucky enough to get any at all. And the profoundly depressing feeling of being locked up, even though he knew he and his solicitor would be out of there within the hour. Besides, he never liked parking his car anywhere near a prison. It wasn't the prisoners he was worried about, it was the screws.

He looked at his watch. They had been doing this for two hours. He had hoped to be able to wrap this up earlier. Now he wouldn't be able to change before the reception at Ellenburg's firm. Nothing like the smell of prison and cigarette smoke on your clothes to make friends and influence people.

'You don't believe me, do you?' the young man asked.

Amery almost laughed out loud. If he'd had a fiver for each time he had been asked that question, he would be even richer than he was already. Why did defendants always want to know whether you believed them or not? As if it mattered. They always asked, and he always gave them the same answer.

'Of course I believe you, Steve.'

Stephen Payne relaxed into his chair again. 'Good. The guys in here, they really rate you. Word is, the Rottweiler is the business, you know? Especially for this sort of thing.'

'Well, lucky for you you don't have previous for "this sort of thing" – although the others could come out in court.'

'They were a long time ago, man. What's that got to do with anything?'

'They weren't that long ago, just a couple of years. Petty dishonesty. Violence. The prosecution could say to the jury, if you were dishonest before, how can they trust you now? As for the violence, well, rape is considered an act of violence. Of course, whether they can refer to it depends on what you say. It's unlikely to come out, though. And you're a reformed character now, aren't you, Steve?'

'That's right.' He smiled at his barrister, evidently a stranger to irony. At last, someone who understood him. 'Anyway, I don't need to rape. I got 'nuff women out there – black, white, all kinds.'

'So you told the police. But this one's a real looker. You'd have to go a long way to beat that.'

'True, but it's not always the face that I'm interested in, know what I mean?'

'Yes, I know.' Amery walked back to the table, smiling. He was beginning to like this man. He looked over at the only other person in the room, a young trainee solicitor who was doing her best to hide her discomfiture. Well, if women wanted to do these cases, they just had to tough it out. Besides, he didn't want a man. In the light of the recent publicity, she was just the window-dressing this case needed.

'Funny thing is,' Steve continued, 'I was beginning to like this one. She wasn't clingy, like the others. I wasn't going to give any of them up, mind you. But I could have cut back for her. She could have been my number one.'

Amery threw the small folder of photographs, taken by the police, down on the table. 'So how are we going to explain these injuries, then?'

'I told you, sometimes we just got carried away.' Steve paused. 'I knew her from school, man.'

'Were you sleeping with her then?'

'No, but I heard things.'

The young trainee piped up. 'Well, hearsay isn't relevant . . .' Amery quietened her with a look.

'Go on,' he said.

'She was very popular in school, know what I mean? From

about fourteen. Nobody could control her – not that she had any family around to do that, anyway.'

'Hmm. Interesting. So she wasn't exactly saving herself.'

'No, but she'd probably tell you that herself. She doesn't pretend to be something she's not.'

'Sounds like my kind of woman. If I weren't a happily married man, of course.' The young solicitor looked at him with open disgust, but Amery didn't care. The man she worked for was a good friend of his, and the client liked him, so what could she do?

'She's got this other friend who went to school with her. I met her the night we all went out – you know, the night she claims I raped her. She's in your line of work too, I think. Liza, Leanne – something like that.'

'Really? Any last name?'

Steve thought for a moment, then shook his head. 'Can't remember, but I saw her on the news a couple of months ago, just briefly. Black woman. Tall, darker than me, short hair.' Steve wrinkled his nose in distaste. 'One of them no-nonsense women. She was with that guy who had been in all the papers – you know, the young one with all the money. That big court case.'

Recognition hit. 'Her last name's not Mitchell, by any chance?'

'Yeah.' Steve slammed his hand down on the table. 'Yeah, that's it. You know her?'

'I met her recently. Well, well.' Amery leaned back. 'Were they friendly at school?'

'Nah. She kept herself to herself. Always in a book. Quiet. She was in Simone's class, though. I heard Simone slept with some guy she liked one time.'

Amery was writing furiously now. 'Could be useful. We'll see. Anyway, what about you? Anyone who could come to court to say how wonderful you are? What about all your women friends?'

'Well, the one I was with when the police arrested me, she's married, so she won't come. The others, well, they don't exactly know about each other.' Steve paused. 'I'm sure I can find someone. I'll just have to think, that's all.'

'You do that.' Amery stood up abruptly. 'Listen, Steve, I've got to go. Duty calls.'

'So when will the case come up then? I can't stand it in here.'

'Don't worry. You'll be out by Christmas. Keep the fags.' He turned to the young woman. 'Can I give you a lift anywhere, Stella?'

'No, thank you,' she replied shortly. She stalked out of the conference room in front of him. Amery smiled at her as he stood aside to let her pass. The view from behind wasn't bad. Not bad at all. Luckily for her he never took these things personally. And besides, he could afford to be indulgent. Looks like this was going to be even easier than he thought.

Chapter Nineteen

Ray heard footsteps behind him as he walked from his car. He almost turned round to see who it was, which wasn't like him. He was surprised at his own reaction. After all, no one would give him any trouble, not round here. He'd lived here all his life; half the area knew him and the other half were afraid of the Willis family.

He never parked directly outside his house, not if he could help it – he couldn't be too careful, especially now – but he usually tried to get fairly close. Having to walk two hundred yards to his front door in the rain wasn't his idea of fun on a Saturday night.

As he neared the gate, it was clear that the party next door was in full swing. He didn't mind, it wasn't as if they did it every night; and they had invited him, but he'd refused. Still, the walls would be jumping tonight.

Ray Willis, having a quiet night in, he thought grimly. Who'd have believed it? But he hadn't felt much like going out lately – he wouldn't until he'd settled a few scores. Best to let Lee finish her trial first. He owed her that much. Besides, then she'd be free to defend him again.

A car was double-parked outside his house. From next door, no doubt. That always happened when there was a party round here. Nice motor, though. His step slowed as he realised whose it was. How long had he been here? he wondered. Still, there was no way he'd be running and hiding from him, not round here. This was his turf. And his visitor needed setting straight on a few things.

He walked up to the side of the car and tapped sharply on the rear passenger window. It glided silently down.

'What the fuck do you want?' Ray asked.

The man in the back laughed. 'Well, well, Ray, is that any way to greet a business associate?'

Ray put one hand on the roof of the car and leaned inside. He spoke deliberately and slowly. 'I said, what the fuck do you want?'

The laughter died. 'I need to speak to you.'

'Go on then.'

'Not out here. Where's your manners, Ray? Aren't you going to invite me in?'

'Piss off. You're not setting foot in my house. I don't want anything more to do with you or your poxy solicitor.'

'Come on, Ray. I thought you had more sense than that. Fifteen minutes, that's all I want. Do you really want to have a public conversation with an accused criminal right in front of your house? Surely we can do our business quietly without drawing attention to ourselves?'

When Ray didn't respond, Clive shrugged. 'Oh well, have it your way. Parker?' His driver picked up the car phone and began to dial.

Ray's mind was racing. He could call his bluff, but he didn't want the police snooping around at the moment. He was still on a suspended sentence. Besides, Clive might think he had something to hide.

'You're getting ten,' he said finally. He turned and walked to his front door.

As always, Parker accompanied Clive. Ray looked at him scornfully. 'Christ, it's Me and My Shadow.' He looked down at his feet. 'What's that doing here?'

'He's my protection.' Clive bent down and patted the Rottweiler's head. 'But don't worry, he's harmless. He only looks the business. You know what I call him? Judas.'

Ray looked at the animal. He'd been around dogs all his life, so it didn't scare him. It was on a leash, even though it wasn't muzzled. Indeed, it seemed abnormally docile, almost as if it had been drugged. All the same, he was glad he had the knife. He didn't check his pocket – he knew from experience that Parker never missed anything.

The front door opened straight on to the small living area and stairs. There was no hallway. The way Clive was looking around the unkempt room made Ray even more angry.

'You got anything to say about my sister, then?' he demanded.

'She told me she was only your half-sister.'

'She's still family. She'd just turned sixteen, for Christ's sake! You think you can come slumming anytime you need a good blow job?'

'Nothing like that happened. Don't you believe what you read in the papers?'

'Don't take me for a fucking fool.' Ray took a step towards him. Parker and the dog also stepped forward, putting themselves between him and Clive. 'It was only because she begged me on her knees not to touch you that you're not in hospital right now.'

'Yeah, she told me last night what a favour she'd done me.'

Ray bristled.

'Except there's the little matter of your suspended sentence, let's not forget. And Sergeant Lambert.'

'I've been inside. You think I'm scared of that?'

'God, you can hardly hear yourself think around here.' The music from next door was reverberating through the walls. In contrast to Ray's anger, Clive's tone was calm and nonchalant, almost as if he was discussing the weather. 'Anyway, relax, Ray. It *was* her sixteenth birthday that night. And I didn't make her do anything she didn't want.' He smiled, remembering. 'It's a wonder I didn't crash the car.' Before Ray could react, Clive wandered over to the small coffee table. There was a stack of books and magazines piled underneath it. He squatted down and looked at them carefully. When he stood, he had a bemused look on his face. 'So it's really true; a Peckham lad who reads Shakespeare as well as *Loaded*.'

Ray tasted bile in his throat. He had to play this one carefully. 'Yeah. Amazing, innit? Anyway, what's it to you?'

'I've been told you and my barrister have been getting quite cosy.'

Ray didn't even bother to ask how he knew. 'Don't know what you're talking about.'

'Now who's taking who for a fool?' Clive was still smiling, his tone still conversational, but as he walked towards Ray his eyes were glacial. 'I've got her earmarked for myself. You muscling in, Ray?'

So that's what this was all about. Ray would have breathed a huge sigh of relief had not both his visitors been watching him like hawks. 'You haven't seen the guy she lives with, have you?'

'Oh, but I have. He's a musician, and right at this moment he's somewhere in America on tour.' He saw Ray's surprise and remarked, 'I'm the reason he's still there, Ray. I've taken over the financing of his tour. Extended his stay, though he doesn't know why. So come on, what were you two doing, meeting at a pub in Brixton, discussing Shakespeare?'

'Having a drink.' Ray stared him straight in the eye. 'That's what people do in pubs, or hadn't you heard?'

'You're a real comedian tonight,' Clive said. He wasn't smiling now. 'Don't you think so, Parker?' His driver nodded. 'One last time, Ray. What did you tell her?'

'Like I said, we were just having a drink together. She's been my brief for years.'

Clive appeared satisfied with this, because once again he was smiling. He stepped back. Parker was still facing Ray. Clive turned and walked towards his driver. When he had gone a few steps past him, he stopped and turned to face Ray once again. 'OK. No hard feelings, Ray. I had to ask. I just want you to know I'll always consider you a friend.'

As he uttered the last word, Parker let go of the leash.

Clive had never seen a dog jump for a man's throat before. Or realised a human being could make such inhuman noises. Good job the party was on next door. That was a real stroke of luck. He looked at Ray writhing on the ground, completely unaffected by it all, and continued to watch until the only movement his body made was caused by the dog.

'Well, it's obviously true, then,' he commented. 'You don't have to say kill for a dog to attack.'

'No. Any trigger word will do, even friend,' Parker replied. It was the first time he'd spoken that night.

'There's nothing on the dog to link it with me, is there?'

'No, I made sure of that. What shall we do with it?'

'Just leave it here. It's not the kind of dog people would associate with me, anyway. That should throw police off the scent.' Clive looked at Parker and laughed at his own appalling pun as he left the house.

Giles Townsend looked up impatiently as he heard the knock on his door. He glanced at his watch. Not yet nine. As far as he knew, the only other people in this early on a Monday morning would be the clerks. He had hoped he wouldn't be disturbed. It had been so long since he'd prosecuted a criminal trial that he could certainly use the extra hours of preparation. It was either that or 'confer with his colleagues' – in other words, ask their advice. An honourable course, but not for him. Not for the Head of Chambers. He wouldn't give them the satisfaction. The knock came again.

'Oh, come in then, Tom,' he said irritably.

The door opened. It wasn't Tom.

'Good morning, Giles. Could I have a word with you, please?' Lee asked.

Giles groaned inwardly. A real criminal lawyer, and the last person he wanted to see. 'Can't it wait, Lee? I'm awfully busy at the moment.'

'No, it can't,' she replied, politely but firmly. 'I'm sorry, Giles, but I've been trying to speak to you for some time and it always seems to be inconvenient. This can't wait any longer.'

Giles let out an exaggerated sigh. 'Will it take long?'

'Not really. I've got work to do too.'

'Very well. Have a seat.' He motioned to a chair near his desk – not the soft armchair Simone had sat in but a straight-backed, upright wooden chair, the one he always gave people when he wanted them to spend less than five minutes.

Lee had been in Chambers too long not to know that trick. She sometimes used it herself. 'Thank you,' she said as she sat in the armchair. She stared at the array of books and papers on the desk. 'Is that it, then? Simone's case?'

'It's the prosecution brief in the case of Regina v Payne, if that's what you mean. You know I act on behalf of the Crown, not Mrs Wilson.'

Lee tried to remain pleasant. 'Yes, Giles, I do know that.'

'I'm not about to discuss the prosecution evidence with you, Lee, even if you are her friend.'

'I know. I wouldn't ask you to do that.' In any event, she could get as much from Simone herself. 'I just wanted to say,' Lee leaned forward, her voice earnest, 'if I can be of any assistance, in any way, you will let me know, won't you?'

'Thank you for your offer, but I can manage,' Giles replied stiffly.

'I didn't mean that the way it sounded. I'm glad Simone has someone as senior as you prosecuting this case.' She paused.

There was no tactful way of putting this, especially to her Head of Chambers. It was a pretty presumptuous thing to do, even for her, but for Simone's sake she had to try. 'But it's been a while since you prosecuted a criminal case, and I thought—'

'Are you doubting my competence?' Giles snapped.

'No,' Lee replied slowly, 'but—'

'Good, because I don't recall your ever having prosecuted a criminal case. Something about the greater power of the state ranged against the poor helpless individual, wasn't it? Well, now Mrs Wilson is relying on "the greater power of the state" to put her rapist in jail. It's different when it's someone you know, isn't it?'

Touché. If Lee had been white, her face would have been red. She and Giles had never been close, but she suddenly realised how much worse their relationship had become in the past few months – ever since she got the Omartian brief, in fact. But at least if he was this sharp, maybe Simone wasn't in such bad hands after all. 'My political views are my own, Giles. I just came to offer you my support, that was all.' She paused. 'There was one other thing.'

Giles made no attempt to hide his impatience.

'A month or so ago, when I was due to start the Omartian trial, I understand from Tom that you instructed that my pupil should be kept free for the duration of the trial.'

Giles hesitated for a second, then said robustly, 'Yes, I did. She had a number of small, rather inconsequential court appearances booked in; I thought it would be far more beneficial for her to watch her pupil-mistress try a big case. After all, a pupil learns as much by observing and taking notes as by doing.'

'With all due respect, Giles, that's a decision for me to make, not you. I'm the one supervising her. You know six weeks is a lifetime to someone at her stage. She could have attended the trial on her days out of court. I really don't appreciate your undermining me like that, both with her and with Tom.'

'I'm sorry you feel that way, but as Head of Chambers I felt it was both more important and more appropriate for her to sit in on the Omartian trial. After all, she did the Mention.'

Giles was pulling rank. At any other time, Lee would not have been surprised, but at this she was taken aback. The barrister-pupil relationship was sacrosanct. Interference, even by the Head of Chambers, was almost unheard of.

'Fine. If that's the way you feel, *you* can supervise her.'

'That won't be necessary.'

'Why not?' Lee shot back. 'You can still do it. You haven't taken silk. Yet.'

She'd hit a raw nerve, as she intended. Giles's voice was quiet but full of venom. 'You will find that not all of us need to be appointed Queen's Counsel – or do show trials – in order to prove our worth.'

'Good. I'll tell her she can start with you next week.'

'You'll do no such thing.'

'I beg your pardon?' Lee was becoming as angry as clearly he was.

'How the devil can I supervise her?'

Damn it. Giles was silent for what seemed like a very long time. He was acutely aware of his younger colleague staring at him. Whatever he said now about Anne-Marie would cause an unpleasant reaction. He decided to opt for the lesser of two evils.

'She's my niece,' he said sulkily, like a naughty schoolboy. 'Not that I see it as any particular concern of yours.'

'Your niece?' Lee repeated flatly. 'Your *niece*?' She sank back in the armchair. 'Why didn't you tell me before?'

'Because I knew this was precisely how you'd react.' All the same, Giles looked guilty.

'Do the clerks know?'

'*I* haven't told them.' When she said nothing, Giles continued,

'For heaven's sake, she hasn't caused any major disasters, has she? And she's getting work, so evidently she hasn't alienated any of Chambers' solicitors. So what difference does it make?'

'Did she go through the Chambers recruitment procedure, Giles?'

Now it was his turn to say nothing.

'Eight years ago when I was looking for pupillage places, you know how many applications I sent off? Forty-nine. Forty-nine, when others had sent off less than half that number. No connections, a comprehensive school education, and black to boot. Forget my upper second law degree or my volunteer work in the law centre. I chose to come to these Chambers because I thought things like that wouldn't matter here.'

'I'm sure Anne-Marie was as good as anyone else,' Giles eventually replied.

'Given the competition out there, there were probably some who were better, and you know it, Giles. There are literally a hundred pupils for every place, and you gave it to your *niece*?'

She got up and had reached the door when Giles said, 'Just a minute.' She looked over her shoulder at him. He, too, was standing now. 'You see why I can't supervise her. You know how it would look. That would be carrying nepotism a bit too far. But there's nothing to stop me *borrowing* her – with your consent, of course.'

Lee gave him a cold stare.

'Didn't you just offer me any assistance I wanted? I'm sure you'd want your friend Simone to get the full benefit of your pupil's research skills, which I am sure by now you have perfected.'

'I don't really have a choice, do I, Giles?' Lee said stiffly. The only reason she didn't slam the door was because that was precisely what he expected. On the other side of the door, she leaned against it and closed her eyes. The sound of Dean's voice made her open them again.

'Miss Mitchell!' He came running towards her. 'I've been looking for you everywhere. I was afraid you'd gone to the Temple library.' He paused, trying to catch his breath. 'You had a call from the hospital.'

'What?' She suddenly felt cold. 'Not my mother?'

'No. They said it was a man. They want you to come right away.'

'It's a miracle he's still alive, considering his injuries,' the young doctor said. He lit another cigarette. He looked at Lee quizzically. 'Are you his girlfriend? Partner, I mean.'

'No, no.' Lee didn't know what to do with herself. One minute she was sitting down, the next pacing the anteroom in an agitated state. 'We have a business relationship. Plus, he's a . . . a friend.'

The doctor shrugged and let it go at that. 'He was admitted in the early hours of Sunday morning. Apparently a neighbour came round to see whether he'd changed his mind about attending some party or other, looked through the curtains and saw him there. The dog was whining, too.'

'Dog? He doesn't have a dog,' Lee said.

'Well, no one has it now. It's been put down.' He took a last drag on his cigarette before stubbing it out. 'He's lost a lot of blood. In fact, he's only just regained consciousness – that's why we rang you. He was very badly mauled. Most of the side of his face has gone. He'll need reconstructive surgery.'

Lee nodded. She didn't trust herself to speak. 'Can I see him now?'

The doctor stood up. 'If you're sure you're up to it.'

She gasped when she saw Ray. She couldn't help it. His neck and most of his head were bandaged; only the right eye and right ear were visible, and part of his mouth. His lips were swollen and discoloured. He was unrecognisable. Both his hands and arms were heavily bandaged too. He must have used them to protect himself.

Lee went to the head of his bed and, tentatively, stroked the tuft of hair poking through the bandage covering his crown. The doctor stood a respectful distance away. She wanted so much to tell Ray he was going to be all right, that he would eventually be his good-looking, cocky self again, but she had never lied to him and she couldn't now.

He seemed to take a while to recognise her, but when he did, his one eye filled and tears rolled silently down into the bandages. He opened his mouth to say something, but no sound came.

The doctor put his hand gently on Lee's shoulder. 'Perhaps we should leave him now.'

Lee didn't need persuading. She couldn't bear to see him like this. As soon as they were out of the ward, she asked, 'Will they be able to fix his face? Make it like it was?'

'His face? We're just glad he didn't lose an eye.' He sighed. 'I'm afraid even with the best work, he won't be quite so handsome in the future.'

'He was trying to say something.'

'He can't. His vocal cords have been too badly damaged. Your card was in his pocket, that's how we were able to reach you. It's too early to say, of course, but the chances of him being able to speak again are not good.'

Lee was still staring at the doctor when everything started to go blurry and unfocused. She realised she was crying. Not quiet tears, but loud racking sobs. He had tried to help her. He had warned her things could get nasty, and now this . . .

She was dimly aware of the doctor putting an arm round her shoulder. She could feel his embarrassment.

'Would you like a cup of tea?' he asked.

Tea. The panacea for all ills. 'No,' she said, between sobs, 'but I would kill for a cigarette.'

Chapter Twenty

Lee had been ringing Simone all day, without success. That evening after work she drove round to her house. It was in darkness, but she rang the bell repeatedly all the same, then waited outside in her car so long that the next-door neighbour opened the door to see what was going on.

Reluctantly she drove away. When she stopped at the traffic lights, she quickly searched the glove compartment with one hand until she found what she was looking for. Since she'd started smoking again, she'd done it with a vengeance. There were packets of cigarettes everywhere – in her desk drawer in Chambers, in her handbag, on the bedside table, even in the bathroom, as well as in the car.

As she parked on the gravel driveway, she finished that one. By the time she reached the front door, she had lit another. By ten that evening, she had finished off the packet. When he came back, David would be able to tell that she'd started again as soon as he opened the front door. A non-smoker always could. She would deal with that when it happened. He still called her regularly but right now she wondered whether he was ever coming back.

She was giving herself a manicure and watching MTV when she heard the doorbell. She wasn't expecting anyone. She wasn't taking any chances. She picked up the entryphone.

'Who's there?' she asked cautiously.

'It's me.'

Simone was standing there in jeans and an oversized sweater, even bigger than the ones she usually wore. She was carrying a small case.

'The trial's tomorrow,' she said, baldly. A pause, then, 'Can I stay?'

It was the first time she'd asked for any sort of help. 'Of course.' Lee stood aside to let her pass.

In the hallway, Simone looked at her as if she was seeing her for the first time. 'You look like Ena Sharples.'

Lee caught a glimpse of herself in the hallway mirror. She had curlers in her hair and a cigarette clamped at the corner of her mouth. The only difference was, her nails were better. Any other time she would have laughed, but not now.

'You hungry?' she asked as she led the way into her living room.

'I can't eat this late. But I could do with a nightcap. Nice. Very nice,' Simone added as she looked round the large, well-furnished room.

'Sit down. I'll get you one,' Lee said. Simone could hear her in the kitchen. When she returned, she brought two steaming mugs, one in each hand. 'Hot chocolate or Milo – which do you want?'

Simone looked at her. 'I wasn't talking about that kind of nightcap.'

'Oh. Well, all I have is half a bottle of wine.'

'OK. Anything to take the edge off, you know?'

Lee came back with the wine and two glasses. Simone was on the sofa, staring into the fireplace. 'I like how you've done this room. Did the fireplace come with the flat?'

'No. I had it put in.'

'I've always wanted to do that but I could never afford it.'

Lee sat at her friend's feet, on the large rug in front of the fireplace. 'Me and David have had some good times in this very spot.' She smiled, then caught herself. Maybe it wasn't right to talk about things sexual with Simone, given the circumstances.

Simone looked at her friend. 'I bet. You miss him, don't you?'

'Yes. Yes, I do.' Changing the subject, she asked, 'You watching this?'

'No.'

Lee picked up the remote and switched off the television. They both sipped from their glasses in silence. Simone lit a cigarette and blew a smoke ring into the air. 'I heard from Michael today.'

Lee stared at her. 'What?'

'Yeah. I was shocked too. He knows about the trial – Giles must have let him know. I gave him our solicitor's address, though I didn't say he could contact Michael. But how else would Michael know my number? I'm ex-directory, and I've changed my number twice – first after we split, and then after Steve.' She shrugged helplessly. 'He says he's coming tomorrow.'

'So, how much do you think he knows? About the rape, I mean?'

'Well, he knows Steve was a guy I was seeing. I told him he may . . . hear things, things said about me, and not to come if he wasn't completely sure he could handle it, but he said he still wants to come.' She took another sip of her wine. 'He also said maybe we could talk about getting back together.' She gave Lee a half smile. 'He certainly picks his moments.'

'Is that what you want?'

Simone sighed. 'I don't know, Leanne. A big part of me, yes. He's the most decent man I've ever met. I was so happy with him. You know all those things they say black men don't do? Buy flowers or cards or chocolates when it isn't your birthday; hold your hand in the street; go out of their way to please you? Michael did all that.'

'David does too, even after all this time,' Lee remarked. 'But then, I never believed that stuff anyway.'

'But when he left after the baby . . . I wouldn't wish that on anyone. I honestly didn't think I would live through it. So, if I did take him back, I could never trust him, or rely on him, in quite the same way again. Not ever. And I don't want to rely on his support through this; I couldn't bear it if he let me down again.'

Lee patted her hand. 'Well, right now let's hope he sticks with you at least through the trial. The jury will like that if they know he's there; Giles can make a lot of capital out of it.'

'Anyway, I don't want to talk about him. What's your week been like?'

'Fucking terrible, if you must know. Give me one of those, will you?' Simone passed her the cigarettes and matches. 'An old client, someone I'd grown to like – well, he's in hospital now, fighting for his life.'

'Oh, shit, Leanne, I'm sorry. What happened?'

'I don't know exactly. Seems he was attacked by a dog. Chewed away half his face. Got him by the throat, too. They don't know whether he'll ever talk again. It's a miracle he's still here. The worst thing is, I think it was because he tried to help me.'

'Why do you say that?'

'You know I'm in the Omartian case? Well, something's not right. I thought he had the answer, or at least would be able to point me in the right direction. He told me it was dangerous, and now . . .' Lee squeezed her eyes tight shut. When she opened them again, Simone was looking at her sympathetically.

'How do you know it was because of you? If he's been in trouble before, it could have been something else, someone else.'

'I just know, that's all.'

The silence now was uncomfortable, not like before.

'Hey!' Simone said suddenly. She was trying to sound upbeat. 'You know who I saw the other day? You remember Winston Talbot? Used to be in our year at school.'

Lee thought for a moment. 'Light-skinned boy, just under average height? Quiet. Used to get bullied a lot.'

At the mention of bullying, Simone averted her eyes. 'Yeah,

well, I saw him the other day in the market.'

'Didn't you used to go out with him?'

'Christ, Leanne. I hate to tell you this, but I didn't sleep with every guy in the year. Not that he would have been interested, anyway. He was gay.'

'What?'

'Yeah. He knew since he was ten or eleven. He never said. Well, that wasn't a school you would want to come out in.'

'So how did you know?'

'He never told me, I just guessed. Anyway, I was looking at this really beautiful black woman walking along. She was turning heads, I can tell you. Anyway, she came right up to me and said, "You used to go to Fordyce Park, didn't you? Simone Joseph? It's Tonia. I used to be Winston".'

'What? God, what did you do?'

'You know, I was more jealous than shocked. I'm telling you, he looked *good*! His grip was really strong though, like a man's. Anyway, we went and had a coffee. He's been inside, you know. I didn't ask what for. Poor thing, it must have been difficult for him. Steve's name came up. I didn't tell him what he'd done to me but Winston remembered him as having given him the hardest time in school. I got the feeling there's some scores to settle there. I told him I would soon be putting him away for a long time. He was dying to know the story, but of course I didn't tell him. He gave me his number, though, said I must call and let him know what happens.' She took a long last drag on her cigarette. 'Just think. This time next week, at least the trial will be over. Then all I have to do is live with what happened for the rest of my life.' She stubbed out her cigarette and stood up. 'I think I'll go to bed now, Lee. Big day tomorrow.'

It was strange for Lee to come to court not as a barrister but as an ordinary citizen, not as someone having an input, and possibly some influence, on the outcome of a case but as someone who could only sit by helplessly and watch. Even her pupil, who had been helping Giles, had had more to do with this case than she had.

They had arrived at court a full hour before the case was due to start but as they went up to the area outside the courtroom where the case was to be heard, Giles was already there with Anne-Marie, at the far end of the corridor. Lee's heart sank when she saw the barrister he was talking to. No, it couldn't be him. Not him.

'What's the matter?' Simone asked.

Anne-Marie saw them first, and gently nudged Giles.

'Nothing,' Lee said. She looked down at Simone. 'Nervous?'

'What do you think?'

'Well, here he comes now,' Lee said as Giles strode purposefully towards them, with Anne-Marie trailing in his wake.

'Good morning, Mrs Wilson. Lee.'

'We've got Judge Morton, I see,' Lee commented. 'He's not too bad. Very non-interventionist, in my experience, but his summings-up are usually right on the money.'

'So I understand,' Giles replied. He looked at Simone. 'Well, I won't ask you how you feel, but I'm glad you're here nonetheless.'

'Why wouldn't I be?'

'You'd be surprised. Some women in these types of cases, for whatever reasons, don't always turn up.'

'Well, Simone's not that scared, and she's telling the truth,' Lee retorted. 'She just wants to see justice done. And,' she added, silkily, 'she knows she has a barrister who will try his very best for her, won't you, Giles?'

Lee could see Simone looking first at her, then at Giles. She wasn't fooled. There was definitely something amiss, over and above the tension of the morning. Simone opened her mouth to speak when something caught her eye.

'Excuse me, please,' she said abruptly.

Giles and Lee watched as she walked towards a youngish black man of average height, wearing a dark jacket and jeans. They watched as, for a moment, the couple just stood and looked at each other, then the man pulled Simone into his arms and simply hugged her, resting his chin on top of her head. They remained like that for a long while. In the bustle outside court, the stillness they created around themselves seemed so intimate that, even from a distance, Lee felt she was intruding just by looking at them.

She didn't notice Amery's approach.

'Good morning, Ms Mitchell. We meet again, and so soon.' His smile was confident.

'Are you defending in this case?' she asked.

'Yes. Hasn't Giles spoken to you yet?' He looked at her Head of Chambers.

'Well, as I'm sure you know by now, the victim is a friend of mine—'

'Alleged victim. Alleged.'

'So, as a friend of the *victim*, I really don't see we have anything to talk about.' She gave him a tight little smile. 'If you'll excuse me.' She went to move away.

'Can't do that, I'm afraid. You see, I intend to call you as a defence witness.'

Lee spun round. 'What?'

'Just thought you ought to know before you sat in court. Can't have one of my witnesses contaminated by hearing evidence in the case, can I? And now you've been told, I know that, as a member of this honourable profession, you won't attempt to listen to any part of the trial.'

Lee was incredulous. 'If you think I'm going to do anything to help the man who raped my friend, you must be mad. Besides, what evidence could I give that you could possibly find of use?'

'Oh, I just want to ask you a few questions about the evening you all spent together the night of the *alleged* rape.'

Lee frowned. 'But how could that possibly help you? I wasn't a direct witnesses to the rape. I don't know what happened after we all left the restaurant.'

'Quite so,' Amery observed. 'But you're willing to condemn my client out of hand, just the same.'

Lee hesitated, then said stubbornly, 'He's just another defendant to you. She's my friend. And if she says she was raped, I believe her. She wouldn't lie to me.'

'Really? Tell me, was Ms Joseph – I mean Mrs Wilson, *always* this perfect?'

Lee heard the clear emphasis on the word 'always'. The use of her maiden name was no accident, either. Steve Payne must have told Amery they had all been to school together. But he wouldn't dare ask her about anything that far back, would he? It wouldn't be relevant. Anyway, why was she even speculating about this? It would be a cold day in hell before she gave evidence for the defendant in this trial.

'Look, I just know what she says is true, that's all. I just know, and I won't be giving evidence, you can be sure of that.'

'Ah well, that's a pity,' Amery said, 'because I'll be forced to issue a witness summons against you.'

'Do whatever you want. I won't be changing my mind.'

Giles had been hovering behind Lee. Amery looked over her shoulder at him. 'Is that so? Well, perhaps you'd like to have a chat with your Head of Chambers about that, because I *will* issue that summons if I'm forced to do so.'

Giles stepped forward. 'Lee, could I have a word, please?'

Lee turned to face him, a tart reply only just restrained by the knowledge that Amery was watching and listening to everything. Giles opened the door to a small waiting area set aside for prosecution witnesses. As soon as he closed the door behind them both, Lee said, 'Surely you're not going to try and convince me, Giles?'

He leaned against the door and took off his wig. From the way his hair was plastered to his head, Lee could tell he was sweating, and it wasn't that warm a day. He ran an exasperated hand over his forehead.

'Are you mad, Lee? Do you want the general public, not to mention the judge, to hear an application for a witness summons to force you to give evidence? Do you realise how embarrassing that would be for you? You, a barrister?'

Lee was astonished. 'Are you, as prosecution counsel in this case, seriously asking me to give evidence for the defence? Against my friend?'

'Oh, for God's sake,' Giles snapped. 'It's not a question of it being for or against her. The profession demands that we assist the court in any way required, including – no, especially – giving evidence. It's the administration of justice that we're all concerned about, surely.'

'Giles, you know as well as I do that justice and the law have very little to do with each other. I co-defended with George Amery on Omartian, remember? He's good, very good. He's also completely without conscience. That's a very dangerous combination. All he wants to do is present to the jury a friend of the victim, a barrister, no less, who will be giving evidence for the defence – not to mention having a poke at me for Omartian. Besides, I can't see how anything I could say could possibly help him.'

'What *did* happen that evening?'

Lee frowned. 'Nothing much. We went out for a meal—'

'We?'

'Me and David, Simone and Stephen Payne.' She could hardly bring herself to say his name.

'Where's David?'

'On tour in America. I don't know when he'll be back.'

'Good. At least Amery can't witness summons him too. Did anything significant happen between Mrs Wilson and Payne?'

'If it had, I would have remembered it.'

'Any tension between them?'

Lee thought for a moment. 'No.'

'What did you think of him?'

Lee shrugged. 'I didn't like him.'

Giles raised his eyebrows. 'Oh?'

'I don't know. It's just a feeling I had about him, you know?'

Giles didn't seem too impressed by that. 'Anything else?' he insisted, leaning forward. 'Are you sure there's nothing else I should know about?'

Lee shook her head. 'No.'

Giles straightened up again. 'In that case, I don't think either you or Mrs Wilson have anything to worry about; there's nothing in what you said that could harm the Crown's case.'

'Then why would Amery want me?'

'Who knows what Payne told him? Maybe it's just as you said, he wants the kudos of being able to call a barrister to give evidence on behalf of the defendant.' He replaced his wig. 'Take my advice, Lee. Save yourself the embarrassment of being forced to give evidence. I think it would look as if you had something to hide.'

'But Amery couldn't tell the jury I refused.'

'No, *he* couldn't, but who knows what Payne could "accidentally" let slip, especially if he's primed.'

Lee was silent for a long time. Finally, she spoke. 'This just doesn't feel right, Giles.' She paused. 'You were right. I've never prosecuted before. So, from your point of view, are you sure this won't damage the case?'

'If what you say in court is what you've told me, I don't see—'

A knock interrupted him. Anne-Marie tentatively put her head round the door and said, 'The judge is ready for us now.'

'Thank you, Anne-Marie,' Giles said, without looking round. His tone was a clear dismissal. Anne-Marie scuttled away.

'I ought at least to speak to Simone first; let her know what's going to happen.' Lee walked towards the door.

'No,' Giles said quickly, putting his hand on the doorknob. 'You know you can't speak to her if there's any prospect of you being a defence witness, however reluctant.'

'Shit! Yes, you're right. It's so easy to forget when it's someone you know. But how will she get back? Besides, she's staying with me.'

'I'll explain the situation to her and make whatever arrangements are necessary.' As Giles turned to go, Lee stopped him.

'Giles, I know how this is going to look to Simone. You will explain it fully to her, won't you? Let her know that I didn't want to do this? That I didn't betray her? But not until after she's given evidence – I don't want her to be upset.'

'Don't worry, Lee.' Giles gave a half-smile. 'I'll speak to her myself. You have my word on that. You forget, I want to win this case too.'

'Mr Townsend,' said the judge.

Giles stood up. 'Thank you, Your Honour.' He turned to his right, looking over the head of George Amery, who was still seated, pen poised to note down everything he was about to say, towards the twelve men and women seated in two rows.

'Ladies and gentlemen of the jury, I prosecute this case, and my learned friend Mr Amery appears for the defence.' He looked slightly over his shoulder at Steve Payne who was seated in the dock at the back of the court, a worried expression on his face. Giles looked back at the jury, and held out a sheaf of documents. 'I have copies of the indictment for you, one between two. Madame usher?'

A bespectacled middle-aged woman in a black robe took the documents from his outstretched hand and began handing them out to the jury.

'You've heard it read out by the clerk, and can now see for yourselves, that the defendant faces an indictment containing a single count, that of rape. Most people think of rape as a violent sexual attack by a man upon a woman he does not know, perhaps walking home late at night. "Date rape" is a term given to us by our American cousins. Very often, people tend to dismiss this kind of rape because the parties are known to each other, often with some kind of sexual history between them. Some misguided people even think that it is consensual sexual intercourse that just got slightly out of hand, slightly too rough, for instance – but not rape, forced rape. Well, ladies and gentlemen, if those are your views, put them out of your mind because this type of offence is not only rape in all senses of the word, it is, I suggest, in some ways even worse than an attack by a stranger because it is a total and complete violation not just of the body, but of trust. People are often wary of strangers, but not of friends, not of lovers; not of people you allow into your home to use the lavatory, as Mrs Wilson did that night.'

As Giles continued to outline the case for the Crown, Anne-Marie, taking notes behind him, was pleasantly surprised by the strength of his speech. Maybe he did believe in the rightness of the cause, after all.

'. . . And with Your Honour's leave, I call the first witness, Simone Wilson.'

As Simone entered the court, she felt very grateful that she had followed Lee's suggestion and sat in on some cases before the trial, as the layout of the court and the people she could expect to see there were now no surprise to her. But the walk to the witness box, only a few yards away, still seemed like the longest she had ever taken. As she stood there and faced the jury, a feeling of helplessness overwhelmed her and she had to clutch the wooden sides for support. The judge, the barristers – this was now completely out of her hands. And the jury, seven men, five women. Young and middle-aged. No one particularly old. No one black. She wondered whether that would make a difference. Possibly not, what with both her and Steve being black. And she could have had one of those old black church women. But then again, she thought cynically, maybe this bunch would just see it as two black people quarrelling among themselves, not knowing where the truth lay, and caring even less.

All this was racing through her mind even as she tried to smile at the twelve men and women before her.

She could barely hold the Bible when she was asked to take the oath. She tried to read the words on the card in front of her, but they were blurred. She hoped she wasn't about to cry; she hadn't even started to give evidence. She tried again. 'I'm sorry, I . . .'

'Perhaps you'd like to repeat the oath after the usher, Mrs Wilson,' the judge suggested in a sympathetic voice.

Simone could only nod in gratitude. The court usher smiled at her in an understanding way and read the words from the card so that she could repeat them.

She looked at Giles as he stood up to take her through her evidence. The strain of trying to keep her emotions in check was threatening to overwhelm her. Her body felt like a battleground. She so wanted to cry, to let out everything that had been inside her for so long. But there was another, more resilient part of her that refused to let the anguish escape, not here. What would be the point of tears, anyway? At any time in her life, had it ever helped? Tears never changed anything. She had cried bitterly when Michael left; as Steve pushed inside her yet again; after the baby . . .

She composed herself, straightened her spine, turned to face Giles, and tried her best to look confident. She was careful not to look at the man in the dock.

As she answered his preliminary questions, Giles looked over the top of his spectacles at her. He didn't really need them; he only wore them for effect. He could see the strain on Simone's face, then surprisingly that seemed to pass to be replaced by a new, more confident persona, which seemed to strengthen as she recounted what had happened that terrible night. She even maintained steady eye contact with the jury. And still no tears. Women didn't recall such an ordeal and not cry about it, surely. Either she was completely devoid of normal human feeling, or she was a very practised liar. Right now, Giles wasn't sure which.

He asked his final question, 'Is there anything else you'd like to tell the court about what happened that night, Mrs Wilson?' and glanced at the jury as she shook her head. From their expressions, it was hard to tell what they thought, though one young woman looked obviously sympathetic; she had also already started taking notes of what was being said. A good sign.

As Giles sat, Amery rose. Simone stiffened, preparing for the onslaught.

'Are you happy to continue, Mrs Wilson? Or would you like a short break?'

Simone was caught off guard, but replied, 'No, thank you.'

'Would you like some water?'

'Er, no.' She looked down at the untouched glass given to her earlier by the usher. 'I still have some, thanks.'

'Now, Mrs Wilson, I would just like to establish the points upon which we agree. There were no witnesses as to what happened between you and Mr Payne that night. That's right, isn't it?'

Simone couldn't believe what she was hearing. 'What?'

'I'm sorry, precisely what part of that question didn't you understand?'

'Only the reason for you asking it,' Simone shot back. 'Do you think I would have wanted an audience?'

'Mrs Wilson, I'm asking the questions here. A simple yes or no will suffice.'

The judge intervened. 'Mrs Wilson, it isn't for you to go behind the reason for counsel's questions, although, Mr Amery, I think that has already been clearly established, hasn't it?'

But when Amery still looked at her expectantly, Simone replied, 'No, if there had been, they would have been here to support my story.'

'Your story?'

'My account,' Simone countered.

'Quite. And it's also right that there is no forensic evidence in this case – specifically, any semen taken from your body, scrapings of skin from under your fingernails as evidence of you fighting off Mr Payne—'

'Your Honour,' Giles stood up, 'the Crown has already made an admission as to this. There is no purpose in this question save to further humiliate and embarrass the witness.'

Simone turned to the judge. 'I'd like to answer that, please.' She ignored Giles's warning look, knowing instinctively that any answers to this question would be better coming from her than apparently hiding behind an admission by a lawyer.

'Very well,' said the judge.

Simone turned back to face Amery. 'In answer to your question, there are three reasons for that. One, I have, and have always had, small hands and very short fingernails, as you can see.' She held up her hands. 'Secondly, I washed myself as soon as I could – as soon as I was sure that he wasn't coming back.' She squeezed her eyes tight shut, then opened them again. Her voice cracked a little as she continued, 'I ran downstairs, locked the door, then ran a bath as hot as I could stand it. I wanted to wipe away every trace of him, inside and out.'

'What do you mean, inside and out?'

Was she to be left with no dignity whatsoever? 'I douched.' She paused, and looked at the jury. 'With bleach.' Several of the women winced visibly. Turning back towards Amery, she continued, 'The third reason was because I didn't immediately report what happened to the police.'

'Ah yes, I was coming to that.' Amery leaned on the lectern, clearly warming to his task. 'How long was it between the time of the alleged rape and your reporting it to the police?'

Simone thought for a moment. 'About ten days, I think.'

'Why the delay?'

'Because I wasn't going to make a complaint. I didn't want to have to . . . to go through this . . .' Her voice trailed away.

'What? Not report it even though you say you've been raped?'

'I *was* raped.'

'Mrs Wilson,' Amery was looking at the jury as he spoke to her, 'I suggest that anyone who had suffered a violent sexual assault such as the one you described would want the police involved as soon as possible.'

'Really? I wasn't aware that you had ever been raped, Mr Amery,' Simone snapped.

Amery turned back swiftly at that response, clearly angry. Before he could say anything, Judge Morton spoke. 'Mrs Wilson, please. I know this is upsetting, but counsel is only doing his job.' As gentle as the judge's tone was, Simone wasn't about to apologise. She was doing what she always did when she felt cornered, fighting back.

'Anyway,' she continued, 'that wasn't the first time I told anyone about it.'

That seemed to take Amery by surprise. 'Really?' he said, clearly not believing her. 'And to whom did you make your first complaint?'

'A friend of mine.'

'Male or female?'

The implication was clear. 'A woman,' Simone answered

shortly. 'Her name's Leanne Mitchell. She's also a barrister.' She guessed, rightly, that the jury would be impressed by that.

'And how long afterwards was this?'

'About four or five days later.'

'Not exactly immediate, was it?' When Simone didn't reply, he asked, 'Do you know whether she made a statement?'

Simone thought back to the day Lee had found her. 'She wanted to,' she replied slowly. 'She wanted to look at my bruises, so at least she could say she saw them. I told her no. I didn't want anyone else to see me naked. And, as I said, I had no intention then of going to the police.'

'So why did you?'

The courtroom seemed eerily quiet as Simone replied, 'I couldn't let him get away with what he did to me.'

'Didn't you have Leanne Mitchell's phone number?'

'Of course I did.'

'So why didn't you ring her earlier?'

'I told you, I wasn't going to report it. She was the one who persuaded me to even think about doing that. Plus I . . . I was ashamed. About what happened.' She stopped speaking. Again it appeared she was fighting to retain her composure. When she spoke again, her voice had a harder edge to it. 'Besides, I'm used to dealing with things by myself.'

'What, even when you were married? You *are* divorced now, I take it, Mrs Wilson?'

'No, I'm not. I'm separated.'

'So you were still legally married when you and Mr Payne embarked upon your relationship.'

'I told you, I was separated.'

'Were you still legally married, Mrs Wilson? Yes or no?'

'Yes,' she replied, almost in a whisper.

'I'm sorry, I didn't quite catch your answer.'

Simone looked him straight in the eye, and said loudly, 'Yes.'

'And that was your status throughout the relationship?'

'Yes.'

'Where is your husband now, Mrs Wilson?'

'With me here today, in court.' She smiled triumphantly and looked at Michael. It was the first time she had felt able to do that. He looked distinctly uncomfortable.

'Was Mr Payne the reason you and your husband separated?'

'No, of course not. That had happened long before.'

'Who left who?'

'He left me.'

'What was the reason?'

Oh no. Anything but that. Simone looked imploringly at Giles, who rose to his feet.

'Your Honour, I really don't see the relevance of that question to the issue at hand.'

'I quite agree,' said the judge. 'Mr Amery, I think you've gone far enough down that road.'

Amery looked about to object, then changed his mind. 'As Your Honour pleases.' Turning back to Simone, he tried a different tack.

'Did you love Mr Payne?'

Simone looked at Giles and read the expression in his eyes. He had told her an affirmative answer would really get the jury on her side. In fact, she opened her mouth to give such a response when she saw the Bible, upon which she had taken her oath, out of the corner of her eye. She couldn't remember the last time she'd been in church, but she had a feeling that, one way or another, she was about to start needing God very soon. Now would not be a good time to begin lying.

'I liked him, at first,' she said finally, 'but I didn't love him.'

'You liked him at first,' Amery repeated derisively. 'Is that all you felt for him?'

'I don't know how he felt about me.'

'I suggest to you that he loved you very much.'

'What? He told you that? You must be joking! He was sleeping with at least two or three other women at the same time as me.' She looked at the jury, and instantly wondered whether she should have said that. Some of them looked as if they found the whole thing, including her involvement in it, very sleazy. And put that way, she couldn't blame them.

'Is that why you reported what happened as a rape, Mrs Wilson? Because of your belief that he had other sexual partners?'

'It wasn't a belief, it was a fact. And no, I reported it because that was what happened. I didn't care whether he had other women or not. I wasn't that serious about him.'

'Because you didn't love him.'

'That's right.'

'You were just using him for sex, to conveniently satisfy your needs during your husband's absence.'

'Just as men have done for years, Mr Amery. Our relationship was primarily sexual, yes.'

'And you were hoping to be reconciled with your husband.'

'I didn't think that was a possibility at the time . . . but it is something that perhaps I would have considered, yes.'

'Mrs Wilson, you talk about being raped, about being dominated and forced to have sex against your will. But I put it to you that not only did this not happen, but you were the emotionally dominant one in the relationship because you had so much less invested in it. You wanted your husband back; wasn't that less likely to happen if he knew about you and the defendant?'

It was all too much. 'How dare you! How can you say that? Do you know what he did to me, that piece of—' She felt, rather than saw, the judge's warning gaze. She caught herself in time. 'Look at the pictures, then. Go on, look at them! Are you saying that I did this to myself?'

'Did you?'

'Mr Amery, that will do!' the judge said sharply. 'Mrs Wilson is not on trial here. I won't warn you again.'

'I apologise, Your Honour. Well, Mrs Wilson, let's talk about the pictures. I suggest that those bruises were due to sexual activity that was a little more, shall we say, energetic than usual.'

'I don't get excited by being hurt, Mr Amery.'

'And what does, to use your words, Mrs Wilson, "excite" you?'

Giles rose to his feet in protest. 'Your Honour—'

'What's that got to do with anything?' Simone blurted out. 'I was raped, don't you understand? Raped! That has nothing to do with sexual enjoyment. That's violence.' She paused. When she spoke again, it was in a quiet, plaintive voice. 'It hurt.'

'Anything that happened on that night was consensual, Mrs Wilson.'

'It wasn't. How many times do I have to tell you?'

'But it was before, wasn't it, when you had sex with the defendant?'

'But not on that night.'

'Yes or no, Mrs Wilson?'

'Some of the things he did to me . . . he'd never done that before . . .'

'Let's see now, you claim the defendant held you down forcibly. You asked him to do that, didn't you?'

'No.'

'As part of a sexual game.'

'No.'

'And you'd asked him to do that in the past.'

Simone sounded as astonished as she looked. 'No!' She stared at the man she had thought she had known well enough to allow him to share her bed. 'Steve! You told him that?' His face was impassive but he could not meet her gaze.

'Mrs Wilson.' Amery wanted her attention on him. He looked down at his papers, then back at her. 'You claim the defendant tried to sodomise you that night.'

'Yes.'

'On more than one occasion.'

'Yes.'

'But was unsuccessful.'

'That didn't stop him trying, Mr Amery. I think my screams put him off,' she replied baldly. 'And before you ask, no, that wasn't something I had ever asked him to do to me in the past.'

'You also say he forced you to perform oral sex.'

'Yes, he did.'

'But that was with your consent, wasn't it?'

'No!'

'But you had consented to this in the past, hadn't you?'

Simone felt the blood rush to her face. Why wasn't Giles objecting or something? She turned to the judge. 'Is he allowed to ask me these questions?'

'Yes. Whether or not you consented is at the heart of this case. You must answer all questions unless I indicate otherwise.'

She looked at Michael out of the corner of her eye but couldn't make out his expression. Maybe it was just as well.

'I'd be happy to repeat the question if you'd like, Mrs Wilson.'

Yes, and underscore it in the minds of the jury. Simone thought bitterly. 'No, I heard you. The answer is yes.'

'In fact, you had volunteered to perform oral sex on the defendant on more than one occasion in the past.'

Simone closed her eyes. She remembered one occasion in particular. That had been such a happy day . . .

'Yes.'

'You also say, and I quote, "Throughout the whole time, the defendant used his greater size and strength to bend and twist me into different positions, like a doll." I suggest this also was something you had consented to.'

'No.' Her voice was weary.

'And on previous occasions. Different, inventive positions.'

Was there to be no end to this? Simone sighed. 'Yes.'

Giles heard the sigh for what it was. For the first time since he had met Simone, she sounded utterly defeated. But then, in his opinion, the sympathy vote had been lost long ago. Silly bitch. As if all this honesty and integrity was going to help. Whoever said the best witness was the truthful one? How truthful did she expect Payne to be? He didn't even want to look at the jury.

In the pause that followed her answer, everyone present could hear the double doors to the courtroom banging together. Evidently someone had either entered the room or left it. Simone didn't have to look to know who it was.

Chapter Twenty-One

It was like a game of chess, played by a master. Amery's cross-examination of Simone had expertly paved the way for Steve Payne, making it easier for him to give his evidence the next day. So easy, in fact, that Amery found himself mentally stepping back, observing as well as hearing the way he gave his evidence in a completely detached way. Odd, he thought, how very different he looked today compared to the scruffy, unshaven man he had seen in Brixton prison. Today, he was clean-shaven and conservatively dressed – courtesy, Amery was sure, of some doting woman or other – the image of a wronged man whose only crime was to love a woman who was only interested in one part of his anatomy. Yes, Amery thought suddenly, he liked that line. He might use it in his closing speech. Being good-looking didn't hurt either. Funny, that, how good looks worked against a woman in a rape case but in favour of the man. After all, why would a good-looking man need to rape?

Amery took a sidelong glance at the jury. Even he, for all his cynicism, never ceased to be amazed at how gullible they could be. Even more incredible, it was the *women* who were lapping this up.

He glanced over at Simone Wilson. She looked drawn and very tired. He knew Giles Townsend would have told her she didn't have to come back now that her part was over, so why had she chosen to return? Lying or not, there would be no benefit in it for her, hearing Payne give his evidence so convincingly, knowing the jury would be comparing the two. The thought crossed his mind that she might actually be telling the truth, but he quickly dismissed it.

'Thank you, Mr Payne,' Amery said finally. 'Could you wait there, please?' Looking across at his opponent, he added, 'There may be some more questions for you.'

But there were surprisingly few. Giles's cross-examination was desultory, and with every reply Payne came across as even more believable. At its conclusion, Amery didn't even bother to re-examine. He knew he had reasonable doubt right there.

Now for the icing on the cake.

'Your Honour,' he said to the judge, 'I have two further witnesses to call. I don't know about my learned friend, but *I* shall be brief. The first is Ms Sylvia Thomas.'

At the mention of the name, Simone raised her head slowly as if she was trying to remember where she had heard it before, even though it was one she heard every day of her working life for the past five years.

The usher left the courtroom to call for the witness, and moments later reappeared with a tall, attractive, dark-skinned black woman, casually dressed in jeans and trainers. There was a brief moment of hesitation when she saw Simone, then she gave the smaller woman a confident, reassuring smile and walked smartly up to the witness box.

Why was she here? Simone struggled to make herself pay more attention, but she was tired, very tired . . .

Sylvia took the oath in a strong, steady, clear voice. After giving her full name and address to the court, she stood expectantly, waiting for Amery's next question.

'Ms Thomas, how do you know Simone Wilson?'

'We work together, at Fordyce Park Comprehensive. We're both teachers.'

'And how long have you known her?'

Sylvia thought for a moment, then replied, 'About five years.'

'How would you describe your relationship with her?'

'How do you mean?'

'Well, would you consider her to be a friend, acquaintance, or work colleague?'

'Well, we're not round each other's houses all the time, if that's what you mean. She's friendly, but very private. But I consider her a friend. I like her, and I'd like to help her.' She smiled at Simone encouragingly, who managed to smile back.

'I'm sure you would. And you want to help us all by telling the truth, is that correct?'

'Of course,' Sylvia said indignantly. 'I didn't come all the way here to lie.'

'Have you ever seen the defendant, Stephen Payne, before?'

'Yes.' Sylvia looked directly at him. 'Once before, round about the end of April or early May. I can't remember exactly.'

'I'm sure you must have met a lot of people in passing since then, Ms Thomas. Why does the defendant stick in your mind?'

'Well, I'm not likely to forget someone who looks like that, am I?'

Some members of the jury started laughing, and Sylvia was momentarily flustered. Her reply had been honest but she hadn't expected Steve Payne to look quite so smug at her response. And surely this was no laughing matter.

'Was Mrs Wilson also present?'

'Yes, she was with me. We were leaving school together.'

'What was the interaction between them like?'

'Well, I didn't see much. I remember this boy, a kid at our school, came running up with some flowers for Simone. He said that he,' nodding in the direction of Steve, 'had asked him to give them to her.'

Giles stood up, a fraction too late. Judge Morton was already on to it.

227

'You know better than that, Mr Amery.'

'Yes, Your Honour,' Giles added, somewhat unnecessarily, seeing as the judge had spotted the infraction, 'that is hearsay. That boy is not here to say whether or not that actually happened.'

'Quite so, Your Honour,' Amery conceded, 'but I'm only calling this evidence as to the fact of its occurrence, not as to the truth of any alleged conversation between the boy and the defendant.'

Judge Morton turned to Sylvia. 'Ms Thomas, did you hear the alleged conversation between the boy and the defendant?'

'No, Your Honour.'

'Did you see the boy bring some flowers for the defendant?'

'Yes, I did.'

'But you don't know for a fact who they were from.'

'No, I don't.'

'I see. Thank you. Mr Townsend, Mr Amery, I will instruct the jury to disregard the alleged conversation.'

Both men nodded. Giles sat down again.

'Now, Ms Thomas,' Amery continued, 'what was Mrs Wilson's reaction on getting the flowers?'

'Well, shortly after that, he – that is, the defendant – came over. She didn't seem very happy to see him.'

'In spite of the flowers?'

Sylvia nodded. 'Of course, I don't know what happened between them earlier; he might have done something he had to make up for—'

'Ms Thomas,' Amery interrupted her, 'as you yourself just said, you don't know what happened earlier, so please don't speculate. The jury is only interested in what you saw, or heard.' His voice now sounded harsh. 'Now, what else did you either *see* or *hear*?'

'Well,' Sylvia said, imitating his tone, 'I *saw* and *heard* him offer her a lift home.'

'And what was her reaction?'

'She was very reluctant. He had to insist. So did I, come to think of it. It was raining, you see; I couldn't see the point in her walking if she could get a lift. If I had known then what would happen . . .' she muttered darkly.

'But you know the alleged rape didn't take place that day, don't you, Ms Thomas?'

Sylvia hesitated, then replied, 'Yes, that's right.'

'When did you hear about the alleged rape?'

'I can't remember exactly. It would have been towards the end of the week following the early May bank holiday. The head told us the news. She didn't go into detail, but then we didn't need it.' She shuddered.

'So all you know is what you heard second-hand.'

'Yes, but—'

'Thank you, Ms Thomas,' Amery said, intending to silence her. It didn't work.

'No. You don't understand. What woman would lie about something like that? And you don't know her; she doesn't lie, not about anything.'

'You did not see it, did you? Yes or no?' Amery asked, enunciating every word clearly. He knew there was only one answer to that, and he was determined to get it, especially after that outburst.

'No.'

'Thank you.' Amery sat down.

Giles looked at Sylvia as he rose slowly to his feet. There was nothing that she could usefully add to the Crown's case. He had a feeling that she had come to court to try and help her friend but by drawing attention to the defendant's good looks and romantic gestures she had inadvertently made it worse. Another honest, well-intentioned, misguided witness.

'I have no questions, Your Honour.'

Amery rose again. 'No re-examination. Does Your Honour have any questions?'

'No. Thank you for coming, Ms Thomas. You can stay or go as you wish.'

'I'll leave, if you don't mind. I have a class this afternoon.' As she walked past where Simone was sitting, Sylvia gave her a puzzled, confused look. Then she was gone.

Amery shifted his position slightly, in order the better to observe the look he fully expected to see on Simone's face any minute now. 'My last witness, Your Honour, is Leanne Mitchell.'

He wasn't disappointed. Simone's head snapped up. She looked both stunned and bewildered.

Giles turned to Anne-Marie, sitting behind him. 'You *did* speak to her, as I asked, didn't you? About Lee giving evidence.'

Anne-Marie looked surprised. 'No, I thought you were going to do that.'

'Bloody hell! Well, it's too late now.'

Lee entered the courtroom, hoping against hope Simone wouldn't still be there. But she was, sitting directly to her left as she entered, literally on the edge of her seat. Lee glanced over quickly at her but that was all she needed to register the confusion, anger, and something that looked very much like contempt on her friend's face.

At that moment, Lee knew. Giles hadn't told her.

In her jury speeches, Lee had often commented that the longest walk was the one defendants made from the dock to the witness box. She now learned it applied to reluctant witnesses, as well. As she stood there, she realised she had never seen a jury, or any other aspect of a courtroom, from that vantage point before. She suddenly felt very exposed – she, who entered court nearly every day of her working life. She could only imagine how Simone must have felt.

Both Judge Morton and the usher smiled in recognition. She

often appeared in this court, under very different circumstances. The usher offered her the Bible, but she declined. 'I wish to affirm, Your Honour.' The judge nodded his assent and as the usher picked a white card with black lettering and handed it to Lee, she commented, 'I don't need that. I know the words.'

As soon as she had made the affirmation, Amery asked Lee for her full name and address. He noticed that she gave her professional address, but he didn't press her. The judge wouldn't have allowed him to, anyway, and there was no point getting on Lee's bad side so early in the proceedings. Getting what he wanted was going to be difficult enough as it was. Mind you, he was going to enjoy taking this arrogant bitch down a peg or two.

'We've worked together before, Ms Mitchell. May I call you Lee?'

'No, you may not.' She gave him a smile as bright as it was false. 'It's customary to address a witness in the more formal style, Mr Amery. Why don't we stick with that?'

'I see. What is your occupation, Ms Mitchell?'

'How is that relevant?'

'You forget, you're not asking the questions today, Ms Mitchell. But if it's something you feel you want to hide from the jury . . .'

'I'm a barrister,' Lee replied, tersely.

'And how long have you been in practice?'

'Over seven years.'

'How do you know the complainant?'

'I went to school with her.'

'The school at which she now teaches, is that right?'

'Yes.'

'And how would you describe your relationship?'

'She's a friend.' Lee looked over at Simone. 'A very good friend.'

'And have you always been this friendly?'

Lee knew where he was going with this but he'd have to do it without her. 'At the relevant time, the time of the rape, we were very friendly, yes.'

'Were you aware that Stephen Payne also attended Fordyce Park School at the same time that you and Mrs Wilson were pupils there?'

'Not at that time, no.'

'When did you become aware of that fact?'

'I'm still not aware of it as a *fact*, but the defendant told me he had attended Fordyce. I certainly don't remember him attending back then.'

'I repeat, when did you become aware of it?'

'Myself, my partner, Mrs Wilson and the defendant had been out as a group earlier on the evening of the rape.'

'Ms Mitchell, I will ask you to try and preface your description of what happened with the word "alleged". You of all people shouldn't have to be reminded. Now, could you please tell us what the atmosphere among you was like?'

'It was . . . pleasant.'

'And Mrs Wilson and the defendant – how did they appear to be in relation to each other?'

'How do you mean?'

'Did they appear to be getting along well?'

Lee wasn't going to help him at all. 'Well, that would only be my perception . . .'

'You know, Ms Mitchell, a simple yes or no to that question would suffice.'

'They appeared to be getting along, yes.'

'Very well? Mrs Wilson had been smiling at the defendant, touching his shoulder, his arm?'

Lee's mind flashed back to that evening. 'Yes.'

'She even had her hand on his leg.'

'I don't know about that,' Lee snapped. 'And as to the rest of it, surely you're not suggesting that she deserved to be raped?'

'No. I'm suggesting that there was no rape; that what happened that evening was a preview of the forthcoming attractions.'

Lee looked at Steve, then at Amery, with open disgust.

'When did you next see the complainant?' Amery continued.

'The Wednesday after the Bank Holiday.'

'You seem very sure of the day. How can you be so precise?'

Lee folded her arms and stared at him. 'Because that was the day I first met you, Mr Amery.'

Someone on the jury laughed.

'Five days later.'

'That's right.'

'Did you see any injuries on the complainant's body?'

'She wouldn't let me examine her. I wanted to, so I could make a statement about what I'd seen. She said she didn't want anyone else to see her naked. I did see a bad bruise on her right wrist, though.'

'Was that all you saw?'

'Yes.'

'Isn't it right, Ms Mitchell, that everything you know about what happened on the night in question came from the complainant herself?'

'Yes, but—'

'One final question. That evening, when you all went out together, what did you think of the defendant?'

'I didn't really take to him.'

'Even though your friend clearly had.'

'Mr Amery, that's comment,' the judge warned.

'And you don't think anything you say in relation to the defendant would be coloured by that dislike, or by your friendship with the complainant?' Before Lee could reply, Amery concluded, 'That's all I wish to ask. Thank you, Ms Mitchell. You've been most helpful.'

'I believe her,' Lee burst out.

'The jury are not interested in what you believe, they're interested in what you know. And the fact is you don't know what happened that night.' Amery sat down with a flourish.

Lee waited, willing Giles to cross-examine her so that she could correct any misconceptions the jury might have of Simone as a person. More than anything, she didn't want Simone to be left with the suspicion that she, of all people, was the one who had sealed her fate.

But he didn't. Neither did the judge. There was nothing left to say.

The judge cleared his throat. 'Due to the lateness of the hour, I'll hear speeches today but I won't sum up this case until tomorrow morning. Mr Townsend?'

Lee stepped out of the witness box as Giles rose to his feet. As she did so, she looked at Simone once again. There was only one emotion on her face now, sheer contempt.

Chapter Twenty-Two

The next morning was wet and gloomy – miserable, even for autumn. Lee stared morosely at the windscreen wipers, on at full speed, as she drove back to court yet again for the conclusion of the trial. Part of her wondered why she was even bothering. Her clerks had been less than understanding about her taking yet another day out of court to be a mere spectator at a trial, instead of trying one herself. And Simone couldn't stand the sight of her now, she had made that perfectly clear the previous evening when she'd walked past her outside court without saying a word. Not that Lee blamed her; she felt as if she had handed Amery the acquittal he wanted on a plate. Logically, she knew that wasn't true. She had only described what had happened earlier in the evening, when they had all been out together. Date rapes were hard cases to prove at the best of times, and the fact that there had been a delay in reporting it didn't help. But that didn't make her feel any better. In any event, whether Simone wanted her there or not, she had to go. She had to try and set things right.

The courtroom was locked when Lee arrived. She wasn't surprised. Judge Morton was not due to sit until ten thirty and there were no other matters listed to be heard in his court. She sat outside, lit a cigarette, and waited. There were only two people she really wanted to see.

Giles didn't come up to the courtroom until ten thirty. He blanched when he saw Lee, but he didn't break his stride.

'Good morning, Lee. I didn't expect to see you here today.'

Lee looked at him through a haze of smoke. 'I'm sure you didn't.' She looked at Anne-Marie who was standing a few feet away, nervously playing with her shiny new wig. 'Would you excuse us a moment, please?'

Giles knew what was coming. He tried the handle of the door to the court. Still locked. There was no escape. He decided attack was the best form of defence. Why should he have to justify himself to this young woman, anyway? He was, after all, the Head of Chambers, and it was time she was reminded of that fact.

'Whatever it is, it will have to wait. I really have nothing to say to you now.'

He had the nerve to be angry with her! Lee stood up, her eyes narrowed to slits. In her heels, she was easily his height.

'You didn't tell her, did you?' she asked, without preamble.

'I asked Anne-Marie to speak to Mrs Wilson. Evidently she forgot. It is unfortunate, but sometimes these things happen.'

'Giles, you assured me that you would speak to her yourself. You gave me your word. When I give mine, I consider it binding, but evidently yours means nothing.' The time for niceties had passed. Lee looked at him with ill-disguised contempt and shook her head, as if she could not believe what he had done. 'You bastard!'

'How dare you!' Giles crossed his arms and looked at her. 'You know, in the past I have attributed your hysterical outbursts to cultural differences, but now I've had quite enough of them. I think you ought seriously to reconsider your future at Maple Court.'

'Oh, no. Don't think you can get rid of me that easily.' Lee didn't raise her voice at all. She didn't need to. 'First of all, you have to have a Chambers meeting with a two-thirds majority to get me out, because I'm not leaving, not till I'm good and ready – although to be honest, I don't know how much longer I can stomach working with you. Secondly, I'll deny this conversation ever took place – and I don't see any witnesses, do you? Thirdly, if you feel you must take this to a Chambers meeting, I'll make sure everyone knows not only how badly I think you handled this case, but that you're not to be trusted, that you break you word and practise nepotism without the knowledge of other members of Chambers. You see, at that point I really won't have anything else to lose, will I? But you will.'

'Don't threaten me. You wouldn't dare.'

'Try it, Giles. Just try it.'

'I know a lot of people at the Bar. Don't push me too far. I'll make sure the only place that will have you is one of your ghetto Chambers.'

'I'll still have my practice, Giles. And right now, any Chambers that doesn't have you at its helm would be good enough for me.'

Giles paused before replying, bitingly, 'Don't try to assuage your guilt by attacking me, Lee. It lacks conviction. And, I can assure you, it won't work.'

In the silence that followed, the sound of the court door being unlocked from the inside was clearly audible. Giles said nothing further and stalked into court. Lee remained outside. Her hands were shaking as she lit yet another cigarette. It seemed the further removed she was from her past, the more it claimed her, especially in situations like this. Giles would never know how perilously close she had come to slapping him.

And still no sign of Simone.

She saw her pupil. 'Anne-Marie,' she called out.

Anne-Marie hesitated. Lee wasn't surprised. She was angry, and it showed; but it wasn't directed at her pupil. Most of that was still reserved for Giles. The rest was directed inwards.

'Come over here a minute, please,' Lee said, walking towards a small room – the same room where she had allowed herself to be persuaded into giving evidence. In that respect, Giles was right, she thought bitterly. Any anger at him, however well deserved, didn't make her feel any better.

Anne-Marie started to object. 'But I'm needed in court. I—'

'Look, the jury have heard all the evidence. Giles can take his own note of the summing-up; after all, he'll be getting paid for this, not you.' When she still looked unsure, Lee added, 'I'm still officially your pupil-mistress, don't forget. If he says anything, you can blame it on me; let him come and take it up with me, if he likes. Don't worry, it won't take long.'

The room had no furniture, save for a table and three chairs, none of which matched. Lee perched on the end of the table, swinging one long leg in front of her, being careful not to drop ash on her suit or blow smoke in her pupil's face. Anne-Marie remained standing near the door, looking for all the world as if she was ready to bolt. It suddenly occurred to Lee that, save for their very first meeting, she always appeared this nervous. Lee wondered whether there was something in her that made Anne-Marie twitchy or whether she was always like this.

When Lee spoke again, she was surprised her voice sounded so patient. 'Don't worry, I'm not going to bite your head off. But I need to know, did Giles tell you to speak to Mrs Wilson? About me giving evidence?'

When she didn't reply, Lee could feel her patience slipping away, fast. But then she remembered, the girl was in an awkward position. Giles was not only head of the Chambers at which she was a pupil, but also her uncle. Professional and personal loyalty. Maybe she should cut her some slack.

'Look, I don't blame you. He was the one who promised me he would speak to her, and it's not something that should be left to a pupil anyway. I won't tell him, but I've got to know.'

Anne-Marie looked at her, clearly deciding what to do. Finally, she said, 'He didn't tell me anything like that. I expect he meant to. He probably forgot. There was so much to do on this case,' she added lamely.

Lee noticed that Anne-Marie could not look her in the eye but she had no doubt that she was telling the truth. 'OK,' she said wearily. 'At least I know now.' She paused, then asked, 'How did she do?'

'I thought she was very good. Very believable.' Anne-Marie had now moved a little away from the door but she would not look directly at Lee. 'At least, I believed her. She was very brave too. It can't have been easy for her.'

'What do you think the jury thought?'

Anne-Marie shook her head. 'I don't know. Some of them were definitely on her side, but . . .' She shrugged.

'And the trial generally? I know date rapes are hard to prove but what do you think?'

Anne-Marie hesitated before speaking. 'Well, the defendant did come over quite well . . .'

Lee didn't want to hear any more. She stood up abruptly. 'Thanks. You'd better go back inside.' As Anne-Marie reached the door, Lee added, 'I'm sure your *uncle* is wondering where you are.' It was a nasty, bitchy thing to say but Lee didn't feel like being fair to anyone at this particular moment. And, although she had nothing against Anne-Marie personally, the way she had joined Chambers still left a bitter taste in her mouth.

Anne-Marie turned. For the first time, she looked her pupil-mistress full in the face. Lee was shocked by the depth of bitterness she saw there. 'You think he's really my uncle, don't you?' Anne-Marie suddenly looked, and sounded, much older than her twenty-three years. 'He just likes me to call him that. Always has.' She laughed. It was not a pleasant sound. 'He says it turns him on.'

Lee wished she was still sitting down. 'Is that what you had to do . . .'

'To get into Chambers? No. It's been going on for years.' Anne-Marie opened the door and left the room.

The summing-up couldn't be faulted. Amery and his solicitor were both taking a careful note of what Judge Morton said to the jury. Anne-Marie was also writing; Giles was not. But Lee was only half listening now. Simone had slipped in, almost unnoticed, just before the start of the summing-up, and sat as close as possible to the door. Lee couldn't speak to her now, or even move to sit next to her, not during the summing-up. She tried to catch her eye, but Simone deliberately avoided her, her eyes fixed on the judge.

As soon as the jury had retired to consider their verdict and the judge had risen, Simone moved swiftly round the back of the court and spoke to the prosecution team – Giles, Anne-Marie, the representative from the Crown Prosecution Service, and the police officer who had conduct of the case. Lee couldn't hear, but whatever was said, the conversation was very brief. Then she returned to where she had been seated, collected her bag and coat, and left court, without looking back. Lee rushed out of court behind her.

'Simone! Simone! Wait up!' Lee had to shout her name down the corridor. People in the passageway, including barristers and solicitors, turned round at the commotion, but she didn't care. She ran after Simone, catching up with her at the lifts.

Simone was jabbing the Down button impatiently.

'Simone, I . . .' Lee reached out to take her arm, but Simone shrugged it off as though she had been burnt. Just then the lift arrived, its doors opening to show that, mercifully, it was empty. Simone quickly stepped inside. Lee followed immediately behind her.

'I don't want you in here. Get out, or else I'm getting out.'

'Simone, let me explain. I . . .'

Simone made a move to leave, but the doors closed before she could do so. She turned and looked at Lee. Lee expected her to be angry, and had steeled herself for that. What she wasn't prepared for was the complete lack of expression on her face. It was as if a door had slammed in front of her.

'There's nothing you can say to make this better, Leanne. Nothing, you hear?' Simone folded her arms. 'You waited a long time for this, didn't you? A long time to get your own back on the mouthy girl who used to bully you and poke fun at you in school and got the one guy you really fancied. And what a way to do it.'

'It wasn't like that at all, and you know it. I—'

'You really put one over on me, I have to give you that. Remember when you came round to see me that day, after it happened? "I'm your friend. Your friend, Simone",' she mimicked. 'You knew I never wanted to report this but you made me feel I ought to. Just two days ago I spent the night at your house and you never, not once, told me what you were going to do.'

'But I didn't know, not until the morning of the trial. Simone, you can't believe I planned this. I had no choice. You heard me in there. I didn't want to do it. Giles was supposed to tell you . . .' But Simone wasn't listening.

'You know, the only thing I was surprised about was that you didn't tell them I was the slut of Fordyce Park, dropping my knickers for anyone. I mean, so what if someone like me gets raped? Or gets raped again in court? Because that's what you helped him to do. Neither you nor your fucking boss lifted a hand to help.'

Lee was close to tears. 'Simone, how could you even think something like that?'

'At school I was so jealous of you. I always thought you had class. Well, you might have more money, drive a flash car and wear expensive clothes, Leanne Mitchell, but you're more of a gutter brat than you ever were. I should know.' She paused, almost as if she was gasping for breath. 'I wouldn't have treated a dog the way you treated me. You set me up from the start.'

The lift doors opened on the ground floor and Simone walked

out as other people entered. For no particular reason, it suddenly occurred to Lee that they had managed to travel all the way to the ground floor without someone else coming into the lift.

'What floor?' someone asked her. She looked at them blankly before she realised where she was.

'This one, thanks.'

She rushed out, not to catch up with Simone – it was too late for that, in every respect. But she had to get out of this place. She thought of Ray, how he used to be – and how he was when she last saw him. She was hurting people she cared for, all for this job.

For the first time since she had come to the Bar, she seriously wondered whether it was all worth it.

After the verdict, which took longer than either he or Amery had imagined, Giles was astonished, on leaving court, to find Oliver Morrison, QC, waiting for him. He knew he wasn't trying anything in the court building, and he hadn't been watching the proceedings. What was he doing here?

Morrison stepped forward, grasped his hand and vigorously pumped it up and down. 'Congratulations,' he said.

Clearly he hadn't heard. 'But I lost,' Giles protested, glumly.

'Giles, you didn't have to win. Everyone knows these cases are impossible. One can't help it if the case is weak, or the complainant lying. The important thing is, in the current climate you've done a criminal case which cannot help but bring you to the notice of the powers that be. What with your extensive civil experience, I think this will clinch it for you.' Morrison smiled broadly. 'Yes, I think this could just do it.'

Lee was staring at the bottom of her empty glass when she realised part of the clock was reflected in its surface. Why hadn't she noticed that before? She squinted at the image, not bothering to raise her head to look at the real thing on the wall; she wasn't entirely sure she was able to, anyway. Four o'clock. She'd been in this bar for hours. The sandwich she had ordered for lunch was still untouched, and was now beginning to look distinctly unappetising – hard and curled up at the edges, soggy in the middle. She ate it anyway. She had to eat something if she was going to be able to drive home.

She rang Chambers and spoke to Tom, who told her the verdict. It was another three hours before she left.

She drove slowly, and particularly carefully. In spite of what had happened earlier, she thought about going to see Simone, but then dismissed the idea. Besides, she suspected it wouldn't be the first twenty-four hours that were the hardest, but the next thousand or so, after it had sunk in. When she reached the Elephant and Castle, she saw the light on in Brendan's office. That was unusual. His secretary had said he had been visiting relatives in Ireland. Plus, as a family man, he usually took his work home with him rather than stay late at the office. But she knew it wouldn't be anyone else. He couldn't afford to pay for this kind of overtime, and he employed too few people to be able to give anyone time off in lieu.

No time like the present. She pulled over, got out of the car and rang the buzzer.

After the fourth ring, she was about to give up when a voice came through the entryphone. 'You're too fucking early. You said eight, eight thirty.' The voice sounded slightly slurred but it was definitely Brendan's.

'Brendan, it's Lee. Open up, I have to talk to you.'

His surprise was obvious. 'Lee? What are you doing here? Look, can't it wait? I'm expecting someone.'

'So I gather, but it can't wait, Brendan. I've got to talk to you. Now. It won't take long.' That last was a lie. If she didn't get the answers she wanted, it might take all night. Then again, what would she do if she did?

It seemed a long while before she heard the click of the door as he pressed to let her in. She walked upstairs to his office. The whole place was clean and tidy but had clearly seen better days. A coat of paint wouldn't have gone amiss, not to mention new desks, new chairs, new carpets. The door to Brendan's office was ajar. She pushed it open to find him sitting at his desk, his head in his hands. A pile of papers was pushed carelessly to one side. Evidently he had been drinking too; his choice was single malt whisky.

He looked up as he heard the door. There were bags under his eyes, and deep grooves around his mouth that Lee couldn't remember having seen there before.

'I've been calling you,' she began. 'They told me you were away.'

'Hector's out of it,' he said.

'I know. Peter Fairfax told me. That, plus the old man's health, means he's going for an expedited hearing date for the trial.' She paused, then added, 'You heard about Ray.' It was more statement than question.

'I saw him today.' Brendan poured some whisky into a coffee mug in front of him.

Lee stood in the doorway, just looking at him. She knew what she wanted to ask him, and sensed that, even in his inebriated state, she would have to use a great deal of tact to get what she wanted. Unfortunately for her, like most occasional drinkers, alcohol seemed to cancel out tact. 'Why did you do it, Brendan?'

He stared at her as if he was struggling to keep her in focus. 'I don't know what you're talking about.' He was making an effort to pronounce every word clearly but it was still unconvincing.

'Yes you do.'

'You think I'd be mad enough to do something like that to Ray Willis? I'd be too fucking scared to. Besides, I liked the bugger.'

'Last time I saw you together, you didn't seem very close. In fact, there was downright hostility between you two, as I recall. Remember? At Clive's bail hearing?'

Brendan kept staring at her. He hadn't quite drunk his way into a stupor but Lee could see he had made a good start.

'So he took his business elsewhere. I was pissed off. So what? If I had every client who pissed me off sorted, I wouldn't have any left.'

Lee came forward and sat down in the chair opposite his desk.

'Ever read Shakespeare, Brendan? *Julius Caesar*?'

'Jesus Christ, Lee, what is this? Twenty fucking Questions? First you accuse me of putting Ray in the hospital, then—'

'Ray gave me the clue, right there. Cassius and his "lean and hungry look". Bet you didn't even know he'd read any Shakespeare. All those years representing him and neither of us knew . . .' Lee shook her head slowly, as much to clear it as anything else. 'I didn't want to believe it, not at first. But it was definitely you he tried to warn me about. And he knew he was taking a risk. He said things could get nasty.' She leaned forward. 'Why, Brendan?' When he said nothing, she continued, 'He could die, you know. You're a good Catholic, Brendan. You really want that on your conscience?'

He turned away, almost as if he couldn't bear to look at her. When he finally did, his eyes were full of tears. 'When I went to see him, I . . .' He stopped. With an effort, he continued, 'I went to say sorry.' Suddenly he reached out and grabbed her hand in his, his words coming out in a rush. 'I didn't do that to him, Lee, honest. I had no idea. I would never have any part in anything like that. You must believe me.'

Lee looked down at her dark, elegant, manicured hand in his paler, rougher one. Slim hands; another thing they had in common. His were as slim as the rest of him . . .

He was willing her to believe him, and she did, at least about this. 'I didn't think you could do anything as barbaric as that,' she

245

said slowly. 'But you knew about it, didn't you?' When, again, he wouldn't answer, she asked, 'Why did you two really fall out?'

He gave a heavy sigh, his shoulders drooping as he did so. He looked like a man desperate to unburden himself, to confess and be absolved. 'You know that young girl Clive was with? That time he was arrested and we had to get him bail? That was Ray's half-sister.'

'So? Sixteen-year-olds sneak into clubs all the time. What's that got to do with you?'

'That was no accident. I sent her there.' He paused as he poured himself another drink. 'Ray didn't know.' He gulped down the whisky. 'Clive likes women, different types for different moods. He was in a mood for something young and fresh that night. I didn't have to sell him very hard to Kelly; virtually every woman this side of sixty is practically throwing her knickers at him anyway.' He paused. 'That stuff in the papers? That was true. And seeing as I already feel like something you would scrape off your shoe, you might as well know that wasn't the first time. Remember when you came to see him at Miller Street? "Don't forget to bring what we discussed," he said. Well, he wasn't talking about his clothes. I had a girl in there less than six hours after you left.'

'How did you get her past the front desk?'

'With Lambert as Custody Sergeant?' Brendan's laugh alone told her how easy that would have been. 'He wanted to watch.'

'What about the drugs? From when he was arrested?'

'Come on, Lee. How many people you know drive fast on grass?'

Lee remembered asking herself that same question. 'But the police said—'

'I know what the police said. I was there, remember, when Lambert told us? The same Lambert who, before his *very* recent promotion, was involved in Ray's arrest at Miller Street.'

Lee remembered how adamant Ray had been about not saying

who gave him the drugs. But where would Ray go to meet someone like Clive? They might as well be from different planets, their lives were so totally different.

'Ray and Clive have a connection?'

'Drug connection, no. Ray's not his supplier, if that's what you mean.' Brendan took another gulp of whisky. The words were tumbling out, now. He might regret this later, but right now he felt better for it. Better than he'd felt in over a year. Besides, what could Lee do about it? Ray had pleaded guilty long ago. Even if it could be reopened, who would be believed? Him or Clive? It was old news now, dead and buried.

'I persuaded Ray to take the rap for the cannabis. It was Clive who was stopped that night, not Ray. Ray had been nicked again, as usual, and had called me from Miller Street. An hour earlier, Clive had also called me. Like I said, he'd been arrested in Maida Vale, but I'd managed to get my old friend Lambert to have him transferred to Miller Street, where he was waiting for him. Clive paid Ray enough to make it worth his while.' His laughter sounded harsh in the quiet office. 'You know, Ray only agreed to it provided I got you to represent him.' Brendan paused, then continued, 'Even though he's been cautioned, Clive hasn't got any drug *convictions* in this country – I've made sure of that. And the stuff he has in the States, well, they're only a fraction of what he could have had. He doesn't know I know about those. I decided to make my own inquiries. And everyone knows that in the Land of the Free, the rich white man with a couple of grams of coke in his pocket can drive right past a team of police officers rousting some poor black sod for crack. That's what this is all about, drugs. Right from the very beginning. He didn't want his father to know but the ironic thing was, he always did. Clive had to pay some suppliers, otherwise he would have been toes up in the Everglades. That's why his dad took the money – to help the prodigal son.'

'So the confession was true? Clive didn't do it?'

'Clive didn't do all of it, just the forty. The hundred grand wasn't enough, but by then Clive knew exactly what to do. I daresay he was very good at his dad's signature by the time he'd finished practising. The handwriting analysis was inconclusive, remember?'

Lee paused. Her mind was racing. 'But Frederick's loaded. That kind of money's peanuts to him. Surely he could have raised it legitimately.'

'Not in forty-eight hours. Not if you've just underwritten your elder son's gambling debts. Not to mention the matter of a very private, very expensive drying-out clinic after Hector hit the bottle during his divorce.'

'So all that stuff about picking him up as a duty solicitor client when he was arrested for the fraud—'

'—was not complete bullshit, Lee. I really was acting as duty solicitor the first time I met him. Back then, he'd been arrested for cannabis possession. Clive's a dabbler, you see. Grass, coke, Es sometimes. Anyway, it was nothing much, just personal use, but the police weren't going to caution him again, so it would have been all over the papers. It's one thing getting arrested in the States, but not here where his father gets invited to the Queen's Garden Party and has never had so much as a parking ticket. I managed to "persuade" them to give him one more chance. That was five years ago.'

'How did it come to this, Brendan? You used to stand for something, remember? Now you're just his fixer and his pimp.'

'Don't get on your bloody high horse with me, Lee. Have you returned that suit yet? Oh, yes, he told me. Said he didn't realise you'd cost him so much.'

'Well then he didn't tell you everything. I sent it back Brendan, so don't try and put that one on me. I won't say I wasn't tempted' – she remembered with a momentary pang how it had taken her a while to get it sent back – 'but at the end of the day, I haven't done anything other than represent him in court to the best of my ability. I haven't tried to find him women, or persuade innocent men to take the blame for his wrongdoings.'

'Innocent? Don't make me laugh! When was Ray Willis ever innocent?' Brendan stood up so suddenly his chair fell over behind him. 'You think I like what I've become? Six years of training, and what did it get me? Two kids, a wife at home with a third on the way, and me running a tiny legal aid practice in the armpit of South London, worrying every month whether I can pay the staff. All my clients are like Ray. Correction – I wish they were; some haven't even got his brains. You think I like working from this shit hole? You think I like going to firms like Robbs Ellenburg Bennett and feeling I have to apologise for my very existence?' He walked over to the window and looked out, his back to her. 'I'm as good as they are, Lee. Any of them. When I helped Clive out I thought he could put in a good word for me with his father and his other rich friends. But no, all I get to do is his dirty work – clean up the mess that firms like Robbs Ellenburg Bennett wouldn't soil their hands with.' He shrugged. 'But it pays, I suppose – better than legal aid, at least.'

'Did he do that to Ray?'

'Ray had a lot of enemies, so I understand,' came a voice from the door.

Both Lee and Brendan jumped. Clive held up a small bunch of keys. 'I let myself in, as you can see.' As Brendan instinctively patted his pockets, Clive continued, 'Oh, they're not yours. You lent me a set a long time ago and I took the precaution of having spares cut. Isn't it amazing what you overhear when you're not expected?' He leaned against the doorway.

'How long have you been here?' Lee asked, amazed at how calm she sounded.

'Long enough. Brendan was expecting me. I suppose he forgot.

Seems you forgot some other things too, didn't you, Brendan? How to keep a confidence? Never mind. I don't expect it will change anything.'

Lee stared at him as he leaned nonchalantly against the door frame. Clive might be capable of many things, but she couldn't believe attempted murder was one of them. What had happened to Ray was one of the most grisly things she had ever seen. He had overheard their conversation. If he had done it, he couldn't possibly look so calm and agreeable – not unless he had ice-water in his veins. Could he?

'Well, Brendan,' Clive continued, 'mustn't keep a lady in suspense. Do you think I was responsible for what happened to Ray? Well?' he repeated, after he heard no reply. 'Do you?'

Lee watched as Brendan tried to look Clive in the eye and couldn't. He looked pitiful. Abruptly he reached out for the whisky bottle, but Clive came over and took it from his trembling hand.

'I think you've had enough, don't you?' Clive said in the kind of voice reserved for old people and small children. He looked over his shoulder at Lee. 'He probably won't remember any of this tomorrow. Good job he wasn't giving evidence on oath; no one would believe him. The state he's in.

'I've met Ray a few times through Brendan and what little I know of him I liked. That's why I've made sure he's getting the best possible care – well, the best you can get in an NHS hospital, anyway.'

Lee looked at Brendan, then back at Clive. 'You two deserve each other. Keep the rest of your fee. Find yourself another barrister. I'm sure you won't have any problem, even now. After all, everyone wants a piece of this trial.'

Clive chuckled softly, looking for all the world as if he'd just heard the most wonderful joke at a cocktail party. 'And exactly what are you going to tell the judge? Or the Bar Council? That, suddenly, you're double-booked – for the case all those other big boy lawyers were drooling to get on to? Because you don't really think I'm going to agree to let you go, do you?'

'I'll tell the judge what Brendan told me.'

'The evidence of a drunken solicitor. I don't think he'll thank you for that. Everyone's thinking I did him a huge favour by getting him on board this case in the first place. Besides, just supposing any of what he said was true, you wouldn't want to get him struck off, would you? What would happen to his practice? His family? And I'm not a lawyer, Lee, but won't you be breaching some kind of lawyer-client privilege yourself?'

Lee met his gaze. There *was* ice water in his veins. 'But surely you can't want me that badly,' she said calmly. 'There are dozens of lawyers who'd jump at the chance to represent you. Besides,' Lee paused for effect, hoping insults would succeed where reason clearly wasn't going to, 'I can't stand the sight of you.'

Clive did not look in the least offended. 'Do you know why I wanted you to represent me, Lee? Pride and ambition. Your great strengths, but also your great weaknesses. And I can use the odd weakness or two. I'm a specialist in weaknesses.' He grinned at both his lawyers. 'You know, that's what we three have in common. We all have the immigrant drive. We're all outsiders. This country was built on the backs of people like us, busting a gut to prove ourselves. I recognised that in you the first time I met you. In Brendan, too. And I wasn't wrong, about either of you. Besides,' he looked her up and down, 'I quite like the sight of you. And I'd like to have you – around for the trial, that is.' Then almost as an afterthought he asked, 'How's David? Still in the States, I understand.'

Lee remembered an oblique reference to her lover once before, in the cells in the police station. 'How do you know about him?'

'Just one of my interests, encouraging and promoting new talent. These music tours, they say they're for a couple of months but then they just get longer and longer. Sometimes they seem to go on for ever. And then you hear about stuff happening to musicians all the time – overdosing in hotel rooms, that sort of thing. Follows in the long, noble tradition of tortured genius.'

Lee tasted bile in her throat. She opened her mouth to speak but suddenly felt overwhelmed by nausea. She put her hand swiftly to her mouth. First Ray, then Simone. She wasn't going to sacrifice David, too.

Brendan stepped forward, galvanised into action by his last remark. 'Christ, Clive, don't make things any worse for yourself.'

'You know, you two are so touchy. Imagining things where there are none. I was just stating a fact. But I don't think there's anything we can usefully discuss, Brendan.' He gave them both his most dazzling smile as he looked at their stricken faces. 'I know I can rely on my legal team to do what's best for the client. Enjoy the rest of the evening. Don't worry,' he said, jangling the duplicate door keys, 'I'll let myself out.'

Chapter Twenty-Three

Life settled into a depressing routine in the four-week lead up to the trial. During the week, Lee would hurry home and spend as much time as possible waiting for the telephone to ring. Weekends, too. In fact, David had rung two or three times but evidently he'd forgotten the time difference; on each occasion she was in court. It may have been her imagination but it seemed to her that his calls were becoming less and less frequent. At that point she rang the promotor, only to find that the tour had run into financial difficulties and the new backer — who insisted on anonymity — had changed the itinerary. Lee felt more panic-stricken than ever.

The other thing she did, every day without fail, was to drive past Simone's house. Since their confrontation at court, she had neither seen nor heard from her. Her telephone number, always ex-directory, had been changed. Lee had made inquiries at Fordyce; the distinctly chilly reception she got there, especially from Sylvia Thomas, told her that Simone still largely blamed her for what had happened. None of the staff would tell her anything at first and when they eventually did, it was only to say that Simone had resigned from her post within a week of the verdict. Lee wasn't surprised. Try as you might, there was no way you could keep something like that a secret. She wondered whether she herself would have wanted to show her face after being so publicly disbelieved, especially to a class of teenagers.

Today found her, yet again, on Simone's doorstep. At first, Lee had been truly afraid Simone would do something drastic, but then she noted with relief that the post was being cleared daily. But the curtains remained drawn, and at night there was no light to be seen.

After the fifth, prolonged ring, Lee decided to give up for that day, but as she was walking back down the ramshackle garden path she felt she was being watched. She looked back abruptly, quickly enough to see the curtains twitching at the front bedroom window.

Lee stood in the middle of the path and shouted up at the window, 'Simone! You'll have to speak to me one day! You know you can't hide in there for ever!' But there was no reaction. She hadn't really expected any. She was about to call out again when she noticed the woman next door giving her a hostile stare. It was the way strangers had always been treated round here. She was most definitely a stranger now.

She sighed and turned away once again. She'd try again tomorrow.

Simone stood by the side of the window and parted the curtains an inch, no more. She watched as the sleek black car pulled away. It would be a cold day in hell before she ever spoke to her again. With the passage of time, she no longer blamed her for what had happened in court. If nothing else, she was realistic, and knew that, all things considered, she had been taking her chances pursuing her attacker through the courts; that was why she hadn't wanted to report it in the first place. But it was Lee who had been instrumental in persuading her to do so; Lee, the same woman who had given evidence on behalf of her rapist. Simone usually found it very difficult to trust people, but she had trusted Lee. She didn't care how reluctant Lee had been, or what her reasons were; the sense of betrayal, and in such a public way, ran so deep she couldn't see how anything her former friend had to say could possibly erase it.

What was that saying about God not giving you more than you could bear? It had been said by someone in the children's home as a prelude to some punishment or other. Well, Simone thought, He must think I can bear a lot. Anyway, her preference was 'God helps those who help themselves'. She picked up the telephone and dialled a number. It was answered on the second ring.

'It's me,' she said.

'I wondered when you'd ring back. You worked out what you want to do?'

'I've been asking around. He'll be at Jezebel's next Saturday – you know, that club in Croydon? One of his singers is doing a live PA and I know he'll be there.'

'How are you so sure? That's not the only act he handles.'

'One, he's fucking her. Two, and more important where he's concerned, he's got a lot of money invested in her. Trust me, he'll be there.' She paused, then asked, 'Can you make it?'

'Just try and stop me.'

Jezebel's was busy, as was usual on a Saturday. Steve finally found a parking space for his BMW a few streets away. Not that he minded, he thought as he carefully reversed into the space. It would mean a short walk; all the better for people to see the merchandise. He glanced sideways at the young woman sitting beside him. Yes, he could really hit the big time with this one. The music industry being what it was, there was always a market for white girls who sounded black. And it helped that this one had the hots for him, too.

His passenger looked over and smiled softly at him. She raised her hand to touch his cheek. 'Still thinking about last night?' she asked him.

Steve continued to look at her, studying her in a rather detached way that belied the smile he was wearing. Everything about her was soft now – her smile, her touch, her eyes as she looked at him. It never ceased to amaze him how women changed after you had slept with them a few times. Their brains became soft, too. As a control technique, it hadn't failed him yet. Not that he was complaining, not with this one, given their professional relationship, but women could never hold his interest after that. All except Simone. She had been on to him right from the start. In bed, he always felt as if he had to please her rather than the other way round. Kept him on his toes, though. His smile deepened as he remembered. Maybe that's why he still thought about her, even now. He didn't think there was any way she would have him back, though. After all, he couldn't exactly convince her it was a misunderstanding.

His companion saw the change in his smile. She moved her hand from his face to his knee. She was slowly moving it upwards when the smile vanished.

'Behave yourself, Claire. We haven't got time for that.' He looked at his watch. 'Let's go.'

She snatched her hand back immediately. She was still looking chastened as they started to walk to the nightclub.

'What's up with you?' Steve said impatiently. 'You can't go in there looking miserable. That's not what they've come to see. Remember that.'

The manager was on hand to greet them. 'Y'all right, Steve? This must be Claire.' The manager's accent changed from Jamaican to Cockney. 'All right, darling?' He looked the scantily-clad woman up and down. 'I can see you've got a lot of talent. And Steve tells me you can sing, too.'

'Yeah. Just wait till you hear her.'

Claire walked ahead of Steve towards the dance floor cum stage. The music was deafening. As he started to follow her, a small group of black women looked admiringly at him, and askance at Claire. The manager whispered in his ear.

'I like the other one better.'

'Which one?'

'You know, the little one. Whatever happened to her?'

Steve was surprised he hadn't heard. He shrugged and said, conspiratorially, 'You know how these things go, Tony. Anyway, let me go and sort this one out.'

It was a couple of hours before Claire had to sing, during which time Steve was able to check out the crowd. It was predominantly black, with a few white faces, mostly women. Some Asian people, too. It was hard to get a good look at the women, what with Claire hanging around all the time, but he had been in this position before; he always managed somehow. One in particular caught his eye, mainly because he thought she was so beautiful he couldn't believe she was there on her own. He looked around for Tony; he would know who she was. But he was nowhere to be seen. From the length and shape of her legs he could tell she was tall for a woman. Being only average height for a man, he usually preferred smaller women, but her legs alone would be more than worth the effort.

He hardly paid any attention when Claire started singing. She really was quite good. Halfway through the first song she had clearly won over the crowd, which was no mean feat, but he had heard it all before. Besides, his attention was now fixed elsewhere. He tried to catch the woman's eye, but couldn't. That wasn't something he usually had a problem with. Strangely enough, she didn't seem to be paying too much attention to the music either. He was beginning to wonder whether she was deliberately avoiding his gaze.

Then suddenly she looked directly at him, gave him the most dazzling smile, and he knew he was in.

Almost before he knew it, he was standing next to her. She was still seated. He tried, with difficulty, to keep his eyes on her face. 'Is anyone sitting here?'

She looked at him. 'There is, now.'

There was barely enough room for two at the small table, but Steve didn't need to be asked twice. As he sat down, their legs touched. He could feel the outside of her thigh rubbing against his as she languorously crossed her legs. Firm. He liked that in a woman. She must have to work out every day to get a body like that. She looked just as good up close. They sat in silence for a few minutes, the woman slowly sipping her drink. Clearly she wasn't the talkative type.

'So, do you come here often?' It slipped out before he could stop it. Shit! Where did that come from? She must think he was a complete idiot.

He was right. She laughed softly but he heard the mocking tone loud and clear. 'Can't you do better than that?'

'Yeah. Sorry. What I meant to ask you was whether you'd like a drink.'

She raised her glass and looked at him. It was half-empty. 'I'm fine for the moment.'

'What are you drinking, anyway?'

She looked at him quizzically. 'Can't you tell a champagne flute when you see one? And not the rubbish they usually sell behind the bar. The good stuff.'

From her manner, Steve was becoming more and more convinced that she was here by herself, so either she knew the management or she had money. But best to make sure.

'Where's your man then, a good-looking woman like you?'

'I don't know.' She took another sip and looked at him speculatively. 'Right beside me, I think.'

He hadn't expected such a direct come-on, and it took him completely by surprise. He didn't even know this woman's name. He was still searching for a reply when she added, 'But I forgot – you came with someone.'

So she *had* noticed him. 'You mean the singer? No, it's not like that. We just work together.'

'Really?' She nodded towards the stage. 'Maybe you should tell her that.'

Steve looked over to where Claire was standing in front of the mike. She had come to the end of her set and was staring at them both, seemingly oblivious of the calls for an encore from the crowd. Clearly, she wasn't happy. She was about to walk over but something in Steve's eyes stopped her where she stood.

His companion suddenly downed the remainder of her drink, picked up a small handbag and started to get up.

'Don't worry. I'll still be here when you get back.'

She had turned away from him by now. Thank God for stretch Lycra. She looked over her shoulder at him. 'I'm not coming back. I'm going home.'

'Already?' He inspected his watch. 'But it's only half twelve.'

She looked slowly around the club and finally back at him. 'Nah, it's dry tonight. That girl's good, but if I'd wanted to see a singer I could have watched *Top of the Pops*. I didn't come here for that.'

'So what did you come down here for, then?'

'Well, I guess you'll never know now. I have to get a cab. Maybe I'll see you around.'

The way she looked at him left Steve in no doubt about her meaning. She had been making a serious play for him, even though they had only just met. It was almost as if she had deliberately picked him out, like a steer for branding, and waited until he fell right into her lap. It was a little disconcerting. In his experience, black women weren't usually so upfront about their interest in a man, particularly if it was sexual. But hey, it was the most exciting thing that was likely to happen to him tonight. And even he didn't get offers like this every day.

She was already collecting her coat by the time he had decided what to do. He came out just in time to help her put it on. All the men were staring at her. As he'd suspected, she was almost as tall as he was, and she wasn't even wearing heels, but she looked just as fantastic in the glare of the cloakroom lights – a little too much make-up, but no matter. And all that hair – man, she was just his type.

She smiled at him. 'At least you're a gentleman.'

'So why don't you let me take you home?' When she hesitated, he continued, 'Come on, it's cold outside. And why take a cab when you can travel home free, with my pleasant company thrown in? What's your name, anyway?'

'Is that the price I have to pay for getting a lift?'

'Well, I don't offer just anybody a ride in my car.' He gave her time to answer but she was just looking at him. If she wasn't so fuckable, he would have changed his mind then and there. Maybe she was married. He looked down at her hand. No ring, though that didn't necessarily mean anything; she could have taken it off.

Who cared about names anyway? Time enough for that later. 'Don't tell me then, if it's such a big secret.'

'I wasn't going to. What about your friend?'

'What about her? I'll be back to take her home, don't worry.'

Again, that speculative look. 'OK.'

That was all she said, but as they walked to his car, Steve already felt as if he had scored a small victory. She didn't live far, or so she said. The drive home was quiet, with music from Choice FM filling the empty spaces in the car. More than once he looked over at her. She had settled back comfortably in the front passenger seat, her eyes closed. She looked for all the world as if she was sleeping, except that occasionally her head would nod up and down, in time with the music.

'This is it, over here,' she said, pointing.

'You live here?' The words slipped out of his mouth before he could stop himself. He couldn't imagine a classy-looking woman like this living on this notorious council estate. It was the place everyone wanted to move from. Most of it was boarded up, and of the people living there, the majority were refugees, squatters, and students who couldn't afford to live anywhere else. Rumour had it even the drug dealers wouldn't trade here; no money in it.

'Well, not all of us can live in style like you do,' she remarked.

Steve furtively scanned the surroundings. Well, if she expected him to walk her to her door, she had another think coming. He couldn't drive any closer, and there was no way he was leaving his BMW round here, unattended, for any woman, no matter how enticing.

But even as he looked at her to tell her this, she smiled at him. 'Well, thanks for the lift. Listen, I know you have to head back, but would you like to come up for a drink before you go?'

The offer was tempting but he was going back to a place where he could have all the drinks he wanted. She would have to do better than that. Looking at her, he was sure she could.

She began to gather her things together. 'Sorry, I should have guessed. That leash of yours stretches only so far.'

'Just hold up there. No woman has me under manners. Never has, never will.'

'Good, I'll remember that.'

'You do that.'

'So, now we've sorted that out, you coming or not?'

It was both a challenge and an invitation, like the woman herself. The combination was irresistible. He couldn't get out of the car quickly enough. He still didn't like the area, though. Full of 'mugging alleys' – narrow, poorly lit walkways littered with rubbish. Even the police, when they came here – which was often – came mob-handed. She had better be worth it.

As they walked, he rested his hand on her hip just low enough to make his intentions clear. She didn't push it away.

'How much further?' he asked.

'You sound like you want something. Think you can handle it?'

'You got that right.'

'Don't worry, we're almost there. Tonight, you're going to get more than you ever dreamed of.'

Steve was grinning broadly now. It was always nice to have a sure thing. Who knows? If it was good enough, maybe he could nip back to the club, take Claire home, then come back for seconds . . .

Out of the corner of his eye, he saw something moving in the shadows. He stopped. As close as they were, his companion felt the tension in his body immediately.

'Did you see that?' he asked her.

'No. But even so, I'm not worried. I've got a big strong man to protect me.'

Steve smiled as she ran her hand down his back. He was about to move off when he saw it again. This time there was no mistake. The face came slowly into view, like the moon from behind a cloud. In the semi-darkness, Steve had to focus before he recognised who it was.

'What are you doing here?'

'I could ask you the same.' With a nod towards the woman with him, Simone continued, 'I see it didn't take you too long to find a replacement.'

'Steve, do you know this woman?'

'Nah,' he said dismissively. 'Just someone I had a thing with, you know? A sore loser.'

'I know. She told me all about it.'

It all happened so quickly that, later, all Steve would remember was pain. The pain of being taken in a headlock, so very suddenly, and having his head smashed against a wall. The shame of being beaten to the ground, face down on a bed of rubbish. And then the tearing, the ripping away – never in his worst nightmares had he imagined ever experiencing this.

Pain and shame. And all the time Simone was watching.

As Simone watched Winston and Steve, she was surprised at how dispassionate she felt. It was just a score she wanted settled. The books would be balanced. She would get on with her life as best she could, but the rape would always be part of her, like wearing glasses.

Steve would just have to learn that too. At least he wouldn't have to go through a trial. He would never report this to the police. Never in a million years. He wouldn't be coming on to any woman for a long time, either.

Simone leaned back against the wall and lit another cigarette.

Chapter Twenty-Four

Four in the morning found Lee with the shift workers, party-goers and other insomniacs at the local Seven-Eleven, which wasn't really all that local. Even the staff seemed to be sleepwalking. She picked up three packets of B&H, several magazines she neither needed nor was really interested in, a giant-sized packet of crisps, and a large tub of Häagen-Dazs ice cream. She looked down at what she was carrying. She seemed to be eating a lot of this recently. Comfort food. The last time she did that was when she was a teenager, back at Fordyce, and the resulting weight gain had only made her feel worse. She was eating so much of this junk recently that if it wasn't for the cigarettes she'd be as big as a house by now.

She saw her reflection in the glass doors on the way out. No one looked good at 4 a.m., but by any standards she looked a mess. Big, baggy jeans – not fashionably big, just big. An old Spike Lee sweatshirt of David's. A baseball cap that had definitely seen better days, worn mainly because she hadn't bothered to comb her hair. It took less than thirty seconds to walk from the counter to the door, but already she had a cigarette clamped between her lips. She looked anything but the principled, successful barrister. She certainly didn't feel very principled at the moment. How far did you compromise before you realised that you were on a slippery slope? And by the time you realised it, wasn't it already too late?

She started the engine, and put on a tape of David's own music.

It was a mixture of things he'd recorded, some with him playing violin against a reggae backdrop, other tracks with him playing bass guitar.

Tears pricked the back of her eyes. She didn't know why she played this stuff, or slept in his sweatshirt. It only made her feel miserable and wasn't any substitute for the real thing in any event. Perhaps she shouldn't worry about him. She knew he could handle himself in a fight – he'd been doing that since he was fourteen. But if your enemies come for you, when is it ever a fair fight? And what about what Clive had said about musicians overdosing?

It was now Sunday. In less than thirty-six hours the trial would be starting. She would have to make a decision.

She put her foot down on the accelerator. She had only been gone fifteen minutes, but maybe he had called.

There was no message when she returned home. Four fifteen. Lately she seemed to be living on her nerves. Sleep was out of the question. She didn't know whether to watch the repeats on TV or read one of the magazines, so she did both, with an interest in neither.

When the phone rang, it was 5.30 a.m. The early morning news had just started, and the airtight room was beginning to disappear under a fog of smoke. Usually she hated to hear the phone ringing at that time of the morning. It usually meant something bad had happened; that was how she had heard about her father. Now she scrambled to get it.

'At last. You know how I hate speaking to machines. You're the only person I would do that for.'

'David?' The line was bad but his voice sounded deep and reassuringly normal. 'You don't know how glad I am to hear from you. Where the hell have you been?'

He didn't sound too pleased. 'Well, that's nice. Not "How's the tour going?" or even "I miss you, D".'

'I do miss you. But D, listen to me. You've got to come back. Leave, right now. Don't tell anyone.'

'What? This line must be really bad. I thought you said I've got to leave.'

'That's right. Right now.'

'You mad? You know how long it took me to get this gig.'

'I know, but I wouldn't ask if wasn't really important.'

'Is your mother sick? I'd come back for that, even though she can't stand me.'

'No, it's not that. She's fine. So am I. Look, I . . . I can't tell you why. Just come home.'

'Are you seriously asking me to drop everything to come home, to give up the chance of a lifetime, just because you say so? I'm not going to do that, Lee. And you know I wouldn't ask you to if you were in my place. If there was an emergency, then yes, but not just because you say so.'

'David, I—'

'Didn't you hear me? I said no. Don't ask me again. Look, I'm on my break, so I just thought I'd call to see how you were. Maybe our next conversation will be better. Take care of yourself.' Click.

It was only after he'd put down the phone that Lee realised she still didn't know where he was, or when she would see him again.

'I know this is a cemetery but you look real miserable.' That was Verna Mitchell's pronouncement. 'Plus, you're as quiet as one of these graves.' She scrutinised her daughter's profile as intently as she could, given their differences in height. 'So, what's wrong?'

'Nothing, Mum.' Lee was standing slightly away from her father's grave, being careful not to let cigarette ash fall on the red and yellow flowers, or to let the smoke drift in that direction. He'd always hated smoking.

So did her mother. She looked at the cigarette with obvious

distaste. 'I see you've started again. Mind you don't do that in my house.'

'Fine. I'll just drop you off and go straight home.'

'What? You mean you won't stay for something to eat? I haven't seen you for a while.' Something in her voice clearly indicated that she needed her daughter's company.

'I'll be smoking,' Lee warned.

Verna frowned. 'You mean you can't do without them even for a few hours?'

'They help, at the moment.'

Verna said nothing more until they were driving back to her house. 'So,' she began, 'you going to tell me what's wrong or not?'

Lee sighed. 'Nothing. Just work.'

'Don't give me that. I made you. I know you. And I've seen you when you've been worried about work before. This is different.'

'Clive Omartian's trial is tomorrow.'

'I know.' Verna suddenly became very animated. 'I told them all at church to look out for you in the news.'

'Believe me, Mum, it's not all it's cracked up to be. Besides, it's not about me. I'm going to try and avoid the media as much as possible.'

'Oh.' Her mother was obviously disappointed. Then, out of nowhere, she said, 'I'm sorry about your friend.'

They had come to a red light. Lee stopped, and looked at her mother. 'You mean Simone?'

'Yes. That's who you're worried about, isn't it?'

Better to let her think that. Besides, she wasn't completely wrong. 'How did you find out?'

'When she lives round the corner from me? Did you think I wouldn't? You know what these people are like when it comes to keeping a secret.'

'Did they say anything . . . about me?'

'Just that you had some part in it, nothing else.' Verna paused, then continued, 'I believe her.'

'I thought you didn't like her.'

'What's that got to do with it? She's a young girl, she's on her own, anything can happen.' She paused again. They had pulled up outside her house. 'It nearly happened to me once, you know.'

Lee switched off the ignition, turned fully in her seat and stared at her mother. 'You never told me about this.'

'Well, it's not the kind of thing you tell your daughter. And it was a long time ago, before I met your father. Besides, nothing happened, not like what happened to her. But it almost did. Maybe that's why I still remember it . . .' Verna was staring straight ahead now. Lee didn't know what to say. She squeezed her mother's hand where it lay in her lap. They sat like that, in silence, for what seemed a long while.

'Come on,' Lee said finally, 'let's go inside. I'll stand in the garden and smoke whenever I need to so long as you don't put any meat on my plate.'

'A black vegetarian.' Even after all this time, Verna still couldn't fathom it. She wondered whether she had failed as a mother. 'Who would believe it?'

Hours later, Lee passed Simone's house on the way to her own home. Something had changed recently, because the curtains were open more often and the lights would be switched on. Whatever it was, it was definitely a welcome change. She thought about stopping, but decided against it. It was late, and there was only so much rejection a person could stand. She would try again tomorrow.

Since their last conversation in his office, Brendan hadn't spoken to Lee directly, only through her clerks. That was weeks ago. It was clear she didn't want to speak to him. Knowing her as he did, he was sure she was trying to do her level best to divest herself of this case. Unfortunately for her, she had one of the world's most active consciences, a luxury no barrister could afford, in his opinion, particularly not one in her position. Clive had her exactly where he wanted her.

Brendan knew she liked to arrive early, especially on the first day of trial – even more so now, he reckoned, given the circumstances. In the past, she had often had to insist that he was early too. He knew that she would be surprised to find him waiting for her.

He was right.

He was leaning on the wall near the Robing Room set aside for female counsel when Lee arrived. He guessed it was she from the footsteps – quick and purposeful, even now. Her step faltered just for a minute when she first saw him, but all the same she walked right up to him, looking him coldly up and down.

'What are you doing out here, Brendan? Looking for a date?'

'Seems I've found one.' Keep it light, he thought. He tried to smile. It was the kind of jocular thing that she would have said to him back in the good old days, when they had been friends as well as professionals. But his smile died when he saw her expressionless face. That really was a lifetime ago now.

'You look fucking terrible,' he said, gazing intently into Lee's face. She was as smartly dressed as ever, but the tension and strain of the last few weeks was deeply etched into her face.

'I know,' she snapped as she tried to open the door. The damn thing was stuck. Again.

Brendan watched her struggling with the handle for a full minute before saying, 'Let me do it.' He put his shoulder to the door and with a sharp twist of the handle, it sprang free.

'Thanks,' Lee muttered as she walked into the room. She put her bags down and immediately lit a cigarette. It was empty, as she'd expected, which was just as well, as this was a non-smoking room. But after all, it was only 8.30 a.m.

' "Thanks",' Brendan mimicked as he stood in the doorway. 'Why the hell bother to say anything if you're going to sound so ungracious about it?'

'Well, forgive me if I don't feel like being too gracious this morning,' she said sharply. 'I've got a liar, a fraudster and a manipulative psychopath for a lay client, and as for my solicitor . . .' she folded her arms and looked at him.

Brendan flushed, a mixture of embarrassment and anger. He stepped inside and closed the door.

'How could you do it, Brendan? After all the years we've known each other? I don't know how you got in so deep in the first place, but why did you have to get me involved in it?'

'Oh, come on, Lee, you wanted that case as much as any other barrister in the Temple, don't forget. And when was the last time you were sure you had a truthful client? What made you think you could expect that from him?'

'The difference is, you knew he was lying all along. I didn't. I may suspect people aren't telling me the truth but I don't have them come right up to me and as good as admit it after stringing me along for months, and then still expect me to lie to the court and the whole world by telling them he's innocent.' She paused, then continued in a quieter voice, 'You shouldn't have done that to me, Brendan. I thought we were friends.'

Try as she might to disguise it, Brendan could hear the hurt underlying Lee's last comment. He looked away from her. 'Have you thought about what you're going to do?'

'What the hell *can* I do?' she asked. 'It seems to me I've got three choices: plead and beg with Clive to let me out, which I'm sure he's bound to do,' she added sarcastically. 'Go and see the judge in Chambers, tell him what's happened and declare myself professionally embarrassed, in which case I may never see David again—'

'And Clive knows where you live,' Brendan added.

'I know. Did you tell him?' Lee felt herself getting angry again. It felt good though, better than feeling compromised and blaming herself.

'Christ, you really don't think much of me, do you? I didn't even tell him where *I* lived, but he knows. Don't you think he's capable of finding out on his own?'

Lee didn't answer that. Instead she continued, 'The other option is to go ahead and do what he wants.'

And become like me, Brendan added silently. He watched her as she fished another cigarette out of the packet and lit it from the stub of her first one. He had never seen her look quite so haggard before.

'So?' he asked gently.

'What choice do I have? Still, maybe if I speak to him he might change his mind.'

'Well, it's worth a try,' Brendan said, trying to sound cheerful, but it was a forlorn hope and both of them knew it. 'Let's go and see whether he's arrived.'

'Now?' She looked at the clock. It was eight fifty. 'He won't be here yet. He won't want to miss his big Kodak moment. Especially not now.'

'It can't hurt to check, can it? Anyway, I'm sure the press are already out there.'

Another woman barrister entered the Robing Room as they left. She gave Brendan a surprised look but said nothing. Then Lee saw a familiar figure.

'I've got to speak to Peter,' she said to Brendan. 'I'll see you downstairs. I won't be long.'

Peter Fairfax greeted her cheerfully as she approached. He had the confident look of a man fully ready and prepared for trial.

'Morning, Lee. All set then?'

'I was going to ask you the same thing. Do you have all your witnesses here?'

'Come on, Lee, it's not even nine o'clock yet. Since when do witnesses arrive an hour and a half early? But everyone's expected, including the handwriting experts. We're calling Hector, as you know.'

'Yes. I'm surprised you're still proceeding against the father.'

'Well, that's up to Nicholas. He was trying to get his interview excluded, but in the light of the handwriting evidence, I don't know. I haven't heard from him or his solicitors, surprisingly.'

'I read in the papers that he hadn't been well recently.'

'That's as may be, but the Crown want pleas from both the father and Hector for everything. You know, your client would really be doing his father a favour if he pleaded. Have you spoken to him again about that?' When she didn't reply, he asked, 'Are you all right, Lee? You look very tired this morning.'

'I'm fine, Peter. You know how it is with a big case. You're always tired. Nothing a good night's sleep wouldn't cure. In fact, I'm going to speak to Clive now, but don't hold your breath on that.' She paused, then added, 'I don't suppose you've considered dropping the case against Clive?' But even as she said it, she knew he wouldn't. If she had a case as solid as his, she wouldn't either.

Her former pupil-master was too polite to laugh in her face, but he smiled indulgently as he remarked, 'Nice try, Lee. I'll be in the Bar Mess should you wish to speak to me after you've conferred with Omartian junior.'

Lee watched as he swept away, his robes flapping behind him, then made her way downstairs. Brendan was waiting near the front entrance. No sign of Clive. A few more people had arrived for other cases, but it was still fairly quiet. Inside, that was. Outside, the scene was just as she had expected and feared. The press were already out in force on the steps of the court building.

'I told you he'd wait to make his big entrance,' Lee said as she stood beside Brendan.

'And speak of the devil,' he replied, directing his attention outside.

A sleek, familiar-looking sedan drew up. Parker got out and opened the rear passenger door. As Clive stepped out, instantly the assembled throng homed in like moths to a flame. Lee couldn't hear anything but she could see that, as he made his way up the steps, shielded by Parker, he wasn't speaking to any journalists. He was, however, smiling and waving, and moving just slowly enough to provide quite a few photo opportunities. He had the air of a man who had everything arranged to his advantage. Lee felt a nasty taste in her mouth.

He spotted his lawyers as soon as he entered the building, and walked directly over to them.

'Good morning,' he said. He looked around. 'Is my father here yet?'

Somehow that wasn't the first thing Lee had expected him to say. 'I haven't seen him yet, nor his lawyers. He's been very ill, I hear.'

Clive shrugged. 'Apparently. I read about it in the papers. I hope that doesn't hold things up. Are we all ready to go, at least?'

'Why don't the three of us find somewhere to have a chat?' Lee said, steering him away from his driver. There was something very sinister about Parker. She wondered why she'd never noticed it before.

'So, have you spoken to the prosecution yet?' Clive asked, as soon as they had found a room where they could talk privately.

'Only about his witnesses,' Lee replied. They were all standing, she and Clive on opposite sides of the table, Brendan leaning by the door. 'He's expecting them all to attend, including the handwriting experts. Look, Clive, Fairfax wanted to know whether you would consider pleading.'

'You told him my answer, didn't you?'

'But if you do, you'll only have to plead to the forty grand.

Your father's putting his hands up for the rest.'

Clive folded his arms. 'I don't think so. Really, Lee, I'm surprised at you. I thought we'd settled this.' There was a menacing edge to his voice now.

Lee tried a different tack. 'What if your father doesn't come today? He's old and ill. The prosecution might want an adjournment.'

'No. No more adjournments. I want to go ahead today. I'm fed up of this thing hanging over my head.'

'It mightn't be up to you. As your lawyer, I must advise you that if the prosecution ask for an adjournment in those circumstances, they'll probably get it.'

'Well, consider yourself instructed to object strenuously, very strenuously indeed.' He looked at them both. 'I know my legal team will defend me fearlessly; after all, you're both so upright and principled.'

Lee didn't know which was worse; the fact that he was openly mocking her, or the fact that he felt so free to do so. Gritting her teeth, she pressed on.

'If, in spite of my objections, they get the adjournment, the trial could be put back for months. Time enough for you to instruct another barrister, someone who doesn't know the truth.'

'Lee, for the last time, I'm not going to sack you. And I think it would be . . . inadvisable, shall we say, to get yourself removed from this case. If we're going to keep going round in circles, we might as well end this discussion here.'

Lee stared at him. 'Very well, then,' she said finally. 'Wait here a minute while I go and speak to Peter again. I may be able to find out something more.'

'You do that,' Clive said. He watched her as she opened the door to leave, then added, 'Lee, I just want you to know how very pleased I've been with your work. I'm sure I'll have matters in the future where I'll need your special expertise.'

274

Lee turned round and looked at him. Those vivid blue eyes showed, as clearly as if he had said it in words, that he had her right where he wanted her – bought and paid for, just like Brendan. This wouldn't end, not with this case. It would never end.

Right then, she knew what she had to do.

Clive laughed as his barrister slammed the door shut behind her.

Brendan looked at him. 'You just have to rub it in, don't you? What the fuck was that last comment about?'

'So what's your problem, then?'

'You. You're my fucking problem. You make me sick to my stomach.'

'Yes, but not so sick that you won't take my money and do anything I tell you. Isn't that right, Brendan?'

Brendan paced round the small room. 'Let her out of this, Clive.'

'Just what *is* going on between you two?'

'Not what you think. It's just . . . I've known her since she started. I got her into this. We used to be friends. Real friends – not that I suppose you'd know what that means.'

'Such concern. I'm touched.' Clive was sitting down now. He leaned back in his chair. 'Go on, Brendan, I could use a laugh this early in the morning. Tell me why I should let her out.'

'One, she could go to the judge anyway.'

'She knows the risks she runs if she does that.'

'She could do it anyway. And it's not even so much about the principle of the thing, now. Don't let that exterior fool you. Bottom line, you know Lee's a street fighter. That's what makes her such an effective jury advocate. The cut and thrust of life at the Bar, that's child's play compared to where she grew up. The thing about street fighters is, once their backs are against the wall, they don't have anything to lose. She could tell the judge *everything*, don't you understand? Not just about this case. About you and Ray, her boyfriend – everything.'

'No, I don't think so. Whatever else she is, she's not stupid.'

'No, that she's not. She could carry on with the trial, of course, but Clive, do you really want to be represented by someone who clearly hates the sight of you? She told you as much herself.'

'And I told her, as you may recall, that it was immaterial to me how she felt about me.'

'Two, she knows you did it, you've admitted as much. She can't allow you to give evidence, not if she knows you're going to go into the witness box and lie. The Crown have a strong case, what with your father's confession and Hector. If you don't give evidence, the way things are going, your chances will be significantly worse.'

'Oh, but I have every intention of giving evidence.'

'Then she can't let you do it. If you start to lie on oath, she's duty bound to withdraw from the case.'

'Next thing, Brendan, you'll be telling me I'll be the first guilty defendant to lie with the full knowledge and complicity of his barrister. In the circumstances, I think Lee knows where her duty lies.' He was beginning to look slightly bored now. 'Any other convincing arguments?'

Brendan took a deep breath. He clasped his hands together, almost as if he was praying. 'I'd take it as a personal favour if you'd find another barrister, Clive. All those years I've known you, I've done whatever you asked.'

'Because I paid you good money. You didn't do it out of the goodness of your heart.'

'But we both know I've done things for you no lawyer should have to do for his client, things I'll have to live with.' He looked down. 'But that was my choice. I'll have to live with it. Lee shouldn't have to.'

'No one held a gun to her head and forced her to take the case.

She was dying for it, just like every other brief in the Temple.'

'But she didn't know the truth. Now she does, everything's changed. She wants out. Look,' he added eagerly, 'I'll talk to her, if you like. She can say she was professionally embarrassed. That way you can save face and get a new brief, plus I'm pretty sure she'll be bound by the Bar Code of Conduct not to tell her replacement what she knows.' Brendan paused. He didn't know what else to say. The only thing left for him to do was beg. 'Please, Clive.'

It was an impassioned argument. For a moment, Brendan thought he'd succeeded. Clive stood up and walked over to him. He put his hand on his arm and gave him a sympathetic smile.

'Not a chance, Brendan. You see, I just don't feel like it. Now, I'm going to see whether my father has arrived. Coming?'

It was a while before Brendan could bring himself to speak. 'You really are a bastard, you know that, Clive?'

'Well, I'll be sure to ask my father about that when I see him.' He smiled at him. 'Don't forget to switch the lights off on your way out.'

'He's not going to plead,' Lee said to Peter as she sat next to him in the Bar Mess.

He shrugged. 'Pity. He's putting his father through it unnecessarily. Would you like some coffee?'

'No thanks.' Lee was in the process of lighting yet another cigarette when she noticed Peter looking at her strangely. 'Do you mind?'

'Not at all,' he replied, not very convincingly. He watched her as she lit up before he even finished the sentence. 'I didn't know you'd started again.'

'Yeah, well, it's better than drinking, plus it's cheaper.' She thought about exactly when she had started again. 'You heard about Ray Willis?'

'Yes. Dreadful business. Some friends of mine on the force told me. Seems he's lucky to be alive.'

'I bet they're really tripping over themselves to investigate this one.'

'You know, Lee, you must stop thinking everyone you've ever defended is the victim of some state conspiracy. I know you were quite fond of him, and I must admit he did have a rather endearing quality, but he was a career criminal, don't forget. I'm sure the police are doing as much as they can but they haven't got much. I've already expressed my interest to both the police and the CPS in prosecuting whoever did this to him.'

'Don't the police have any ideas on who could have done it?'

'I doubt it. If they have, they haven't said anything to me. No witnesses, you see. There was a party next door with a hundred or so people but everyone there was so busy imbibing various substances, both legal and illegal, that no one can say what happened. Ray's in no fit state to give any information, even if he wanted to. The police think it's most likely an underworld related attack, Ray being who he was.'

Lee wondered whether the police really believed that. Whether they did or not hardly mattered. If that was their approach, no one would talk. They'd be too scared to. After a couple of months the investigation would be scaled down, or even closed – 'due to lack of evidence'. Clive would win again.

'What if I knew someone who knew something?' Lee began slowly.

'I'd tell you to tell that someone to go to the police, obviously. They have no concrete leads at the moment.'

Lee shook her head. 'It's not as straightforward as that. The situation's . . . complicated.'

'No it's not. It's just that straightforward. Look, I'm sure you've told them there are ways to ensure their safety, if that's the main concern.' Peter stared at Lee, who returned his gaze, a bland expression on her face. 'This isn't something minor, Lee. Willis isn't out of the woods yet. He could die. Tell your friend, or whoever this person is, to get themselves to the nearest police station *tout de suite*.'

Lee was staring at him, hoping she was conveying her message without having to put it in words.

'At least,' he said slowly, as realisation dawned, 'that's what I would say to that person if they were sitting in front of me right now.'

'Really, Peter? Even if this person has a confidential, professional relationship with the person behind the attack? Even if he's the last person on earth the police would suspect?'

Peter leaned forwards so suddenly that Lee instinctively moved back. 'For God's sake, Lee. If you know something, you've got to come forward. Lawyer-client privilege only covers this case, nothing else.'

Lee gave him a tight little smile. 'Wherever did you get the idea that it was me, Peter?' She paused to light another cigarette. 'But don't worry. I'll make sure I tell my acquaintance what you said. Speaking of Clive, though, you seem very confident about this case.'

She saw the confusion in his face. He opened his mouth to say something and for a moment she was afraid he was going to press her. She was relieved when instead he leaned back once more and, taking his cue from her, replied, 'Wouldn't you be, in my place?'

'Not if I didn't have a motive. Especially if the father's confessing to the lot.'

'I don't need a motive. I've got some pretty damning handwriting evidence.'

'Which isn't conclusive.'

'Says one expert. The other doesn't think so. Plus, I've got Hector.'

'Ah, yes. The jealous older brother who makes all these wild allegations in his statement about my client doing hard drugs.'

'They're more than just wild allegations, Lee. He's been seen taking the stuff.'

'Do you think you're going to get any jury to believe that my good-looking client is a junkie, Peter? He looks healthier than both of us. Plus he's got no convictions for drugs in the UK.'

'He has cautions.'

'For soft drugs. Personal use only. Not the kind of thing you'd commit fraud for.'

She was right, and Peter knew it. It certainly weakened the Crown's case against the younger man, but the overall thrust was still strong. Even if the powers that be weren't so keen on pushing this case, he'd still want to carry on.

Finally he said, 'Even if the father did it all, which I doubt, I'm convinced the son was behind it. Someone like Frederick doesn't keep his nose clean for seventy-odd years then steal thousands of pounds from his own company, especially when his own net worth is several times that.'

'Well, I'm sure you'll tell that to the jury. Speaking of Frederick, have you seen Nicholas Robbins yet?'

'Not yet.'

That was an ominous sign. Lee would have been worried, but she had no room left to worry about anything else. She looked at her watch. Nine fifty. Forty minutes to go. 'I'd better go and look for him. No point in discussing anything further without him being present.' She stood up. 'Keep an eye on my notes, will you?'

'Of course, if you feel you can trust me.'

'Peter, you're the one person in this whole case I do trust. Besides,' she smiled, more genuinely this time, 'I won't be gone long.' Just long enough.

Peter watched her as she left the Bar Mess. A complex woman. Friendly though they were, he had never completely understood her, not when she was his pupil and certainly not now. That earlier conversation about Ray, he could have sworn she was trying to tell him something. And, even though they got on well, it spoke volumes when the only person you could trust in a criminal case was your opponent.

He looked at her papers, neatly stacked in a pile opposite him on the table. He tried not to look too closely but there was one sheet of paper that caught his attention, criss-crossed as it was in yellow highlighter pen.

He got up and went to buy another cup of coffee. He came back to his place and tried to read his newspaper, but to no avail. The highlighted page, sitting on top of Lee's papers for all to see, seemed to be drawing him with a laser-like intensity. Finally, he folded his copy of *The Times*, drained his cup, put his chin in his hands and stared at the sheet.

It was easy to read upside down, especially as the words 'Clive's convictions: US' were written in block capitals.

Peter sighed. He might be trustworthy, but he never claimed to be a saint.

'You must be mad!' Robbins spluttered, looking at Clive.

'Is that why you wanted this conference?' Lee asked. 'To insult my client?' She was once again in the same windowless conference room where she had been with Brendan and Clive less than an hour earlier, except that there were now six of them. The sense of claustrophobia heightened the tension, which was already so tangible you could taste it. The room smelt of perfume, expensive aftershave, traces of cigarette smoke and fear. Frederick Omartian and Arthur Forman, his solicitor, the oldest men in the room, were the only ones sitting down.

'But you can't possibly win.' Robbins turned to Lee. 'You have shown him Hector's statement, haven't you?'

'Of course I have!' Lee snapped. 'If Clive wants to fight this case, that's entirely his prerogative, and I shall do my very best for him in that regard. And anyway,' she added, glancing at Frederick Omartian, 'you're not particularly concerned with *my* client's best interests, are you?'

Robbins reddened. 'I'm still going to make my voire dire argument to try and exclude my lay client's interview, because, as you know, without it the prosecution's case is significantly weaker. But if that doesn't work then our best option would be to change our plea, before the trial gets under way proper. Of course,' he added bitterly, 'it won't make much difference, not without your client's plea. The Crown want a package deal on this one. If your client insists on fighting the case, why fight just one case when you might as well do both?'

'The judge might have something to say about not accepting your client's plea,' Brendan said, speaking for the first time.

'Perhaps. But I'd be a lot happier if I could walk out of here knowing we were all of one mind.'

Lee looked at Frederick as she spoke to Robbins. 'Is your client still willing to plead to the whole amount?' she asked quietly. It seemed so rude to be making these inquiries while Frederick was in the room, but professional etiquette meant she couldn't speak to him directly, not while his lawyers were there.

'He always has been, and still is, although it's very much against my better judgement.' Robbins looked at Clive. 'I don't happen to believe he's responsible for it all.' Frederick opened his mouth to speak, but Robbins carried on, 'Yes, I know, I know, Frederick. I act under your instructions. But that's my view.' Turning back to Lee, he added, 'Frederick knows how I feel.'

Now Lee looked at Clive, searching his face, but there was nothing there but apathy. Nothing to indicate any remorse for, or concern about, his father. And this was the man she had to do her professional best to defend. 'Well, my client's position is still the same, Nicholas. He's not going to plead.' She looked at Frederick.

'I'm sorry.' More sorry than he knew.

'My son must do what is in his own best interests,' Frederick replied. It was the first time he had spoken. 'After all, he always does.' Although clearly not a well man, it was the resignation in his voice rather than his appearance which was truly shocking, all the more because it stood out in sharp relief against that of his son. Clive looked and sounded as if he could not lose; Frederick, as if he had already lost; and not just in terms of the case.

Frederick needed the assistance of his solicitor to get out of his seat. Watching them, Lee remembered how Frederick had twice spurned his older son to lean on the younger one. Now, Clive simply watched as his father was slowly helped to his feet. Then he spoke.

'Thank you, Father. I have every confidence in Ms Mitchell. It's a shame you apparently don't feel that way about Mr Robbins.'

Frederick turned slowly and gave his son a look that was equal parts pity and sadness and slowly shook his head. Robbins gave him a contemptuous look.

'Leave it alone, Clive,' Lee said.

Clive put up his hands in a gesture of mock surrender. 'Consider it left,' he said, and got up and left the room.

Lee was the last to leave, directly behind Brendan. As she did so, she saw Peter standing a few feet away, holding the set of papers and documents she had left with him.

'I'm sorry,' she said as she walked towards him. 'It took a bit longer than I thought.'

'I thought you might need these,' he said, handing over her papers. His expression was rather grim, unusually for him. 'After all, you can't have a conference without your case papers, can you?'

'Thank you.' She was about to say something more, but decided against it. 'I'd better robe up, and I need to ring Chambers. Excuse me.'

As she started to walk off, Peter said, 'Lee, is there anything else you need to discuss with me? About your client? Anything at all?'

'No. No, I don't think so.'

'Very well, if you're sure. I'll see you upstairs.'

There were two other barristers in the Robing Room. Neither looked up as Lee entered. She put on her robe, and fastened her bands round her throat. Maybe if David had changed his mind . . .

The telephone was answered on the first ring.

'Dean, it's Lee. We're just about to start, but I was wondering whether I got any phone calls this morning . . . You're sure? Could you check with Tom, please? Perhaps it hasn't been written down.' There was a pause, then she said, 'Oh. Well, if David, my partner, rings, could you Tannoy for me at court as soon as you get it? It's very important.'

She replaced the receiver, then assessed her options as she straightened her wig in the mirror. She looked at her papers. She was sure the top page had been the other way round. But it didn't matter. If Peter hadn't taken the bait and nothing in his manner indicated that he had – her options had narrowed down to one, which was to tell McCallum. Getting a judge involved might increase David's chances of coming through this unscathed but there were no guarantees. It could also mean her being reported to the Bar Council, perhaps the end of her career at the Bar. But she couldn't let Clive go into the witness box and lie, that was for certain. She had so few cards to play with, but somehow she had to produce a winning hand.

Chapter Twenty-Five

Ten minutes to go.

Lee leaned against the wall and lit another cigarette. The packet was almost empty now. She'd have to get some more at lunchtime – if she could last that long.

As she took the first drag, she closed her eyes, trying to block out the commotion around her, if only for a minute. She felt, rather than saw, someone at her shoulder.

'Don't start on me, Brendan,' she said, wearily.

'What's going on, Lee?'

Peter's voice jolted her back to reality. She straightened up and looked at him suspiciously. 'What do you mean?' An old lawyer's trick, answering a question with a question; it gave you time to think on your feet.

'Don't play games with me, Lee. I taught you that one. It's clear, to me at least, that there's a problem with you and Omartian.'

It was useless to deny it. 'Does anyone else know?' she asked immediately, and instantly regretted it.

'So I was right,' he said quietly. He looked around. Everyone was still too busy trying to get into court to pay any attention to them. 'Don't worry, Robbins is not the most perceptive of men. Even I wasn't sure, until now. This is a case everyone wants a part of – except you, it seems. Why?' When she didn't answer, he added, 'You don't leave your case papers with prosecution counsel, no matter how well you know them. Especially when you obviously need them to confer with Robbins or your client. I've prosecuted you several times, you've never done that with me before.'

Lee didn't answer. She didn't look at him either. Peter lowered his voice, speaking more urgently now. 'Lee, if you know something . . . you know you won't be able to let him give evidence.'

'I'm not saying he did it.'

'You're not saying he didn't, either.'

Before either of them could say anything further, the court usher approached them. 'Judge wants to come in.'

'Yes, in a minute.' Peter's tone surprised Lee; he was never that sharp with court staff.

'Let's go in, Peter.'

'You can ask the judge for more time if you want. I won't object.'

That *was* what she wanted, but how could she be seen to be the one asking for it? She couldn't, not without Clive's authority, and he would never give it. As far as he was concerned, the matter had already been decided.

'Mr Fairfax, you know he doesn't like to be kept waiting,' the usher persisted.

Peter looked at Lee, who was still avoiding his gaze. Finally he turned to the usher. 'Very well, but I'd like a quick word with the clerk first, if I may.'

'It had better be quick, Mr Fairfax.'

There were at least five times as many files and documents than there were people in the court. It was obvious from even the most cursory glance that several hundred hours of preparation had gone into bringing this case from the time of the first allegation to where they all were today, ready and fully prepared for trial. Each solicitor and barrister, for the defence as well as for the Crown, had a complete set. So did the judge, who appeared to be in an ebullient mood. Lee wondered whether he had read all the papers.

She hoped he hadn't. That way, it would take twice as long; the prosecution would have to outline the case and set out its evidence that much more carefully, for his benefit as well as that of the jury.

Robbins was already seated as Lee took her place in Counsel's Row. Peter was deep in conversation with the court clerk. Lee saw the clerk shrug. 'I'll have to speak to the judge about that,' he said, before he disappeared into an anteroom at the side of the court. As he did so, Peter came over to Lee and Robbins.

'I've asked if the judge will see us in Chambers,' he said.

'He's coming in?' Robbins asked.

'No.' Peter glanced briefly at Lee. 'In his room.'

'You don't think he'll agree to that?' Robbins said. 'Why can't he just clear the court? It's nothing the defendants can't hear, surely.'

'Maybe he won't,' Peter admitted, 'but I would prefer it that way. Anyway, it doesn't make any difference to your client, does it, Nicholas? If you feel we've discussed something he should know about, I'm sure you'll tell him. Do you have any objections, Lee?'

Lee knew what he was trying to do. He was providing her with an audience with the judge. Not private, of course, Robbins would be there, but away from Clive and Brendan. This was her chance.

'None at all.'

They had their answer almost immediately. When the clerk came back, he could barely contain his surprise. 'He said he'll see you.'

Lee stood up. As Robbins bent down to gather his papers, Peter whispered quickly to her, 'Ball's in your court now.'

Lee walked over to Brendan. 'Judge wants to see us in his room.'

Brendan paled, then glanced over quickly at Clive who was staring at them intently. 'Are you going to tell him?'

Lee remembered this morning, and the way Clive had spoken to her. 'If I give in to him now, I'll be bought and paid for, just like you.'

'Well, at least I know where my family is, and that they're safe. What about you, Lee? Excuse me, I'm going to see our client.'

Whatever was said, it took no time at all. It was impossible to see what was going on, Brendan's tall frame completely obscured Clive who was still seated. In any event it was over almost as soon as it began. Brendan's face was like thunder as he walked back to his seat behind Lee.

'He said to give you this,' he said in a low, terse voice, holding out a sheet of thick, creamy vellum, folded in half.

The message contained only five words: 'I hope you're feeling lucky.'

Lee stared at Clive. Their eyes met, and held. She walked over to the dock, holding the note, and stood in front of him. She leaned over the rail, as if she was about to say something to him. Then, without taking her eyes off him, she crumpled up the note in one hand and dropped it in his lap.

Then she returned to Peter and Robbins. 'Ready, gentlemen?'

McCallum was in his room, the trial papers and a cup of coffee in front of him on his large desk. He was fully robed, except for his wig. Lee was struck by how young he seemed without it.

'You know I don't usually see people in my room,' he said, 'but I'm sure the Crown would not have asked unless there was a very good reason. Well, Mr Fairfax, Mr Robbins, Ms Mitchell, are you ready to proceed?'

'The Crown is ready, Judge,' Peter replied, using the less formal mode of address.

'Good. At last.'

'Have you had the opportunity to read all the papers in this case?'

McCallum glared at him. 'Unlike some of my colleagues, I believe in coming to a case fully prepared, as I'm sure you do.'

'Of course, Judge,' Peter replied quickly. 'I meant no disrespect by my observation. It's just that there is a great volume of papers . . .'

'Don't forget, Mr Fairfax, this is the second stab we've had at trying to get this thing off the ground. I think you can safely assume I'm now very familiar with this case. I see the Crown has dropped proceedings against Hector Omartian.'

'That is correct. He will now be called as a witness for the Crown.'

'I see. I've read his statement. Very well, how does that affect the estimated length of trial?'

'I estimate it will now be no longer than two weeks.'

'Two weeks? As short as that? One would never guess from the volume of papers.'

'Much of it is uncontested, Judge, and so will simply be read. In fact, in the way I propose to present the case against the defendants, much of the Crown evidence over the next three or four days will be read.'

'Really,' McCallum commented drily. 'I'm sure the jury will be as excited as I am by that prospect, Mr Fairfax. You must, however, take your own course.'

'Your Honour, I know my learned friend for the first defendant will have a point of law to raise regarding Frederick Omartian's interview. Depending on the outcome, that may shorten things even further.'

'Is that right, Mr Robbins?'

'Judge, yes.'

'How long will this take?'

'About thirty minutes all told. I'm sure my learned friend for the Crown will be objecting. And you may of course need time to consider the matter.'

'Quite. Do you propose to do this straightaway, or just before Mr Fairfax seeks to submit the offending material in evidence – which, on my reckoning, will be about the third or fourth day of the trial?'

'Straightaway, Judge. I think for various reasons my learned friend and I would want this matter resolved as soon as possible one way or another.'

'Very well, then. I don't want to keep the potential jurors waiting any longer than they have to, so I'll have them brought in, swear them, then send them out for a coffee break while we deal with it. At least they'll know what's going on. I don't want them kept in the dark about anything in this trial if it can possibly be helped. I suppose the press will have to come in as well, then.' He sighed at the thought. 'All of this could have been done in court, in the absence of the jury, but in the defendants' presence. I don't think it's right that matters like these should be aired in their absence. Was there any other issue anyone wanted to raise?' When no one answered, McCallum said, 'What about you, Ms Mitchell? You haven't said anything so far. Is there anything you want to address me on?'

Lee hoped her surprise wasn't showing. She felt as if she'd been caught hiding some guilty secret which, under the circumstances, was entirely appropriate. But she didn't expect to be addressed so directly. For a moment, she wondered if McCallum knew. Out of the corner of her eye she could see Peter studying her. Now was her chance.

But what about David's chances? Her earlier show of defiance notwithstanding, she just didn't feel that lucky.

'Well, Ms Mitchell?' McCallum said, impatient now.

Lee couldn't bring herself to look at Peter. 'No, Judge. There's nothing I wish to raise at this point.'

'Very well. I see Mr Amery is no longer with us, so I'm sure it won't be necessary to remind any counsel presently before me that the purpose of this trial is to administer justice as fairly and efficiently as possible, not to play to the gallery or to create tomorrow's headlines. I intend to come into court in precisely three minutes.'

Lee was the first to leave the room. Clive was still seated in the dock, with Brendan standing nearby. She took her seat without speaking to either of them. As Brendan approached her, she deliberately turned her back towards him. He leaned over her shoulder, and was about to speak when the court usher announced, 'All rise!'

Everyone present stood as McCallum entered. As soon as he sat down he said, 'Jury please, Usher.'

Lee could clearly hear Brendan's sigh of relief behind her, and heard him quickly get up to speak to Clive. He would know, Lee thought, that McCallum would never have called for the jury if she had told him the truth. And now Clive knew it too.

Law as entertainment.

Swearing the jury took longer than anyone had thought, mainly because some potential jurors, who were initially very pleased at having the chance to sit in judgement on what promised to be a real live soap opera, became distinctly unhappy at the thought of having to do so for two whole weeks, especially when they would not be able to discuss the juicy details with anyone outside the jury for the duration of the trial. A handful excused themselves. Of the twenty or so remaining, those whose names were called grinned as if they had just won the Lottery. It was obvious that, once the case was fully under way, a packed courtroom would give the whole proceedings an almost game-show atmosphere. The jury was a fair mix in terms of age, sex and race. Maybe Clive would get off, Lee thought morosely; there were just enough young women on it to make a hung jury, if not an outright acquittal, a distinct possibility. The sworn jurors looked expectantly at the judge, waiting for the case to begin.

'Yes, Mr Robbins?' McCallum said.

He rose to his feet. 'Your Honour, there is a point of law I wish to raise in the absence of the jury.'

There was an almost audible groan from the jury. Sent out so soon.

'Very well,' McCallum replied. Turning to the jury, he said, 'Ladies and gentlemen of the jury, I wanted to have you sworn as soon as possible, not only so that the defendants can be put in your charge, but also because I personally am a firm believer in keeping jurors aware at all times of what's going on at every stage of a trial, rather than making you wait for no apparent reason. Counsel for Frederick Omartian has told me this matter should take about thirty minutes, so you can treat this as an early coffee break, if you will.'

Robbins stood silently, waiting for the jurors to file into the jury room. When the last one had disappeared from view and their door closed, he spoke.

'My learned friend for the Crown is aware of my submission, Your Honour. Perhaps I can outline it to you before detailed argument is given. It concerns the interview given by the first defendant upon arrest. Your Honour will find it in Exhibits File One.'

'Yes, I have it. It's quite lengthy, Mr Robbins.'

'That is precisely my point, Your Honour – one of them, at least. The first defendant was seventy-seven at the time of the said interview. He has now just turned seventy-eight. He is a man of good, in fact exemplary, character; he was, and is, not in good health, and has not been for some time; and at the time of the interview he did not have the benefit of legal advice. The Crown's case against the first defendant rests substantially on this piece of evidence, which they claim was voluntarily given. It is my submission that the interview was obtained through fundamental breaches of the Police and Criminal Evidence Act 1984 and its Codes. If I can direct Your Honour to Archbold—'

'Before you do, Mr Robbins – I'm grateful for your outline – I'd like to hear briefly from Mr Fairfax. I take it you're objecting to this submission?'

'Yes, Your Honour.'

'On what grounds?'

'On the grounds that the confession made by this defendant in his interview was freely given, and that he voluntarily waived his entitlement to legal advice; he says as much in his interview. If the defendant was being coerced in any way, it was not by the police.' Peter looked over at Lee, sitting next to Robbins. 'It has always been the Crown's case that this defendant was being coerced by his younger son. This is now supported by Hector Omartian's statement.'

'Very well. Now I know the parameters of the argument, please take me to your authorities, Mr Robbins.'

As she listened to full argument from both sides, Lee wondered what Robbins would do if he won. Peter could still proceed against him, he had the handwriting evidence, after all, and she was pretty sure he would. As the debate unfolded, it seemed increasingly unlikely that he would lose.

But not, apparently, impossible.

Ever mindful of the possibility of appeal, McCallum's own detailed ruling was almost as long as the argument that preceded it. However, he made it clear that, although the defence argument had some force, he was narrowly persuaded by the Crown's submissions. When Robbins rose again to address the judge, he had an air of defeat that went beyond the loss of the voire dire.

'In the light of Your Honour's ruling, could I have some time to confer with the prosecution counsel and the defendant? It may shorten matters considerably.'

McCallum didn't need to ask why. 'How long will you need, Mr Robbins?'

'Fifteen minutes should be sufficient.'

'Are you sure that's all the time you'll need?'

Robbins looked over his shoulder towards Frederick Omartian, sitting in the dock. 'Quite sure, Your Honour.'

'Very well. None of this affects you, Ms Mitchell.'

'Not directly, Your Honour.'

'Very well, I'll rise. Please send word via the court clerk if you need further time.'

As soon as the judge had risen, Nicholas and his solicitor went to where Frederick Omartian was seated, and helped him out of the witness box. Then the three of them, as well as Peter, left court together. Apart from the court staff, Lee, Brendan and Clive were the only ones remaining.

'Let's go to the Bar Mess,' Lee suggested to her solicitor. It was the one place Clive couldn't accompany them.

As soon as they sat down, Lee said, 'Robbins is going to plead Frederick out.'

'I guessed as much. Peter may not go for it, though.'

'Not after the judge's ruling. Robbins nearly succeeded; in front of another judge it could have been very different. Peter knows that. Plus, he's a percentage player. He'll agree the plea, if it's still on offer.'

'Are you kidding? Robbins is on his knees even as we speak. It's Frederick I feel sorry for, poor bastard. He's not even carrying the can for someone who appreciates his sacrifice. He might get an open prison, but that's the best he can hope for. He'll lose his reputation and everything he's worked for; his health has definitely deteriorated as a result of these proceedings, his family's split in two, and for what? A lying, ungrateful shit he calls a son.'

'To be fair, even to Clive, his reputation was shot from the time he was charged. Who's going to trust him with their money again? And have you noticed that, since his arrest, every paper, even the broadsheets, has mentioned the fact that he was originally from Eastern Europe, even though he's been naturalised over fifty years?'

'Yes. Well, they're going to have a field day with this when we get back in court. It will cut the trial time virtually in half. That doesn't give me much time.'

'Do you still think you can find a way out of this?'

'I've got to try. I'm not beaten yet. I can't let him give perjured evidence, Brendan. I'm walking a very fine tightrope, morally and legally, as it is.'

As if on cue, a message came over the loudspeaker. 'Would all parties in the case of Omartian and Omartian please return to court immediately.'

Lee and Brendan looked at each other. 'Already?' Lee said.

As they entered court, Lee saw a very relieved Robbins sitting in his appointed place. Neither the judge nor the jury had yet come in, but the court, unlike before, was now packed. Peter was seated also. They barely had time to resume their places when the jurors filed in. As soon as they had taken their places, the court usher stated, 'All rise!'

Once Judge McCallum sat down, so did everyone else, all except Robbins.

'Thank you for your time, Your Honour. Might the indictment be put again to the first defendant?'

'Is the defendant fully aware of the possible consequences for him of this proposed course?'

'He is, Your Honour.'

'Is this an agreed course, Mr Fairfax?'

'Yes, Your Honour.'

'Very well, let the indictment be put again.'

There was a low murmur from the more seasoned court

reporters as the clerk stood up. When an indictment was put again, it meant only one thing. The murmur grew significantly louder when Frederick Omartian, in a quavering, but dignified, voice, said 'Guilty' to the charge against him. Journalists started writing furiously. Some of them left court with as much speed as decency would allow to telephone their copy.

Lee looked back at Clive. He was completely unmoved.

'Is the plea acceptable to the Crown, Mr Fairfax?'

Peter looked quickly at the dock, then at Lee, before replying, 'Yes, Your Honour.'

'Mr Robbins, I take it you don't wish to mitigate now.'

'No, Your Honour. Your Honour might find pre-sentence and community service reports of assistance.'

'Mr Robbins, given the amount of money involved, and the fact that the defendant stole money entrusted to him by his clients to invest, community service is wildly optimistic, even if he were young enough and fit enough to carry out such work. The defendant must be under no illusions about the likely disposal of this case. In fact, it is only because of his age and his state of health that I'm not going to remand him in custody. He can have bail, with an additional condition that he surrender his passport, pending the preparation of the reports. I take it your client's plea is still the same, Ms Mitchell?'

Again, now would be the time to say something. Lee felt all eyes upon her as she stood up. 'Yes, Your Honour.'

'This shortens things considerably, doesn't it, Mr Fairfax?'

'Yes, Your Honour, it does. The trial should now be no more than five to seven working days. Certainly I expect to finish the Crown case this week.'

'Very well. Frederick Omartian, stand up. Your part in this case has been adjourned for four weeks, so that pre-sentence reports can be prepared on your behalf. Please do not feel that because you have been admitted to bail this is any indication of the likely sentence in this matter. Very well, you can go. Mr Robbins, there's no need to wait.'

'Thank you, Your Honour.'

Lee got up in order to let Robbins out. As she did so, she watched Frederick being helped, once again, from the dock, except this time he was leaving his good character behind. He had made his fortune long ago, but now that was all he had.

Chapter Twenty-Six

It was an impressive opening speech.

Peter nailed his colours very clearly to the mast. Right at the beginning he told the jury that, despite Frederick's plea, they still had to give separate consideration to the guilt of the only remaining defendant. It was the Crown's case, he told them, that Clive Omartian had coerced his father into committing this offence; if that was also their view, he, too, was guilty of this offence. Clive had also been interviewed, Peter added, in the presence of his solicitor, and although he had the right not to say anything, having been cautioned by the police, he neither denied the police allegations nor positively asserted his innocence, as one might expect. Peter told the jurors that they would hear a great deal of evidence, in particular from the defendant's brother, Hector Omartian, to support the Crown's contention that Frederick Omartian was merely a conduit through which the defendant could commit this offence, in order to finance his cocaine habit. As if to cover himself, however, he also warned the jury about being swayed by media coverage of either this court case or of Clive Omartian himself. They were to try this case on the facts, nothing more.

Clive visibly relaxed when he heard this last comment. For a moment he had been worried. He could control his own lawyers, but Fairfax was an unknown quantity. He had always appeared so affable, as if he wanted everyone to like him. Weak. He hadn't expected him to be this good. But now hadn't the very person who was supposed to prosecute him told the jury they should disregard gossip column publicity about him and drugs?

Lee was impressed too, but for different reasons. In setting the scene, Peter was using his likeable personality to win the jury over to his side; he had to, because with the amount of statements to be read, and so little live evidence, he was forced to attract, and hold, their interest right from the start. He was also taking all her good points – the father's confession, the adverse publicity – and deflating them. In addition, because of the dramatic turn of events as far as Frederick was concerned, the handwriting evidence was no longer of any real significance. After all, the Crown by accepting Frederick's plea were no longer saying that Clive committed the offence himself. Hector would be the trump card, and his evidence would be kept, tantalisingly, until last.

The assembled journalists were not used to hearing such an impassioned opening from the Crown. A few of them even stopped writing.

By the beginning of the fourth day, however, everyone, including the judge, was visibly wilting. All except Clive. Lee wondered whether some of the women on the jury were wilting over him. Given the way he was looking, better than she'd ever seen him, she couldn't entirely blame them. They had no idea how different the inner man was from the outer. McCallum had been at pains to point out to the jury that statements to be read were as important as if the evidence was coming live from the witness box, and that in fact the reason for their being read was because the defence did not require the live witness to be brought to court. Important, however, was not necessarily the same as interesting. The jury had heard very little evidence so far and seen hardly any of the interplay between barristers and witnesses that gave criminal trials their distinct character.

Everyone stood up as McCallum entered court to start the day's proceedings.

'Good morning. Are we ready to proceed, Mr Fairfax?'

'Your Honour, yes.'

'Will this evidence be in the form of statements to be read?'

'No, Your Honour.'

There was an audible sigh of relief from one of the jurors.

'I call Hector Omartian.'

There was a rustle of excitement and expectation. Everyone watched Hector as he strode to the witness box. He had a purposeful walk, and an almost military bearing. Lee remembered what his father had been like the first time she had met him, how he had walked and carried himself, in spite of his advanced years and ill health. In this regard, Hector was definitely his father's son. As he took the oath in a deep, steady voice, Lee could hear something of his father in his voice as well. But she would never have guessed he and Clive were related in any way. At fifty-five, Hector was old enough to be Clive's father himself. Short where Clive was tall, bald where his brother had a full head of hair, clearly not a follower of fashion, and with a face only a mother would love – the differences were too great to explain simply by the fact that they were only half-brothers. No matter what he said, whether he was going to speak the truth or lie on oath, whether his evidence was motivated by malice and envy or by much higher, nobler feelings for his father, some of the jurors and most of the press would already have judged him and found him wanting.

After he had stated his name and address for the court, Peter asked, 'The defendant, Clive Omartian, is your brother, is that right?'

'No. We're half-brothers. My father married his mother after my mother died.'

'I stand corrected. But it *is* right, is it not, that you have no previous convictions?'

'None whatsoever.'

'I know you're anxious to be totally honest with, and helpful to, this jury, so it's right they should know you too were originally to face trial with the defendant and your father over this matter.'

'Yes, that's correct. The case was discontinued against me.'

'You were first arrested in December of last year in connection with this matter?'

'Yes.'

'Some weeks before your half-brother?'

'Yes.'

'When you were interviewed after your arrest, did you make any kind of statement?'

'I denied having any part in any fraud, or any dishonest dealings.'

'Apart from that interview, did you make any other statement about what happened?'

'Not at the time. Not until two or three months ago, in fact.'

'Was there any reason for that gap of several months?'

Hector hesitated. 'I had wanted to come forward and tell the truth about this whole thing for several months. But my father wouldn't let me.'

Somewhere in the public gallery someone sniggered. McCallum looked up sharply, then turned to the witness. 'I apologise for the interruption, Mr Omartian. Please continue.'

'What I meant was, my father had made it clear that he was prepared to take the blame. He didn't want Clive getting into trouble. It's always been like that between them.'

'If that was the case, what made you change your mind?'

'Clive can do no wrong in my father's eyes. I don't think he knows what he's doing. Whatever my father does won't change him. It'll never change him. Clive doesn't appreciate the sacrifice my father has made, even now, because he's never had to sacrifice anything, for anyone, in his life.' He was getting angrier. 'My father is an old, sick man. Because of him,' pointing to Clive, 'he's almost certainly going to prison.'

Lee believed every word Hector had said so far but as long as she was still representing Clive, however reluctantly, she had to object.

She rose to her feet. 'Your Honour, is my learned friend for the Crown intending to direct this witness to the evidence any time in our future, as in his statement, or has he brought him merely to air his personal grievances?'

'My learned friend knows me better than that, Your Honour.'

'Maybe, but she does have a point. Please get to it, Mr Fairfax. And Ms Mitchell, sarcasm has no place in my court.'

'You've said you've come here to tell the truth, Mr Omartian. What is that truth?'

Lee rose again. 'Truth is a matter for the jury to decide, Your Honour.'

'Point taken, Ms Mitchell. Mr Fairfax, surely you can ensure the witness expresses himself in some less emotive way.'

'What really happened, Mr Omartian?'

Lee found herself holding her breath. What Hector would say next would have far-reaching consequences.

'Clive came to my father. Said he was desperate. He owed some money to some people in America. I think it was for drug dealers—'

'The witness doesn't know this, Your Honour,' Lee objected. 'He's here to give evidence about facts, not his opinion.' She placed a determined emphasis on the word 'facts'.

Peter looked at her deliberately before turning back to Hector. 'Go on,' he said after a pause.

'He forced my father to take the money. Said if he didn't do it, he would do it himself. And I wasn't speculating. I've *seen* him take cocaine.'

Lee suppressed a sigh of relief. She stayed in her seat. No grounds for objection there. Hector had risen to the bait. For the first time in a long time, she felt the thrill of a small personal victory.

'My father's stubborn,' Hector went on. 'He'll also do what he thinks is right. He thinks it's right to protect Clive, even from his own wrongdoing because, as he sees it, he has his whole life ahead of him. But I think it's right that the truth be known. Clive's not a child. He's a man, and should be man enough to shoulder his responsibilities rather than let them be carried by an old man who may not see out the year.'

It was a good, sympathetic note to end on. 'Thank you, Mr Omartian.' Peter looked at his former pupil. 'I'm sure my learned friend will have some questions for you.'

The room was deathly quiet as Lee rose and turned to face Hector.

Attack was definitely the best form of defence here. In fact, in the circumstances, it was the only defence. Especially when Clive wanted to see her put through her paces.

'You stated earlier you wanted to help the jury, Mr Omartian. Let's start with this allegation of drug-taking, taking cocaine, that you mentioned. Did you say that to help the jury?'

'No. I said it in answer to your objection. You made it look as if I didn't know what I was talking about.'

'But when you said, "I think it was for drug dealers", you don't know whether that was true, do you?'

Hector paused a long while before finally answering, 'No.'

'So, in relation to that, you don't, in fact, know what you were talking about.'

Again, there was a long pause before Hector said curtly. 'If you put it like that.'

'Yes or no, Mr Omartian.'

'No.'

'Thank you. Now, about this alleged drug-taking, where did it occur?'

'At my father's place in the country, last summer.'

'Any particular reason why you remember it?'

'It's not every day I see a member of my family, however distant, taking cocaine. It's not something I'd like to see again, either.'

'Wasn't that about the time you were going through your very costly divorce?'

'What's the relevance of that, Your Honour?' Peter asked.

'It's this, Your Honour. Mr Omartian, you were also receiving treatment for alcoholism around that time and for several months afterwards, weren't you?' As Peter rose to object, Lee countered, 'Your Honour, it was the witness who introduced the issue of substance abuse quite without cause. Whether or not Clive Omartian took drugs on that occasion bears no relevance to the issues in this case.'

'It came from your witness, Mr Fairfax. The defence are entitled to cross-examine it. You can call rebuttal evidence later if you want.'

'Thank you, Your Honour. Well, Mr Omartian?'

'I was having treatment then, yes.'

'Bearing that in mind, would you have been sober enough to remember what the defendant was doing?'

'I know what I saw.'

'Are you sure?'

He paused just for a moment, but that was enough.

'You don't have to answer, Mr Omartian, we'll let the jury decide. Now, as to your statement, you accept you only came forward very late in the day to make it, don't you?'

'I didn't make it at the time of my arrest.'

'No, you waited until just before the case was discontinued against you. Any connection there, Mr Omartian?'

'No! I resent that. I told you I would have made it earlier but for my father's objections.'

'You're a fifty-five-year-old man, Mr Omartian. Do you always do what your father tells you to?'

'How dare you!

'No, how dare *you*, Mr Omartian. You agreed to make this statement in return for the Crown's discontinuing the case against you, that's the *truth*, isn't it?'

'No.'

'And it's motivated not so much out of concern for your father but because of the antipathy you feel towards your brother, particularly because of the close relationship he had with your father.'

When Hector spoke again, his voice was quieter, calmer – still dignified, but clearly wounded. 'My father and I have never been as close as I would have liked. That is, and always will be, a continuing source of sadness to me. As for Clive, it's no secret how we feel about one another, and I can assure you it's not all one-sided. But you don't know him. I know him. He's my brother—'

'Half-brother.'

'I don't know what he's told you. He's always been good with women. He may even be acquitted, who knows? But I *know* him. I know what he did. And I want the truth to be known.' Hector looked directly at the jury. 'I hope you do too.'

'Thank you. I have nothing further.'

Peter looked at the clock. It was after one. 'Your Honour, this may be a convenient moment.'

'Yes, I agree. Very well. Court is adjourned until five past two.'

The court stood in silence as the judge left. Then Peter crossed the few feet that separated him from Lee.

'Well, I hope you're feeling proud of yourself,' he said disapprovingly.

'Good cross-examination, Peter,' she smiled ruefully. 'I learned it from a master.' Quickly she gathered up her papers. 'Excuse me.'

305

Clive was waiting with Brendan outside court. He was very pleased, as well he should be. 'That was very impressive, Lee.' It was the first pleasant thing he had said to her since the trial began.

'Why didn't you tell me about the coke, Clive?'

'Oh, that. I didn't remember.'

'But I bet you remember now.'

He smiled. 'Funny enough, I do. I think hearing about it must have jogged my memory. Well, see you at two. Come on, Brendan, I'll buy you lunch.'

As the two men were about to move away, Peter approached the group.

'A word, Lee, please.'

The two of them moved away into the corner of the hallway, about twenty feet away. Close enough to be observed but not to be heard.

'What do you think that's all about?' Clive asked.

'I don't know. But at this stage of the trial, I don't think we should be going anywhere until we find out.'

Brendan used his height as discreetly as possible to try and make out what was going on, but all he could see was Peter showing Lee a document.

The conversation didn't last long. When Lee came back, she looked from one to the other. 'We need to talk. It won't wait until after lunch.'

They found a quiet interview room.

'You didn't tell me you had convictions in the States, Clive. For drugs.'

Clive looked startled for a moment, but only for a moment. For a minute, she thought he was going to deny it. Instead, he merely shrugged. 'I didn't think they'd find out about those.'

'Well, Peter just showed me the list, hot off the fax from Miami, I understand.'

'So? How is it related to what I'm charged with?' He walked

over to a chair and sat down, putting his feet up on the table. The soles of those shoes had clearly never seen a city street. He rocked gently back and forth. 'Anyway, I can't see how it can damage our case, not now.'

'Really? Well, the whole issue of your coke habit has now been brought into the case because of something you failed to tell me. The Crown are proposing to submit the list of convictions in evidence.'

'So what? The prosecution can't rely on my American convictions, particularly if I deny them.' He looked at Lee and Brendan. Clearly they were taking this very seriously. He stopped rocking. 'Can they?'

Neither of them said anything. Finally Lee spoke, mentally crossing her fingers as she did so.

'Brendan, remember that Johnson case we did?'

Like a shot, Brendan took the cue. 'Of course. It's not every day a prosecution witness gets flown over from Anchorage, of all places. Johnson kept putting it off, didn't believe they would actually do it.'

Lee looked at Clive. 'And Anchorage isn't even on a direct flight path. Not like Miami.'

For the first time since she had visited him in that police cell all those months ago, that smooth, polished veneer was cracking before her very eyes.

'You can't be serious,' he said, looking from one to the other. 'How could this happen?' He jumped up suddenly from his chair, almost kicking the table over in the process. 'How could this happen – to me?'

Instinctively Brendan moved towards Lee, a small movement but one that placed him close enough so that one more step would put him between barrister and client.

'Did you do this to me?'

'No, Clive, you did this to yourself. You never told me you had convictions abroad. Did he tell you anything, Brendan?'

'Nope. And I thought you told me everything, Clive.'

Clive knew he hadn't told anyone about this. It was bad enough in America. He didn't want anyone here to know, as well.

'The question is,' Brendan continued, 'what do you do now? If you don't give evidence, you're as good as convicted. If you do, well, I don't need to spell it out.'

'There is another alternative, of course,' Lee said. 'You could sack me. Get another barrister. Because of what I know, I'd be professionally embarrassed, and you'll be able to save yourself. Otherwise, you might as well plead guilty now. I don't think you'll get an open prison, either.'

'We're halfway through this trial. The judge wouldn't let me sack you even if I wanted to.'

'You're a paying client, Clive. Legal aid, well, that's different. You'd be stuck with it then. You might get stung for costs, but think of it as a kind of business loss. We'll leave you alone to consider your options. Of course, you can always carry on with the trial – if you feel lucky.'

Outside the room, Brendan said to Lee, 'But the Johnson case was about a sex shop tourist in Soho.'

'Yes, I know,' she grinned. 'Never said it wasn't. Prosecution did fly him over, though.'

It took a lot to persuade McCallum. It was just as well the court had been cleared, save for the lawyers and the defendant. If it wasn't for Peter Fairfax taking a united stand with her on this one, she wasn't sure whether she would have pulled it off. It was good to have the prosecution on your side at a time like this.

As the judge announced his decision in open court, Lee could have written the headlines herself: 'Celebrity Trial Screeches To Halt', 'Omartian Fraud Case Adjourned'. The message, however put, would be the same. She hadn't said anything about Ray, and she wouldn't, not until she knew David was safe. But she wasn't as worried about him now, even though she hadn't heard from him; Clive had too much to lose to let anything happen to him now. He no longer had a hold over her. They both had sticks of equal size.

Relief might set in later, but for now she felt completely drained. Peter was waiting for her as she left the Robing Room.

'Do you need a lift back to Chambers?'

'No, I'm driving, thanks. Anyway, I'm going straight home.'

They waited for the lift in silence. When it came, it was mercifully empty; Peter had something to ask her.

'How did you know?'

She looked at him. 'Know what?'

'That I'd look.'

'I didn't. You were always so principled.'

'Apparently not.'

Lee wanted to laugh but she didn't have the energy even for that, so she just smiled.

'I knew you wanted out of this case, I think the judge sensed that too. You also know I couldn't have used those convictions even if I'd wanted to.'

'Yes, but Clive didn't know that. Don't worry, I didn't tell him you could. He just assumed it.'

'Who do you think he'll get now?'

'That's the least of his worries. Even now, there's someone waiting to jump into my shoes. He'll probably tell them how awful I was and how he couldn't stand it, so he had to sack me. Believe me, it's a small price to pay.'

'Well, you now have the distinction of being the only barrister in the country who didn't want to defend Clive Omartian.'

'That's something I'm proud to claim.'

As the lift doors slid open on the ground floor, he said, 'You were taking a big chance, you know.'

'One of these days, Peter, I may tell you how big.'

★ ★ ★

When she arrived home, the red light was flashing furiously on the answerphone.

'I'm catching the next plane out. This had better be good.'

Lee let out a sigh that had been building up for weeks.

Yes, it would be, now.

Epilogue

'Phone call for you, Miss Mitchell,' Tom said. He was cordial enough these days, but Lee suspected he still hadn't forgiven her for getting sacked from the Omartian case, especially since Clive's new Counsel seemed to be heading for victory. In her place, he would have moved heaven and earth to keep the brief. But then, he hadn't known the half of it.

Lee was in the Clerks' Room with some other members of Chambers. They had clubbed together to buy some champagne and now everyone was full of the Christmas spirit. Giles in particular. He seemed to think next April would bring him the appointment he had craved for so long. Unfortunately, it appeared this time he would be right.

She thought about Frederick. No champagne for him. This would be his first Christmas as a convicted man. Open prison was all very well, but it was still prison. But at least he wasn't approaching the future with a face he didn't recognise, unlike Ray.

It was rare to find so many people in Chambers at this time of year. People were usually on holiday, skiing or catching some winter sun. It wasn't full, by any means, but there were enough people to make a pleasant change.

'I'll take it in my room, Dean.'

She took another sip before she answered the telephone. The line was very bad, but gradually she could make out a familiar voice. 'Simone? Is that you?'

311

'Yeah, it's me.'

'Where the hell are you?'

'At the airport. Do you know what Heathrow is like just before Christmas? Terrible.'

'Well, if you're ringing me from the airport, presumably you're not there meeting someone.'

'You're right. I finally did it – finally saved enough money to make it to West Africa. Who knows? I might even find my roots. Well, my dad, anyway.'

'I thought we were going to do that together.'

'Come on, Leanne. We're getting on better, but it's not like it was, you know that. At least, not yet.'

When Lee said nothing, Simone added, 'Besides, I don't know when I'll be back. Not for a good few months. That's why I wanted to ring you. I . . . I don't blame you any more, not for what you did. I can't pretend to understand your reasons, but I know you wouldn't have done it unless you had absolutely no choice. So, I'll see you when I get back. Have a good Christmas. Give my love to your mum, not to mention that gorgeous hunk of man you have there.'

'He's not getting anyone's love but mine. Simone?'

'What?'

'It's a start, isn't it?'

'Yes, it's a start.'